Mystics of Sonoduhl

Rudy Lopes

BRONX
RIVER
PRESS

Mystics of Sonoduhl is a work of fiction. Names, characters, incidents, and places are the product of the author's imagination and are used fictitiously. Any resemblance to actual persons, living or dead, locales, or events is entirely coincidental.

Published by Bronx River Press

BronxRiverPress.com

Paperback ISBN: 979-8-9917307-0-9

eBook ISBN: 979-8-9917307-1-6

Second Edition

Cover and map designs by Diane Lopes

DEDICATION

For my mother, who planted within me a profound love of reading,
and for Mary, who helped me to believe in myself.

To my invaluable alpha and beta readers Kathleen, Tony, Michael,
and Niels: your feedback was invaluable.

To Bill, Steve, Brooke, Toyi, Cassie, Debi, and everyone at my
writing and critique groups: your encouragement and suggestions got
me over the hump more than once. Prospective writers out there, be
sure to find (or create) your own groups.

Lastly, kudos to Laurence and the gang with the SFWA mentorship
program.

You all helped to make me a better writer.

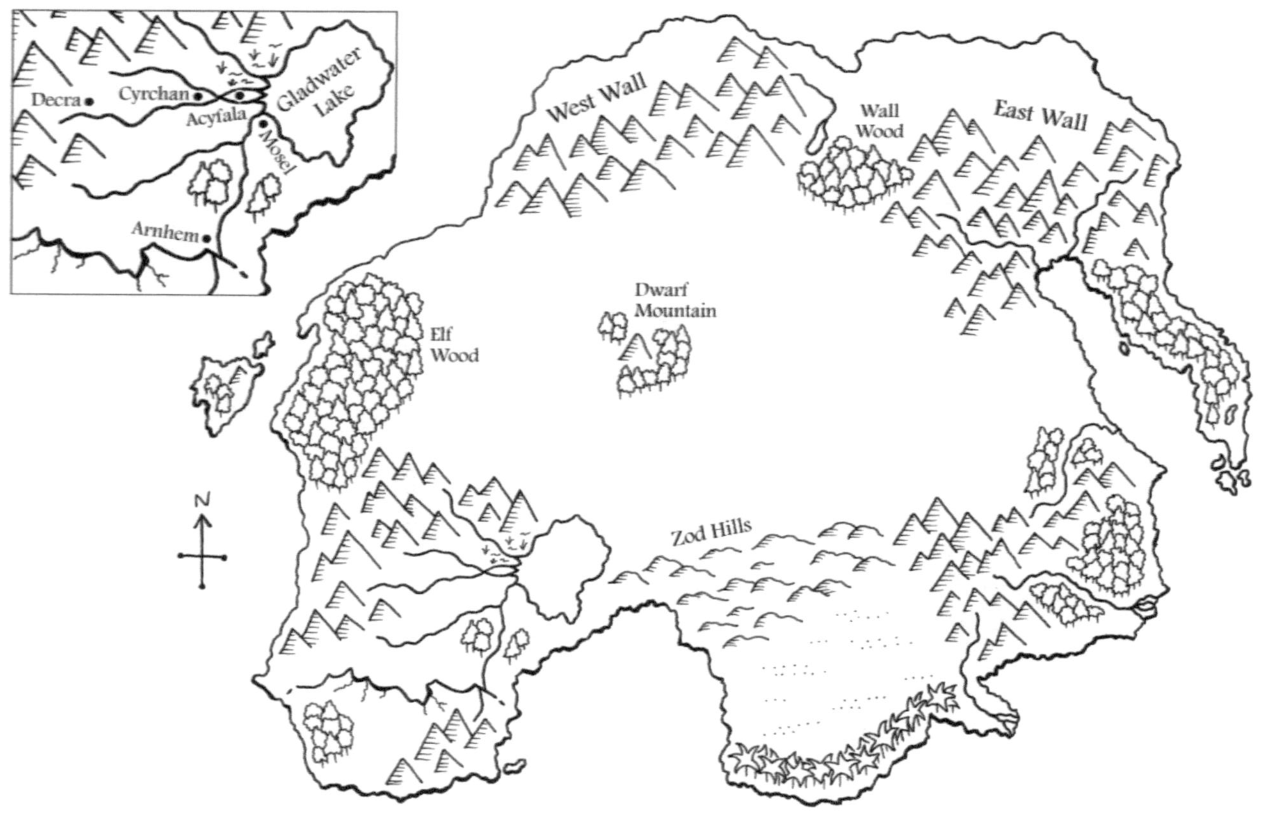

East Wall
Wall Wood
West Wall
Dwarf Mountain
Zod Hills
Elf Wood
Gladwater Lake
Mosel
Cyrchan
Acyfala
Decra
Arnhem
N

CONTENTS

Part 1

PARADISE LOST

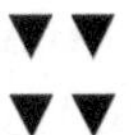

This horse hates me.

Maghrurio was convinced of it. After getting shouldered into the stall door for the fourth time, he finally lost his temper. "What is your problem, Snowfall? Don't you like getting brushed?"

The dappled gray and white mare turned her head and stared. Maybe it was his connection with the animal, or more likely just his own conscience, but the meaning seemed clear.

I'm very disappointed in you.

Snowfall appeared to sense his changing attitude, a dissatisfaction Maghrurio began to feel last week. A strange dream of smoke, blood, and death left him shaken. The unrest dissipated, replaced by a growing feeling that perhaps it was time to move on. It was a familiar sense of ennui he'd experienced with so many jobs before. The lethal combination of boredom and restlessness, the fear of being trapped, and the need to break free.

"Come on, Snowfall, it's not so bad. I haven't decided anything yet."

With a huff and a stomp, the perceptive horse turned her head away from him.

Do you expect me to believe that?

"I don't know, girl, really I don't. Working for Abner is fine, I guess, but sometimes I feel like I can do better than this." He sighed. "I'm not sure what I should be doing with my life."

Recognizing his honest admission, Snowfall nickered and turned, nuzzling him affectionately.

Maghrurio absently stroked her head and gave her an apple core from his pocket.

"Thanks, girl. Let's get you hooked up to the wagon so I can get some breakfast of my own. Don't worry," he reassured the mare. "It's not like I'm quitting this morning. I'm still making up my mind."

Only he wasn't, really.

• • ● • •

Washed and refreshed, the horse and wagon readied, and his chores completed, Maghrurio returned to his small room in Abner's house. He quickly donned a fresh set of his usual pants and tunic, as unremarkable and nondescript as he himself. Slightly taller and thinner than most people, he could not be considered imposing or even notable by any stretch of the imagination.

A familiar nagging thought rattled around in his mind.

I'm approaching middle age. Will I ever amount to anything?

Maghrurio followed the aroma of fresh breakfast to the sparse kitchen, where the housekeeper was busy washing pots in the sink. "Good morning, Bacarus."

Bacarus was a slight woman with dark hair and eyes. A bit shorter and younger than he, she wasn't much for small talk, but her energy level made hard workers seem lazy by comparison. Because of her work ethic, perhaps, she favored pants rather than the house frocks typical of other housekeepers he'd encountered. She was usually even-tempered with him, but when suitably provoked, she could frighten the fur off a wild wolf.

She inclined her head in greeting. "It's porridge and fruit this morning. The herbal tea is fresh. Help yourself," she added.

Discordant humming drifted down the hall, preceding the approaching master of the house. "Good morning, all," Abner said with a twinkle in his eye.

He was easily one of the tallest men in town, with white hair and a flowing beard he kept well-groomed. His piercing blue eyes missed nothing, and his sharp wit and ready laugh were often on display. He was a treasure trove of stories and advice and quite a friendly sort once you moved past the idea of him being one of a handful of magic-wielding Mystics in all of Sonoduhl.

"Porridge again, my dear?"

Maghrurio sighed at the morning ritual. The affluent and powerful of Sonoduhl sought out Abner for his wisdom and guidance. Why then did he seem to delight in provoking Bacarus' temper? She returned Abner's stare evenly. "I know how to make many dishes, Master. But for those that sample too many of them, a bit of porridge will keep their hems from bursting."

Abner laughed at her riposte. "Such a wonderful, sharp wit. Never lose that, my dear; it is among the finest of your many talents."

Bacarus responded by sniffing loudly, turning back to her dishes in silence, and scrubbing twice as hard.

Responding to Abner's good mood, Maghrurio gave an exaggerated sweeping bow, "By my hands has yonder wagon been readied, my liege."

Abner's smile vanished. "You, on the other hand, are quite adept at keeping your talents well hidden. We'll be chatting about your future, Maghrurio, and far sooner than you might prefer."

Clutching a cup of tea, Abner retreated into the hallway. Maghrurio's humor vanished abruptly as he exchanged wary looks with Bacarus.

• • ● • •

The trio set out shortly afterward aboard the rickety Snowfall-drawn wagon, Abner and Bacarus in the cramped front seat and Maghrurio, as usual, alone in the back with his thoughts.

Did I hear what I thought I heard? Am I getting fired?

Oblivious to the incongruity of worrying about firing even as he contemplated quitting, Maghrurio tried to distract himself by focusing on his surroundings. Decra was an interesting place, more than a town and less than a city. Nestled in the shadow of the Blade Mountains to the north, it boasted all the hallmarks of civilization, such as temples to several gods, a library, and a branch campus of the larger University of Learning in Acyfala, Albiona's capital to the east. It also boasted the provincial touches of a small town--a thriving market, family farms, and a casual familiarity its inhabitants shared. People in Decra were friendly, quick to greet and chat with each other.

There was friendliness and warmth all around as they rode toward the market.

Just not within the wagon itself.

Abner seems uncommonly silent, as if he had harsh news to deliver and didn't quite know how to begin.

At their first stop, Bacarus left the pair waiting while she visited the general store to replenish their foodstuffs. Once they were alone, Abner fixed Maghrurio with a hard stare.

Here it comes.

"Maghrurio, the time has come to re-examine our arrangement. You've performed various errands for me and assisted me in my work, but I don't think you can continue in that role any longer."

"Master, whatever I've done to disappoint you…"

Abner shook his head. "There is no disappointment, but it is clear you can no longer work for me." He sighed. "You've gone through many jobs over the years, Maghrurio, none of which you were particularly suited to or inspired by. This job has been no different. You deserve a calling that will challenge you and inflame your passions."

"But I have enjoyed…"

"Really, Maghrurio, you've enjoyed the people you encountered. But the job itself? No, this running, fetching, and carrying is a waste of your potential."

Maghrurio saw Bacarus emerge from the store with her arms full and, without thinking, jumped down to help her into the wagon.

"We'll talk more later, Maghrurio, but I'm afraid my mind is made up."

After an awkwardly silent ride to their next stop, Bacarus departed to get some sewing supplies at a dress shop. Abner climbed to the ground and stretched his back.

"Please wait with the wagon, Maghrurio. The apothecary next door has asked for my opinion about an odd shipment she received." The Mystic shambled off, leaving Maghrurio to wallow in despair and self-pity.

He was fired. Again. He just couldn't seem to help it. He'd get an itch to do something and just as quickly lose interest. Sure, there would be a new job and a new place to live--he'd always managed to before--but still… How many jobs had he gone through? How many more before he found something that suited him? Maghrurio was by no means a young man, but he still hadn't found an answer to the fundamental question.

What do I want to be when I grow up?

The apothecary burst from her store, yelling as she ran toward the wagon. There was a burst of bright light and a thunderclap of sound, and Maghrurio was thrown to the ground.

He slowly regained consciousness, dazed and bloody. *The sounds, the smells, the feeling of danger… Was this that dream again? No, this was reality.* He lay on the ground in front of the smoldering wreck that, until moments before, had been the shop.

His ears ringing from the explosion, Maghrurio lurched to his feet. He ran, choking, into the burning building, his cloak a flimsy shield against the flames. Unfamiliar with the layout, he found the interior a maze of shelves and tables obscured by billowing smoke and chaotic destruction. Flames were everywhere, with random tongues of green or violet as some exotic ingredient was consumed.

Where could Abner be?

Dodging flames and falling debris, Maghrurio weaved around obstacles he couldn't move and tossed aside ones he could. Another fallen shelf, another pile of broken crockery, but still no Abner.

Time is running out.

He cast about desperately, searching through the smoke for any sign of his master's body. Then, a chunk of the roof collapsed, a near miss that peppered him with debris. He ducked under a cross beam and crawled toward the back of the shop, the smoke and flames closing in from every direction. He despaired of ever finding his master when he spotted the man sprawled near the counter. He scrambled over shattered shelving until he stood next to the body. Reaching down, he felt the old man's neck for a pulse.

He's still alive.

Hurling debris aside, he hoisted Abner's body across his shoulder and staggered to the doorway, barely reaching it before the roof collapsed behind them. Somehow, he struggled to the wagon and dropped the unconscious Mystic in the back as Bacarus and the apothecary ran up. They immediately started working on Abner's wounds in a desperate attempt to save his life.

Abner was in bad shape. He was badly burned in many places and riddled with cuts and bruises from flying debris. His eyes fluttered open and fixed on Maghrurio's face. He waved his fingers as if washing a window, and Maghrurio felt a strange breeze blow on his face.

"Our conversation is private. I don't have much time, Maghrurio." The injured man coughed up blood and continued. "Someone has been assassinating Mystics throughout Sonoduhl, and I fear I am their latest victim." He gritted his teeth as a wave of pain swept through him. Maghrurio ripped cloth from his tunic and applied pressure to an oozing head wound.

A wracking cough seized Abner, and he fought to draw breath. His throat was ravaged, and he could only whisper. "You thought I fired you earlier, but you mistook my intention." Straining, his charred right hand pulled a golden ring from his left and pressed it into Maghrurio's. "Put this on. Never take it off. You are the Mystic now." He smiled weakly. "Dream of me…"

Abner cried out and went limp. His eyes fluttered, then closed for the last time.

ACCESSION

Maghrurio sat in his austere room, still in a daze. The memorial service was elaborate and well attended by the rich and powerful because Abner was that famous. He accepted condolences when people offered them, and he ate what Bacarus put in front of him, but still, he felt disconnected from all that transpired.

He tried to start small... his job was gone. Not that big a deal--when you've drifted through life, you grew accustomed to a certain fluidity. Abner was dead... that was a kicker. Abner was a powerful Mystic, maybe the best in all of Sonoduhl. Still, death comes for everyone eventually, right?

No, the thing that really had Maghrurio off-balance was sitting snugly on the small finger of his left hand. The Mystic Ring. Golden it was yet set with an ordinary stone. Its simplicity belied the effect it had on his life. It was the reason people were paying their respects to him. It marked him as Abner's heir.

A Mystic! Me!

Maghrurio knew no magic, nor did he possess any wisdom or insight of value. He felt like a toddler wearing his father's shoes. He wasn't worthy of the Ring and fully expected to be exposed for the fraud he was.

He continued to stare through the window of his room, uncertain of what to do next. Smiling, Bacarus poked her head around his open door and let herself in. She'd taken it upon herself to care for him these last couple of days and seemed determined to continue in her new role.

"The last of the well-wishers have left, and Sheru is helping me tidy up."

"Who?"

"Sheru. She ran the apothecary and lived there, so she had nowhere else to stay. I put her in the spare room until she figures out what comes next. If that's acceptable to you, that is."

"Sure."

She examined his face closely. "This has been quite a shock for both of us. How are you holding up?"

"Fine."

Bacarus frowned at him. "Fine, my left foot. You haven't slept a wink since the accident. You're practically unconscious on your feet."

"Mmm…"

"How eloquent." Her face hardened. "That's it, no arguments. You're going to bed right now."

She grabbed his arm, marched him over to his small cot, and pushed him down onto it. Removing his shoes, she flipped his legs around until he was in a proper recumbent position.

"Sleep!" she commanded and left the room.

Exhausted as he was, it took him a long time to comply.

• • ● • •

His dreams were vague and troubling, with nothing clearly seen but a pervasive sense of danger closing in from all sides. He fled through fields and towns, but something ominous continued to follow. When he could run no longer, he hid behind doors and under beds, but peril continued to draw closer, poised to seize him. His fear grew until he finally cried out into the darkness.

"Help me, Abner!"

The change was abrupt and profound. One moment he cringed in the darkness and in the next he stood in a pleasant glade shaded by ancient trees and surrounded by stone benches arranged in a circle. Between the benches and the trees stood a low granite wall, weathered by age and expertly built without crack or crevice. Absent were the sounds of birds and beasts, but not alarmingly so. The air was filled instead with the heady aromas of rich earth and growing things. He had no idea where he was but somehow felt safe and secure.

"Where am I?" he wondered aloud.

"An ancient place called the Circle of Friends," said a voice behind him. Maghrurio spun around.

"Abner!" he cried, incredulous.

"Hello, my friend." Abner stood before him, whole and hale and robed in deepest blue.

"I… you…" Maghrurio sputtered, confusion and surprise warring for supremacy.

"The Abner you knew is dead. I am not him. I am neither ghost nor shade but merely an imprint upon the Ring you wear. And yes, this is a dream. But at the same time, yes, this is real." He lowered himself onto one of the benches. "Why don't you have a seat?"

Maghrurio slumped onto a bench and continued to stare, dumbfounded. "You're not dead. So I guess you can't tell me about… what comes next?"

"I'm sorry, Maghrurio, but I'm as in the dark in that respect as anyone."

Machrurio opened his mouth to ask another question, but with so many jumbled in his head, he couldn't pick one.

"I imagine you're wondering why you're here? I certainly did when I was in your place. I'm here to help you become a Mystic. You'll need a teacher, someone to instruct you and help you polish your skills. Someone to discuss your ideas and observations with. That will be me. I'm not omniscient, but hopefully, we can figure things out between us. Just dream of me, and we'll be together." He smiled encouragingly, and Maghrurio guessed he was trying to convey support and confidence.

Maghrurio decided to accept the explanation. Gazing into Abner's eyes, he asked, "Why me?"

"You might suspect you were simply in the right place at the right time, but you'd be wrong. No, Maghrurio, I knew I would be in mortal danger that day but had hoped I was clever enough to avoid serious injury. Alas, I was mistaken."

He arose and began pacing. "But I was not mistaken when I said you needed something to ignite your passions. My instincts, and what you'd shared of your recent dreams, told me you were the apprentice for whom I'd been searching. Of course, I'd rather hoped there would be more time to prepare you, but this," he gestured around him, "will have to suffice."

Maghrurio shook his head as he spoke. "I don't know if this is going to work, Abner. I have no magic, no special insights, no skills to speak of. I'm not ready for this. I'll never be ready for this."

"Would it surprise you to hear that I had the same reaction when I was recruited? The idea of doing magic, of being a Mystic, frightened me terribly at first. But my Master worked with me, and when I finally inherited the Ring, I was ready. We'll have to improvise a bit with your training, but we can make it work." Abner smiled and sat back down. "Your first lesson in magic is simple. Are you ready? Here it is: anyone can do it."

"What? That's crazy!"

"Oh no, it most certainly is not. The Mystic Ring helps to focus your power and makes the magic easier to learn, but anyone sufficiently skilled and practiced can do it. Normal people just don't know how."

A worried expression crept across Maghrurio's troubled face. "If anyone can do it, then that means…"

Abner nodded. "Yes, Maghrurio, that means you can do it, too. Would you like to try? Of course, you would." Abner rose. "Stand up, please. Now, clear your mind, flap your hand like this, and conjure a breeze."

Maghrurio slowly rose to his feet, trying in vain to conceal a look of panic. He shut his eyes, took a deep breath, flapped his hand as Abner had, and thought about breezes. Nothing happened. He opened his eyes, concentrated harder, and flapped again. Nothing continued to happen. Embarrassment and frustration rising, he flapped angrily toward Abner, and… Abner's hair moved. It actually moved! There were no winds here in the Circle of Friends, but he had somehow conjured a breeze!

"Congratulations, Maghrurio. You've taken your first step on a long road."

Maghrurio was shocked that he had performed actual magic. Incredibly minor magic, certainly, but it was magic just the same.

"The key to magic is focus. If you can learn to eliminate distractions and focus on what you're doing, you'll be able to create a breeze every time you try. I suggest you start meditating every day to help with your concentration. And, of course, practice conjuring the breeze."

Abner put a hand on Maghrurio's shoulder. "You must also let go of your negative thoughts. I know you're plagued with self-doubt and feel inadequate to this challenge. Don't believe it! You are a Mystic, and you will master these lessons. With hard work and a bit of luck, you could become the greatest Mystic in Sonoduhl--IF you can cast aside your mental baggage." Smiling, Abner added, "I believe in you, Maghrurio. You should believe in yourself as well."

Abner glanced up as the sun inched toward the horizon. "Our time grows short. I can come to you only once per day. Calling for me during sleep would be the simplest." His expression turned somber. "Remember, someone out there is trying to kill Mystics. Find out who and why they're doing it and stop them. Be careful until we meet again!"

Night descended on the Circle of Friends and, with its mists, obscured Abner and his surroundings. Finally, Maghrurio drifted away from his mentor into a deep and untroubled sleep.

THE DARKNESS AND THE LIGHT

Maghrurio awoke, refreshed and exuberant, ready to face a new day. Then the reality of his situation hit him, and anxiety once more took hold. After his morning ablutions, he followed the sweet aroma of breakfast to the kitchen. Bacarus and a strange woman were whispering over tea and abruptly halted their conversation as he entered the room.

"There's tea and muffins for breakfast, Master."

Maghrurio grimaced, "By the Twelve Gods, Bacarus! Please don't call me that."

"I can't very well call you by your name. It wouldn't be proper."

"Fine, then don't call me anything." Between the recent events and the shock of realizing he was the master now, his appetite was quite spoiled. He ate to give his hands something to do.

"You remember Sheru, Mas…" Bacarus caught herself. "She's staying here with us for a while."

Sheru was shorter and much slimmer than Bacarus. Her dark shoulder-length hair framed a pleasant face that seemed friendly and outgoing. He'd passed her on occasion in town but had never actually met her before today.

Sheru extended her hand. "It's a pleasure to meet you, Sir. I am sorry for your loss. I liked Abner. He was a good man who always treated me with respect."

Maghrurio shook her hand. *Well, Abner asked him to investigate his murder, so he might as well start here.* "What can you recall about the… incident?"

"Earlier this week I received a shipment of herbs and powders from the normal trade route through Albiona, but there was an extra box that seemed odd. It wasn't anything I'd ordered, and the markings were unfamiliar. In my line of work, you learn to be cautious with unknown materials, so I set it aside for Abner to examine. When he saw it sitting on my counter, he yelled about danger and shoved me out the door. I'd only taken a few steps before it exploded."

Unfamiliar markings weren't much, but it was their only clue so far. "What can you tell me about the markings? Were they something decorative, or were they runes or strange letters?"

"They were definitely some kind of writing, but nothing I'd ever seen before."

"Would you recognize these markings if you saw them again?"

Sheru nodded. "Oh yes, I have an impeccable memory for that kind of thing."

Bacarus cleared her throat, "Could there perhaps be pieces of the box in the rubble? Something with the writing on it that might have survived the fire?"

Maghrurio recalled how encouraging Abner used to be when he or Bacarus had a useful idea. "That's an excellent suggestion, Bacarus. We should go at once."

Bacarus beamed at him. "Give me a minute to straighten up, Master."

'Master' again. Sighing, he went outside to ready the wagon.

Soon they were riding across town, returning to the scene of the crime. Maghrurio saw the butcher staring his way, but before he could wave hello, the butcher turned away to speak to his wife. He saw the same behavior repeated by several more people--each stared in his direction but looked away when he turned toward them. People were talking about him, apparently.

He was living on borrowed time, and the goodwill people expressed during the services was already waning.

They reached the ruins of Sheru's store soon enough. It had rudy not yet been cleared by the cleaner crew, so they slowly sifted through the debris. Open to the weather, the interior was littered with glass shards, chunks of scorched furniture, and broken pieces from the roof and walls. The stench of soot and burned wood permeated everything. Little, if anything, was salvageable. Maghrurio recognized the sorrow and loss on Sheru's face. He certainly had his own troubles, but she'd lost her home and livelihood in the fire. Still, they had a job to do, and he'd keep at it until it was done. Or until they ran him out of town for the charlatan he was.

Picking through the rubble was a tiring, thankless chore, but after two fruitless hours, it finally paid off.

"Over here!" called Sheru from a far corner by the remains of her main counter. As the others hurried over with care, she hefted a foot-long section of charred wood. "This was part of the box."

Maghrurio stooped to examine her find. Wiping away the soot, he revealed strange characters etched into the wood in a line. Bacarus had no ideas, but the shapes seemed familiar to him. His mind searched back through some of his former 'careers'--jobs he'd held for months or weeks or less. He recalled one with an unpleasant armorer obsessed with generating intense heat for his forgings. The job itself wasn't a good memory, but he recalled special coal shipments from the Zod Hills, packaged in boxes with markings much like these.

"The Graavt," he said suddenly, startling the other two. "They ship varieties of coal from their homeland in the Zod Hills. This box came from them or from someone who gets shipments from them. Since coal doesn't normally explode, I'm betting someone reused this box."

"If this came from the Zod Hills, then it had to pass through Albiona to get here," pointed out Bacarus.

"And if it came through Albiona, we should think about Cyrchan-- it's the closest Albiona town on the trade route," added Sheru.

Maghrurio slowly straightened himself. "Good points, all. Let's take this bit of evidence back with us and think about what it might mean." They dusted themselves off and remounted the wagon for the return home.

· · • · ·

Unfortunately, thinking about the evidence was the last thing he'd get to do. As they arrived home, they found an officious older gentleman waiting for them.

The man was shorter than Maghrurio, with close-cropped white hair and a hint of a beard. His dress was of the court, marking him as one of the Duke's men. As he eyed Maghrurio, his expression suggested he was inspecting an unusual bit of refuse requiring disposal.

"The Duke of Decra extends his greetings and salutations. He understands that he intrudes on your grief, but the needs of the high and mighty know no pause. Thus, the Duke requests and requires the presence of Decra's new... Mystic." There was a slight pause and a flicker of his eye, as if he knew Maghrurio wasn't really a Mystic and the whole twisted affair would be straightened out presently.

Maghrurio gestured with his soot-covered hands. "As you can see, I must wash first, but please inform His Grace that I will be along immediately thereafter."

The messenger paused momentarily as if to convey his contempt. "You misunderstand. I am to return with you."

"Ah. Very well, then, if you'll give me a moment." Head down, he headed for his washroom.

This is bad. Maghrurio had heard the stories. The Duke was a greedy, power-hungry despot who only treated well those subjects who could do something for him.

What does he want with me?

Unfortunately, he had little time to ponder the question. A quick wash and change of clothes were all he could manage, and he emerged from his room to find the messenger waiting impatiently. Trying to hide his rising trepidation, Maghrurio gestured toward the front door. "Shall we?"

· · ● · ·

Sheru and Bacarus exchanged worried looks as the door slammed shut.

"That didn't seem like a neighborly hello," said a concerned Sheru.

"No, it seemed more like being called to the headmaster's office."

"Is there anything we can do?"

"Do you mean besides worry? No, we have to hope Maghrurio can handle himself over there and return in one piece."

"If that's possible. This is Duke Bileyo we're talking about."

"I expect this will be his first real test of being a Mystic. I'd better get the wagon packed and ready for Cyrchan in case there's any trouble."

Sheru hesitated. "I could help if you like."

"You're our guest. I wouldn't want to impose."

"It's the least I can do after the kindness you've shown me." Sheru sighed and looked out the kitchen window. "Bacarus, can I be honest with you? I've lived in Decra for over a year now, and I spent all that time trying to make my shop a success. Sure, I chatted with customers, but I never really connected with anyone. That's why I'm so thankful you let me stay here." She lowered her eyes and mumbled, "Right now, you're the only real friend I have."

Bacarus cupped Sheru's chin and lifted, making eye contact. "I haven't known you long, Sheru, but I consider you my friend too. Let's get the wagon ready."

• • ● • •

Maghrurio followed the messenger to his coach, a far more ornate and luxurious vehicle than the rickety wagon Abner had left him. Exotic woods, precious metal clasps, and embroidered tack all seemed designed to convey a simple message: Duke Bileyo was a Very Important Man and you weren't. Maghrurio's anxiety grew.

The coach made its unhurried way through the marketplace as his mind raced. What did the Duke want of him? His grasp of what it meant to be a Mystic was still nascent and tenuous. Surely the Duke didn't expect miracles already?

Or was that the problem? Was a new Mystic supposed to arise fully formed through an apprenticeship he'd never had? Was the Duke rightly expecting expertise that he, Maghrurio, didn't possess and couldn't deliver?

The coach crept closer to the Duke's castle, and panic seized hold in Maghrurio's belly as his brain fought to calm his jangled nerves. He had little choice but to either run and hide or face the Duke. His expression grew firm; he would not run. He would face the Duke and see what he wanted and let the chips fall where they would.

His belly, on the other hand, advocated running and hiding.

The coach pulled to a halt at the castle entrance, and they disembarked. The messenger guided Maghrurio through the castle, past hallways adorned with paintings, sculptures, and tapestries depicting conflict and might of arms, and into the Duke's primary receiving room. Maghrurio gave a small sigh of relief; he was afraid they'd bring him to a smaller room of lesser import which would be an overt insult to his position as Mystic.

Not that I could do anything about it…

The messenger reminded him that the Duke should be addressed as 'Your Grace' at all times.

Maghrurio nodded--*I already knew that*--and was left to wait.

At first, he whiled away the time by examining the room. A fire blazed unnecessarily in the overlarge hearth, tinging the air with the scent of smoke. Lavish seating for six was arranged in front of it. Large stained-glass windows flanked the fireplace on either side, decorative yet bright enough to illuminate the setting. Impressive war-inspired artworks graced the opposite wall, while ornate wooden bookshelves dominated the remaining two walls. He inspected their contents for a while, noting one wall contained only military titles while the other boasted history, agriculture, and political treatises.

The time did not pass swiftly, and his anxiety level increased despite his efforts to calm himself.

Show me a stack of boxes to carry, wood to chop, or a thousand other tasks I have mastered. I know almost nothing of this Mystic business. Why do I remain in this horrible position?

He tried distracting himself by skimming a treatise on the Black Empire War, in which Nahrein and Albiona revolted successfully against the Black Empire and regained their independence. He was surprised to learn a young Abner had played no small part in that struggle. Unfortunately, the subject matter wasn't nearly distracting enough to make his current situation any less stressful.

When Duke Bileyo and his guards finally swept into the room, two hours had passed, and it had been all Maghrurio could do to not soil himself. The Duke was an older man, a soldier in his youth who had fought in the Black Empire War. His campaigning days were well behind him and he had put on some weight, but he still looked fit enough to handle Maghrurio without breaking a sweat. He exhibited a confident and superior demeanor, as if he knew he held all the cards in this encounter.

"Thank you for waiting, my boy. Affairs of state, and all that. First, let me congratulate you on your…" He waved a hand at the Mystic Ring.

Maghrurio inclined his head. "Thank you, your Grace."

The Duke gestured toward the chairs. "Shall we sit?"

A servant appeared bearing light refreshments, and at a wave, she and the guards left the room. They were alone at last.

"So, you're my new Mystic…" The Duke seemed to be appraising him, and his expression said that appraisal was less than satisfactory.

Maghrurio fought to control his trembling hands, recalling all Abner had ever said about his role. "Technically, your Grace, I am the people's Mystic. I just happen to live in Decra."

"Mmmm, yes, of course," the Duke responded, sitting back. "So show me something. Dazzle me with your talents." His eyes pierced Maghrurio like a hawk.

Sweat began to form on the crown of Maghrurio's head. *He knows! He sees through my facade and knows I am a fraud!* He forced a chuckle and tried to regroup. "I was warned of your humor, your Grace. Your jest is a good one."

"I'm not joking. Show me something."

Maghrurio frowned. He didn't know everything about Mystics, but he did know from his time with Abner that this wasn't how they were treated. "Duke Bileyo, this is a highly unusual request. Mystics are accommodating, but only up to a point. They… We… don't perform on command like trained dogs."

The Duke leaned forward and reached for Maghrurio's knee. His grip was hard, firm, and increasingly painful. "Show. Me. Something."

Maghrurio held his gaze as long as he could, which wasn't long at all, and finally exhaled. "I regret that I am still in training, your Grace, and have nothing of substance to show you yet."

"As I suspected. I'm told new Mystics apprentice prior to assuming their positions. You, on the other hand, were a simple laborer before Abner died. You are quite unqualified and therefore undeserving of both Ring and position."

The Duke leaned back in his chair, his face the epitome of decisiveness. "It is clear what must be done. You will give the Mystic Ring to me, and I will become the first Duke Mystic."

Horror and disbelief crawled across Maghrurio's face. He was entirely in Duke Bileyo's control, but he couldn't yield the Ring. *Abner had chosen me!* He inhaled deeply and mustered his flagging courage. "I'm sorry, my Duke, but I cannot comply."

"Come now, be reasonable. You have no training, no inherent abilities, and no understanding of power and its uses. I beat you in two of those, and I'm sure I can figure out how it works far more quickly than you. Still, you will be compensated for your troubles." The Duke withdrew a pouch from his pocket and tossed it on the table between them.

Maghrurio could hardly believe his ears. *Is he seriously trying to buy the Ring?* "A generous offer, your Grace, but again I cannot comply. Abner bequeathed the Ring to me, and I cannot contravene his last wish."

The Duke's serious face slowly grew a wicked smile. "I suspected that would be your answer, but I had to try. Being a Duke, though, means I tend to get my way." He clapped twice, and four soldiers burst through the chamber door. "Hold him," he ordered, the smile never leaving his face.

The soldiers pinned Maghrurio's arms to the chair. He was powerless to stop them. The Duke strode forward, seized his left hand, gripped the Ring, and pulled.

There was a burst of light, and Duke Bileyo was thrown across the room. Stunned, Maghrurio looked down at the Ring resting innocently on his finger.

The Ring had defended itself!

The Duke, unaccustomed to being denied, stormed back in a rage. "You dare to strike at your Duke?!?"

His face, twisted in fury, betrayed a hint of uncertainty. Or was it fear?

Is he afraid of me?

Whatever it had been vanished in a moment. The Duke drew himself to his full height and roared, "Consider your options, boy.

One way or the other, that Ring will be mine. Throw him in the dungeon!"

The soldiers manhandled Maghrurio to a standing position and headed for the door. His ineffective struggles were rewarded with a swift blow to the back of his head, and the room quickly faded to black.

IF WISHES WERE HORSES

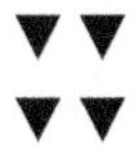

Maghrurio regained consciousness on the floor of a dark, musty cell he assumed was somewhere in the depths of the castle. His head throbbed, and he wished for a cold cloth and a comfortable bed. He expected neither.

The room was small, some four or five paces square, with a single solid wooden door. A small window located high in the wall opposite the door admitted little air or light. Dirty straw was strewn haphazardly across the floor, and the place stank of mildew and filth. The room's only contents were a small bucket in the corner and a rickety cot with a threadbare blanket.

The reality of his situation hit Maghrurio like a hammer blow, making his earlier anxiety with the Duke seem like inner peace. He searched the walls for any sign of vulnerability, but nothing was immediately obvious. It was a dungeon cell, one that had probably broken countless prisoners before him. He didn't expect to fare any better than its previous occupants.

This was a side of Decra he'd never seen before and hoped never to see again. Assuming, of course, he found his way out of there. Alive.

Fear gradually turned to despair. With nothing else to do, he sat gingerly upon the cot, as concerned with whether it would support him as he was with whatever vermin it might harbor. Hands folded, elbows on his knees, he contemplated his Ring. He looked at it, really looked at it, for the first time. It was gold and of reasonable size, not so large as to be ostentatious yet not so small as to be overlooked. The bezel had a golden filigree of clearly superior craftsmanship; otherwise, it was not terribly impressive.

Secured within the bezel rested a stone. It wasn't precious or even semi-precious--just a regular looking smallish rock, roughly cut, as if the crafter realized at the last moment he had forgotten to procure a gemstone and grabbed a random stone from the ground. If he didn't know better, he might have suspected the gold was fake, and the whole piece was little more than worthless scrap.

But he did know better. The Duke had imprisoned him for it and would probably harm him for it. Given Abner's fate, might the Duke even kill him for it?

He thought back on his exchange with the Duke. It had gone disastrously, but try as he might, he couldn't identify anything he'd done wrong. Clearly, the Duke had investigated his background and realized he wasn't Mystic material. Just as clearly, the Duke seemed enamored with the idea of wielding Mystic power. He was Decra's town leader and, thus, a member of the Nahrein Confederacy's ruling council. Adding Mystic's powers to his political ones might be enough to vault him into a greater role. Council leader? King? Anything was possible.

All the more reason to deny the Duke this prize. But how to do so?

His only saving grace thus far was that the Ring had defended itself, and the Duke was leery of what else it might do. *What else might it do?* Maghrurio suspected it only reacted to the Duke's attempt to remove it and would not act in defense of its wearer. And even if it did, there were methods by which the Duke could get his way without endangering himself. Fire, starvation, rabid dogs…

There had to be something he could do.

Maghrurio tried to recount the stories Abner told over meals or around a campfire, the tight spots he'd landed in, or the clever solutions he devised. Was there something there that might help him?

Abner had once described being captured by the Black Empire early in their civil war. He had gone to deliver a message under a flag of truce, knowing there was a strong chance he'd not be allowed to leave. Somehow, he'd managed to escape from captivity even though they'd bound him. How had he done it?

Try as he might, Maghrurio couldn't recall the details. The depressing and increasingly chilled environs were too much of a distraction. Miserable, he closed his eyes and wished he'd never come to the castle. He could have remained at home, safe and content. He saw it in his mind's eye--the warm kitchen, with fresh bread on the sideboard and honey at the ready. The ancient oven, which Bacarus scrubbed every day but could never quite get completely clean. The bay window looked out onto the front yard, with the aromatic herb pots arrayed on the sill beneath it. Between the oven and window, a battered embroidery sampler--an oddity in a house full of oddities. It was quite old but in reasonable repair. Its once-vibrant colors faded to hints of their former glory. The message itself was odd, too.

What did it mean?

"Dangers strike, troubles come; seek the solace of hearth and home?" he wondered aloud.

A flash of blinding light, a brief lurch, and he was sitting in his kitchen. The sun was shining outside, and he could hear Bacarus and Sheru arguing in the hall. Somehow his wish had been fulfilled. He had escaped!

Shocked, he glanced down at the Mystic Ring. This must be how Abner had escaped those many years ago, some interaction between Ring and sampler. And the magic must transport only to wherever the sampler awaited, he reasoned, else Abner would have had no need of a wagon for travel.

Surely this was another aspect of his magical inheritance, revealed to him at an opportune time.

Maghrurio glanced over at the sampler where it hung on the kitchen wall. Did it seem a bit more frayed than he remembered? Perhaps each use exacted its toll until, eventually, the thread fell apart and the sampler disintegrated. He would ask Abner about it, but something told him the sampler was only to be used in the direst of needs.

After all, it didn't make one immune to danger--otherwise, Abner would still be alive.

He rose from his chair and entered the hallway. Bacarus had opened her mouth to speak but shrieked when she saw him. "Master, you're back!"

Sheru spun about, too stunned to say anything.

"Where did you come from? We've been waiting here by the door."

"Never mind that. I've just escaped from the Duke's dungeon." He quickly related the tale.

"You've left him a sticky puzzle," said Sheru.

"Yes, but we should leave at once to avoid any further... unpleasantness."

He looked around, but Bacarus interrupted him. "Not to worry, the wagon is loaded and ready to go."

"One moment." He dashed back to the kitchen and pocketed the sampler. *If it helped once, it might help again.*

They hastened outside, locked up behind them, and quickly boarded the wagon. "Duck under here," suggested Sheru, holding up a large blanket spread over the cargo area. "In case the soldiers are looking for you."

Maghrurio couldn't argue with her logic, so he climbed into the back of the wagon and covered himself. He felt bags and other parcels tossed on or near him for camouflage, and with a *snick*, the horse and wagon departed.

It normally didn't take long to reach the town gates, but today it felt like hours to Maghrurio. Every jostle brought a sharp stab of fear, every sound an expectation of discovery and capture. The minutes dragged on until, finally, he could hear the gate guards yelling at people nearby.

"State your name and business," a gruff voice shouted at the front of the wagon.

"My name is Bacarus. I'm taking my friend Sheru here to see her mother in Albiona. Her store was destroyed by fire the other day, did you hear?"

"Yeah yeah yeah," muttered the guard, "Keep it moving."

Maghrurio breathed a sigh of relief. They were getting out.

"Hang on a minute," shouted the guard.

He held his breath. *They saw something!* His mind raced for what to do, unable to think of anything. He could hear the guard walking around to the back of the wagon where he was hidden. He shut his eyes as he waited for the inevitable, and then... *plonk* A bag was thrown against his leg.

"A bag fell off your wagon. You can go now," advised the guard. "Next!"

Maghrurio willed his pounding heart to slow. They were past the gates and safely away.

· · ● · ·

He remained under the blanket for a long while. When they finally stopped for a break, they were well away from Decra and safe from prying eyes. Once they resumed their journey he remained in the back, wanting to be alone with his thoughts. Bacarus and Sheru sat up front, mostly silent and focused on their eastward journey to Cyrchan.

Maghrurio sighed. Unless he somehow managed to get a lot better at this Mystic business, he could never return to Decra. The Duke with no local Mystic would likely lose status in the council, so he might send people after them. In fact...

Could the Duke be behind the Mystic murders? Perhaps as part of a conspiracy to replace independent Mystics with nobles?

It was a thought but not one he could investigate. After all, any evidence would be back in Decra, and he couldn't go back there now. No, their best bet was to continue to Cyrchan and see what they could turn up on the explosive package.

His brief burst of determination was dampened by a lingering sense of futility. He was supposed to be a Mystic, yet he couldn't prevent the Duke's actions. Even now he relied on flight as his only defense. He had escaped captivity, but that was the sampler's achievement, not his. Hardly the stuff Mystics were made of.

Maybe the Duke was right after all. Maybe I'm not Mystic material.

Maybe he just needed an afternoon nap and another chat with Abner.

· · ● · ·

He drifted into darkness, calling out Abner's name. Slowly the darkness lifted, and he could see his surroundings taking shape around him. Sturdy tree trunks were all about, replete with large heart-shaped leaves. They were linden trees, which suggested he was somewhere in the far north--probably the Wall Wood, a large forest nestled between the mountain ranges of the Eastern and Western Wall.

"Good day to you, Maghrurio," came the familiar voice.

"Good day, Master," said Maghrurio, relief evident in his voice.

"Oh no, I am not the Master here. We are merely colleagues discussing our craft. Please call me Abner."

Reminded of his earlier conversation with Bacarus, Maghrurio made the effort. He described the events of the past day, leaving out his own misgivings and feelings of inadequacy. "What do you think, Abner?"

"Duke Bileyo was always going to be a problem. He tried pressuring me for years to align myself with him, to help him politically. I always refused on the same grounds you did--we work for the people, not for leaders. And you're right, you won't be safe returning for a while yet. Let's put your sampler question aside for the moment. So you think the package originally came from the Graavt?"

"Yes, I recognized the writing. We think it came through Albiona by way of Cyrchan, so that's where we're headed. Hopefully, we can dig up more clues there."

Abner nodded thoughtfully and then abruptly changed the subject. "It's getting late, and we don't have much time. Let's talk about Mystic magic. At its foundation the magic is based on the four elements--air, fire, water, and stone. Some spells are straightforward, like producing wind or flame. Some are more challenging and involve combining the elements. We'll get to those soon enough, but let's get you comfortable with the basics. Now, wind is the simplest--the breeze spell I showed you last time. The rest are similar."

Abner flicked his fingers and produced a flame. "Concentrate on the image of fire and move your fingers like I did."

After several attempts, Maghrurio finally managed to create a flame. He jerked his hand back in surprise, dropping the flame onto a pile of leaves and setting it alight.

"Now, concentrate on water and wiggle your fingers like this."

Maghrurio again tried several times before producing a small spout of water, which he used to extinguish the burning leaves.

"Now for stone," Abner said, flipping his hand. "Again, think of what you want and repeat the gesture."

On his first attempt, Maghrurio conjured a pebble the size of an eyeball. His smile was much wider.

"Excellent work, Maghrurio. We'll make a Mystic of you yet!"

The forest shimmered, and Maghrurio looked around in alarm. "What did I do?"

"Someone is trying to wake you. Remember, practice what you've learned and have confidence in yourself!"

The scene faded to black, and Maghrurio woke up.

Sheru leaned over him. "Sorry to wake you, but we have company."

CALL TO ARMS

Maghrurio wiped the sleep from his eyes and took in the scene. The wagon was at rest amidst a handful of scrubby trees. There was no one around for miles except for the six gruff-looking men on horseback arrayed around them. Sheru sat nervously in the front seat next to Bacarus, who was talking to the apparent leader. He couldn't see her face, but he could tell by her stiff posture that she was struggling to maintain her temper.

"Hey, look, the sleepy baby woke up!" joked one of the men, to general laughter.

Maghrurio smiled lightly. He tried to appear unconcerned about the potential threat but knew that even were the riders weaponless, he could barely take one of them in a fight.

He turned and addressed the leader. "How can we help you today?"

The leader leaned back in his saddle. "We've been riding all morning, you see, and we're getting hungry."

"Not just for food," the joker added, leering at the women. Sheru shrunk at the comment.

The leader gestured widely. "Since you have so much here, we thought you wouldn't mind sharing."

To Maghrurio's alarm, the outlaws dismounted and moved the short distance toward the wagon. He had only seconds.

"Stop!" he shouted, and oddly enough, they did. "You know not your peril, for I am a Mystic from Decra and a wielder of elemental magic. Leave this place and live!"

The men looked at each other, momentarily unsure, but when nothing else happened, they started forward again.

This was it.

He focused his mind and flicked his fingers. Nothing happened. He tried again and managed to call up a small tongue of flame in his hand. He paused for a second, unsure what to do with it, before hurling it at the ground in front of the leader, who took a quick step back.

The tiny flame sputtered and went out. Nothing further happened. The men roared with laughter, to his embarrassment and horror. He could do nothing to stop what was coming.

The joker was the first to the wagon. Laughing, he reached up for Bacarus. She grabbed his hand, twisted his arm, spun him completely around, and pushed him to the ground with her foot. His friend grabbed at a screaming Sheru. Bacarus lunged across the wagon seat and, with a snap of her leg, kicked the ruffian away. She dropped to the ground by the wagon, facing the surprised outlaws.

With a shout, the joker and his friend rushed her with fists flying. Shifting her weight as she swept her arm, she deflected the friend's charge head-first into the wagon. Spinning about, her hands and feet were a blur. In a moment only four outlaws remained standing. Nobody was laughing anymore.

"You heard the man," Bacarus declared. "Leave this place and live." She struck an aggressive martial pose of a style Maghrurio had never seen before. With a quick glance at each other, the outlaws grabbed their downed fellows and hurried away on their horses.

Sheru and Maghrurio stared in shock at Bacarus, who blushed and said, "We should get moving. They might come back." She remounted the wagon and, with a flick of the reins, resumed their eastern progress.

The remainder of that afternoon's journey was marked by continued silence. Sheru spent most of it staring at Bacarus, her mouth open and poised to ask a million questions but unable to articulate a single one. Bacarus, in turn, focused on her driving, her gaze fixed on the path ahead. Her stiff posture firmly communicated that she didn't want to talk about it.

Maghrurio, while both shocked and impressed by her display, was struck with a bitter sense of his own inadequacy. He had tried to be a hero, but all he managed to do was get laughed at.

Some Mystic I turned out to be. The Duke was right to insist that I had no right to my position.

• • ● • •

Late in the day and miles from Decra, they halted to set up camp. Sheru curried and fed Snowfall while Maghrurio collected firewood and ignited their cooking fire with a lackluster flick of his hand. Bacarus prepared their evening meal, and sunset found them eating a quiet dinner. It didn't take long before Sheru finally found her voice.

"So, are we going to talk about this afternoon?"

Maghrurio sighed and put down his plate. "I'm so sorry. I was completely hopeless. If not for Bacarus…"

"You have nothing to be ashamed of," Bacarus said as she set down her plate and faced him. "You've been a Mystic for less than a week. You can't expect to be an expert instantly. Complex skills take time and hard work to acquire."

"Speaking of complex skills," interjected Sheru, "what the hell did you do back there?"

The question hung in the air like a storm cloud. Bacarus leveled a hard stare at Sheru, who returned it undaunted. Maghrurio was busy wallowing in shame, but he couldn't help but be curious as well.

Where did those complex skills come from?

Bacarus blinked first, then looked down. "I don't like to talk about it." She resumed her meal and would say no more. Ignoring all further attempts to elicit a response, Bacarus collected the dinner dishes and left to wash them in a nearby creek.

Sheru stared into the fire, lost in thought, until she finally blurted, "It's all gone."

"Excuse me?"

"My shop, my home, my career. My life. It's all gone."

Maghrurio didn't know how to respond.

"I thought things were going well for me, that my life was finally turning around. And then that box showed up."

"I'm sorry you were dragged into this, Sheru."

"By all rights, I should be angry with you and Bacarus, but you've been the only ones in Decra to be nice to me. Apart from Abner, and he's…"

"You're welcome to stay with us as long as you like." Maghrurio put a consoling hand on her shoulder.

Sheru shrank from his touch.

Maghrurio pulled back his hand as if burned. "I'm sorry, Sheru. I didn't mean you any harm."

Sheru wrapped her arms around herself, avoiding his eyes.

"She doesn't like to be touched," said a returning Bacarus.

Maghrurio glanced back and forth between the women, not entirely certain of what had just transpired. "My apologies," he said as he rose and left them in the camp.

He walked down to the creek himself to wash his face and hands. Clearly, something was troubling Sheru, something more than losing her home and livelihood. Like him, she was adrift without direction, trying to find her way in a changing world. Like him, she needed to make the best of the current situation.

He kept twitching and flipping as he walked, producing fire, water, stone, and wind. The spells weren't much, but if Abner had taught them, then he should master them. He needed to have faith that, eventually, the practice would pay off. He needed to remember that he wasn't the only person with troubles. He needed to stop wasting time feeling sorry for himself.

He just wished it all was easier to do.

• • ● • •

The night passed quickly. Maghrurio took the first watch, practicing his basic spells under the light of the two moons. Sheru took the next watch and Bacarus the last. She woke her companions with the enticing aroma of scrambled duck eggs she had found down by the creek. They ate quickly and resumed their eastward trek to Cyrchan.

Maghrurio tried engaging Sheru and Bacarus in conversation, but neither was in a talkative mood. After a while, his thoughts returned to his own problems. Quite frankly, he just wasn't Mystic material. Sure, he'd managed to master the basics, and his spells rarely misfired any longer, but if he couldn't rely on them when it really counted, then what good were they?

Part of him longed to jump off the wagon and run away. Another part longed to fling the Mystic Ring as far as he could or to give it to someone better suited to use it--Duke Bileyo? Bacarus? The next person they met on the road? But the greater part of him knew he could do none of those things. He was stuck with the Ring, his position, and his fate. He sighed again and let his mind wander.

They passed through an area of rolling hills and trees, mostly varieties of maple and birch that offered sparse cover from the storm clouds heading their way. It would be a race as to whether they would eat lunch before or after the skies opened up. Either way, he foresaw a wet and miserable evening ahead.

He turned his attention to the evidence that originally inspired their journey, the piece of wood from Sheru's shop. It was Graavt writing, certainly, but he'd never learned to read or speak the language. They needed to find someone who could interpret it for them, but Graavtish was little spoken outside of the Zod Hills. Since he'd first encountered the writing while working for one armorer, he reasoned, maybe another would be a place to start?

They stopped for a brief lunch and managed to get back on the move before the rains started. The ground was fairly level and hardened by much traffic, so apart from being personally soaked they weren't terribly inconvenienced. Visibility was reduced by the downpour, and they encountered few travelers for the remainder of the day. Spotting a small hill with a stand of red maple, they decided to halt and set up camp for the evening.

Maghrurio's ability to produce flame again came in handy, as the firewood they collected was too wet to light by normal means. He took small comfort in this meager contribution. Sheru continued to stare at Bacarus as she had all day. Whether because of Sheru's silent onslaught, or the result of some internal debate, Bacarus finally relented.

"I was born in a small village near the Greytops on the east coast. My parents were traders, and we used to travel all over the Barrier Woods. When I was still a little girl, my parents were swept away when a bridge collapsed over the Caqaba River. I was stranded on the wrong side with no idea what to do. A group of monks found me and took me back to live at their monastery. They taught me many things, including how to take care of myself."

Ever curious, Sheru asked, "Why didn't you stay with them? Did the training get too hard"

"I could handle the training, but the elders foresaw in me a great leader." She shook her head. "I didn't want to lead anything. I just wanted to keep things ordered. They kept pushing, I pushed back, and eventually, I left. But I've kept up my fighting skills."

Bacarus paused for a moment, then stared fully into Maghrurio's eyes. "My abilities took a long time and a lot of hard work. That's why I'm telling you, Master, not to be so hard on yourself. Put in the time and the work, and before long you won't need my help any more than Abner did."

The rain became a deluge, which literally dampened all further attempts at conversation. Finally, too exhausted to set a watch, they built up the fire, rolled into their bedrolls, and one by one drifted off to sleep.

• • ● • •

"Abner?"

Maghrurio found himself this time at the edge of a sprawling desert. Hunting birds circled overhead, searching for prey only they could see. The air shimmered with the heat, and he felt as if all the moisture was being extracted from his body. A series of broken and rolling hills lay scattered behind him. Spinning around to take it all in, he spotted Abner sitting nearby on a large rock.

"Welcome back, Maghrurio. It would appear we're at the southern edge of the Zod Hills overlooking the Zod Desert. It's a most uncomfortable place." Abner scrutinized him sharply. "You look upset. What's the matter?"

Maghrurio wanted to be brave about his shortcomings, but as he started to relate his tale, the frustration and shame poured from him unchecked. When he finished, shaken and close to tears, Abner put a hand on his shoulder. "A Mystic's life is not easy, especially in the beginning. Yours especially so, since you were never properly apprenticed. I'm glad Bacarus was able to calm things down."

Maghrurio gazed at Abner, his voice stony but his face beseeching. "I feel like such a failure, Abner. Is there any hope for me?"

"My friend, you must trust me that things will get better. Here's something that might raise your spirits. You must know you're not the only Mystic in Sonoduhl, right?" At Maghrurio's nod, he continued. "A Gathering of Mystics takes place twice every month--when Vadha rises in full and two weeks later when Ghata is full. You can join them in the same manner as you join me, by sleep or trance. Some Mystics are older and more experienced like I was, and some will be younger and newer to the role like you. There, you will be among friends and allies. Ask questions and share your experiences. You may find things aren't quite as bleak as you think."

It wasn't a panacea, but the idea of interacting with other Mystics did seem to help a little. The thought made Maghrurio feel, if not quite better, definitely less miserable.

Abner seemed to see something encouraging in Maghrurio's face, so he stood up. "Good. Now for today's lesson. You've mastered the basic forces, so let's work on magnitude. After all, you've already seen that a tiny flame is only good for starting a campfire. To make the flame larger, you need to visualize what you want it to do and believe you can do it. The stronger your belief, the more effective your spell will be."

Maghrurio was stunned. "You're kidding, right? I just poured my heart out about feeling inadequate to this whole task, and you tell me the only way to get better is to believe in myself?!?" He paced the arid ground and shouted. "Self-confidence is in short supply these days, Abner, and every failure makes things that much harder!"

Abner just shook his head and spoke more softly. "I empathize with your difficulties. Believe it or not, I had them as well in the beginning. Just keep practicing Maghrurio. Meet with your peers. Keep your eyes open. And, most of all, believe you can be better."

The mists rolled in, signaling the end of their session.

WHEN IT RAINS…

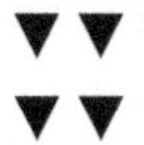

A light rain doused the soggy travelers the following morning. Nevertheless, they continued their eastward trek as they took stock of their situation.

"We should reach Hasa before nightfall, barring any problems," said Bacarus. "It's a small town, but it has a decent inn."

"I could use a nice, warm bed for a change," muttered Sheru. "I've never been a fan of rainy days, especially when I'm in them."

"I was thinking," began Maghrurio. "Last time I encountered Graavt packaging I was working for an armorer. Does Hasa have one?"

"I'm not sure," Bacarus answered. "We can ask around."

The wind squalled, and the rain grew in intensity, killing further conversation. They retreated into their cloaks and their private thoughts.

Maghrurio pondered the previous night's lesson. *So I need to practice my spells and grow my confidence.* The first part was fairly easy, the second not so much. His confidence would surely get a boost from some success, but he couldn't expect any success without confidence. How was he to unravel this knot?

The rain continued, falling straight and heavy, so he decided to practice summoning wind. He flapped his hand and could see the raindrops move slightly in the wind he made. *Great, once more, with confidence!* The raindrops again moved slightly. And again. And again. He worked on it for the rest of the morning, and by the time they found a copse of willow trees to shelter for lunch, he had managed to get a tiny bit more movement. It was something--not much, but something.

The rain persisted all afternoon, sometimes light and breezy, other times heavy and oppressing. When it wasn't his turn to drive, he continued to practice with little improvement. By the time the sky began to darken and they drew near to Hasa's town wall, he was thoroughly soaked and altogether frustrated with the whole exercise.

A few more minutes through the soggy town brought them to the Excelsior Inn. A strong lad helped unload their luggage and led their horse and wagon to the stables. Escaping the downpour, they passed through the doorway into the bustle and warmth of the Excelsior.

The wide entryway opened into a large and inviting tavern, dimly lit by candles and crowded. A central fireplace shed warmth, and the air was thick with laughter, smoke, and off-key singing. Most of the participants were dry, so clearly they'd been indoors for a while.

A short, balding man in a bright red smock approached, shouting instructions to three different workers. It was hard for Maghrurio to make out who was supposed to be listening to what, but they seemed to have the chaos under control. As quickly as it began, they each dashed off to complete whatever tasks had been assigned. Content, or at least momentarily satisfied, the man turned to the three. "How can we help you this evening? Dinner, drinks, rooms?"

Bacarus spoke up. "All three would be great. With a bath, if possible."

"We have a suite upstairs with three beds and a sitting area. Would that work?" He stopped a passing worker, gave some whispered instructions, then resumed his attention with a hopeful look.

"Sure, that would be fine."

He clapped twice, and two young lads appeared to bear away their luggage. Following them to their rooms, the man continued, "Please, make yourselves at home." Then, opening their door, he pointed, "Beds are through there, and the bath is on your right. Just ring for hot water to be brought. The tavern is downstairs, as you saw. Call if you need anything." He and the lads swept from the room in a flash.

Sheru looked at the other two. "I've had enough water poured over me to last for a while. Why don't we change into something dry and head downstairs for something to eat?"

• • ● • •

The trio returned to the chaos of the tavern for their evening meal. Glancing around from their table, Maghrurio spied farmers, laborers, merchants, and tradesmen--a solid cross-section of Nahrein citizenry. A handful of soldiers drank at the bar, and women and children scattered throughout the room. *Surely somebody here must know how to read Graavtish or knows someone who can.* He pushed away his half-eaten stew and stood up. "I'm going to mingle and try to find someone who can translate that piece of wood we have upstairs. I'll see you later."

Maghrurio eyed the soldiers in the room, all resplendent in their Nahrein uniforms. *They could be from any town in Nahrein, not necessarily from Decra.* It paid to be cautious, though, so he avoided them on the off chance that Duke Bileyo was searching for him.

He exchanged small talk with some merchants gathered at the bar before asking if they knew anyone who could read Graavt script. None did, so he excused himself and wandered around. It didn't take many brief conversations before he'd decided the search was pointless. Disappointed, but not terribly surprised, he returned to the bar for some wine before bed. No sooner had he taken a sip when a woman slipped into the seat next to him.

"Hi there. I'm Nepri," she said to him, smiling. She was tall, with dark hair and eyes, nicely dressed and bejeweled. In a word, attractive.

In two words, very attractive.

"Hello, I'm Maghrurio." He smiled and gestured around the room. "It certainly seems to be a busy night."

"Oh yes, it's usually like this. I don't recognize you, so I'm guessing you aren't from around here. Are you in town for business?"

"Just passing through, actually. I have business in Albiona."

"Really? I've always wanted to go there. It must be very exciting!"

"I, uh, imagine it will be."

"That's a very unusual ring you have. May I see it?"

Maghrurio held his hand out, and Nepri grasped it with the slightest touch. *Her hands are really warm and soft.* He sipped his wine while she inspected his Ring.

"I've never seen a stone like this before. What kind is it?"

"I'm not quite sure, but I do know this ring is rare. There are only eleven others like it in existence. I... inherited it."

Nepri's eyes perked up. "A dead relative, perhaps?"

Maghrurio sipped some wine, thinking of how best to describe the situation. He settled on "Something like that."

"I'm so sorry to hear." Despite her comment, her smile grew, if possible, even more dazzling.

Maghrurio could feel the effects of the wine starting to loosen his tongue. "Oh yes, it was quite sudden. One minute I'm a regular working man; the next, I have this Ring, a house, a staff..."

Nepri inched closer to him. "You must be a very important man now and doing very important things."

Without thinking, Maghrurio leaned closer as well. The noise level, already loud when they'd first met, was growing by the minute. Singing, shouting, loud conversations, and ever greater numbers surrounded the pair. Pretty soon, they'd have to shout in each other's ears to be heard.

Nepri was a pleasant listener, so Maghrurio captivated her with stories of some of his former jobs. She showed interest in his every utterance. *No way she could hear me over this racket. But, whatever.* He knew he was no ladies' man, and he wasn't really trying. But, for tonight at least, everything he said seemed to work.

I'm not drunk, but I'm not sober, either. Then, remembering his mission, he steered the conversation back to his main objective.

"While I'm in town, I'm actually looking for someone who can help me with something."

"Ooh, do tell!"

Soldiers at the other end of the bar burst into song, prompting Maghrurio to speak into her ear.

"I have Graavt writing on some wood upstairs in my room. Would you happen to know anyone who can read it?"

It didn't appear that she'd heard much of what he'd said over the singing, but she smiled and gestured upstairs. He rose and led the way.

The rooms were empty and far quieter than downstairs. Nepri swept in after Maghrurio, glanced around quickly, and lounged against the armchair by the fireplace. Smiling innocently at him, she asked, "Now, what were you saying about wood?"

Maghrurio, focused on the possibility of solving a mystery, rushed into his bedroom to retrieve the evidence. Returning to the main room, he presented it to her.

Her smile quickly fell away. "What's this?"

"The wood with the writing I told you about," he replied eagerly.

Nepri stood abruptly, stiff with anger. "Is that what you said? Are you kidding me?"

At that moment, Sheru and Bacarus entered the room. They halted by the door, unsure about the stranger ranting at their friend.

Nepri took in the cut of his clothing and the quality of his room and snorted in disgust. "Ugh, I'm an idiot! I can't believe I wasted an hour listening to your inane blathering. I thought you were some kind of bigshot nobleman or something, but no, you're just another idiot drifting through town. What a pathetic loser!"

She stormed out of the suite, slamming the door behind her. Maghrurio sputtered in confusion, "What was that about?"

Bacarus had the decency to look shocked. Sheru, meanwhile, fought to keep a straight face.

His confused expression slowly turned to understanding, and finally to horror and embarrassment. Sheru burst into howls of laughter that chased Maghrurio to his bedroom, where he remained for the rest of the night.

• • ● • •

The next morning, a deflated and still embarrassed Maghrurio found his colleagues already eating breakfast downstairs.

"Good morning," he muttered sheepishly, joining them at their table. He took a quick glance around to make certain Nepri wasn't around. Too embarrassed to eat, he ordered a pot of tea and some toast, more to occupy his hands than anything. He sat silently, at a loss for what to say.

Sheru saved him. "I'm sorry for laughing at you last night. But you must admit, it was kind of funny…"

Bacarus gave her a look, and she wiped the smile from her face.

Sheru tried again. "Listen, forget about that woman. She was bad news. We should focus on what we came here to do--see if we can get the Graavtish translated and then continue on east."

"Apology accepted, and thank you, Sheru. Clearly, this hasn't been a good week for me." As shamed as he felt, he was relieved to see her opening up again. A waiter swung by with his breakfast order, and he tucked in.

Putting down her teacup, Bacarus interjected, "We need to talk about funds. I think we should pool our money together to get us through this trip. We can think about what we'll do after it's over."

The others agreed and, after fishing through their pockets, came up with a small pile of coins. Not bad, but not great, since there were no prospects of getting more anytime soon.

Maghrurio asked, "Bacarus, I know I'd feel more comfortable if you kept the money. After all, you ran Abner's household all those years."

"Fine, but you two should hold something just in case." She handed over a few coins and put the remainder in an inside pocket. "So where to now?"

Sheru piped up. "Why don't we split up and see if we can find anyone that can read Graavtish? As he said earlier, you and I can hit the marketplace, and Maghrurio can try the smithy types. We'll meet back here before lunch and follow up then."

Nodding his assent, Maghrurio ran back to his room and returned moments later with a satchel slung over his shoulders, the charred piece of wood secured within. With a plan in place, they left the dining hall and ventured forth into the rainy streets of Hasa.

Maghrurio had some difficulty finding his way through the winding streets. A fair number of people were out and about despite the rain, so he was forced to ask for directions once or twice before eventually finding his goal.

The old armorer stood on a covered porch, holding an oblong piece of glowing metal with battered tongs against the wrought iron anvil. His hammer falls were loud, forceful, and rhythmic, alternating between the glowing metal and the anvil itself. Maghrurio waited patiently, recalling his past experience of getting yelled at if he interrupted his master's work. The armorer eventually plunged the metal into a liquid bath with a resounding hiss and laid down his tools.

He paused for a drink of water, wiped his brow, and turned to Maghrurio. "Can I help you?"

"Good day, sir. I was admiring your setup here. It's been a long time since I worked a forge, but I feel it's not totally lost to me."

"It sticks in your blood, doesn't it?"

"Indeed. I was wondering if I could ask a question if you have a moment?"

The armorer seemed pleased by Maghrurio's display of respect, so he nodded.

"I have a piece of a box here with what I think is Graavtish writing on it." Maghrurio pulled it out of his satchel. "Would you be able to tell what this says or where it came from?"

The armorer wiped his hands on his apron and reached out for the wood. "This is definitely Graavtish. I recognize many of the letters. I can't read it all, but this word here," he pointed, "means Cyrchan. If I had to guess, this was part of a shipment to somebody there."

"My thanks, you've been most helpful." Maghrurio knew metalsmiths like this man would be insulted by a monetary reward, but he deserved something for his assistance. Eyeing a weapons display near the front, he asked, "May I?"

The armorer nodded, and Maghrurio stepped over to inspect the assortment of blades. "Impressive. I find myself on the road with no weapon and could certainly use a good dagger."

After some discussion and requisite haggling, Maghrurio left with a well-balanced dagger, sheath, and whetstone for a fair price.

He made his way back to the inn and ordered tea while he waited for his companions. He chose a spot near the back, but in a somewhat sheltered spot, so he could watch the entrances easily without necessarily being seen himself. There weren't many diners and drinkers at this hour--a family with several children, a cleric of some type, and a soldier hunched at the bar, whispering with someone obscured by shadow. The children were complaining loudly about their meal, and the cleric was plainly rethinking his decision to dine here. The soldier leaned back, and Maghrurio caught a glimpse of a familiar face--dark hair, dark eyes, attractive...

Nepri.

Maghrurio's face flushed as he watched her. She could be quite captivating when she wanted to be, but right now, she was getting as angry as she had been last night. A lull in the children's screams carried her voice to where he sat.

"I'm telling you, I met the guy you're looking for last night. If your captain has the coins, I can tell him all about it."

Maghrurio's heart quickened as the pair rose and left the inn. *That was close.* He rose himself when he saw Bacarus and Sheru enter the room and quickly hustled them out. "We need to leave immediately. Some of those soldiers we saw last night were sent by the Duke!"

They grabbed their belongings from their suite, sneaking past a pair of soldiers by the stairs who were more interested in watching women than looking for Maghrurio. Bacarus settled up with the innkeeper, mentioning several times they planned to spend the day meeting with customers before heading southeast for Lanh after the evening meal. If this ruse worked, the soldiers would waste a day searching for them in Hasa, allowing them to get off the road at Cyrchan well before any pursuit reached that far.

They hurried to the stables and readied the wagon. With Maghrurio hidden in the back once again, they made for the rain-sodden road to Cyrchan.

THE CIRCLE

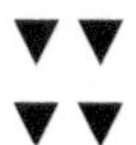

The road to Cyrchan continued eastward through flat, lightly forested terrain. Apart from the occasional merchant caravan or stray traveler, they saw no others on the road. Even so, Maghrurio remained wrapped in a concealing blanket until they stopped for lunch several hours later. Sheru provided him with a shawl to throw over his head so that he would appear as an old woman from a distance. So long as Duke Bileyo's soldiers didn't get too close, this casual disguise should suffice.

The masquerade did little to improve Maghrurio's mood.

That very night would see the greater moon, Vadha, rise in full. It would also mark his first Mystic Gathering. Once more, his stomach fluttered, only this time in anticipation of the event. The idea of being around Mystics who knew what they were doing was daunting, despite Abner's suggestion that there would be some with skills closer to his own.

The afternoon passed without incident, and the rain finally tapered off. As the day grew older, Maghrurio abandoned all pretext of contemplating anything but the impending Gathering.

Who would be there? What might they be like? Would they accept him?

When evening approached, they found a dry stand of willow trees off the road in which to make their camp. As if on cue, they each fell to their evening duties of horse, fire, and food.

Over dinner, Maghrurio related what he knew of the coming event. "When Vadha rises in full, I will be transported in my sleep to the Gathering. Hopefully, I will learn something about being a Mystic and, with luck, something to help our investigation."

Sheru asked, "Do you mean you'll be carried off by magic?"

"I don't think so. I'm pretty sure I'll still be here physically, but some part of myself will join the group. Maybe my spirit or something." He chuckled, "I guess I'll have to let you know afterward. I don't expect it will take all night long, so be sure to wake me for the third watch." Collecting their utensils, he washed them in a nearby stream. He then spread his bedroll and went to sleep.

At least, he tried to.

Maghrurio lay quietly, eyes closed, waiting for… What? Abner hadn't given any instructions for joining the Gathering, so he hoped it would just happen. Excitement and apprehension kept sleep at bay, so he tried to relax and calm his mind as best he could.

In an instant, he felt part of himself flying from their campsite. Away east, he soared past Albiona and the Gladwater Lake, over the hills of Zod, and descended at last to a sheltered hill surrounded by ancient trees. He recognized the Circle of Friends from his first training session with Abner. This time, however, unfamiliar faces marked his arrival.

From his left, a dark-skinned woman approached. She was roughly his build and dressed in a black tunic and dark blue pants. She flashed a cheery smile. "Hi there, you must be new. My name is Buhlo, and you are…?"

"Maghrurio, pleased to meet you."

Hand over heart, she bowed in greeting. He copied her in return.

"How long have you held your Ring?"

"It's only been a few days since Abner's death."

"WHAT?!?" The shock was evident on her face, but the others conversed among themselves and paid no mind to her outburst. "By the Twelve Gods, this is bad. Really bad. They're going to want to hear all about it, for sure."

Maghrurio didn't feel like recounting the wretched details, but he knew he'd have to. Delaying the inevitable, he changed the subject. "Who are all these people?"

Buhlo, still stunned by his revelation, quickly recovered. "This is my third meeting, so let me share what I know." She gestured to their left at an overweight, balding man with body language that screamed distrust. "That's Varka. He's been a Mystic longer than anyone. I guess he's the senior Mystic now. He's very cautious, though, maybe too cautious to lead. If not him, then The Hidden One over there."

She nodded toward a tall inscrutable figure wearing a gray full-face mask and matching cloak, silently scanning the throng until his eyes fixed on Maghrurio. He bowed, and Maghrurio responded in kind. There was something about his bearing that made Maghrurio think he might make a good ally.

"The Hidden One has also been around for a while, just not as long as Varka. He's vocal at meetings. He asks lots of questions and is helpful when needed, but nobody knows who he really is. He says the mask is for his protection." Her shrug told Maghrurio that was as much as she could explain about the enigmatic Mystic.

A dark figure appeared at the edge of the clearing. He eyed the attendees one by one, locking his suspicious eyes momentarily on Maghrurio before taking a seat facing the trees at the outer edge. The man's diminutive stature and traditionally sallow complexion betrayed his origins. Hooking a thumb, Maghrurio asked, "Who's the Graavt?"

"That would be Usnik. If he says three words the whole meeting, I'll be surprised. Mostly he just sits there, listening. Never offers up any information."

Curious. I'll have to keep an eye on him.

She pointed at a pair to their right. "I call them the Twins."

Maghrurio raised his eyebrow because they couldn't be more dissimilar. The man was short, soft, and rounded, with thin sandy hair and an unpleasant expression. The woman, on the other hand, was tall and lithe with long blond hair. While physically attractive, her demeanor suggested she found the meeting and its attendees beneath her. The pair was focused on their whispered discussion.

"Those two always gravitate together. Miya may be beautiful, but she's condescending to us newbies. Obolon is a bit nicer, but not by much. They usually support whatever The Hidden One suggests." She scanned the group once again and added, "That's pretty much everybody I know."

It was a lot to take in. Maghrurio would probably need reminding, but it was good to have made a friend so quickly. He only wished the rest of the Gathering would be as accommodating. "Thanks for showing me the ropes, Buhlo."

"No trouble." She nodded her head, adding, "It looks like Varka is convening the meeting. Just follow my lead, and good luck."

Varka cleared his throat and spread his arms in welcome. "It seems we are all of the twelve that could make it tonight. As the longest-serving Mystic here, it falls to me to convene the Gathering." Folding his arms, he walked to a low altar near the perimeter and moved his hands. When he stepped away, a tiny whirlwind hovered there.

Maghrurio noticed there were four such altars, equally spaced at the cardinal points around the Circle. Varka proceeded to the next one and summoned a tongue of flame. At the third, he produced a small stone, then at the final attempt, a large drop of water. When he had completed his circuit, he stood between the wind altar and the outer wall and gestured to the other Mystics. One by one, they rose and followed Varka's path, adding their own conjurings at each altar as he had done.

Buhlo nodded as Maghrurio followed her to the end of the line. He added his own elements as best as he could manage, noting the variation in size, shape, and style that the other Mystics had produced. He then joined the other Mystics near the wind altar.

Surrounded by the manifestations of wind, fire, stone, and water and standing in front of the central fountain, Varka's voice rose in the night. "By the everlasting elements, I welcome you all." He gestured for everyone to be seated in the inner part of the Circle and turned his attention to Maghrurio. "You are new to the Gathering, so please introduce yourself."

Maghrurio glanced at Buhlo, and at her encouraging smile, he stood. "My name is Maghrurio, and I bear sad tidings." He paused, considering. These were all Mystics, but something told him he shouldn't be too open about what he suspected. Fighting back the grief that threatened to overcome him again, he continued. "Abner is dead. He was killed by an explosion at an apothecary in our town."

His revelation set off an uproar among the Gathering. Even Usnik spun around, abandoning all pretense of disinterest. Varka called for order and eventually managed to calm everyone down. "This is sad news indeed. Tell us your tale."

Maghrurio described the events of that fateful morning, including the part where Abner gave him the Ring but excluding the private comments that passed between them. He saw familiar expressions of sadness and loss. Ones mirrored in his own face over the past several days. Varka seemed close to tears. Not only did he mourn a long time colleague, but now he was the senior Mystic. Maghrurio sat down amidst the stunned silence that followed.

Obolan stood after a short time. "I'm interested in our newcomer's opinion. Was this a tragic accident, or has something more sinister transpired?" He looked expectantly at Maghrurio as he sat back down.

Maghrurio felt all eyes upon him as he stood. Again, instinct told him to stick to facts and not share what Abner suspected. Still, he didn't want to lie, so he chose his words with care. "I saw nothing at the time to suggest foul play. It seemed to have been an unfortunate accident with an unstable shipment." Relief colored some faces while others remained pensive. "I can only hope to honor his memory by earning the confidence he placed in me."

Varka rose. "Let us all stand in silence to honor our friend one last time."

Hands over hearts, the assembled Mystics said their goodbyes. Even Usnik wore a mournful frown. After a minute, they all regained their seats except for Varka.

"We have lost too many Mystics of late. But the sun rises again every morning, and the world continues. Unless there is anything else pressing, I'd suggest we leave things as they are until the next meeting."

Nobody responded. It seemed no news could compete with what they'd already learned.

"Then I declare this Gathering closed. Go forth and serve."

Buhlo leaned over. "Steady yourself. They'll all want to speak with you now." She gave his hand a friendly squeeze and walked away. Turning, he was surprised to see Usnik approach.

"I grieve with you. Abner was the best of us, Mystic or otherwise."

Maghrurio thanked him and asked, "Did you know him well?"

The reticent Graavt nodded once, then leaned in and whispered, "Take care, young Maghrurio. All is not as it seems in the Circle of Friends." On that cryptic note, he stepped away and vanished.

"He's an enigma, that one," said an amused voice. Maghrurio turned to find himself face-to-face with The Hidden One. He accepted the other's expressions of sympathy. "You must be pretty raw in your mastery if you've only been a Mystic for a few days."

Maghrurio smiled weakly, "I could be doing better, certainly."

"Well, if you have any questions, just let me know."

Maghrurio sensed the smile beneath the mask. "Thanks again," he nodded.

A flash of yellow caught the corner of his eye, followed by a woman's cold voice.

"You'll be taking over for Abner, then?"

Maghrurio turned to find Miya standing beside him, arms crossed and looking every bit as confident and assertive as he wasn't. He could envision her leading troops into battle or maybe usurping a kingdom. Obolan was at her elbow, smirking.

"I am so charged," Maghrurio replied, trying and failing to match her bearing.

"Oh, I'm sure you'll do just fine." With a smirk, she turned away, whispering with Obolan. The sarcasm couldn't have been any heavier.

"Don't mind her," The Hidden One whispered. "Everything is a battle with her, but she's mostly harmless."

Before Maghrurio could acknowledge this, he was interrupted by Varka. "Welcome again, Maghrurio. I trust you are growing comfortable with your new role?"

"I am trying, Varka. Thank you."

Putting an arm around Maghrurio's shoulder, Varka turned him away from the others. "I'm hoping we can be honest and open with each other, Maghrurio. I'm concerned about your news beyond just the loss of a colleague and a friend." He paused as if trying to figure out how much to say and how to say it. "I've attended these Gatherings for a long time. We've been losing the best of us to sickness or accidents over the past several years, and I wonder whether someone here might be responsible. Can you tell me with all honesty that Abner's death was not deliberate?"

Maghrurio thought of what to say. Varka seemed genuine, but Usnik's warning still rang in his ears. He still didn't want to lie. "I've seen nothing yet to suggest this wasn't an accident," he replied carefully.

That seemed to satisfy Varka for the moment as he smiled and patted him on the back. "Very good. Keep your eyes open, then, and good luck with your training."

Varka walked away, and The Hidden One rejoined him. "I see you've mastered the four basic elements already."

"I can summon them at will," Maghrurio replied, "just not impressively."

"That'll come in time. The important thing is to keep practicing every day. Practice builds confidence, and confidence builds capability."

Maghrurio nodded. It made sense if you thought about it. He was already past the point of worrying whether or not he could make the spells work--he could do it every time he tried. His problem remained that without confidence, the results continued to be frustratingly minor. Knowing he needed confidence did nothing to engender confidence when his results remained meager. If he could be half as confident in his abilities as The Hidden One seemed to be, he'd have no troubles with Duke Bileyo or anybody.

The Hidden One departed, leaving Buhlo as his sole remaining companion.

"So what did you think of your first Gathering? It's nice to have other Mystics to talk with, isn't it?"

Maghrurio found himself at a loss for words. Surprise? Curiosity? Many emotions clashed within him, so he settled on one. "Confused."

"That was my initial reaction as well. After a couple of these, you'll get a better sense of what's up. We tend to jockey for alliances or information about each other, with nobody wanting to give up too much." Smiling, she added, "And by we, of course, I mean them. In case you hadn't noticed, I'm a bit more social." She shook her head as her smile melted into a frown. "No, we don't often get real shockers like the one you delivered, but there have been deaths. Relatively recent ones."

"Yes, Varka mentioned that. I'm not sure whether that's normal for the group or if it means something more." He gave a tight smile. "Time will tell, I imagine."

She nodded in response. "I don't suppose anyone told you how to leave?"

Maghrurio shook his head to a chuckle from Buhlo.

"Nobody told me my first time either, and I had to sit here all night until I woke up. Just concentrate on your sleeping form, and that'll take you back."

Maghrurio placed his hand on his heart and bowed. "Thank you so much, Buhlo, for making this a bit less intimidating than it could have been."

Buhlo smiled and returned his bow. "See you next time."

She vanished like all the others, leaving Maghrurio alone in the Circle. Before he could focus his mind, though, an unfamiliar voice rang out from everywhere and nowhere.

"Heed these words, wind-walker." A flash of light appeared, and then the image of an unfamiliar smithy tucked between a nondescript warehouse and a merchant's office. "In Cyrchan, the blacksmith is the key to the beginning and end of your search. Heed these words."

The mists swirled around a startled Maghrurio, and before the echoes had died, he slipped into a deep sleep.

• • ● • •

A savage kick to the ribs brought Maghrurio abruptly to consciousness. He looked around and saw Sheru's frightened face and Bacarus' silent anger. They were surrounded by two dozen soldiers, swords drawn and pointed right at them.

WHAT YOU LEAVE BEHIND

Maghrurio rubbed the sleep from his eyes and glanced around. Swords, scowls, horses, many men. This was no social call.

One man stepped forward. "Good morning," he said to Maghrurio. "I apologize for waking you so early, but we're looking for a wayward guest of the Duke." Fixing his gaze upon Maghrurio's face, he called out, "Is this the one?"

Another soldier stepped forward. "Yes, sir, this is the prisoner we secured in the Duke's dungeon."

Maghrurio rose slowly to his feet. The second soldier was one of the four that had manhandled him back in Decra. The first was an officer--a captain, based on the Nahrein uniform markings. He was tall and muscular, with black hair close-cropped in military fashion and a scar that snaked across his right hand and disappeared under his sleeve. He exuded the confidence of a man accustomed to command, and the smile on his face suggested pleasure in a mission completed successfully.

Sheru whispered, "I'm sorry, Maghrurio, they snuck up on me before I could raise the alarm."

"Don't worry, it wouldn't have mattered. Besides, I'm the one they want."

The officer held up his hand. "Please, no talking." He stepped forward until he was face-to-face with Maghrurio. He clasped his hands casually behind his back, his eyes were sharp and fixed, his expression one of triumph. "My name is Captain Azak. You are Maghrurio, I presume?"

Maghrurio held his gaze. "I am."

"Thought you could fool us with talk of diverting to Lahn?"

"It was worth a try."

Azak responded with a tight smile. "You are charged with escaping from His Grace's custody. Whether your companions will be charged as well depends upon your willingness to cooperate."

Maghrurio glanced at his companions, noting the worry on Bacarus' face and the fear on Sheru's. They had assisted him for no reason other than friendship, and he owed them his protection. "These women are on their own journey. They know nothing of the Duke or our dispute. If you allow them to continue unharmed, I promise to willingly accompany you."

Azak ignored the offer. "You led us on a long chase, and my men are itching for some payback. Tell me why I shouldn't let them take it out on you?"

Maghrurio did not like where this conversation was going. A beating, at the very least, seemed imminent, and who knew what might happen to the women? *I have to somehow take charge of this situation.* "Captain, why don't you ask your man what happened to the Duke right before I was imprisoned?"

Azak's face clouded, recalling no doubt how the Duke had been blasted across the room when he attempted to take the Ring. Maghrurio knew he'd scored a hit and pressed the captain before there was time to consider further. "I say again, let them go, and I promise to accompany you."

Azak stepped back. "I have decided to accept your offer. You will be bound and placed on a horse. If you do this willingly, I will allow the women to depart. I will, however, dispatch two guards to accompany them until noon to ensure they continue on their way."

Azak signaled. Men seized Maghrurio, bound his wrists, and put him roughly onto a spare mount. Maghrurio cooperated fully, silently thankful that with his hands tied in front, he could at least grasp the saddle horn to stay seated.

"Thank you for the ride, and good luck on your journey," Maghrurio told his friends. "I'll be fine, don't worry about me." He watched a pair of soldiers mount their horses as Bacarus finished loading the wagon, and they soon left him behind. Sheru's nervous face didn't leave his until they rounded a curve and dipped out of sight.

"I don't want any trouble from you," warned Azak.

"I haven't forgotten my promise."

"Good, because we still owe you for our troubles."

The company set out in short order. They rode in a loose cluster, with Maghrurio's horse at the center. Several soldiers ranged fore and aft to scout the terrain. Azak remained at the head, calling instructions and conversing with his men. Nobody spoke with Maghrurio or rode near him, but his every move was watched by many eyes.

Every hour or so, Azak would call for a halt. The men would range around, scouting the area, checking the horses, or simply relieving themselves. Maghrurio would slide out of his saddle, stiff and sore. He would stretch his aching muscles, reveling in his brief reprieve while surrounded by swords. After too short a time, the company would remount and resume their ride.

While they rode, Maghrurio willed himself to ignore his increasing discomfort. His anxiety, of course, was a different story. Once again, he found himself in desperate need of magic to aid him, yet with a skill that was insufficient for the task. He didn't dare try any spells with the soldiers watching, but he knew he could produce the elements on demand. He just couldn't as yet produce anything of substance, anything to extricate himself from this mess.

Eventually, Azak called a halt for lunch. Maghrurio fell from his saddle, too sore to properly dismount. He lay on the ground as the company set up a temporary camp. Food bars were handed out, and one was tossed on the ground near his head. He pulled himself into a seated position against a tree and fed himself while dwelling on his miserable predicament.

Clearly, he was in trouble. The Duke was set on getting the Mystic Ring and would keep him locked up until he handed it over. If he was lucky, that is. He was certain the Duke had people skilled in the art of persuasion, armed with tools both frightening and painful. Not for the last time, Maghrurio cursed his meager skills and wished the improvements his colleagues promised would hurry up and arrive.

Azak approached from behind and sat on the ground next to him. "You ride well for someone trussed up."

Maghrurio gave a tight smile. "One does what needs doing."

"Agreed, which is why your hands are tied. We'll be sharing this road for a few more days, so why don't we pass the time pleasantly? Were you born in Nahrein?"

Maghrurio silently counted to ten. "Captain, I appreciate that you're trying to be friendly. But you and I both know what awaits me at the end of our journey. A pleasant conversation won't change that fact."

Azak nodded. "I understand you have something the Duke wants. I also understand his attempt to wrest it from you by force was not... effective." He finished his food bar, wiping his mouth on the back of his hand. "Not very tasty, are they?"

"They excel as a chewing exercise."

Azak chuckled. "True. So tell me, Maghrurio, how can we resolve this? As you say, we both know what will happen when I bring you back. The Duke only wants the Ring, and I'm guessing he won't get it until you agree to hand it over."

'Until' I hand it over, not 'unless.'

"Give some thought to how we might proceed. I'm an honest man, Maghrurio, or at least I try to be. If you can think of a way to give the Duke what he wants without harm to yourself, I will consider it."

Azak called out, and the men began breaking camp. Azak rose to greet the two soldiers he'd dispatched earlier to shadow the women. Maghrurio noticed one had a pronounced limp he didn't recall seeing before.

"Azak, what about the women? Are they safe? Are they unharmed?"

"I would be more concerned with your own safety if I were you."

Did something happen with his friends?

The company remounted (Maghrurio painfully so), and they set out once more. Maghrurio had some thinking to do. Either Azak wasn't actually that bad or he was a decent actor. Either way, as the journey progressed, he had no doubt there would be increasing pressure on him to give up his Ring. He had to escape, but with so many eyes on him, he'd never get loose from his bonds. Sneaking away from a mounted company would be even more unlikely.

Cursing his rotten luck and saddle sores, he thought back fondly to the "comfort" of their wagon. At this moment, he could have been reclining on a soft blanket, his head propped on his pack…

His pack.

It had the sampler in it!

Maghrurio's heart quickened as he realized a means for his escape. But the wagon was less than a day's ride away, and while the company's horses could move at a decent speed, Snowfall was old and slow. If he vanished now, the soldiers would catch up to the wagon far too quickly. He'd have to wait until the dead of night to try it, to give his friends time to reach Cyrchan.

Assuming the sampler worked again.

• • ● • •

The captain pressed on until dusk before halting for the night. Like clockwork, the soldiers busied themselves making camp while Maghrurio rested his weary body under a gnarled oak tree. Before long, Azak appeared with dinner for another chat.

"Stew and bread. Eat up."

Maghrurio accepted the plate with bound hands. "Thank you."

They ate in silence, Azak barely bothering to chew.

"So, have you given any further thought to our conversation?"

"I've had nothing but time to think, Captain."

"And?"

"As you suggest, I prefer to avoid unpleasantness if possible."

"Excellent. And how do you propose we do that?"

Maghrurio put his half-empty plate down and hesitated. "If I were to… give you my Ring, would you be willing to let me go?"

Azak's eyes lit up. "Nothing would please me more. I'd fulfill my mission, the Duke would get what he wants, and you'd avoid punishment. Everybody wins!"

Sure, everybody except me. "But can I trust you, I wonder?"

Azak nodded. "A fair question. I can be rough, but I believe in honoring my promises. If you give me the Ring, I swear to let you walk away without reprisal."

Maghrurio looked hard into Azak's unflinching face. His instinct told him he could trust the captain, so he nodded.

Azak held his hand out expectantly.

"Ah, there's the problem," said Maghrurio. "You see, the Ring can only be removed at dawn. That's why it blasted the Duke. He tried removing it during the daytime. Not even I can take it off before then. Only when the morning breaks can I give it to you."

Captain Azak looked suspicious. "You aren't trying to fool me, are you? Because I appreciate honesty, but I deal ruthlessly with deception."

"Fool you?" Maghrurio asked as he raised his bound hands. "To what end? Where can I go?"

Azak stared at him thoughtfully for a long while. Finally, he rose to his feet. "I'm going to believe you, for now. We'll be bedding down for the night, so we'll get you a blanket. And I'm sorry, but I will need to secure you against escape."

He waved over one of his men, who hammered a spike into the tree behind Maghrurio and attached a long chain to it. The chain ended in a manacle, which he locked around Maghrurio's ankle.

"That will prevent you from wandering off in the night. Come morning, as we discussed, you'll hand over the Ring, and I'll let you leave. Sleep well!"

Maghrurio lay in the dark, willing his racing heart to calm. His ruse had worked, for now. He'd bought himself some time, and hopefully, he would be well away before Azak was any wiser.

Assuming, of course, the sampler trick worked again.

He worried about his options if it didn't, but that was too frightening to contemplate. He also worried about Bacarus and Sheru. Azak hadn't said anything about them, and one of the guards had come back limping. Nursing his concerns, he rolled himself into the threadbare blanket and settled in for the night.

The wait was excruciating. Several soldiers left the camp to patrol the perimeter, but it seemed to take forever for the balance of the company to settle down to sleep. Vadha joined Ghata in the blackened sky, and still, the camp was active. Eventually, things quieted down long enough for him to make an attempt. He cleared his mind and whispered the words on the sampler.

"Dangers strike, troubles come; seek the solace of hearth and home."

Nothing happened.

Maghrurio panicked. He had scant hours until dawn. If he was still here, Azak would surely make him pay for his deception. His mind reeled. How could the magic abandon him? Did the sampler need to be hanging in Abner's kitchen to work? He tried to breathe deeply and clear his mind--panic was not going to help. So what was different from the first time he tried this? He recalled in the cell, he visualized the kitchen and its contents. Maybe he needed to picture the sampler in his mind for it to work?

He took another look around, making certain he remained unobserved. He took a deep breath, drew a clear picture in his mind, and once again whispered, "Dangers strike, troubles come; seek the solace of hearth and home."

He vanished silently from Captain Azak's campsite, leaving both rope and manacle lying on a blanket in the dark.

REJOINED

Maghrurio found himself lying on the floor next to his pack. He looked around and spied the balance of their luggage, presumably in the sitting room of one of Cyrchan's many inns.

The sampler had worked again!

He dug it out of his pack and examined it. *Am I imagining it, or does this seem a bit more faded than I remember?* He could hear Sheru and Bacarus arguing in the next room.

"I'm not saying we abandon him, Bacarus. I'm saying we can't charge into the night without some kind of plan."

"We just can't sit here talking about it, Sheru. We have to do something!"

Maghrurio stood in the doorway. "May I suggest that we order something to eat?"

Bacarus whirled around, screaming, "Maghrurio! By the Twelve Gods, where did you come from?!?"

Sheru stared at him, dumbfounded.

He embraced them with relief. "I've never been happier to see you both. What say we order something and have a chat?" In ten minutes, they huddled around the fire with late dinner orders in place and a well-deserved bottle of wine in hand.

Maghrurio related his tale quickly enough and brought out the sampler for their inspection. "This must have been something Abner created or perhaps found during his travels."

Bacarus furrowed her brows. "Wasn't this hanging in the kitchen?"

"It was, and it's proven incredibly useful so far. I think you should probably hang onto it, just in case." He handed it over to Bacarus, who pocketed it. "So what happened with you two?"

Bacarus, normally not prone to oratory, remained silent. Sheru, usually the talkative one, likewise said nothing.

Something happened. "Bacarus?"

Bacarus sighed and reluctantly recounted their journey. "The soldiers followed us all morning. They kept their distance but occasionally made unsavory comments at our expense." Sheru lowered her eyes at this, clearly uncomfortable with the memory. "They made no attempt to lower their voices. The comments became worse as the morning passed, and I started getting worried about whether they'd graduate from talking to acting before long."

Sheru snarled in anger. "They were horrible. No one should talk to a woman like that, let alone…" Her voice trailed off.

Maghrurio looked at Bacarus in alarm. She continued her tale. "It seemed my fears were justified. When mid-day rolled around, we stopped near a copse of trees by the road to give our horse a feed and a rest." She paused, scowling. "I was hoping those filthy pigs would give their voices a rest."

Sheru wrapped her arms tighter around her body and said nothing.

Bacarus took a breath to compose herself and continued. "Anyway, once we stopped, the comments got cruder and louder. I told them they were free to return to their captain, but that only prompted more crude remarks. When I told them to go do to themselves what they wanted to do to us, it was the spark that turned their crude talk into action."

She glanced over at Sheru, who had grown angrier in the telling. Sheru picked up the tale.

"They both went after Bacarus. I guess I was too frightened to pose a threat, so they felt justified ignoring me for the moment." Sheru's attention wandered momentarily as if recalling a different time and place. With an almost imperceptible shake of her head, she returned to the story. "They came at her with daggers raised. They said they'd teach her a lesson for her sass. Only they were the ones to get schooled. I'm not even sure what happened after the first soldier reached for her, but the next thing I knew, the soldiers and their daggers were scattered on the ground around us."

Bacarus scowled, "Clearly, nobody ever taught them how to speak to women properly. Or how to handle a dagger, for that matter."

Sheru gave a grim smile, "Well, you taught them something. One of them cursed us both and tried to get up, but Bacarus put him down with a kick to his knee. She suggested they remain on the ground until we were far away and advised them to think about how they should address women in the future. We boarded the wagon and left them moaning in the dirt, giving Bacarus the evil eye as we drove away."

"I don't know what to say," said an embarrassed yet relieved Maghrurio, "I'm sorry you had to endure that."

Bacarus smiled to ease his discomfort. "They were idiots and, in the end, caused us no real trouble. We continued on to Cyrchan, but once we got here, we couldn't agree on what to do next. Your appearance settled that argument nicely."

Sheru added, "It's really good to see you safe again."

"I'm glad we're all safe." There was a knock at the door, and Maghrurio opened it to a pair of kitchen hands who brought their food. In a coordinated ballet of movement, they set the table and bowed themselves out.

Bacarus raised his glass. "To the successful conclusion of our journey!" They clinked glasses and tucked into their meal.

The conversation soon turned to other topics. Maghrurio recounted his first Gathering in brief, leaving out some of the one-on-one conversations for later contemplation. He also described his subsequent vision, and they discussed what it might mean.

"I was planning to track down another armorer, but the vision changed everything," Maghrurio began. "'In Cyrchan, the blacksmith is the key to the beginning and end of your search.' is what the vision said," he quoted. "We need to find the blacksmith and get him to help us unearth the truth about Abner's murder."

"Do you think he'll help us?" Bacarus wondered.

"Of course, he'll want to drop everything and help us," Sheru responded. "With a righteous cause and a vision to boot? We're on a mission from the gods!" Her optimism was infectious, and even Maghrurio began to feel cracks in his wall of anxiety.

Weary of the day's efforts, they bade one another good night and bedded down in better spirits than they'd known in a while.

As he lay in bed, Maghrurio's mind whirled. His failures so far in living up to Abner's confidence laid a disquieting foundation. His experience as Captain Azak's prisoner remained a raw wound, as was his anxiety over the forced separation from Bacarus and Sheru. Frankly, it was a wonder he could function. Still, a comfortable bed and a full belly can do wonders for calming one's nerves, and his luck had yet to completely run out. He took a few deep breaths and tried to push his unsettling thoughts into the deep places of his brain.

In the absence of sleep, he mulled over what had transpired during and after the Gathering. Buhlo and The Hidden One seemed friendly, and Usnik was an enigma. He wasn't sure whether Varka was concerned with Maghrurio's well-being or merely his own. He was pretty sure about Miya and Obolan, though. They were unreliable and untrustworthy as allies, and he suspected they felt the same way about everyone but each other.

His vision was a mystery as well. It appeared the blacksmith was the solution to the question of Abner's murder if they could find him. In a town like Cyrchan, he didn't expect that would pose much of a challenge.

Of course, his conclusions assumed he had correctly interpreted the clues of the past few days. His guesses seemed to make sense, but he knew he was no genius. Had something transpired at the Gathering that he had overlooked? Some clue, perhaps, that his limited observational skills failed to catch? Maghrurio was sure that had Abner attended the Gathering, he'd already have solved the mystery. How was he to live up to that example? Flustered and unsettled, he slowly and reluctantly succumbed to sleep.

• • ● • •

Once more, Maghrurio called to Abner in his dream state. This time, their meeting place was a dreary marshland surrounded by a dense canopy of trees, vines, and other noxious growths. The malodorous air was permeated with flying insects and the calls of unseen birds and beasts.

This must be somewhere in the Black Marsh, north of the Gladwater Lake, several days east of Cyrchan.

Abner appeared as before, resplendent in his blue robes. Maghrurio greeted him and launched into the highlights of his experiences. As he described the disembodied voice and image that followed the Gathering, Abner nodded his head.

"What you described was almost certainly your first Mystic vision. No one knows where they come from, although I've always believed they arise from the magic itself. Regardless of their source, they are powerful clues for us to interpret as best we can."

"I'm guessing the vision means the blacksmith will help us find your murderer. Is that right?"

Abner shook his head. "I'm sorry, Maghrurio. I exist here in your dreams, so my knowledge is limited. Your thinking seems logical to me, but I can't know for certain whether it's correct or not."

Maghrurio sighed. He'd have to rely on his own deficient deductive skills, after all. "So what about the Gathering? What can you tell me about the other Mystics?"

Abner sat upon a weathered tree trunk. "Varka and The Hidden One are the senior Mystics now. Varka's been around for ages, a bit longer than The Hidden One and almost as long as I was. It always seemed to me The Hidden One was the more talented of the two. I'm not sure where Usnik fits in; he's always been somewhat of a recluse. My guess is he's right behind those two, but he doesn't disclose much, so it's hard to say. Obolan and Miya are pretty much as you've described--they always bear watching. I didn't really know the new one, Buhlo." He shrugged. "Sorry, I can't help much there. For what it's worth," he added after a moment, "there used to be more of them. At one point in my early days, there were as many as eleven. We've suffered losses, or some Mystics haven't been attending."

That gave Maghrurio something to ruminate on. There were only seven at the Gathering.

What happened to the rest?

"I'm glad you put my sampler to good use," Abner continued. "Over the years, it proved a lifesaver on multiple occasions. I inherited it from my master, who found it uncounted years before. You must be sure to use it only in extreme need. Every use weakens it until it eventually becomes drained of magic and passes away. There are other similar artifacts scattered throughout Sonoduhl, or so I was told. As with everything else, keep your eyes open."

Something tickled Maghrurio's memory. "The Hidden One. Who is he?"

"He appeared at a Gathering many years ago and shortly thereafter began wearing the cloak as you described. He said he'd been attacked and suspected one of us. He warmed up to the group eventually, but he was The Hidden One evermore. It's been so long I can't even recall his true name or his appearance."

"If you have nothing else," Abner said as he stood, "let's continue with your lessons. How is your mastery of the four basic elements? Can you summon them at will?"

"Yes, I've gotten that far. I just haven't had much luck with increasing their magnitude."

Abner smiled that grandfatherly smile again. "Don't be too discouraged. Time and confidence will help you there. Now, if you recall, all Mystic magic is based on elemental magic. You've already got the four elements working. Have you tried combining any of them yet?"

Maghrurio admitted he hadn't even considered the concept.

"Combining elements is what separates the real Mystic from the apprentice because it's all based on your skill and imagination. I'll give you two examples, and you can build from them. Try combining the finger move for fire and the hand flap for wind, or the finger wiggle for water with the hand flap for stone."

Maghrurio performed the fire and wind gestures with his right hand and, after a few false starts, was rewarded with a spurt of flame that traveled a few inches. On his second attempt at combining the water and stone gestures, he was able to produce a glob of mud, which fell to his feet amidst the copious amounts of mud already present in the marshland.

Abner smiled encouragingly as he continued to experiment until he was able to reproduce both combinations at will. "Very good work, Maghrurio. I personally found experimentation to be the most enjoyable part of my training. Some combinations will be useful, while some will be as useless as creating mud in a swamp. Don't forget," he added, "you can use both hands to combine gestures; not all gestures need to be done simultaneously. And remember, through self-confidence, you can increase their power and magnitude."

"Why don't you just tell me what combinations you mastered?"

"That's not how this works, I'm afraid. I can only point the way to wisdom. I cannot lead you there. In my day, I mastered many combinations, but at this moment, I don't recall a single one beyond what I've already described. I know next time, I'll be able to teach you more, but what that lesson might be remains hidden until the time comes. It's a limitation of the magic that brings us together, unfortunately." Abner acknowledged the disappointed look on his colleague's face. "Believe me, I wish it were otherwise."

"As do I, Abner. But I thank you for the assistance and guidance you are able to provide."

The sun was tricky to judge in the misty swamp, but it seemed to Maghrurio's eyes that it was edging toward dusk and the conclusion of this training session. He bid Abner farewell until next time.

Abner smiled in parting. "Keep experimenting and have fun!"

THE FORSAKEN

Maghrurio rose with the sun, mentally rested but emotionally and physically drained. He was worried about the task ahead, with a roiling in his gut that deep breaths were powerless to diffuse. Any breakfast he took would certainly be returned forthwith. He remained in bed, trying in vain to calm his frazzled nerves. The blacksmith was key to solving the murder, so he simply HAD to get him to agree to help. What was he to say? What arguments could he bring to bear? How could he convince him to help?

He'd known a few other smiths. To a man, they had been fiercely independent, focused on their craftsmanship and little else. He would need to overcome that attitude to involve the man in their quest, but how? He shook his head, recalling how optimistic he had been the previous night.

I could use some of that optimism this morning.

He felt immobile, trapped between the need to solve Abner's murder and the fear that his arguments wouldn't recruit the blacksmith to their cause.

The question of Azak, which should have been more pressing, faded into the background. He'd probably assume Maghrurio escaped on foot and would waste the day combing the surrounding countryside. That should leave sufficient time to complete his business with the blacksmith.

That is if he could figure out how to convince the man.

Maghrurio chided himself for his paralysis. Abner had repeatedly told him to be more self-confident and believe in himself. *Well, if I can't feel genuinely confident, I'll just have to trust my luck and fake it instead.* With a deep breath, he cast off his immobility and rose from the bed.

He bathed, dressed with determination, and departed his room prepared to meet his challenge head-on.

His worries pierced his newfound determination before he'd even reached the common room.

Maghrurio chose a table in the far corner and ordered tea and toast. He breathed deeply before attempting his breakfast.

If I take any more deep breaths, I'm going to pass out.

The bit of toast he nibbled lay like a stone in his stomach. His brief burst of determination withered under the reality that he still had no idea how to proceed. He grunted an incoherent greeting as his companions joined him at the table. Potential arguments paraded through his mind as he watched them devour their meals, secure in their certainty that he, Maghrurio, would surely prevail.

Sheru eyed Maghrurio's pallor with concern. "You're pretty quiet this morning. You've barely touched your toast."

"I'm not sure I can do this."

"Do what?"

"I don't think I can convince the blacksmith."

Sheru objected immediately and strenuously. "Maghrurio, don't you dare think that. I haven't known you long, but you've had remarkable accomplishments in the past week. You escaped from the Duke's clutches twice. You've begun to master the Mystic arts with no preparation or real training. You untangled this mystery and brought us to where we can finally solve it. What more did you think you could do?"

Maghrurio shook his head throughout her litany. She had it all wrong. Those escapes were due to the sampler, not any skill he might possess. His so-called mastery of the Mystic arts was pathetic. As for getting them here, well, all they'd done was follow the road eastward. Bacarus had been far more useful on their journey, saving them from harm twice. No, he wasn't really responsible for any of those 'accomplishments,' and he remained undeserving of her praise.

"You don't understand," he insisted. "You've grossly exaggerated my value to this investigation." His eyes shifted back and forth between them but avoided direct contact, his face a study in despair.

"The prophecy says we need the blacksmith to solve Abner's murder, and I still have no idea how to convince him."

A speechless Sheru glanced at Bacarus, beseeching her to set Maghrurio straight. Bacarus reached across the table and grasped his hand firmly. "Listen to me. Self-doubt is a real thing. I experienced it many times in my monastery days. If you let it fester and grow within you, pretty soon, you'll be unable to leave your bed." She locked his eyes with her own, and he sensed her attempt to bolster his crumbling ego with her strength and confidence.

"Abner believed in you, Maghrurio. I believe in you. Sheru believes in you." She smirked, "Are you trying to make us look stupid?" A hint of a smile touched lightly on Maghrurio's lips. "Then let's get out there and make an attempt. Try and succeed or try and fail. Either way, you have to try." She gave his hand an encouraging squeeze and released him.

Maghrurio felt a bit of her confidence worm its way into his core. He took a deep breath and imagined it fed the fires of his flagging confidence.

It was time. I'll have to figure it out on the way.

"Thank you both for your encouragement." A brief smile, then said, "Shall we meet our destiny?"

• • ● • •

Most towns in Nahrein were a confusing mishmash of winding streets and meandering alleyways. Cyrchan, on the other hand, was laid out in a grid pattern with several main streets running north-south and east-west. It boasted two separate market areas on opposite sides of the town. By luck or chance, their first attempt chose the one where their blacksmith target was not -- at least, the blacksmith shop they found was not the one from Maghrurio's vision. After asking for directions, it didn't take long for them to find the right smithy, sandwiched between a plain warehouse to the left and a merchant's office to the right.

Exactly as he saw in his vision.

The blacksmith is the key to the beginning and end of your search.

He took a moment to examine the structures in more detail. The warehouse stood with its main doors swung wide but displayed little activity. The blacksmith's shop was clearly a working smithy, with the smoke and rhythmic hammering one would expect of such an establishment. It stank of melted metals, smoke, and sweat.

The merchant's office was likewise open, and a tall man with light hair stood in its doorway watching their approach. He was of medium build, and his clothing suggested his merchant practice was successful. He bore a friendly face with piercing blue eyes that seemed to see through all pretense into the heart of anyone he examined. Maghrurio had no doubt that contributed to his apparent business success.

"Good day to you all," the man said as he wiped his hands with a rag. "I'm Gazto, a merchant in these parts. I'd shake your hands, but they're covered in grease." He chuckled, "It's an occupational hazard."

Maghrurio introduced himself and his colleagues. "I don't mean to interrupt. We're actually here to speak with the blacksmith."

"Ah, old Grumpy, eh?" Gazto smiled. "Good luck. He's not the most sociable of creatures."

Maghrurio smiled. "I've worked with smiths before. I know enough to pay heed to the demands of their craft. From the cadence of hammer falls I'm hearing, he's in the middle of drawing a piece of iron. I'd be a fool to interrupt him now."

"I have nothing to do right now, so I can keep you company." Gazto continued wiping his hands. "Not sure why he bothers anyway. I import better stuff than he could ever make." Gazto leaned in and staged-whispered, "Monkey isn't terribly happy about that. But what can you do... it's just water to a pi'pala."

He shrugged at Maghrurio's puzzled expression. "Forget it, just something my grandmother used to say. Hang on a second." Gazto disappeared into his office, returning moments later, pulling cloth gloves onto his hands. "Those chemicals are hell on my hands. My apothecary gave me an ointment, but it doesn't help much."

Sheru's ears perked up. "You should try aloe. It's great for all sorts of skin problems." She grinned at Gazto's questioning look. "Sorry, it's my profession."

The pair traded their opinions on the efficacy of various ointments and salves while Maghrurio's thoughts returned to the blacksmith. The rhythmic pounding hadn't changed, so he still had time to figure out how to approach this negotiation. It was a negotiation, he realized. He wanted something from the blacksmith--his help--and had to somehow convince him to yield it.

He reviewed his options. Appealing to the smith's better nature might work if he were an outgoing, caring person. Maghrurio had never met a blacksmith who could be described as such, so he abandoned that approach. As much as he might like to, he also couldn't ask Bacarus to beat him into submission, assuming she was willing and able to do so. What other choices did he have?

The hammering suddenly ceased, and Maghrurio felt his own heart take up its tempo. "Hey, it sounds like Dumpy is finished," Gazto laughed as he seated himself in front of his office. Clearly, he sensed entertainment value in the impending conversation and wanted a good seat.

Maghrurio's stomach clenched in anticipation. Abner said to be more confident, he recalled. When in his life had he ever been confident? There was that summer he traveled with an acting troupe when he somehow landed the part of a king. He had felt supremely confident in that role. Could that be the answer?

As the blacksmith stepped out of his shop, Maghrurio realized he had a plan after all.

"Hey, Rumpy, these folks are looking for you," called out Gazto. The smith studiously ignored him as he rinsed the sweat from his head using a large ladle from the rain barrel outside his front entrance. After a long drink and a steady stare at his visitors, the blacksmith addressed them.

"The name is Munpi." He extended a hand and shook each of their hands in turn. He frowned in Gazto's direction, and the frown remained when his gaze returned to them.

He doesn't like Gazto very much and expects not to like us either. Good thing I'm not planning to appeal to his better nature.

Maghrurio took a deep breath, channeled his play king, and put his plan to the test. "Good day, Munpi. I am Maghrurio, a Mystic from Nahrein." This brought a guffaw from Gazto, which Maghrurio pretended not to have heard. "We are on a quest vital to all of Sonoduhl and have been guided to your door by a profound vision."

Munpi's countenance remained unchanged, so Maghrurio continued. "First, I have a question for you. Can you identify this writing?" He handed Munpi the piece of wood he'd carried from the wreckage of the apothecary.

Munpi accepted Maghrurio's offering and examined it. "There's too much fire damage to say what kind of wood this is, but this writing is Graavtish," he replied. "It's incomplete, but what I can see looks like it was addressed to me." He lifted the fragment to his nose and sniffed. "I smell fire, coal, and something else I can't quite place. Where did you come by it?"

"This is all that remains of a mysterious shipment delivered to my associate's shop," he said, gesturing at Sheru. "It exploded later, killing a powerful Mystic." He drew himself up to his most imposing and majestic stature. "My vision told me you would be the one to help us solve this murder and prevent countless others."

Munpi stared at Maghrurio like he had two heads. "Thanks, but I'm a blacksmith, not a detective." He turned to re-enter his smithy.

"Wait!" Maghrurio tried to hide the panic in his voice. His plan to act powerfully and presume cooperation had failed. His mind went suddenly blank, and he cast about wildly for something else to say.

"You tell him, Lumpy!" Gazto laughed.

"Yes?" asked Munpi, as his placid expression transitioned to mild annoyance.

"Look, Lumpy…"

"That's Munpi," snapped Munpi, glaring at both Maghrurio and Gazto, who had erupted into a fresh round of laughter.

Dammit.

"My apologies. Munpi, the fate of all of Sonoduhl rests with solving this crime. Surely you will sleep better knowing you helped to save countless lives?"

Maghrurio cursed his foolish instincts. *Did I just appeal to Munpi's better nature?* Gazto's continued laughter seemed directed at him personally.

"Maghrurio, was it? Your time is up." Munpi turned and walked back to his doorway, stopping to shout over his shoulder. "And Gazto? To blazes with you!" He disappeared into the smithy.

Gazto slapped the arm of his chair, laughing louder and harder than before. Maghrurio watched Munpi vanish, and his failure settled on him like a ton of iron. Gazto's laughter was just the icing on the cake.

Great. No blacksmith, no solving Abner's murder. I need to go after him. I need to change his mind. But how?

Maghrurio hesitated in front of the smithy. Gazto clearly assumed the show was over and took his derisive hysterics down the street and around the corner. Maghrurio knew the echoes of that laughter would haunt his dreams for some time, but in the meantime, he had to do something to salvage the situation. The shocked and disappointed expressions on his companion's faces were like daggers in his heart. With no real ideas, he entered the smithy.

There was a burst of bright light and sound, and for a moment, he lost track of time.

Maghrurio found himself out on the street, dazed and unsure of what had just happened. His ears were ringing, and his hands were cut and bruised. He glanced around and saw his friends lying beside him, similarly disoriented but without serious injury. The flaming wreckage of the smithy stood before him, and his brain tried to connect the dots.

Was Abner in there? No wait, Abner is dead. Who was in there?
Munpi.

The realization hit him like a hammer. He struggled to his feet and burst into the ruin, hoping against hope that Munpi had somehow survived. Shielding his eyes from the smoke and intense heat, he cast about in desperation for some clue of the smith's whereabouts. The intensity of the conflagration forced him back outside, but not before he caught sight of Munpi's mangled corpse beside a cracked and blackened anvil. The smithy burned and collapsed upon itself, burying the blacksmith along with any hope of solving Abner's murder.

All Maghrurio could say was, "Shit."

Part 2

CHANGE OF HEART

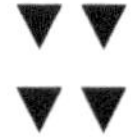

Maghrurio lay curled in the fetal position on his bed at the Salty Frog. Apart from the occasional visit to the privy, he'd remained there since his return from the disaster at the market. Sometimes he slept, but mostly he just lay there contemplating the depths of his failure.

Munpi was dead, and it was all his fault. If he'd been able to convince the blacksmith to join his cause, the explosion wouldn't have harmed anyone. But he failed. A man was dead, and his quest was over.

He could still smell the char from the flames in his hair, still feel the ash under his fingernails. In his dreams, he relieved his failed attempt to save Munpi from the inferno. Gazto's taunting laughter still echoed in his ears.

All that had chased him during the day also chased him under the covers of a night.

What kept him there was the Mystic Ring that stared at him from the nightstand.

Maghrurio could no longer pretend otherwise. Abner had made a grave error by choosing him as his successor. He couldn't do the spells worth a damn, and he'd failed at his one and only quest. He didn't deserve to wear the Ring, so he'd removed it upon his return.

It stared at him from the nightstand, voicing an accusation only he could hear. It taunted him with his failures and passed judgment on his inadequacies. It dared him to choose.

Go forward, or go back?

He lay in bed, unable or unwilling to decide.

• • ● • •

"I'm worried about him, Sheru."

Bacarus and Sheru huddled in their sitting room at the Salty Frog. "He hardly gets out of bed. He barely eats, and he won't talk. And his Ring... he won't say whether he's taking a break or has fully renounced his position."

He wouldn't say anything, in fact. Just that morning, she'd tried to confront him. "It's been days, Maghrurio. What are we going to do? We can't return to Decra because the Duke is still looking for you. We can't stay here because we're running out of money. Are we still trying to solve Abner's murder, or should we just start new lives?"

Maghrurio lay motionless, and his sad, vacant expression made her wonder whether he'd heard her at all. Losing her patience, she yelled, "Choose, dammit!"

Again, no reaction. Frustrated and a little disgusted, she'd stormed out of his room and slammed the door.

Hours later, the women regrouped to discuss their immediate future.

"I'm worried too, Bacarus, although I can understand him a little. I lost my store, my home, and my livelihood all at once. I know what it's like to feel adrift without direction, and I hate it." She straightened her posture and set her jaw. "We're running out of money, and we can't wait for him to work this out. That's why I visited the healing center down the street this morning. They needed someone to handle their medicines, and that someone turned out to be me. That will give me some stability and should provide us with income."

"Bless you, Sheru, that's a load off my mind." Bacarus gazed out the window, a faraway look in her eyes. "Sheru, what have we overlooked? We went through the ruins of Munpi's smithy and found nothing. Surely that can't be the end of our investigation?"

"Our investigation?" Sheru shook her head. "It's been his investigation, Bacarus. We're just along for the ride. Or, in your case, for the muscle."

Bacarus frowned at the characterization but let it go. "Let's reason this through. Our top three problems are money, murder, and Maghrurio. The money we can deal with--you found a job already, and I will too. Murder? I don't know of any other leads to chase, so we're going to have to rely on our currently unreliable Mystic. Maghrurio? We've done what we can for him, so he's just going to have to pull himself out of this."

Sheru nodded in reluctant agreement. "I'll look in on him once more, and then let's explore the town."

• • ● • •

Maghrurio knew he couldn't stay in bed forever. He'd failed with Munpi, and the investigation was at a dead-end. He probably didn't deserve to wear the Mystic Ring. But if he really thought about it, these developments weren't all that different from the rest of his adult life. Being a Mystic was just another in a long line of jobs he'd fallen into and abandoned not long after. Sometimes the job hadn't suited him, and sometimes he hadn't suited the job. So while he hadn't decided to quit just yet, this wasn't uncharted territory. From that realization emerged a tiny spark of self-respect. *Whatever my choice, I will survive this.*

Coming to a decision of any kind fed the tiny spark. He understood that, eventually, he would have to get up and get on with his life. Was now as good a time as any? *Yes!* Slowly he unfolded his body, rose from the bed, and shuffled over to the wash basin. This took longer than usual since he'd not been attentive to his needs this past week. With a fresh change of clothes, he felt he might be ready to face the world again.

What he wasn't quite ready to face was the Mystic Ring. Undecided about wearing it but unwilling to be frozen by indecision, he shoved the Ring deep into his pocket. He noticed his companions were absent, so he grabbed an apple and closed the door on his way out.

While he wasn't physically or mentally at his sharpest at the moment, he retained enough presence of mind to keep a low profile and watch for Captain Azak and his men. He wandered the streets, careful to avoid the vicinity of the destroyed smithy.

It had been years since he'd last been in Cyrchan, but it hadn't changed much. A few new eateries and some new shops, but mostly the citizens endured the passing years.

He hadn't eaten much over the past few days, so his steps were a bit unsteady. He made short work of the apple, which succeeded only in whetting his appetite. A quick stop at a street vendor filled his belly and steadied him.

Late that afternoon, Maghrurio's luck ran out. He'd been slowly meandering in the general direction of the Salty Frog when he caught sight of Captain Azak. Clearly, the man hadn't given up the hunt quite yet. Maghrurio ducked into a crowd and watched the captain continue down the street and around the corner. Cyrchan was part of Albiona, not Nahrein, so technically, Azak had no jurisdiction here. In diplomacy, though, it was always easier to beg forgiveness than ask for permission, so he thought it best not to let Azak catch him.

The thought of capture gave him a sudden start. If Azak took him, what of the Mystic Ring in his pocket? He couldn't allow Azak to have it. Would the Ring defend itself if he wasn't wearing it? He didn't know for sure… Indecision gave way to practicality, and for safety's sake, he slipped the Ring back onto his finger.

He needed to get under cover, so he ducked into a nearby building. It took him a moment to realize he'd sought refuge in one of the town's jewels, the famed Cyrchan Library. Endowed by a wealthy widow with a profound love of books, it grew to become one of the largest libraries in Sonoduhl. The building itself was curiously untouched during the savage rebellion that liberated Nahrein and Albiona from the Black Empire. The entryway was dominated by a statue memorializing the brave librarians who gave their lives to protect the refugees and books from rampaging soldiers. Maghrurio took some solace in the physical reminder of their courage in the face of overwhelming odds.

The interior boasted frescoed ceilings and intricately handcrafted bookshelves holding more books and scrolls than he'd ever seen in his life. Tables, large and small, stood in orderly rows among the shelves. Brown-robed librarians moved silently along the rows, shepherding books and patrons alike. Permeating it all was a mixture of scents--dust, paper, leather, wood polish. He respectfully declined a librarian's assistance and moved off in no particular direction, letting his feet take him where they may.

Like most citizens of Nahrein, Maghrurio had enjoyed a modest education. He attended school as a child, learning about history and the essentials of life as determined by his instructor. He still enjoyed reading when the opportunity presented itself. Standing in the midst of this grand library, an opportunity was clearly present once again.

Turning a corner, Maghrurio found himself pulled from his musing and drawn to a bookshelf partway down the aisle. It was an oddly compelling sensation he'd never felt before. His eye caught a battered old book as the source of this compulsion entitled *In the Beginning*. Curious, he took down the book and found an old, battered armchair on which to peruse it.

He wondered at the unusual sensation. Had the Ring drawn him?

Like attracts like.

Wary of damaging the ancient and fragile pages, he carefully opened the book. Captain Azak and the danger he represented were forgotten as Maghrurio bent to read.

"In the beginning of things, Chaos reigned.
Order wept to see the world as it was.
It resolved to put right the way of things
And vowed to fulfill its virtuous cause.
Order created elemental groups,
Each with a trio of gods to guide them.
***Stone**, the first, upon which all things are built.*
Elayrue, master of rock and soil, led;
His sister Grutam was goddess of strength;
Her twin Esad, the permanence of death.
***Fire**, the second, which drives all things to be.*
Magmus was master of flame and passion;
Sarnas, god of life's flame in animals;
Thebar, god of life's flame in greenery.
***Air**, the third, which surrounds and supports all.*
Wehni, fair goddess of wind and weather;
Regnis, god of the vast heavens above;
Ellast, patron of the breath of wisdom.
***Water**, last, which flows through and around all.*
Boq, the god of all waters, great and small;
Ufnal, goddess of birth and renewal;
Naul, her twin, goddess of health and healing.

Lo, the Twelve could not dwell upon the land,
For their power was great and terrible;
Life could not endure their divine presence.
Yet they delighted in their creation,
Precious fruit of their collective labor
Which they were loath to wholly abandon.
Great debate raged; arguments were exchanged.
In the end, a grand consensus was reached.
Blocks of stone they formed, cured by living flame.
Cubes all hewn and shaped by wind and water.
One created for each god and goddess.
Manifestations of divine power.
Twelve Ules, set to protect their creation.
A single chip was removed from each Ule,
And mounted with skill upon golden rings.
Twelve Mystic Rings, for champions to use
To bring order and justice where needed.
Mystic Rings attuned each to its patron,
And to artifacts strewn throughout the land
So that Chaos could ever be held back."

Maghrurio scanned the chapter further, but the narrative turned to other topics. He flipped greedily through the rest of the tome, but the topic was not resumed. He replaced the book on the shelf, hardly noticing the brown-robed librarian who rushed to ensure it had been properly placed.

He'd never heard the tale before. If true, then his Ring was tuned to one of the gods. He wondered which it might be but soon turned his attention to the other revelation. Artifacts? Did that explain the sampler? And the word was plural, which suggested there were more. Where might they be, and who had them now? He had a lot more to think about on this.

He glanced around the shelves nearby and imagined what further treasures of Mystic lore might be hidden. He closed his eyes, cleared his thoughts, and reached out his mind to search his surroundings. At first, he felt nothing, but soon a familiar sensation pulled him along the row to another set of shelves and a small leather-bound book. He

ignored the title--something about libraries--and scampered back to
the armchair for more reading. A quick scan of the contents led him
to a brief notation in the middle of the book.

*"Among the rarer books to be found are those documenting the earliest Mystics-
-their abilities and their artifacts."*

Maghrurio's imagination ran wild. Finding such a book would be
almost as good as finding one of those artifacts. Of course, would he
even recognize an artifact if he saw one? He decided if books about
Mystics generated mental vibrations, then surely artifacts themselves
would do something similar.

He reshelved the book and tried to find another, to no avail. He
was disappointed, but not overly so. What he had already found was
enough to set his brain reeling. He needed to get back to the inn to
contemplate it all, preferably without being captured by Azak's men.
Distracted by the possibilities, he found himself outside the library,
not entirely certain how he'd arrived there.

The immediate threat of capture focused his mind. With care, he
made his way back through the congested streets, keeping an eye out
for Azak's men. He ducked into a store or two and watched through
the windows, making certain that he wasn't being followed. There
were a couple of times when he thought he recognized someone.
While nerve-wracking, both were false alarms.

After what seemed like forever, he finally reached the inn. Relieved
at the thought of home and safety, he crossed the street to the front
door.

He had scarcely approached the threshold when strong hands
gripped him from behind.

• • ● • •

Bacarus was pleased with herself. They'd wandered most of the day,
getting a sense of the streets, and found a tavern that served as the
town's unofficial gossip hub. The Black Marsh was slightly less dank
than its namesake to the northeast but similarly filled with a variety of
creatures of questionable intent. Bacarus spoke with the owner and
secured the position of evening manager. She solidified her standing in
his eyes by immediately catching and firing a bartender for stealing
from the till.

Employment and income assured, she and Sheru left the tavern with a sense of accomplishment. If Maghrurio would only rouse himself, they could count the day a success.

The late afternoon sun was beating down on their backs, casting a glare into the eyes of pedestrians before them. This bit of luck saved them as they spied Captain Azak and his men before they were spotted. They quickly ducked into a tailor shop and watched the soldiers walk past.

"This isn't good," said Sheru in an understatement.

Bacarus frowned in agreement. "I can only hope they haven't figured out where we're staying." Nervous, the pair re-entered the traffic flow and hurried toward the Salty Frog.

"We're going to need to keep an eye on them."

"Maybe we could spread some rumors about Maghrurio leaving town?"

The pair stopped short, seeing Maghrurio walking toward the inn. Pleased that he'd finally roused himself, they rushed up and grabbed him from behind. Startled, then relieved, he greeted them as they left the dangers of the dusky street behind and hurried into the warmth and safety of home.

PROFIT AND LOSS

The trio compared their day's experiences over a plain dinner of roasted fowl and spring vegetables.

Bacarus drained the last of her ale. "With Azak and his men on the prowl, Sheru and I will need to be extra careful on our way to and from work. You, at least," she pointed at Maghrurio, "should be safe hiding out for a few more days."

"Hiding out? After all your badgering to get me out of bed?"

"Very funny. If Azak doesn't track us down in the next few days, he'll probably move on eastward. I, for one, will feel a lot better when they leave town."

Sheru replied, "Maghrurio is certainly too recognizable to be wandering the streets, and I'll bet some of Azak's men might remember what you and I look like, too. Especially those two that you roughed up."

Bacarus frowned. "True. Perhaps we all need a change of appearance?"

Maghrurio put down his cup. "You mean disguises?"

Bacarus held her arms before her, using her hands to frame Maghrurio's face. "Shaving your scraggly head and not your whiskers might work for you."

Maghrurio gave a grudging nod. He'd tried shaving his head once but was so gaunt at the time it made him look like he was at death's door. He was willing to shed his locks again if it kept him free.

"A change in wardrobe would help us all." Sheru grew more pensive as she stared at Bacarus. "I'll bet those two guards would recognize you, whatever you were wearing. We'd better change your hairstyle and maybe color it too. I can pick up what we need in the morning, but we're going to have to start thinking about money soon."

Maghrurio and Bacarus exchanged frowns, but the need was too obvious. The plan settled, they wished each other pleasant dreams and retired for the evening.

• • ● • •

Maghrurio lay awake in bed for a time, conflicted over whether to call upon Abner. His need to speak with him warred with his embarrassment over his weakness and failures. But, ultimately, his need won out.

Maghrurio found himself at the edge of a towering cliff overlooking a majestic waterfall. He was easily a thousand feet above the broad valley below and could see a river running from the base of the cliff to a large lake far to the north. In the distance, a series of rivers meandered from the western mountain range across the far landscape to empty into that same lake.

The air was thick with waterfall spray and green smells from his lush surroundings. Surely, he stood at the head of the Long Falls with Nahrein and Albiona stretched out before him.

"Welcome back," greeted Abner. He bore a friendly smile, but his penetrating eyes, as always, seemed to pierce Maghrurio's soul.

Ashamed and unable to make eye contact, Maghrurio unburdened himself. He spoke of his responsibility for Munpi's death, Gazto's cruel laughter, his failed quest, and his subsequent crippling depression. He also described his foray into the library and his discoveries therein.

"First, I must commend you on your decision to take up the Ring again. Failure is never easy to bear, but it is one of our best teachers. Also, I must counsel you to avoid jumping to conclusions about your vision. As I said before, visions can be tricky things to interpret. Don't be so quick to assume you've failed. As for the blacksmith, you didn't force him into his shop. You didn't cause it to explode. You are no more responsible for his death than you were for mine."

Maghrurio forced himself to look into Abner's eyes and found a degree of comfort in them. He nodded in response, not trusting himself to speak again.

"Also, congratulations on your discoveries in the library. There are books scattered around Sonoduhl bearing nuggets of wisdom about Mystics, their origins, and their capabilities. Unfortunately, you won't find a list of spells anywhere because we tend to be a rather closed-mouthed lot." He winked at Maghrurio, adding, "As I recall, it took me quite a while to make that discovery myself when I started out."

Maghrurio was taken aback. *I figured out something faster than Abner?*

"Now, last time, we covered combining elemental gestures to achieve enhanced effects. Today's lesson is the last big one, so pay close attention. You can combine spell gestures with innocent ones to create more complex results. We'll start with wind again since that's easiest."

Something clicked in Maghrurio's mind. Abner had mentioned wind being easiest before. Did that mean his Mystic Ring was of the Wind group? "Abner, which god is our patron?"

Abner shook his head. "I'm certain I knew once, but I cannot recall now. That is something you must discover for yourself."

"How about the sampler? Is that one of the artifacts I read about?"

"The threads are the artifact, yes, and the words into which they are sewn trigger their magic."

Maghrurio was pleased to learn he had guessed correctly.

Abner smiled. "Shall we proceed?" At Maghrurio's assent, he continued. "I want you to summon wind, but at the same time, make a pushing motion with your other hand."

Maghrurio did as his master requested and was rewarded with a gust of wind that blew in the direction he had pushed.

"Splendid! That is exactly what I'm talking about. You created the wind with one hand and directed it with the other. Here's another example." Abner turned and walked toward an apple tree growing nearby. "Make the stone gesture with one hand and punch this tree with the other. Be sure to get the timing right, or you'll hurt yourself."

Maghrurio looked at the tree with determination. With his left hand, he made the stone gesture as he swung his right fist at the trunk. He swore aloud when he mistimed it and slammed his unprotected fist into the unyielding tree.

Abner ignored his embarrassment and suggested another attempt. Maghrurio flexed his right hand a few times and gave it another shot. Switching hands, he managed to get his swollen and bloody knuckles to make the stone gesture before the blow. His fist connected a solid, painless blow that shook the tree hard enough to lose a few leaves and an apple. Amazed, he smiled at Abner. "Stone fist!"

"Remember these successes, Maghrurio. Let each one be a building block you use to build an impenetrable wall of self-confidence."

Maghrurio's mind raced as he imagined possible variations of this technique. He found he was actually feeling better about things.

I might master this Mystic thing after all.

"I'm afraid I do have some bad news, however."

Maghrurio's smile quickly vanished.

What now?

"The magic embedded in your Ring enables many things, such as your access to our training sessions and the Gatherings. There are limitations, such as my own inability to recall details from my life." He hesitated, then continued. "The magic also limits the time we have together. I'm not sure how long that is, but it balances against your practice time."

Maghrurio was stunned. "You mean, the more I practice, the less time we have together?"

"Yes, unfortunately. Still, it is vital for you to continue practicing. Practice hones your abilities and builds your confidence. Practice is essential to your continued success as a Mystic. I seem to recall my own master was able to give me some warning of his time limit. I will endeavor to do so as well." He smiled, "There is still time. Do you have any questions?"

Maghrurio couldn't help feeling their time together was an hourglass, with sand slowly dwindling down to nothing. He felt he had a million questions, but one rose above the rest.

"Master, how can I possibly succeed without your guidance?"

"Maghrurio, just try your best, and you'll do just fine."

• • ● • •

Sheru left early the next morning, as she was likely the least recognizable of the three--Maghrurio was, after all, the main target and the two soldiers Bacarus manhandled probably still saw her in their nightmares.

She returned before long, purchases in hand. For Maghrurio, she found a nondescript gray robe to replace the simple pants and tunic he favored. Bacarus would exchange her functional pants for a modest mid-calf dress with matching shorts as a nod to her fighting abilities. For Sheru, an unflattering pants and tunic set that, on her slight frame, would help make her gender indeterminate.

After breakfast, Sheru mixed the powders and chemicals she procured and set about to transform Bacarus' dark hair into a golden yellow. Maghrurio shaved his head and left his facial stubble alone, making him look decidedly graver. For herself, Sheru deliberately hacked her own hair brutally short, giving her a servant-boy appearance.

Sporting their new clothes and hairstyles, they certainly looked different. Whether they looked different enough remained to be seen.

PROGRESS

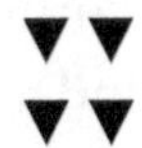

Sheru departed for her new job at the healing center and left her friends to dwell over the remains of their breakfast. Bacarus wasn't expected at the Black Marsh tavern until after lunch, so they discussed their options. They couldn't return to Decra any time soon, so it made little sense to retain their horse and wagon. Any eastward journey would be quicker and easier on the West Marane or Black Rivers, which converged on Cyrchan's eastern boundary, and heading eastward was definitely on Maghrurio's mind.

Ever since he found the Mystic lore hidden in the library, he'd wanted to search for more. If the Cyrchan Library had some, he reasoned, surely the larger Acyfala Library should as well. True, Azak and his men were likely to head that way if they failed to find him in Cyrchan. Still, Maghrurio felt it was a chance worth taking. Bacarus was not so sure and took a fair bit of convincing. Once she finally relented, they decided he should leave that very afternoon. With luck, he'd be in and out of the library before Azak even decided it was time to continue eastward.

Bacarus counted out coins on the table. "Take this money with you. Sheru and I have jobs now, so we can spare it."

"Thanks. I'll be careful with it and, hopefully, bring some back."

"Just use what you need, don't worry about us."

"Keep the sampler handy, too, in case I need a quick escape."

Bacarus patted her pocket and the concealed artifact within. "Good luck and be safe."

Packing his knapsack with essentials, he nodded to Bacarus and headed for the streets. He kept a sharp eye out, hoping his disguise would shield him from unfriendly eyes but, at the same time, unwilling to totally rely on it. The Salty Frog lay in the northwest quadrant of the town, so he made his way across town toward the docks midway between the northeast and southeast quadrants.

As he passed through one of the market areas, he encountered numerous hawkers enticing passersby to sample their wares or appreciate their performances. Turning a corner, he nearly collided with a young man standing behind a small table with three playing cards and a small pile of coins before him.

Maghrurio's ire bristled. This was a "Follow the Knave" game, a basic con meant to ensnare the unwary and cheat them of their money. Three cards are shown, two red aces and a black knave, and the dealer flips them back and forth face down and challenges you to find the knave. It looks easy enough, but it was a sure way to lose all your coins. A younger and decidedly more foolish Maghrurio had fallen victim to such a swindle, and his blood burned whenever he remembered that embarrassing experience. Here, as then, a young fool was being lured into the trap and would soon lose his purse.

Unless Maghrurio did something about it.

He scanned the immediate vicinity and found the accomplice, a larger man with a club at his waist, watching the crowd for trouble. Directly confronting the dealer would bring the club wielder into play, and while Maghrurio was angry, he had no time for such a confrontation.

He recalled his last training session and the trick of combining basic spells with non-spell gestures. On a hunch, he made the wind gesture with his left hand while making a push motion toward the table with his right. A sudden gust knocked over the table, throwing the cards to the ground, where they were revealed to be three red aces. The young fool and several of the onlookers launched into a heated argument with the dealer, which soon caught the attention of the local constabulary. Pleased but distracted by his small revenge, Maghrurio continued on his way toward the docks.

He didn't notice Captain Azak until he collided with him.

Blustering, Azak whirled around and hurled an obscenity at Maghrurio, who repeatedly bowed while mumbling an inarticulate apology. Azak glared at him and stormed off, leaving Maghrurio alarmed but relieved. However uncomfortable his bald head and scruffy beard were, the disguise had worked. He hurried on his way, thankful his mumbled voice hadn't betrayed him but unwilling to press his luck any further.

Fortunately, his luck held. The Acyfala ferry, which departed twice per week, was scheduled to begin its West Marane River run that afternoon. It was a 30-foot monstrosity that would win no prizes for beauty or speed. It was a reliable way to travel, though, drifting downstream to Acyfala in under a day.

Paying his fare, he joined the parade of passengers, livestock, and cargo that boarded the ferry and breathed a well-earned sigh of relief. Azak was behind him, the library was before him, and he'd actually accomplished something good with magic.

Things were looking up for a change.

• • ● • •

Bacarus had managed taverns and large kitchens before, but the Black Marsh was a completely different animal. There were dozens of workers to manage. The inventory rooms were larger than their rooms at the Salty Frog. Most importantly, they are open every day regardless of problems or conflicts. If the Twelve gods themselves were to return to Sonoduhl, the Black Marsh would be ready to serve them food and drink.

She spent most of her first day getting to know the employees, relying heavily on her front-house and back-house managers to keep things running smoothly. She randomly poked her nose into everything as she tried to gain an understanding of how it all worked. By the evening meal, she had a better grasp on general operations as well as the employees-- she identified who she could trust and who bore further scrutiny.

After the dinner rush subsided, she grabbed a bite from the kitchen and seated herself near the bar. She had chosen this vantage point earlier. It was somewhat out of the way, yet she was well-positioned to watch everything from there.

Customers of every social stratum dotted the bar and seating areas, farmers and merchants, and laborers alike. The tavern owner held forth at his traditional corner table, paying no attention to the goings-on at his own establishment. Bacarus could fully understand his need for a tavern manager, as he seemed unable or unwilling to do the job properly himself. It was only blind luck and the popularity of the tavern that kept the doors open at all.

Noise from outside drew her attention to the doorway, where she spied Captain Azak and some of his men as they entered the tavern. On her guard, she double-checked her appearance in the mirror behind the bar. With her new wardrobe and blonde hair, she appeared nothing like the woman from Maghrurio's wagon. Still, she hoped she wouldn't find herself in a position to discover just how good her disguise was.

As the evening progressed into night, the crowd grew larger and more raucous. Azak and his men mostly behaved themselves and had not yet given any indication they recognized her. A new party entered the bar, seemingly tired from a day's work and looking to unwind. They glanced around and chose a large empty table situated near Azak. As they took their seats, Bacarus spied a familiar frightened face-- Sheru!

·· ● ··

Sheru's day at the healing center had been most rewarding. They had put her to work managing the herbs, powders, and potions used for healing patients, and she was in her element. She spent time reordering the mini apothecary and was able to assist with patient care as needed. All in all, she felt gratified to once again be doing work she loved.

When her coworkers invited her to join them at the Black Marsh, she accepted eagerly. It would be an opportunity to settle further into her new role and to get to know them better. She'd also be able to see how Bacarus was doing.

Her stress level spiked once they entered the tavern. Of all the places to sit, her peers had chosen the table next to Azak and his goons. Her face betrayed her panic upon seeing him, but she managed to hide it before anyone noticed. She took the chair farthest from Azak, ordered a glass of ale, and hoped for an uneventful evening.

Unfortunately, her hopes were not to be. Drawn no doubt by the number of women at her table, Azak's soldiers began paying special attention to her group. Her friends spurned the initial crude advances, which caused the soldiers' behavior to grow more obnoxious.

Azak, for his part, worked hard to ignore them.

Some soldiers moved chairs over to join her party, despite vocal objections from her coworkers. One soldier slammed his chair down on her foot and didn't bother to apologize as his attention was focused on her friend sitting next to her. As he glanced around the table, smiling at the women, she realized with horror that this was one of the soldiers from the road, the one Bacarus had rewarded with a limp.

Her friend stormed away from the table, so he turned his attention toward Sheru. He began to say something and stopped, confusion marking his face.

"You look familiar, sweetheart. Don't I know you from somewhere?"

Sheru's eyes widened in panic. *Oh, gods, what do I do now?*

• • ● • •

Bacarus had watched the escalation of boorishness between Azak's soldiers and Sheru's party long enough. She strode over to Azak's table, trusting her bouncers to keep watch over the soldiers.

She planted herself firmly in front of Azak. "Captain, your dogs have wandered off their leash."

Azak smiled, "My men are relaxing after a hard day's work, just like everybody else in here."

"They're disturbing my customers. What's worse, they're disturbing me. Rein them in, or you'll get a personal tour of the local jail." Leaning in, she added, "If you're lucky."

Azak continued to smile as she kept her eyes locked on his.

Does he recognize me?

Finally, Azak leaned back and gestured magnanimously. "As I said, we're just here to relax." He nodded at his lieutenant, who barked out an order. The soldiers scrambled back to their table without delay. He raised an eyebrow at Bacarus. "Satisfied?"

Bacarus relaxed her posture a little. "For the moment, captain. For the moment."

She saw color return to Sheru's face and gave her a wink as she instructed the bouncers to keep a special eye on Azak's table. Retreating to her perch near the bar, she felt better about things than she had all day. Azak hadn't seemed to recognize her or Sheru. Plus, lounging here meant he wasn't chasing after Maghrurio, who should be well on his way to Acyfala.

At that exact moment, by coincidence, Sheru and Bacarus had exactly the same thought as Maghrurio, separated though they were.

Things were looking up for a change.

THE PASSENGER

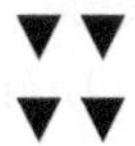

The deck of the Acyfala ferry was crowded. A string of horses and some cattle huddled amidships around the twin masts. Trade goods, cut timber, and assorted bags of produce took up most of the raised foredeck, leaving barely enough standing room for the two dozen passengers. Wanting some solitude, Maghrurio sought a better place to pass the time.

He was turned away from the aft deck--off-limits to all but crew--and so found a small space near a friendly-looking cow. He made a cold dinner of dried fruit and tasteless crackers, more from habit than hunger, and considered the events of the day. He'd escaped Cyrchan right from under Azak's nose and hoped his friends' disguises were likewise successful. Also, for the first time, he had worked a real spell yielding results he had intended. That made him especially proud but also somewhat curious.

Why have I been successful?

Abner would insist he was gaining confidence, but he discounted that explanation as wishful thinking. What was it about the attempt that differed from other occasions where he had been inadequate?

He recalled the scenario, walking around the corner and seeing the "Follow the Knave" dealer. He experienced a flush of anger once again and realized that must be it--anger! He'd been genuinely angry, which must have helped focus his spellcasting. He didn't think he could generate anger on command, but he filed away the idea in his mind for further contemplation. After all, he had a big day ahead of him and an important objective.

The Acyfala Library! He'd been to the city a couple of times over the years, but this would be his first visit to that legendary repository of wisdom and lore. He contemplated the wonders he might uncover amidst the largest collection of books and scrolls in all of Sonoduhl. Like the Cyrchan Library, it had largely been spared the looting and damage visited upon other locations during the Black Empire War. It was bound to have historical records regarding Mystics.

Given his experience in Cyrchan, Maghrurio hoped three days would be enough to search the library. That would leave plenty of time to catch the ferry on its next return trip. In fact, he realized anyone reporting back to Azak that he was in Acyfala would have to take the same trip.

I don't need to be careful at all!

Pleased with himself, he drifted off to sleep as the ferry continued down the river.

• • ● • •

Maghrurio awoke the following morning to the staccato drip of falling rain. Unfortunately, he had nothing to cover his head and was soon soaked. From his vantage point, he could see the other passengers similarly discomfited. Dripping and uncomfortable, he made a quick breakfast of dried fruit and hard cheese and resigned himself to the inevitable.

The light rain quickly grew heavier, and he found himself chilled, waterlogged, and utterly miserable.

This is no way to travel. Is there nothing I can do about this?

He paused for a moment in thought, wondering if his recent training might help. His mind focused, he flapped one hand for wind and gestured upward with the other. To his surprise and delight, a wind barrier formed directly overhead, which forced the rain to cascade alongside him.

I created a rain shield!

He soon discovered if he kept the upward hand steady, the shield stayed in place. Feeling bold with his other hand, he moved his fingers for fire as he raised that hand to match the other, channeling warmth under his shield. With two arms held extended steadily above him, he looked a bit odd, but he didn't care much. It wasn't powerful magic, but he wasn't trying to slay dragons. He was just trying to stay relatively warm and dry.

Maybe this is working because I'm not trying to do much.

It didn't take long for others to notice he wasn't shivering or getting soaked. A small child approached him, standing close to capitalize on his protection. A second child joined the first, and then another. Other passengers started moving down toward him, and the animals were growing alarmed.

"Everyone, please stop pushing before someone gets hurt," he implored. "I will try to use my shield to protect everyone."

The people gave him room as he climbed up to the foredeck, hopeful that he could grant them some small respite from the weather. He stared up at his shield, wondering what he should do. His upraised hands were fairly close together, so he spread them out to shoulder width. As he'd hoped, the rain shield expanded. He moved his hands a bit farther until most of the people were protected. The rest managed to shift their positions to stay within his protective circle.

It wasn't much, but Maghrurio was elated. Once again, he'd managed to make a spell work as intended. He'd helped people, regardless of how minor the help was. But the best part was that he'd used a spell combination of his own devising. His unexpected success and the repeated thanks he received buoyed his spirits.

His arms quickly grew tired, and he struggled to keep them aloft. Luckily, a pair of tall boys let him prop his arms on their shoulders, keeping his spell working for the hour or so the rain lasted.

When the rain had dwindled to a misting, he dropped his hands and stopped his conjuring. There was no point pushing his luck in case the spell behaved differently in the absence of falling rain. He'd hate to frighten or possibly harm the people who thanked him so profusely.

For the remainder of the trip, he massaged his sore arms and exchanged words with everyone who approached him. He'd certainly made quite an impression. He hoped word would filter back to Azak, drawing him eastward just as Maghrurio returned to Cyrchan.

I might as well relax and enjoy this good mood.

• • ● • •

The ferry reached the Acyfala docks after lunch. Once again, Maghrurio accepted heartfelt thanks from the departing passengers and politely refused offers of food and drink. He was anxious to find the library and begin his search.

One passenger lingered, a tall blond merchant named Vodi. With a friendly face and ready smile, he never seemed at a loss for words. Blessed with an uncanny ability to recall names and details to match any face he saw, the merchant also seemed to know everyone. If Maghrurio recalled correctly, Vodi mentioned that he lived in Acyfala.

"Hail Vodi, I was wondering if I could ask a favor."

"For you, my friend? Just name it."

"I have business at your world-famous library and was hoping you could direct me."

Vodi beamed. "Our library is the envy of Sonoduhl. Worry not, Maghrurio. I will take you there myself. If you wish, I can also guide you to a reputable inn. The owner is a good man and will treat you well."

Maghrurio thanked him and followed him from the ferry.

Acyfala bustled in all the ways Decra did not. A steady influx of wagons, pack animals, and carts flowed through the streets. Pungent smells and subtle aromas from animals, shops, and eateries competed for attention. And the crowds! There were more people walking the main thoroughfare than Decra's entire population. Maghrurio felt overwhelmed but tried to maintain some semblance of decorum.

He followed Vodi through the crowded docks and into the city proper. He saw many of the same things as in Decra and Cyrchan, yet more so. Houses both plain and unadorned and mansions fit for kings. Tiny shops and stores boasting a dozen clerks to assist the crowd of customers. Normal pets like dogs and cats, but also exotic birds and monkeys and tamed firisi, their diminutive wings glistening in the sun. Statues of stone and bronze, and marble, intricately carved and almost lifelike in appearance.

Maghrurio had forgotten how impressive Acyfala could be to its country cousins.

After what seemed like hours of walking, Vodi stopped before a large inn. The exterior was clean and inviting, and the sign hanging over the door bore a curled dragon fast asleep on a pile of gold.

"Welcome to the Sleeping Dragon, my friend. Let me introduce you to the owner."

Stepping inside, Vodi looked around quickly and made a beeline toward a short round man with a pleasant, flushed face and fiery red hair. "Ospo, my friend, I want you to meet a very important man. Maghrurio is a Mystic from the west. He's come to Acyfala to do research in our library."

Ospo beamed at Maghrurio and shook his hand vigorously. "I am pleased to make your acquaintance, sir. We haven't had a Mystic in the city for over a year. Please let me know if I can help you in any way."

"Thank you, Ospo. I am actually in need of a room--just a plain room, nothing fancy--but I'm not sure for how long. My research could take two hours or two days. It really depends on what I'm able to find."

"I have just the room for you. It's upstairs in the back, so you won't get much noise, and there's a lovely view of the flower gardens. You can have it for as long as you need it at no charge."

They argued good-naturedly, and in the end, Ospo reluctantly agreed to accept payment that Maghrurio considered grossly insufficient. Still, he was glad to have a base of operations and happy that he'd made some new friends.

After a quick check of the room, the pair departed the inn and headed for the library. Maghrurio paid attention to the route so he could find his own way later, but again the distracting sights and sounds of the city made it a challenge. When they finally arrived at the library, Maghrurio could see why Vodi had been so proud.

The sun peeking through the clouds reflected off its twelve golden spires. Rich wood completed the roof, intricately carved with symbols and animal shapes. The walls were likewise of rich woods, alternating light and dark sections in a checkerboard effect. Majestic stone lions flanked the main entrance, each twice the height of a man. The bronze doors stood open, revealing marble statuary and artwork within.

Maghrurio gasped. *This makes the Cyrchan Library look like a barn.* The columns, the architecture, and the statuary were intricate beyond belief. It seemed as though natural organic forms had been transformed into stone in homage to the wisdom housed within. He could spend days examining every facet of the exterior. It was that impressive.

"Everyone reacts like that, you know," whispered Vodi, not bothering to hide the pride in his voice. "It is the jewel of our fair city and would remain so even if it housed a refuse dump."

Maghrurio replied honestly, "Words can hardly describe the majesty. I'm glad to have seen it." Turning to Vodi, he added, "I'm also pleased to have met you and most thankful for your assistance."

Vodi returned the handshake warmly, adding, "You have but to ask for me at the inn, and I will be at your disposal." Bowing and smiling, he left Maghrurio and disappeared into the crowd.

THE SEARCH

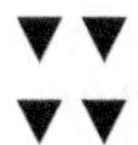

If the library exterior was impressive, the interior was miraculous. The artwork that adorned the walls was exquisite, with eleven panels, each dedicated to the god whose marble statue stood above it. The ornate inner door, crafted of expensive dark woods inlaid with precious metals, depicted the twelfth god--Ellast, god of wisdom, his outstretched arms welcoming patrons to the collected lore contained within.

Maghrurio passed through the doors into the majestic library proper. An immense vaulted ceiling bearing intricate landscapes towered over rows of tall bookshelves ranged as far as the eye could see, laden with countless books and scrolls amassed over the years. Doors and archways scattered about the room hinted at additional treasure troves of knowledge. The susurrus of scattered patrons, the echo of footsteps, and the silence of the wisdom of ages filled the cavernous interior. It was hard not to be impressed with this place. Surely his search for Mystic lore would bear fruit here.

Ignoring the grandeur as best as he could, Maghrurio opted for a systematic search of the library. Assuming he would sense the presence of relevant books and scrolls, he reasoned a slow walk through every aisle of the main room should allow him to find what he sought. He would repeat the approach with the side rooms afterward.

The aisles were long and filled with bookcases, crammed with all manner of books--large and small, new and ancient, bound in leather, cloth, and wood. Their allure was palpable. Absent his quest, he would be tempted to remain within these walls reading book after book until death claimed him. But a quest he did have, so he dampened his curiosity and commenced his long slow trek.

Almost immediately, he sensed his first prize. He glanced left and down, his eyes drawn toward a smallish leather-bound tome. Removing it from the shelf, he sat on the floor and flipped through the fragile handwritten pages.

"...Of the training of Mystics, I have a single anecdote that the very first spell taught is the elemental spell easiest to master. Fire, water, stone, or wind, it identifies the Mystic's patron god as one of the three grouped under that element."

Maghrurio continued to flip through the book but found nothing more. He thought back to his own first training session. He had learned wind first, which meant his patron was of the Wind triad-- Wehni, Regnis, or Ellast. *Wind or heavens or wisdom, which was it?* He replaced the book and continued down the aisle.

He made his way in a slow, methodical fashion and tried not to get distracted overmuch by the dizzying array of books surrounding him. As the afternoon crawled toward evening, he sensed another target on a nearby shelf. He removed a tattered cloth-bound book and, seating himself on a nearby chair, began to read.

"... Most I have encountered have been reticent to speak about the ways of Mystics, but one or two did share some fascinating insights. Some of their tales seem fantastical, but the presence of a Mystic Ring lends credence to their words."

"Each Mystic Ring represents one of the Twelve Gods, that much is known. Each Mystic, therefore, is identified by his or her Ring and its patron God. Mystics can also use artifacts, magical items that come in three varieties."

"Most common are the Omnic artifacts, which can be employed by any Mystic. The View Stones, for example, are common pebbles that can transform a dish of water into a window to places near or far. When I asked how it did this, my Mystic merely smiled."

"Unumic artifacts function for one Mystic Ring only and appear innocuous to all others. My Mystic described the Maizeling, a crude doll made from an ear of dried corn. In the right hands, it could carry tremendous weight for its master."

"Last, just as the gods are grouped into sets of three, the Quartic artifacts function for any Mystic within that triad. With the Thread of Returning, any Wind Mystic could sew words into cloth, and when they spoke those words, they

would be whisked away like the wind, from wherever they might be to wherever the threaded cloth reposed."

"There are other artifacts of each type, but my sources would speak no further of them--neither what they might do nor where they might be found."

Maghrurio sat back, his mind awash with possibilities. There were many artifacts out there, some of which he could use and one of which he already had. Surely his sampler contained the Thread of Returning, which reinforced the idea that he was of the Wind triad. Again, he wondered which of Wehni, Regnis, or Ellast he was.

The docents circulated through the library and informed the patrons that the library would be closing shortly. Maghrurio made a note of where he was in the aisle so he could resume his search in the morning. He replaced the book on the shelf, thanked the docent, and returned to the Sleeping Dragon for food, rest, and some deep thought.

• • ● • •

The following morning, after a hurried breakfast of dried fruit and water, Maghrurio headed back to the library, eager to continue his search for Mystic lore. Along his route, he watched as a matter of habit for any sign of Azak and arrived without incident. Resuming his search from the previous night, he continued his slow tour of discovery. It took him several more hours to complete the main room, but he found nothing further.

Deciding a break was warranted, he took his hunger to the street and purchased a baked meat patty from a street vendor. He sat on the edge of a maritime-themed fountain and ate in silence. The general pace of activity was quicker here than back in Decra. The feel of the marketplace was also different--the shoppers and vendors didn't so much haggle as argue. He also noted a larger number of soldiers than typical, with several patrols within view.

One, in particular, caught his eye, and he did a double take. A soldier eating from the same meat patty vendor looked very much like one of Azak's. Maghrurio searched the marketplace carefully but didn't recognize anyone else. His mind raced.

They couldn't possibly have heard I was here. They must have been heading to Acyfala at the same time I was. I'll need to be much more careful.

If Azak was here already, he no doubt already knew of the ferry incident and eyewitness accounts. Maghrurio made a mental note to adjust his disguise further as he made his way back to the library.

Switching to the outer rooms, Maghrurio noticed that some were lone chambers while others branched into multi-roomed sections. He could still search them systematically, but it would take another day or two to complete. After an hour's exploration through several rooms, he sensed the Mystic presence in a pile of scrolls on a shelf. Picking through the scrolls was tedious, but eventually, his patience was rewarded. He seated himself on the room's chair, unfurled the scroll, and devoured its contents.

"I have endeavored to locate the twelve Mystic Rings in an attempt to shed light on their mysterious nature. Within the confines of the Zod Hills, one of the Stone Rings is in the permanent keeping of the Graavt people. To the west, a Water Ring is likewise held by the hidden people of whom there is no record. A Wind Ring is currently held by a rebel in the Black Empire. The Fire Rings are hidden. I can find no other traces."

Maghrurio wondered about this revelation. If the Stone Ring was with the Graavt, that probably pointed to Usnik. He had no idea who or what the "hidden people" might be, but could the Black Empire rebel have been Abner? The rebellion happened roughly forty years ago when Albiona and Nahrein emerged from the overthrown empire. But forty years?

Just how old was Abner, anyway?

Maghrurio continued his search until closing time. As he emerged from the library, he kept a sharp eye for any sign of his pursuers. He also guarded against the possibility he was being followed by taking a meandering path back to the inn, ducking into a shop or two with rear exits he employed. He finally reached his destination, breathless but still as yet undiscovered.

Maghrurio decided on a private dinner in his room and retired early. He conceded that contacting Abner was pointless until he had finished searching the library. Warm beneath his blankets, he drifted off to a mostly dreamless sleep.

Mostly.

At some point in the night, he heard whispers from the depths of his dream state. Some part of him thought it sounded much like his own calls to Abner, but this was clearly some other voice. He focused on it, and the whispering increased in volume until he could comprehend it.

"Maghrurio, I wish to speak with you. If you ignore my request, the link will be broken. Focus on me, and we can speak as you would with your former master."

Maghrurio didn't recognize the voice, although it did sound vaguely familiar. Should he ignore or respond? There was so much he didn't understand about being a Mystic… After a moment of hesitation, his curiosity won out, and he focused on the voice.

His surroundings melted and reformed into high, rolling hills spread out all around him. A city loomed in the distance. He stood upon a tall hill under a twisted, leafless tree marked with a thick blue stripe about its bark--clearly a milestone or trail marker of some kind. A figure approached from behind the tree, cloaked in black.

"Thank you for coming, Maghrurio. We need to talk," said Usnik as he removed his hood. He stared hard at Maghrurio before continuing. "Do you recall my last words to you?"

Maghrurio thought back to the Gathering and Usnik's cryptic parting comments. "You said I should take care and that all was not as it seemed in the Circle of Friends."

Usnik nodded and relaxed visibly. "You can't be too careful. You and I have been investigating the same mystery and should compare notes, but this isn't the best place to do it." Usnik kept glancing around them as if expecting to be attacked at any moment. "Meet me in Ober City, at the western edge of the Zod Hills. There's an inn called the Rock Garden. I'll leave a word with the innkeeper. Will you come?"

"Can we not speak now?" Maghrurio asked, hesitant to embark on such a long journey alone into an unknown country.

Usnik shook his head firmly. "This communication is not safe; we may be overheard. Will you come?"

Whatever bothered Usnik, paranoia or legitimate concern, was infectious. Maghrurio felt as if hidden eyes were fixed upon him. He didn't really know anything about Usnik, but in their brief acquaintance, he seemed…well…he seemed like a lot of things. Dangerous to the wrong sort. Taciturn, to the point of muteness. Brusque, bordering on rude. Still, he didn't strike Maghrurio as bad-intentioned, and he might have information that could get the investigation into Abner's murder back on track.

Setting his nerve, he nodded his assent to Usnik's request. Usnik nodded in return and promptly vanished along with their surroundings.

THE DIE IS CAST

Over tea and a fruit pastry the following morning, Maghrurio pondered the day ahead. He had the library search to complete and the subsequent journey to Ober City. Plus, of course, he needed to avoid Azak and his men. He knew little of the lands east of Acyfala and nothing of what lay across the Gladwater Lake, so he'd need transportation and a guide. Since he knew few people in the city, he'd have to call in a favor.

He spotted Ospo, the innkeeper, across the room and made his way over. Ospo spied his approach, and his customary smile burst forth.

"Maghrurio, my friend, good morning to you. Are you enjoying your stay? Is there anything I can get you?" His breathless manner could be overwhelming, but Maghrurio had grown accustomed to it.

"Actually, Ospo, I was wondering if you knew how to contact Vodi. I have business away east and was hoping for his advice."

"I will send word for you, my friend. No doubt he can break away for lunch if your need is pressing?"

Maghrurio thought about his library search. "No, I'm not in a rush, but if he could join me for dinner tonight, I would be honored."

Ospo smiled broadly. "I will make it happen!" He clapped Maghrurio on the back and shifted his attention to scolding a passing kitchen boy. Maghrurio chuckled a bit; Ospo appeared the perfect example of a scattered brain, but he seemingly retained everything he said or saw. Satisfied with the evening's arrangements, he departed the inn for his mission at the library.

Knowing Azak and his men were in the city made his trek to the library an exercise in caution. While he did reach the library safely, he couldn't shake the feeling his luck was running out. Ignoring his unease, he entered the library, intent on resuming his search where it had ended the previous day.

Some rooms were dustier than others, betraying both age and disuse. He thought he detected a strange tingling sensation in a side room packed with scrolls, but he couldn't quite place it. After a more careful search still turned up nothing, he decided to continue on and return later.

He walked through room after room for the rest of the morning, extending his senses as he tried to detect traces of Mystic lore. Apart from a growing suspicion that his time was running out, nothing revealed itself. He broke for lunch, tired and disappointed in his morning's efforts. He revisited the street vendors, thinking ahead to his upcoming dinner with Vodi when he heard a familiar voice nearby.

"Our informant said he was last seen in this area. Spread out and find him!"

Maghrurio turned slowly and spotted Azak as he gave direction to a half dozen soldiers, all dressed in civilian clothing and casting about for him. He cursed himself for his lack of attention and thanked the Twelve gods he hadn't stumbled blindly into Azak's lap. His appetite dashed, and he quickly lost himself in the crowd and hurried back to the library.

The afternoon was far different than the morning had been. Where he had roamed the library in carefree pursuit of Mystic lore, now he was constantly and painfully aware of his surroundings. Was that patron staring at him? Is that docent a soldier in disguise? Was he too conspicuous in wandering the rows?

There was no telling how much longer he had. He moved with determination, splitting his attention between detecting Mystic sensations and watching for Azak's men, and completed his tour of the outer rooms without encountering anything noteworthy. He returned to the side room that had earlier confounded him and once again experienced the strange tingling sensation. This time he focused his attention on the feeling itself. It wasn't quite like that which indicated the Mystic lore examples, but there was something familiar about it. He had the impression he'd felt something similar once before.

He paced the room and tried to isolate the source of the sensation. After much effort, he was finally able to narrow it down to a far corner by a wooden bin full of scrolls. Eyes closed, he leaned forward to randomly select a scroll, and the sensation grew a bit stronger. Leaning back to hold the scroll, the feeling grew weaker. Again he leaned forward to select another scroll, and again it grew slightly, then ebbed when he leaned back. Looking around to see if anyone was watching, he picked through the entire bin to be sure. Clearly, the scrolls themselves weren't what he was sensing.

He leaned against the wall above the bin, and the sensation grew again. He stretched and stooped and concluded that, whatever he was feeling, it was stronger toward the floor. He lifted the bin from its position against the wall and moved it to a spot nearby. Scooping the scrolls and replacing them in the bin, he cleared the floor for further investigation. The corner was too dark to see clearly, so with a deep breath and great care, he conjured a wisp of fire. For once, his inadequate skills worked in his favor, as his flame was small enough to keep away from anything flammable. Just in case, though, his left hand was poised to cast a water spell.

In the sudden light, he could see something near the baseboard. Four small triangles were scratched into the wall, arranged two-by-two and pointing downward. It was from this image that the sensation was strongest. Maghrurio reached out his left hand to brush away the dust and cobwebs. The moment his hand made contact, the image began to glow softly. He dispelled his fire, the eldritch gleam casting enough light for a closer look. A recess had formed beneath the triangles, concealing an object the size and shape of an old book. He reached in and retrieved it, and the corner faded back into what he'd found initially--a plain wall with dusty scratches.

Maghrurio examined his find. The object, while the size and weight of a typical book, was, in fact, two thin rectangles of slate, each about the size of his hand. They bore no mark or glow, nor did they emit any magical sensation he could detect. Obviously, this was Mystic-related, possibly even a Mystic artifact, but he had found them in a library.

Should he take them for himself? Propriety warred with curiosity, and in the end, he decided that while library books were for everyone, Mystic items were for Mystics only. He would examine them, and if he couldn't figure out what they were, he would return them. Satisfied, he pocketed the slates and replaced the scroll bin as he'd found it.

• • ● • •

Maghrurio walked back through the library, past the docents and patrons and bookshelves, the artwork and sculptures, and the statues in the main lobby. He wanted to remember the sights and smells in case he never returned. With a final glance, he turned and made his way back to the inn. He was extra careful this time, ducking through shops and alleys, knowing Azak was on the hunt. Fortunately, he managed to avoid any undue notice as he reached his destination.

He encountered Ospo almost immediately as if the man had lain in wait for him. He pushed Maghrurio into the kitchen in an uncharacteristic sense of urgency.

"Soldiers were here earlier, asking about you. I told them I had not seen you but suggested the Laughing Cow Inn across town was where lawbreakers might be found."

"Thank you, Ospo. I hope this won't cause you any trouble. Don't worry, I hope to be leaving in the morning."

"It is no trouble, my friend. Now, go and get ready. Vodi will be here shortly, and I will arrange for dinner in your room."

Maghrurio thanked him profusely and turned toward the stairway. On impulse, he grabbed a piece of chalk from a blackboard by the dining hall and hurried to his room.

He closed and locked his door, not wanting to be disturbed, while he examined the slates he'd found. On the walk back from the library, he pondered his discovery. The triangles were Mystic-related, and they led him to the slates. True, the slates didn't emit any sensation he could detect, but neither did the sampler, which he knew was an artifact.

He could only conclude they must be an artifact of some kind and hoped that, since he could sense them, he could, in fact, use them.

He placed the slates upon his table and sat.

What to do?

He tried placing items atop and underneath the slates, but nothing happened. He took out the chalk and drew an X on one slate. Still, nothing happened. He drew a circle on the other slate. Again, nothing happened. He was still picking up some sort of aura or sensation from the slates but was at a loss to explain it. With Vodi due shortly, he reluctantly stacked and stored them in his knapsack for later.

Ospo led Vodi to his room, and Maghrurio greeted them warmly. A small fire burned in the fireplace, driving the chill from the air and radiating comfort. Waiters followed them into the room with platters bearing a roasted duck and assorted root vegetables. At a word from Ospo, all departed, leaving the pair to enjoy their meal alone.

As they ate, Vodi maintained a steady stream of innocuous chatter that meant little and interfered not at all with their digestion. Once they had finished, however, serious talk commenced.

Leaning forward, Vodi asked, "As much as I enjoy your company, my friend, I sense you did not ask me here for companionship. What is it you require?"

His expression was one of utter sincerity. Maghrurio suspected Vodi might do almost anything he asked. "My friend, I have been called away to meet a colleague in Ober City, and I do not know the way. Any guidance you could give me would be most welcome."

Vodi clapped his hands and laughed aloud. "Have I not said our meeting was fated? I also have business there. We can travel together!"

They made plans to leave in two days in order for Vodi to make the necessary arrangements. They would travel down the Marane River, through the Black Marsh, and south into the Gladwater Lake. Hugging the western shoreline, they would make for Mosel, a town at the mouth of the river that shared its name. At Mosel, they would switch to a more suitable vessel and head due east across the lake to Ober City on the opposite shore. There, Maghrurio would have to rely on Usnik to make the final connection.

Maghrurio only needed to remain hidden and avoid capture until then, and they could stay ahead of Azak's relentless pursuit.

Maghrurio bade Vodi farewell in the lobby and returned to his room. The time they spent was a balm to his frazzled nerves, and not solely because he now had a solid plan for his rendezvous with Usnik.

He enjoyed their moments of camaraderie, however brief, and they reminded him how much he missed Bacarus and Sheru.

Distracted, he retrieved the slates from his knapsack and laid them on the table, determined to unpuzzle their mystery. Two large Xs stared back at him, one on each slate.

That didn't seem right. He recalled drawing an X on only one and a circle on the other. He paused, thinking, then flipped both slates over. Two circles. Hmm…

Grabbing a bit of cloth, he wiped the circle from one slate. It vanished from the other. He flipped them over and cleaned off an X. Both were now clean, front and back. He drew an X on the left slate, and it appeared on the right.

Now we're getting somewhere!

Cleaning off both slates, he placed one on his bed and pocketed the other. Heading downstairs, he ducked through a side exit and found himself outdoors in the flower gardens below his window. He pulled out the slate and chalk to write 'Hello' on it. He hurried back to his room to check its twin. Sure enough, "Hello" stared back at him in his own handwriting.

Apparently, this artifact would allow him and another to exchange messages. He thought immediately of Bacarus and Sheru. Would it be possible to get one of the slates to them?

As he prepared for bed, Maghrurio considered whether to contact Abner. He knew their time was growing short, and he didn't want to waste what little there was, but there was much to share, and Abner's opinions would be of value. Still, nothing was terribly pressing, and he could afford to wait a bit longer. Satisfied, he climbed into bed and closed his eyes.

Sleep was a long time coming.

• • ● • •

The dawn light filtered through the window and awakened Maghrurio. Serenaded by the morning birds, he stumbled past the window to complete his morning ablutions. He was partway through shaving when he realized something was wrong.

He crept back to the window and saw what his unconscious mind had registered. One of Azak's men was in the flower garden, obviously looking for something or someone. He'd heard Azak mention an informant yesterday. Who was it, and just how much had they shared? And were Azak's men still searching, or had they tracked him down?

There were noises in the hallway and heavy footfalls that approached his room. A loud knock echoed from his door.

Had his luck run out at last?

FAVOR THE BOLD

The knock repeated more urgently. Maghrurio had no means of escape. Even if he could leap from the window without injuring himself, Azak's men watched the garden. He was glad of the sampler as a failsafe escape plan, even if that would take him west to Bacarus and days farther from his meeting with Usnik.

The knock sounded a third time. Resigned to his fate, Maghrurio crossed the room and opened the door. Vodi's anxious face appeared, relieved to see him.

"My friend, you are not safe." He slipped into the room and shut the door behind him. "There are soldiers of some kind here, looking for you. Ospo has attempted to divert them, but we should leave with haste."

With a sense of profound relief, Maghrurio grabbed his knapsack, which he'd kept packed for such an eventuality, and the pair slipped through the door into the hallway. Rather than head downstairs, Vodi took them across the hall and through a closed door. They ascended narrow stairs and emerged onto the inn's roof. Vodi motioned him to remain still and inched toward the edge to scan their surroundings.

He crept back and whispered, "There are men at the front entrance and in the garden. As yet, no one has covered the rear, so we'll need to jump to the next building." He flashed a rakish grin and whispered, "I hope you're athletic!"

Hurrying quietly, they made their way to the back of the inn. A second building stood nearby, about six feet away. Its roof was flat, and if one had the nerve or proper motivation, one could jump over to it. Maghrurio had both at the moment, and at Vodi's nod, they both leaped. Maghrurio's leap was ill-timed, and he very nearly fell.

Scrabbling at the precipice, he needed all of Vodi's help to keep from plummeting multiple stories to the street below. It wasn't until they stood securely on the other roof that Maghrurio realized how close he had been to injury or death. He fought to keep from shaking.

"There's a ladder on the far side of the shop," Vodi motioned, and they headed for it. A quick glance over the side showed the coast was clear, and they quickly descended. Vodi paused for a breath and whispered, "I have a friend I can count on who lives nearby. Follow me."

They hurried down streets and alleys and presently found themselves at a plain door on a nondescript lane. Vodi knocked quietly, and the door opened a crack. Maghrurio could make out sharp eyes in the darkness within but little else. He followed Vodi into the shadowed entryway, and the door closed behind them.

A match flared, revealing a man of diminutive stature with a sallow complexion.

No, not a man-a Graavt.

A young one, barely at adulthood, if Maghrurio was any judge.

The Graavt glanced suspiciously at Maghrurio but relaxed visibly at the sight of Vodi. He lit a candle and led them into a small room with a fireplace and several chairs. Tattered gray curtains obscured all daylight from the windows, leaving a gloom barely illuminated by the crackling flames. Their host gave Maghrurio a once-over and left the room. He returned moments later with an older Graavt. Vodi introduced him as Jaysel.

"I am sorry to impose upon your hospitality, Jaysel, but we are being pursued."

Jaysel nodded to his son, who slipped quietly from the dwelling. "My son will scout things out for us. Vodi, my old friend, what have you gotten yourself into now?"

Vodi introduced Maghrurio and related their situation briefly. "So you see," he concluded, "we need to get out of the city as soon as possible."

Jaysel was silent, but his face and body language betrayed his mood. He was angered by his friend's predicament and was probably considering storming out and doing something about it. He mastered his anger with effort and turned to Maghrurio. "And what business takes you to Ober City?" he asked.

Maghrurio thought it best to keep the particulars to himself. Meeting Jaysel's eye, he responded, "Mystic business." Seeing the skeptical look on Jaysel's face, Maghrurio raised his hand and moved his fingers just so. A small tongue of flame appeared, illuminating the surprised look on Jaysel's face. Maghrurio extinguished the flame and said no more.

The door burst open before Jaysel could say anything, and his son returned out of breath. "Father, there are soldiers in and around the Sleeping Dragon. They search for a man who masquerades as a Mystic."

Jaysel looked critically at Maghrurio again, and Vodi spoke up. "My friend, you just saw his magic flame with your own eyes. I myself have witnessed him holding back the rains on my trip downriver. He is no charlatan."

Jaysel considered Vodi's words and nodded briefly. "Vodi is a good judge of character and not easily fooled. We will help you. What do you need?"

"We need passage downriver to Mosel and then on to Ober City." Maghrurio hesitated and added, "There is also a package I need to be delivered upstream to Cyrchan if that's possible."

Jaysel thought for a moment. "I have friends along the way, as do you, Vodi. I'm going to trust that, in this instance, mine will be less likely to talk about what they see." He turned to his son, adding, "my boy here can get your package to Cyrchan. Just give him the details."

Maghrurio produced one of the slates, and the younger Graavt wrapped it. Armed with instructions on how to find Bacarus and what to tell her, he clasped arms with his father and disappeared into the morning.

Jaysel excused himself briefly and returned, bearing a light repast. The morning's adventure had left them ravenous, and they made short work of the bread and fruit. Jaysel bade them rest while he left to make arrangements.

Maghrurio was curious, and they had nothing to do for a while, so he asked a question that had been growing on his mind. "Vodi, I don't want to sound ungrateful, but why…?" He hesitated.

Vodi seemed to read his mind. "Why do I seem so irrationally willing to risk helping you?"

Maghrurio nodded, "Well, I wouldn't have put it quite so baldly, but yes."

Vodi leaned back in his chair. "When I was younger, working the docks in East Arnhem, I always knew I would make something of myself. I aspired to big things; everything I did was just another steppingstone." He smiled a bit, thinking back. "At least, that's what I told myself at first. After a few years on the docks, though, I started to wonder whether I'd ever be able to put down my loading hook."

Maghrurio smiled. "I did a year on a dock myself. Hard work, blisters, little pay, and no fun was what I remember most."

"You recall it perfectly. So I was working myself to death out there, with little progress in my march toward riches, when one day, a merchant offered some of us the chance to sail with him on a special run to Snake Bay. He was in some financial straits himself and needed that deal to bail himself out. He promised bonus pay, so naturally, I volunteered, as did some of my mates. There were a handful of passengers on the ship as well to help cover costs. The voyage began well, but we ran into some trouble and were boarded by pirates near Karn. That's south of the Zod Desert, by the way."

"So there we were, taken by pirates, and I'm just some idiot kid who's about to lose his pay, or worse, his life. They rounded up all the crew and passengers, and things were pretty scary. That's when he stepped up." Vodi pointed at Maghrurio's hand. "An old man who was wearing a ring like that one. He asked the pirate leader if they wouldn't rather be home eating supper."

Maghrurio was nonplussed. "What an odd question to ask."

Vodi nodded. "I know, right? So naturally, the pirates all laughed, thinking they had a fool on their hands. The old man just smiled and asked if they were sure. One or two made noises about tossing him overboard, 'Supper for the sharks,' they joked. Then the old man stopped smiling and asked them once more if they wouldn't rather be home eating supper. The pirate leader decided he'd had enough of the old man and told his men to take him. Next thing I knew, the old man was waving his arms around, and one by one, the pirates were caught by gusts of wind and tossed from the ship."

Vodi's face turned serious. "In the confusion, one of the pirates somehow got behind the old man and pulled out a wicked knife. The old man was looking elsewhere; he didn't know. I was just a kid, but I couldn't let him get knifed in the back. I jumped the pirate and wrested the knife from him, and two of my mates grabbed him and threw him overboard. Pretty soon, all the pirates were in the ocean, and we were sailing away."

"The merchant got down on his knees, thanking the old man for saving his business, and offered him whatever he wanted in compensation. The old man declined anything for himself but asked the merchant to double my pay. He asked my name and saluted me, hand over heart, thanking me for saving his life. He told me I'd been touched by the aura of Mystics and that my fortunes would be forever tied up with them."

"We completed that run, and the merchant did quite well. He doubled everyone's pay in thanks, but because of what the old man said, he quadrupled mine. It was more money than I'd ever seen, I can tell you. When we got back to East Arnhem, I quit the docks and used the stake to start my own merchant business."

He looked at Maghrurio again. "That's why, when I met you on the ferry, I knew I needed to do whatever I could to help you. Not because you protected me from the rain, but because my fortunes are tied up with yours."

Maghrurio smiled. "I have no fortune to speak of apart from the good fortune of making your acquaintance. Hopefully, I can prove worthy of your friendship."

• • ● • •

They waited for hours, sometimes in conversation and other times in silence, until Jaysel returned. He bore groceries--a fresh loaf, some meat and cheese, and a bottle of wine. They supped while he filled them in on his activities.

"I booked passage on a fishing boat leaving shortly. It should get us to Mosel in a few days, and we shouldn't run into any problems. We'll need to find another ship to head across the lake from there, but that shouldn't be too much trouble."

Vodi frowned, "I notice you said 'us' and 'we,' Jaysel. Do you intend to travel as well?"

Jaysel stared at Vodi as if he had two heads. "You are my friend. You are in need. Why wouldn't I go?"

Vodi exchanged a look with Maghrurio, who shrugged. "Very well, then. Welcome to our quest!"

The trio finished their meal and cleaned up while Jaysel packed a few oddments. Wary of their hunters, they slipped from the abode and headed for the docks. Following Jaysel's lead, they used back alleys and ditches even Vodi hadn't known, and soon they reached their destination.

The *Saucy Susan* was an ugly boat, and that didn't even take into account its poor paint job or air of ill repair. Given a choice, they would never have selected it for their journey downriver. Unfortunately, the *Saucy Susan* was one of the few boats remaining at the dock, so they had little choice. Its captain was a grizzled man, guilty of too many dinners and too little exercise. He accepted a small pouch of coins from Jaysel, and the three boarded the boat without ceremony.

"Welcome aboard," he grunted. "I'm Gav. Do what I say, and we'll get along great." Turning toward the wheelhouse, he ordered, "Pull in the ropes and hoist the anchor."

No doubt the easiest way to get along would be to do as instructed, so all three jumped to their tasks and helped ready the boat for departure. Maghrurio pulled in the last of the ropes and glanced up to see Azak staring at him from the far side of the docks. "Shit!" he muttered and ducked behind the wheelhouse. Peaking around the corner, he could see Azak and his men storming down the dock in their direction.

"Azak is headed this way!" he called out.

Gav ignored the outburst, focused as he was on piloting. Jaysel hoisted the anchor and, grabbing a pole, pushed the boat away from the dock. Maghrurio helped him, albeit from the side of the boat opposite of where Azak was.

Vodi watched their approach and finally called out a warning. "They've commandeered a longboat. Damn, I thought they'd be stuck without options."

Maghrurio realized he'd already been spotted, so he stepped out of hiding. He watched as the soldiers hurriedly took their seats and manned their oars. Azak continued to grin in his direction. He knew, like Maghrurio, a longboat with many oars could run down the fishing boat with ease.

Jaysel yelled to the captain, "Does this boat have any weapons?"

"Don't need weapons," came the unfortunate reply.

Vodi armed himself with a makeshift club while Jaysel drew the short sword he had strapped to his belt. Maghrurio stared at the longboat, which was still not yet underway. The soldiers were having difficulties with seating, as they had clearly overloaded the boat.

There are too many of them. We can't afford to let them catch us.

Maghrurio recalled a summer spent in a fishing village when he'd had the opportunity to work all kinds of boats. He remembered longboats could be tricky when overloaded, and this one was so low in the water it was nearly awash. Inspiration struck, and he stood at the stern of the fishing boat facing Azak's men.

He summoned wind and tried to send it toward Azak's boat. What he received was a slight breeze that barely rippled the water.

Damn, I need a wave. How do I make one without wind?

Maghrurio cast about for a solution while his time was running out. He thought about ways to make water move. In a burst of inspiration, he formed the gesture for water with his left hand and the gesture for wind with his right and brought them together in a wide arc. A wave materialized from nowhere, moving in Azak's direction. It wasn't enough to do the trick, though, barely lapping at Azak's boat.

Panicking, Maghrurio tried the gestures again and added a push with both hands. The resulting wave was a bit stronger than before, enough to overtop the sides and swamp the longboat. Azak and his men yelled and cursed, but their boat slipped beneath the surface and dumped them unceremoniously into the river, yards from the dock.

Entirely pleased with himself, Maghrurio smiled and waved goodbye as the fishing boat left its pursuers behind.

Another success!

THE SHIP

With Gav at the wheel and the rest manning poles, they made good time down the Marane River. Maghrurio knew before long, Azak would regroup and resume the chase, so he resisted the urge to lay down his pole and drift with the current. His companions had come to a similar conclusion because, as one, they poled the boat downstream for the balance of the afternoon.

Evening settled around them. Gav secured the wheel and limped over to the stern, drawing with care a fishing line that trailed in the water. It bore multiple hooks, and several had snared wriggling fish when he hoisted it onto the deck. With deft fingers and a sharp knife, he gutted and prepared the fish and placed them in a large pan. He then motioned for Maghrurio to get a fire going on a large flat stone amidship, pointing at a pile of kindling and firewood for his use.

In no time, a supper fire blazed, and the aroma of cooked fish soon had them salivating. Jaysel contributed herbs from a belt pouch, along with a loaf Gav provided, and they had a marvelous feast. The fish themselves were ordinary, but something about the river air and their hard work made the meal taste almost magical.

They left the boat to drift while they ate but rejuvenated by the meal, Jaysel and Maghrurio resumed their pole work. Vodi busied himself cleaning up the fire and the utensils. Gav lit a lantern to beat back the growing darkness and placed it at the tip of the bowsprit. Along with the scant moonlight from both Vadha and Ghata, they had enough light to navigate the river. The trio drew straws for the overnight watch, and Vodi stood first. Gav remained at the helm for a time while the others bedded down on the deck as best they could.

Gentle but firm hands roused Maghrurio from a deep sleep. He was struck by the pervasive reek of rotting vegetation and noted the torches set around the periphery of the boat.

Vodi responded to his questioning look. "Gav set them. He said they should keep us safe through the Black Marsh. We passed into it a while ago." He apologized for waking Maghrurio, then retired himself.

Maghrurio took his place at the watch. He felt at peace, despite the smell. With a splash here and a vocalization there, the marsh by night proved alive with hints of fish, fowl, and beast alike. His companions were asleep, including Gav, and for the present, nobody was snoring. He'd had some experience with a ship's wheel before and thought he could steer if the need arose. His stress level had dropped markedly. As for now, he had only to watch for pursuing lights or strange sounds.

He contemplated his recent Mystic successes. Anger fueled his attack on the "Follow the Knave" dealer in Acyfala, but anger had nothing to do with the rain shield or swamping Azak's boat.

What was the common thread? There was a missing piece to this puzzle, but he couldn't find it.

The river and surrounding bog changed little during his watch, and he roused Jaysel in turn and returned to his blanket. Too tired to think about anything, let alone consult with Abner, he let the gentle rocking of the river lull him to sleep.

$$\bullet \ \bullet \ \bullet \ \bullet \ \bullet$$

Maghrurio woke at first light to find the others already up and about. Gav was back at the wheel, and Vodi was assembling breakfast from their cold leftovers. Once the meal was finished and cleaned up, there was nothing else to do but stare at each other. The stories began shortly thereafter.

Vodi, of course, began with a tale of hijinks from his younger days. He'd made one bad decision after another, all borne of ignorance, yet things somehow still managed to turn out in his favor. Luck clearly played a big part in his career.

Quiet Jaysel spoke of his youth when brawling contests were his entire existence. He seemed proud of the victories he achieved yet rueful of the wasted years. "I made some friends but more enemies and eventually was forced to leave town to seek my fortune. That's how I ended up in Acyfala," he smiled sadly, "and if I don't learn to control my temper, I'll have to leave there as well. Somewhere out there," he gestured randomly, "my true destiny awaits. If I don't wander once in a while, how will I ever find it?"

Gav offered up an abbreviated tale from the wheelhouse. He'd worked the boat for his grandfather and father and inherited it when they'd run into some trouble on a trip. "I wouldn't trade it for anything, though. The river is in my blood."

Maghrurio shared a slightly edited version of his awkward encounter with Nepri in Hasa, downplaying his own mortal embarrassment somewhat. His companions laughed in all the right places, and time passed pleasantly.

They encountered little river traffic for the rest of the day. The marsh spread out on either side of the waterway, thick with swamp grass and literally crawling with rodents, lizards, and other assorted creatures. They spent most of the day fighting a losing battle against flying and stinging insects. Maghrurio even tried his rain shield, including the fire component, but the bugs quickly discovered the gaps in his defenses. It wasn't until nightfall that the cloud of insects relented, leaving them the possibility for undisturbed sleep.

Once more, they drew straws for the watch, and this time Maghrurio was first. He watched the others bed down and stood quietly with Gav for a time. The lantern glowed from the bowsprit, and the torches blazed around the deck. The night seemed to hold its breath, with barely a sound apart from flowing water. That was when the creature attacked.

It was impossible to see exactly what it was, but several long slimy tentacles breached the surface and slammed into the boat from the starboard side. Gav swore and shouted, "He's trying to drag us into the shallows!" He grabbed the wheel firmly and fought to keep them to the river's deepest part.

Maghrurio grabbed a steering pole and swung at a grasping tentacle. The pole bounced away harmlessly, and the tentacle upended him. Jaysel, his fighting instincts triggered, drew his sword and attacked. He deftly weaved between the waving tentacles to strike again and again, with little result. His blade barely penetrated the creature's scaly hide.

More tentacles surged out of the marsh and grasped at ship and man alike. Maghrurio could see they were in danger of being dragged under if he didn't think of something fast. Looking around desperately for inspiration, he saw Vodi use the flat firestone to fend off the creature's attack.

Fire!

Maghrurio dove to his right as tentacles lashed out anew. Regaining his feet, he summoned fire and wind while pushing toward the creature. A small burst of flame shot two feet at a tentacle, which pulled back in response and vanished beneath the surface. He sent another burst that struck a tentacle dragging a dazed Jaysel to the railing. A third blast repelled an attempt to seize Gav in his wheelhouse. Maghrurio summoned burst after burst, using the flames to drive the monstrosity back from the ship. Finally, cowed by the one weapon it couldn't abide by, the creature withdrew its tentacles and retreated into the night.

His breath coming in ragged gasps, Maghrurio labored to calm his racing heart. His flames had been small but thankfully enough to do the job. His companions congratulated his skill and quick actions, but he knew he had much room for improvement. Still, it was another small success.

The men remained awake for some time and watched for the creature's return. Gav told them it had been a giant river squid called a pi'pala. The torches usually kept them at bay, so he placed several more torches around the perimeter to be safe. Whether cowed by the additional torches or the memory of seared flesh, the pi'pala troubled them no more.

As the waning Vadha set, they left the smells and danger of the Black Marsh behind and passed into Gladwater Lake. Gav pulled the wheel about and drifted south along the coast, carried by the current toward Mosel. At the change of the watch, Maghrurio eased himself onto his blanket and eventually fell asleep.

• • ● • •

With the rising sun, the boat was a flurry of activity. Gav's passive fishing line provided breakfast, and it looked to be another pleasant spring day ahead of them. The Gladwater was huge; the coastline to the north and south extended beyond their vision, and the eastern shore may not have existed for all they could see. According to Gav, they would skirt the western coastline for the remainder of the morning until they reached Mosel somewhere around lunchtime.

With little else to occupy their time, Gav set the travelers to minor tasks around the boat, repairing lines and cleaning. It gave their hands something to do while their minds considered the journey to come. Maghrurio, for his part, dwelt on what followed behind rather than what lay ahead. Somewhere back there, Azak was coming for him. He didn't wish Azak killed but hoped the pi'pala would buy him some time.

The day dragged on, and the mind-numbing boredom of maritime life reminded Maghrurio why he had abandoned his brief nautical career that one winter. There was scattered traffic on the water, with little on the nearby shore. There remained no sign as yet of his pursuers. Vodi and Jaysel passed the time with some bizarre card game he couldn't follow, and Gav, as usual, remained silent within the wheelhouse.

When they finally drifted into the docks at Mosel, Maghrurio knew he'd have to push on to Ober City right away. There was his meeting with Usnik, but there was also the head start on Azak he didn't wish to squander. The trio thanked Gav for his service and hit the docks in search of their next ride.

While Maghrurio purchased some street food for their evening meal, Vodi and Jaysel met with several captains. Within the hour, they reconvened, discussed, and decided on their best option over a quick bite of roasted meat wrapped in flatbread. A fast sloop would be departing soon for Ober City, and they meant to be aboard her. With a favorable wind, they expected to reach their destination by late evening. It was the last ship of the day making that run, gaining them another precious day on Azak. They wrapped the remains of their meal and hurried to catch their ride.

Their experience aboard the sloop was different from the fishing boat. As a sailboat with its own crew, their services were not required. They had only to sit and wait for the voyage to end. Vodi and Jaysel whiled away the hours on their card game. Maghrurio spent his time thinking.

As afternoon swiftly became evening, they polished off the remaining foodstuffs Maghrurio had purchased in Mosel and generally tried to stay out of the crew's way. Maghrurio thought back to the adventure tales he'd read as a child, imagining he'd be bored with part of the story because nothing was happening. Now that nothing was happening to him, he appreciated just how comforting "nothing happening" could be.

Well after sundown, the sloop reached the docks at Ober City. The trio disembarked, heading toward the heart of the city in search of lodging and entertainment. They located the Rock Garden Inn with little difficulty and secured rooms for the night.

Once his companions had retired to their rooms, Maghrurio returned to the front desk to retrieve Usnik's promised message. The innkeeper poked around below the desk and brought forth a sealed scroll with Maghrurio's name inscribed on the outside. He thanked her and hurried back to his room to read its contents.

"Take the main gate into the hills and head due east for nearly a day. Seek a hill with a single tree shaped like a hermit holding a lantern. I will meet you there, Usnik."

He had his directions. He would spend the night here, have breakfast with his companions tomorrow, then continue on the last leg of his journey. He went to sleep as he contemplated what revelations Usnik might share.

HOMEFRONT

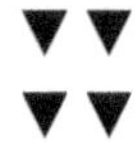

The hour grew late, and the last of the Black Marsh's inebriated patrons were turned out into the streets. Bacarus held the door for Sheru and locked up the tavern behind them. She was grateful Sheru switched to the evening shift, giving them similar work schedules and a companion for the walk to the nearby apartment they called home. It even had a spare room for Maghrurio once he returned from Acyfala.

He should have returned already. I hope he hasn't run across Azak again.

There weren't many people on the streets at this hour, so Bacarus easily noticed they were being followed. A slight turn of her head to scratch an ear, and there they were--three large thugs spread out across the width of the street, positioning themselves to surround and intimidate and possibly to rob and harm as well. She shifted her carryall bag over her head and shoulder to free her arms and spoke casually to Sheru.

"Don't look behind us, but we have unwanted company."

Sheru's eyes grew wide. "What do we do?"

"Stay close. Remember what I taught you, and don't look so scared."

Sheru inched closer to Bacarus, trying and failing to compose her face. They turned a corner, and Bacarus brought them up short, their backs pressed against the building they'd just rounded. The men followed quickly and were almost past before noticing their prey. Grim faces turned their way, and the thugs positioned themselves to prevent escape.

Bacarus recognized one of them, the bartender she'd fired on her first day. "Have you come looking for a recommendation? Because I recommend you keep walking."

Bartender's companions didn't smile, nor did they leave. They advanced within a few feet before he snarled, "You're gonna regret firing me." Bartender brandished a small club, and the men attacked.

Bacarus parried Bartender's swinging arm with a forearm block that sent his club clattering into a refuse pile. She deflected his roundhouse punch and pulled him off-balance, using his momentum to throw him into his companion. She risked a quick glance at Sheru and saw her scuffling furiously with the third attacker.

Her assailants untangled themselves and approached her from opposite sides. With a yell, they both attacked. She blunted the companion's attempt with a leg block but caught Bartender's fist on the side of her head. Fighting against the pain, she lashed out with defensive kicks and punches that were intended to keep them at bay until she could recover. She heard Sheru scream and wished she had thought to pick up some kind of weapon. Another swing connected, and she dropped in a daze to her knees.

As she fought to stand against the fog in her head, she heard yells and the sound of swords being drawn. She struggled back to her feet and saw several men chasing their fleeing attackers. Another helped Sheru to her feet. Bacarus rose to thank their rescuers and came face-to-face with a handsome soldier.

"My lady, I'm so sorry you had to endure that. Rest assured, my men will chase down those scoundrels and teach them manners." He swept off his hat in an exaggerated flourish. "Allow me to introduce myself. I am Lieutenant Dhalil from the land of Nahrein. And you are…?"

"Bacarus," she rasped and moved toward her friend. "Sheru, are you injured?"

Sheru appeared shaken but whole. "I'm fine," she replied through tight lips.

Bacarus gritted her teeth. She could have handled those idiots in her prime, but she was out of practice and allowed herself to be distracted by Sheru. It galled her to need rescuing, but she was thankful things hadn't become out of hand. She regarded the soldier again and wondered where she'd seen him before. "Lieutenant, I must extend my gratitude. We are indeed lucky that you happened along."

She graced him with a ridiculous curtsy, biting back her annoyance at having to play 'the girl.'

"I have seen you at the Black Marsh before. Perhaps I will run into you again there." He flashed one last smile and, with a shout to his men, departed with a short salute.

Now that he mentioned it, I have seen him once or twice at the Black Marsh. The women watched them leave and then hastened toward home.

"Bacarus, are you alright?"

"I'm fine, probably just a bruise on my head. What happened to you?"

"I'm no fighter, but I did what you told me. He went to grab me, and I just kept swinging my elbows. I don't think he expected me to be so lively." Her eyes gleamed, and she held her head high. "I may not have your skills, but I will never again be the frightened victim."

It had been a brave step Sheru took several evenings ago, telling of her past assault. It prompted Bacarus to share some basic defensive techniques to inspire confidence and help restore Sheru's sense of control. She knew a sense of confidence was critical to anyone's mental well-being.

"My skills were years in the making and took great pains to acquire. Even so, we'd be in a bad way now if not for the good lieutenant. Although," she added, "I have to wonder whether both groups showing up on that deserted street was the coincidence it seemed."

"You think he was following those men?"

"Worse, I wonder if he might have paid those men to attack so he could 'rescue' us. Which suggests he knows, or suspects, who we are. Either way, we need to be even more on our guard."

They entered their apartment and locked the door.

Safe at home, Bacarus removed her carryall and placed it on the table. She rooted through it and withdrew the package that had been delivered earlier that evening. She had been perched at her usual table overlooking the bar area when the Graavt had entered. With a quick glance around the room, he moved quickly to the bar and queried the bartender, who pointed in her direction. The stranger had then approached her with a bow.

"Good evening. I have traveled from Acyfala with an urgent delivery from your friend Maghrurio." His hands fumbled through his bag and produced a small package. "Maghrurio extends his greetings and regrets that he has been called away on an errand. He asked me to give you this and to bid you to mark an X on it in chalk."

It had seemed an odd request, but much in her life, these past two weeks hadn't made sense. She thanked the Graavt, put the package in her bag along with some chalk, and resolved to do as he had asked later that night.

It was later now, and she was curious to unlock the mystery behind the gift. She filled in Sheru while she unwrapped it, and they sat at the table staring at the small blank slate.

Sheru remarked, "It doesn't look like anything special."

"True, but it's a small request, so let's see what comes of it." She marked an X on the slate and held her breath, half expecting something wondrous to happen. Nothing did, so she set it down on the table and stood. "Maybe whatever it does takes time. Why don't we get some tea while we wait?"

They prepared some tea and resumed their seats with hot mugs in hand. As she glanced down, Sheru gasped. Bacarus looked down as well. The X had vanished, replaced by one word.

HELLO

Using her sleeve, she erased the word and wrote with her chalk.

WHO IS THIS?

Her writing remained for a moment, then vanished and was replaced by one word.

MAGHRURIO

Bacarus scribbled furiously.

PROVE IT. WHAT'S OUR HORSE'S NAME?

After a moment or two, the slate again erased itself, and they watched new words appear.

SNOWFALL. ARE YOU WELL?

Bacarus breathed a sigh of relief. "It's him."

WE ARE FINE. HOW IS THIS WORKING?

YOU SEE WHAT I WRITE. I SEE WHAT YOU WRITE.

Sheru exchanged an excited look with Bacarus. "This is some kind of magic!"

They exchanged news with Maghrurio for almost an hour before calling it a night. Since they were on a later schedule than he, they agreed to just write down messages at any time if needed. If they needed real-time conversation, they'd try to schedule something. They bid each other luck and signed off.

"I hope he's able to track down the other Mystic," Sheru remarked as she prepared herself for sleep.

Bacarus nodded. "I'm wondering where we should put the sampler, just in case he needs a quick exit. It won't do to have him magically appear in the middle of the tavern."

"Why not just leave it in his room? We don't have a maid, so nobody should ever be in there."

Bacarus removed the sampler from her bag to the nightstand in Maghrurio's room. They then extinguished their own lamps and went to their beds. The day's labors and the night's unexpected conflict were exhausting, and they drifted off to sleep in no time.

EXPLORERS

Maghrurio's late night with the slates meant a late rise, so his companions had already finished their meals by the time he appeared in the dining area for breakfast. Drinking tea to be sociable, they watched him devour his boiled grains in silence until most of the morning crowd had dispersed.

Over another round of tea, Vodi began the conversation. "So, my friend, what comes next?"

Maghrurio put down his teacup tentatively. "Vodi, you mentioned you have business here in Ober City. Jaysel, you have been a godsend in getting us out of Acyfala and down here safely. I can ask no more of either of you, but I must set out at once."

Vodi looked disappointed. "Friend Maghrurio, I cannot lie. I do have business and must see to it this morning. Are you certain you cannot delay a day or two?" When Maghrurio shook his head, Vodi continued. "Then I'm afraid all I can do is await your return."

Jaysel's expression hadn't changed. He turned to Maghrurio and asked, "So when do we leave?"

Maghrurio frowned. "Jaysel, I'd hate to impose on our brief friendship. Surely you have business awaiting your return to Acyfala? And your son, does he not look for his father's return?"

"I admit our friendship would not move me to make this sacrifice. But Vodi is my friend, and I owe him a great debt. Since he cannot accompany you, I will assume his place. Besides," he added while taking up his tea, "you will be headed into unfamiliar territory. You will need a guide if you expect to return alive."

"You would be wise to consider his offer," said Vodi. "The hills are no place for a man walking alone."

Maghrurio pondered Jaysel's cryptic comment. He'd never been to the Zod Hills before and didn't know anyone who had. Perhaps it was wise to have a local to guide him properly, one who could smooth over any cultural issues that might otherwise spiral out of hand.

"Very well, I accept your kind offer."

Jaysel responded with a small nod. "Perhaps I will find my destiny on the way."

Vodi broke into a huge grin. Maghrurio, meanwhile, hoped he'd made the right decision.

$$\cdots\bullet\cdots$$

Packed and ready to go, Maghrurio and Jaysel bade Vodi farewell around mid-morning and left Ober City by way of the east gate. Maghrurio had shared Usnik's instructions with Jaysel-- *"Take the main gate into the hills, and head due east for nearly a day. Seek a hill with a single tree shaped like a hermit holding a lantern."* Jaysel didn't recall ever seeing the tree in question, but the directions were plain enough. They would travel east and trust their instincts.

Of course, "head east" was simple in theory, but it proved more of a challenge in practice. The hills were of varying sizes and heights; some were smooth and grass-covered, while others were craggy and difficult. Often it was easier to go around hills rather than up and down again, so keeping true to the east was a constant challenge. The sun was hot, but the wind was pleasant, and there were plenty of creeks and rills from which to replenish their waterskins.

They stopped on a rocky hillside for a late lunch of bread and fruit. Eating in the shade of an overhanging rock formation, Jaysel shook his head. "The trail is unusually empty today. I've only seen a handful of other Graavt at a distance all morning. There should have been more."

Maghrurio frowned. "It's not a holiday, is it?"

"No. It might just be a coincidence, but we should get moving again in case it's something more."

They made decent time as they continued eastward. The frequency of rough hills dropped, and they began to see more greenery--ground cover, bushes, and the occasional scrubby tree. Animal life also grew more evident as all manner of rodents, birds, and lizards dotted the landscape. Jaysel stopped on one tree-strewn hill and grabbed several short pieces of dead wood. Stuffing them in his pack, he explained, "When it grows dark, we'll want torches to help fend off predators."

"Predators? What kind?"

"Gûr-i, mostly, although larger things creep into the hills from time to time."

Gûr-i… that's just great. Similar to wolves but larger and smarter, they made dangerous predators. No traveler liked gûr-i, but he'd had more than his share of experiences with them. In fact, his left leg sported a wicked scar from a close encounter he'd rather not repeat. He resolved to pick up his slackening pace and hoped they could find Usnik before it turned fully dark.

They crested the next hill, and Maghrurio noted the gibbous Ghata had set. He had another day or two before the moon grew full, which would mark the next Mystic Gathering. He wondered how much he should share of what he'd discovered and which of the Mystics he should (or could) trust. He hoped to find answers to many such questions during his upcoming meeting with Usnik.

A few hours later, footsore and tiring, the pair topped one of the taller hills around and halted for a breath and some quick reconnaissance. As before, there was ample small creature activity but little to none of the human or Graavt variety. Jaysel thought he spied some movement on the last hill but wasn't certain if it was a trick of the failing light. Off to the east, perhaps another hour away at their current pace, they could see an oddly shaped tree that might be the one Usnik mentioned. Mist wreathed the hills beyond, obscuring them from their current vantage point. They readjusted their packs and resumed their eastward progress.

Maghrurio was lost in thought, reviewing the evidence he had so far uncovered when an unconscious observation caught his attention-- the susurrus of small creatures he had grown accustomed to had ceased. He glanced at Jaysel, who had clearly just had the same realization.

"Take care," Jaysel whispered. "Something is on the hunt." He removed torches from his pack and handed one to Maghrurio, who lit them both with a finger gesture. Jaysel also unsheathed his short sword and proceeded up the next hillside. Maghrurio swore silently and drew the dagger he had purchased a lifetime ago back in Hasa. Had it been only two weeks? Its purchase had been a courtesy at the time, but he felt fortunate to be holding it now.

The silence seemed to grow as the daylight faded with the setting sun. The two became more aware of their surroundings and grew convinced they were being stalked. Jaysel pointed at a hollow ahead and gestured for Maghrurio to follow quickly. "This place should be more defensible. Pile whatever scrub and dry brush you can reach. Fire will be our friend tonight."

No sooner had they reached the mouth of the hollow than the first pair of eyes appeared. Blinking in the semi-darkness, they were joined by a second pair, then a third. Maghrurio scrambled, gathering kindling and scrub to pile at the mouth of the hollow. At a nod from Jaysel, he summoned flame to ignite the pile. The gûr-i, discouraged by the flames, withdrew from sight. Maghrurio continued to grab whatever was within reach to feed the flames, but before long, the fire died down to little more than embers.

The gûr-i returned shortly thereafter. Three gûr-i charged the pair, growling and slavering while their brethren howled for reinforcements. Jaysel's sword swept again and again, and Maghrurio's dagger flashed in the dim light. The gûr-i retreated with light wounds but left similar wounds behind as well.

Another attack followed swiftly as three more gûr-i swept into the hollow. Jaysel managed to catch one in the chest, killing it instantly but paid for it with a clawed arm and a gash on his leg. Maghrurio, as he stood near the diminished fire, managed to fight off the lone gûr that came for him.

Wounded and short of breath, the pair watched the gûr-pack inch forward. There were over a dozen, and Maghrurio knew the gûr-i would make short work of them if they attacked as one. His magic might be the only thing that could save them. What could he do?

As he feared, the pack surged forward together, intent on ending the fight quickly.

Maghrurio, intent on conjuring flame with his left hand, swept out his dagger with his right. His dagger instantly transformed into a large flaming sword that cleft a charging gûr in two. The pack, frightened and dismayed by the sudden appearance of the flaming sword, abandoned their attack and fled the hollow. Surprised yet pleased with his latest magical discovery, Maghrurio turned a smiling face toward his companion.

Jaysel was sprawled on the ground and splattered with blood. A gûr stood over him, growling at Maghrurio. Afraid for his companion, Maghrurio leaped at the creature. Down came the flaming sword, and the gûr fell in two.

Maghrurio sheathed his dagger and rushed to his comrade's side. He had a nasty laceration on his left arm in addition to his other wounds and was bleeding profusely. Maghrurio quickly ripped up some makeshift bandages from his robe and bound the injuries, but they continued to bleed unabated. Realizing he had scant seconds to save a life, he summoned fire while drawing his dagger and was rewarded, once again, with a flaming sword. He pressed it against his companion's wound, cauterizing it. Jaysel cried out and lost consciousness, but fortunately, the maneuver stopped the bleeding. Maghrurio then re-bandaged Jaysel as best he could and took stock of his current situation.

The rendezvous point was near, but how near was unclear. The gûr-i had scattered but were still out there, able to strike again given the opportunity. Jaysel was unconscious and would need to be carried. Maghrurio could manage, but not for long. Besides, he couldn't fight while carrying Jaysel. There was no good solution, so he decided to chance the dash to find Usnik.

He replaced Jaysel's sword in its scabbard and hoisted his unconscious friend onto his back. Luckily for them both, a job on the docks taught him how to lift and carry heavy loads. With a quick look around, he headed eastward, searching for the strange tree.

He could hear little from his surroundings apart from his own heavy breathing. Struggling under his burden, desperate to find the rendezvous point, he finally spotted the odd-looking tree on the next hill. Fearing a gûr-i attacked any moment, he put on a burst of speed and reached his destination. He collapsed under Jaysel's weight at the foot of the tree.

Struggling back to his feet, Maghrurio drew his dagger and looked around. The tree did sort of look like a man holding a lantern if you saw it from the right angle. What he didn't see was Usnik. He paused to consider what to do next, and his blood froze as the howling began anew.

Plainly, he could see the hill wasn't defensible. With no choice left, he gathered up Jaysel and ran. His chest burned, and his legs ached, but if he didn't find a better place, they were both dead. He managed to make it halfway up the next hill when he saw the first gûr approach. He lowered his injured friend to the ground, drew his dagger, and prepared to make his last stand.

The gûr charged as he summoned the flaming sword. He struck a glancing blow, but it was enough to drive it back. Two more attacked, with more closing in behind them, and he knew his time grew short. A fourth gûr leaped at him, and his backstroke went wide as the beast hammered into his side. Knocked to the ground, his dagger flew from his hand, and he expected the worst. What he didn't expect was the dense hail of stones that struck the gûr-i, driving them back.

"Grab your friend and follow me!" came a hurried shout as a shape dashed across the hill and down the other side. Maghrurio snatched up his dagger and Jaysel and ran like all the gûr-i in the world were on his tail, which in this case actually seemed to be true. Time and again, he halted long enough to throw a meager flame toward the pursuing gûr-i. It wasn't much, but it slowed them sufficiently to keep him a few steps ahead of them. Arms and legs quivering on the verge of exhaustion, Maghrurio thought he could go no further when they broke through a wall of mist into a familiar place. Ancient trees, a curved granite wall, stone benches…

Maghrurio wondered aloud, "Is this the actual Circle of Friends?"

"Yes," said a familiar voice behind him.

SANCTUARY

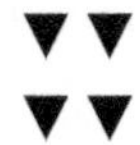

Maghrurio spun around to see Usnik. Behind the Graavt, two gûr-i had also entered the Circle, but they acted more like tame pets than the vicious predators who had just tried tearing him to pieces. He looked questioningly at Usnik.

"The Circle of Friends is a profoundly magical place," Usnik explained. "Some suggest this is the very spot where the gods decided the fate of the world. We are quite safe here. Violence of any kind is impossible within these walls." He gestured at Jaysel, unconscious on the ground next to Maghrurio. "Death, specifically from violence, is likewise impossible here. Now would be a good time to attend to him."

Maghrurio bent to the task, his face serious as he cleaned the wounds and applied fresh bandages. He gave his friend some water, covered him with a blanket, then turned to the Mystic.

"Thank you for your help back there. I wasn't sure we'd survive."

"I asked you to come. I could hardly stand by and do nothing." He motioned toward Jaysel with his head. "You took a risk in carrying him this far. Friend of yours?"

"More like a friend of a friend, but I couldn't just leave him to the gûr-i. As you said, I could hardly stand by and do nothing."

Usnik grunted his assent and fell silent again. The gûr-i, sniffing around, departed the Circle.

Maghrurio stared at the taciturn Graavt. He was clad in a simple brown robe without a weapon or pack--clearly, he had not traveled far to this place. He carried a rough walking stick he probably picked up along the way to help ease his passage through the rocky hills.

Maghrurio noted the Mystic was also studying him and wondered what guesses Usnik drew from his own appearance.

Usnik broke the silence with a chuckle. "The Circle prevents violence, but it seems to allow cautious suspicion. I'll make the first gesture. Would you like to know which god is your patron?"

"I've narrowed it down to the wind triad, but I don't know which one it is."

Usnik gestured toward the small stone structure at the center of the clearing. "Inscribed about the fountain are the names of the Twelve Gods. Pass your Ring hand over them, and your patron's name will glow." He turned his back to Maghrurio. "It is considered bad form to ask another's patron, so I will look away while you proceed."

Maghrurio paused, considering. Under normal circumstances, he might accept Usnik's assurances with some skepticism, but the profound change in the gûr-i's behavior strongly suggested the magical nonviolent nature of the Circle was genuine. Also, while Usnik gave few personality clues at the Gathering, his willingness to help drive off the gûr-i was a point in his favor.

"If I may ask, why rocks? Why didn't you use something against the gûr-i that was more, I don't know, lethal?"

Usnik kept his back turned. "They are creatures of the wild, doing what is in their nature. There was no need to kill them."

Maghrurio frowned. Maybe his simplistic approach of "kill or be killed" wasn't necessarily the right or even Mystic way. He'd have to think about that.

With no response for Usnik, he turned instead to the altar. It had a small circular interior bearing a familiar design. With a start, he realized it looked like the scratchings on the library wall where he found the slates--four triangles in a two-by-two formation. About the rim of the altar were names and icons of the Twelve etched into the stone. Between the two, squarish indentations were arranged--one per name. He had no idea what they signified.

He held his breath as he passed his hand around the perimeter, and to his surprise, the name of Wehni, god of wind, glowed fiercely beneath his touch.

That explains a lot.

He withdrew his hand, and the fountain returned to its placid state. "I am finished," he called.

Usnik approached slowly. "It is better to know than not know, as a rule."

"Agreed. Tell me, if it is bad form to ask about one's patron, is it also bad form to volunteer that information?"

"Courtesy dictates that you should first ask whether I want to receive it. That's because I would be compelled to return the favor."

"Interesting. I had no idea there was such a thing as Mystic etiquette. So, Usnik, you asked me to come to hear what you would share. What is it?"

Usnik seated himself on a bench and waved at Maghrurio to do the same.

"I have kept apart for a long time in mistrust of my fellow Mystics. It is the nature of our profession, perhaps, but in my case, compounded by my own suspicious instincts. But, as you know, Mystics strive to uncover mysteries and are loath to yield the fruits of our labors." He shook his head, a wistful expression on his face. "I realize now that attitude kept me from connecting with good people. Abner was one. I believe you may be another."

Maghrurio was surprised. He had always assumed Abner was a good Mystic, but the idea that anyone could think the same of him was hard to swallow. A frown creased his face as Usnik continued.

"Over the years, we have lost several of our numbers, Abner easily the best of them. I have quietly looked into it, and I suspect Mystics are being hunted." His face grew even grimmer than usual. "I believe one of us is the hunter."

Maghrurio was stunned. Given his own poor skill level, he was more than willing to believe in the idea of a bad Mystic. But a Mystic that was bad, as in evil? It made little sense. He'd had religious instruction in his youth. The gods of their pantheon were neither good nor evil. They didn't always agree, but they strove together to ensure that Sonoduhl thrived. Mystics were similarly committed to a better Sonoduhl. An evil Mystic would mean a betrayal of their patron and the sacred trust between Mystics and the land. To target fellow Mystics would be a sacrilege beyond belief.

But Abner believed he had been murdered, and Usnik seemed to believe so as well. Maghrurio gazed into the trees and tried to pull together all he had learned. Usnik certainly seemed on the level, and as a new and not very skilled Mystic, he could certainly use an ally. He appreciated that Usnik waited patiently for him to make up his mind. In fact, that most of all convinced him to put his trust in the Graavt.

Maghrurio stood. "Usnik, I came by this Ring when Abner was killed. Murdered, from what I can determine, and your suspicions confirm my own. If we share our evidence and work together, we may be able to track down whoever is responsible." He extended his hand, and they clasped wrists in friendship.

"You showed me how to find my patron. Shall we seal our friendship by sharing what I found?"

Usnik bowed. "I would be honored."

"My patron god is Wehni of the four winds."

Usnik smiled. "I am a champion of Elayrue, god of stone. So we are elementals, you and I, leaders of our triads. It appears I have chosen my ally well. So why do I suspect a Mystic, you may ask? Because as near as I can tell, most were killed in the same manner-- some type of explosion."

"Abner was killed in an explosion at an apothecary. He was examining a strange package at the time. I have a fragment here." He dug through his pack and produced the section of wood for Usnik.

Usnik contemplated the fragment for a moment, then returned it. "Yes, this is a shipping address. I believe these attacks were deliberate explosions triggered when a specific target was nearby. None but a trained Mystic could do that."

Maghrurio couldn't argue with his logic.

"There are at most twelve Mystics, one for each of the gods. Varka has been around for a long while, but he doesn't strike me as the scheming type. The Hidden One has been a Mystic almost as long as Varka." He paused, "Of course, The Hidden One survived an attack already but has chosen to withhold details. Other Mystics there were, once, as many as ten, but over the years, they vanished from the Gathering. Three were replaced. I don't know how Obolan's predecessor died, nor Miya's. Buhlo is almost as new as you, and I am certain her master was killed."

"Is it possible any of the missing Mystics are still alive but unable or unwilling to join the Gathering?"

Usnik shook his head sadly. "I have been unable to contact any of the missing ones. And, of course, there are the two I never saw."

"Ah, yes. You've seen at most ten of the twelve, which leaves two unaccounted for."

"Exactly. So, we have the three newest Mystics…"

"Four, counting me."

"Right, four newest Mystics plus The Hidden One, Varka, and myself. That makes seven, which leaves five unknown Mystics. If we suspect none of the current Gathering, then one of the five is the renegade we seek. On the other hand, we could have ten suspects, not counting you and Buhlo, who are newer than the murders. If we eliminate me as well, that still leaves nine."

"Eight, since The Hidden One has already been attacked."

"Right, eight potential suspects, of which as many as five may not exist. We should focus on the three we know--Varka, Obolan, and Miya--and see whether we can rule them out as possibilities."

Maghrurio agreed, but his words were drowned out by the rumbling of his stomach. "Perhaps we should reconvene this discussion over a meal. I trust you have a residence nearby, somewhere we can make my companion a bit more comfortable?"

Usnik smiled. "You are observant, Maghrurio. I'll grant you that. My home is not far from here."

Maghrurio picked up the unconscious Jaysel while Usnik summoned fire and transformed his walking stick into a flaming staff as a ward against the gûr-i. Raising the stick to light the way, they headed through the mist and back into the real world.

It took less than an hour to wend their way through the hills to their destination. The occasional gûr howled in the distance, but they saw no sign of pursuit. Still, they were glad to reach Usnik's abode as night settled about them.

Usnik lived in a small stone house surrounded by a stone palisade. It was basically a single room sparsely furnished with a small side pantry. Maghrurio wouldn't go so far as to call it sloppy, but clearly, Usnik didn't entertain much. Indeed, he took no notice of the disheveled interior when they entered, as he moved instead to light candles and open windows to the evening breeze.

Maghrurio laid Jaysel on a cot in the corner while Usnik moved toward a table near the door. Scrolls, quills, and various odds and ends lay strewn about its surface, which he carelessly swept aside. He arranged bowls, utensils, and a small bubbling pot retrieved from the fireplace around the table, and they sat down to dinner.

Maghrurio found the vegetable stew unusual yet enjoyable, with unfamiliar spices and herbs. He complimented his host, and they set some aside for Jaysel to eat when he awoke. Usnik cleaned the empty pot outside and, leaving it drying by the doorway, resumed his seat at the table.

"So, where were we?" Usnik asked.

"We were going to focus on Varka, Obolan, and Miya."

"Yes. Ghata will rise early tomorrow morning, and the Gathering will assemble with it. Talk to the three and see what you can learn. I will watch from afar as usual. Don't speak with me, or you'll raise suspicion."

Maghrurio agreed and rose to check on Jaysel once again. Satisfied with his friend's comfort, he left a brief slate message for Bacarus.

On his way out the door, Usnik said, "I just need to set my security first." Maghrurio couldn't see specifically what Usnik did, but the gap in the palisade they'd passed through was replaced by solid stone. Usnik saw the questioning look on Maghrurio's face and muttered something about asking him tomorrow.

Maghrurio hoped that meant he'd learn a spell or two from a practicing Mystic.

DEFIANT

Bacarus and Sheru rose in mid-morning. Their shifts didn't commence for several hours, so they visited the inn's dining area for tea and meat pies and discussed their next steps. Bacarus chalked a brief note to Maghrurio on the slate.

RAN INTO AZAK'S MEN AT THE TAVERN, OTHERWISE QUIET

She didn't expect a reply any time soon since he should be otherwise occupied with his rendezvous with the other Mystic.

Sheru gazed thoughtfully into her tea. "That Dhalil guy, he seemed nice. Almost too nice." Her eyes swept the room, but few people were about. She leaned in anyway, lowering her voice. "I think it's safe to assume Dhalil and his men report to Azak. It would be too much of a coincidence to have two groups of soldiers from Nahrein that aren't working together." At a nod from Bacarus, she continued. "With Azak chasing after Maghrurio in Mosel, Dhalil and those soldiers must be here to keep an eye on us."

"So if they already know who we are, can I stop coloring my hair and wearing dresses?"

Sheru smiled, "It would have faded in a few weeks, you know." She grew more pensive and blurted out, "Do you think Azak ordered Dhalil to pay those thugs to attack us?"

"That idiot I fired would have done it for free, but anything is possible. What I can't understand is why. What's Azak's play? What's he trying to accomplish?"

Sheru hid her face in her teacup. "Maybe he's just trying to scare us. Maybe if we got scared enough, we'd run to Maghrurio. And we'd lead Dhalil right to him."

Bacarus stared at Sheru. She'd been trying to puzzle this through all night, and that thought had never occurred to her. "You know what? You are amazingly paranoid. Or you're absolutely right. Perhaps both."

Sheru smirked, "Dhalil watches over us if we stay here and chases us if we leave. So what are we supposed to do? And, before you answer, please think twice about suggesting we leave. I like my job here. It's the first chance I've had to actually do what I love since this whole mess started."

Bacarus frowned. She sympathized with Sheru's feelings. She was enjoying her job at the Black Marsh more than she had expected. She fully understood how Sheru didn't want to be uprooted yet again. Still, Bacarus was committed to helping Maghrurio. Like it or not, she was prepared to leave Sheru behind if circumstances gave her no choice.

Hopefully, that scenario won't come up.

The thorny problem of what to do about Dhalil haunted their afternoon. They parted for their places of employment and went about their uneventful shifts. After hers ended, Sheru passed through the Black Marsh's doors and joined Bacarus at her usual perch. They noted Dhalil's entrance a short time later, and he gave them a nod of greeting. Bacarus suspected this would become a nightly ritual--Dhalil would follow Sheru to the bar and surreptitiously trail them home. It was annoying, but it planted a seed of a plan in her brain.

Sure enough, at closing time, Dhalil and his men were among the last patrons Bacarus ushered out of the tavern. They also discreetly trailed them home. Once safe inside, Bacarus checked the slate to find a message waiting:

AZAK PROBABLY IN OBER CITY

With a swipe of her sleeve, she erased the message and wrote one of her own.

WE NEED TO LOSE AZAK'S MEN HERE, WILL ADVISE

She put the slate away, and they retired for the night.

• • ● • •

Upon waking the next day, Bacarus checked the slate to find a new message.

BE CAREFUL!

Her response was likewise short and pointed.

ALWAYS

The duo descended to the dining area and enjoyed another of the local teas with a cheese and flatbread breakfast. Bacarus shared her thoughts about how they might evade Dhalil's men.

"I'm willing to bet they've fallen into a routine," she began. "They follow us to work, then follow you to the tavern, then follow us back home. If we were to disappear out the back way of the Black Marsh shortly after you showed up, they wouldn't notice for hours. We'd get a head start on them, and they'd have a challenge picking up our trail in the dark." Seeing the look on Sheru's face, she added, "I know you've gotten comfortable here in Cyrchan. I have, too. But we have to shake the soldiers, or else they'll get Maghrurio when he returns."

"I don't like the idea, but I see your point. But even if we do it, then what? Where would we go?"

Bacarus ticked off the options on her fingers. "We could hide out somewhere and wait for them to leave town. We could follow Maghrurio's lead and go to Mosel. I suppose we could always go back west the way we came." Her frown conveyed her opinion of that last option.

"Hmm… staying only works if they leave. Otherwise, we're no better off than we are now. If we choose Mosel, we'd have to go on foot. There are no boats to take during the night. Plus, we'd risk running into Azak there." She looked up hopefully. "You know, they wouldn't expect us to head back home again. West might not be such a bad idea."

Bacarus shook her head. "Forget west, that would lead us back to the Duke. We could go south overland to Lanh and catch a boat there. That would lead us straight to Mosel without having to mess with the marshes. We could be there within a week."

"It sounds like our best options are to go back to Decra or go forward to Lahn and on to Mosel. One takes us closer to home, the other closer to Maghrurio." Sheru frowned. "I really don't want to leave. But if we have to go, I guess Lahn is our best bet."

Bacarus nodded in agreement. "Let's watch our chaperones a bit longer and confirm their routine. Then we can decide when and how we'll ditch them."

• • ● • •

Another work shift, only this time Sheru spotted their escorts as they went to their workplaces. Once again, Sheru was followed to the tavern, and this time Bacarus decided to engage Dhalil in conversation.

He sat alone at the bar while his men chose tables nearby. "I guess you needed a break?" she asked and gestured toward his men.

Dhalil returned a lopsided grin. "They can get on your nerves after a while, but Sergeant Vasagh can keep an eye on them. Would you join me for a drink?"

"I don't drink on duty, but I will have some tea." She caught a waiter's eye and gestured, and he brought her tea and a refill for the lieutenant. "So, to what do we owe your special attention?"

Dhalil hesitated and then relaxed into a sad smile. "I suppose we both know the answer to that question. My Captain searches for your friend, so he ordered me to keep an eye on you. I'm glad we did because I'd hate to think what might have happened the other night had we not been at hand."

"So you had nothing to do with that attack?" she asked pointedly. "Your Captain had nothing to do with it?"

A pained expression crossed his face. "I'm hurt you'd even think that. Look, I joined the military to protect people and serve something bigger than myself. Sure, I am obligated to follow orders, but I would never acknowledge an order to harm civilians." He leaned toward her and confided, "Truth be told, I have reservations about this whole mission, but I intend to make sure it is executed with honor."

Bacarus saw honesty in his face and found it somewhat endearing. "Lieutenant, I'll accept your explanation. For now. So long as you don't interfere with our work, I see no reason for us not to at least be pleasant to one another." Rising, she took her cup in hand. "Speaking of work, I need to get back to it. I enjoyed finally speaking with you, Dhalil. I guess we'll see you around."

He rose also and nodded his head in salute. "It has been my pleasure, Bacarus."

She returned to her usual perch. Sheru, who watched the entire exchange, sipped quietly at her tea. After a few awkwardly silent minutes, Bacarus turned on her. "What?"

"Nothing. I just thought you two made a nice couple."

"Oh please, I was just trying to get information from him." She filled in Sheru with the details.

"If they watch us today, then what's to stop them from arresting us tomorrow?"

"On what grounds?"

"Does it really matter?"

Sheru's question hung heavily between them. They fell into an uncomfortable silence, speaking only sparingly as closing time approached. Again, Dhalil's men followed them home; Bacarus' observations still held true.

They went to bed and resolved to execute their plan the following night.

IN THE PALE MOONLIGHT

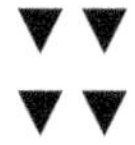

Maghrurio slept poorly, despite his physical exhaustion. He slipped from dream to dream, fraught with fear and danger. It was with relief that he finally saw the brightness that marked the call to the Gathering, and he answered eagerly.

Once again, he found himself within the Circle of Friends. Having just stood in the actual location the day before, he was impressed with the accuracy of the depiction but lamented what was missing--the smell of the greenery, the sound of beasts and birds in the trees. He looked around and realized he was alone. The pale Ghata rose above and, along with the stars, bathed the ancient place in a pale twilight.

Breathe. You have a job to do.

A bright, grayish light flashed within the Circle before him. It dimmed and coalesced, revealing his colleague Obolan. They exchanged nods, and Maghrurio approached him.

"Greetings, Obolan. How goes it?"

"Maghrurio. We must be early."

Again the grayish light flashed, and Miya joined them. She gave a stiff nod in greeting and fell to whispering with Obolan as they abruptly moved away, leaving Maghrurio alone. Old friends anxious to exchange news, or simple rudeness? It was probably a little of both.

Light flashed once more, and a new Mystic appeared. Flaming red shoulder-length hair framed a small, angular face. Short and thin, the young woman glanced apprehensively, her expression similar to Maghrurio's at his first Gathering. He guessed her to be a newly-made Mystic--one of the missing five. She flinched at the flash to her left and was surprised to see Buhlo appear alongside her. Maghrurio approached them in greeting.

"Maghrurio, it's nice to see you again."

"And you as well, Buhlo." He turned to the new arrival, asking," And you are..?"

The woman took a deep breath and replied, "My name is Kuyi, and I'm not sure what's going on. I was being chased by… well, I found a cave to hide in. I was exploring when I found an old skeleton." She raised her hand and continued, "It was wearing this ring."

Maghrurio smiled and gestured around him. "You are a Mystic, Kuyi. Welcome to a wider world."

Kuyi stared at them, awed and speechless, so Buhlo launched into the same welcome speech she had given Maghrurio. He scanned the clearing and their growing number. Varka and The Hidden One were still missing, as was Usnik. He turned back to the conversation in time to hear Kuyi's question.

"I have this Ring and no idea what to do with it. Is there a school or a book or something?"

Both Buhlo and Maghrurio smiled, and Buhlo answered. "The last holder of your Ring can be summoned in your dreams to teach you. Just concentrate on wanting it to happen, and it will."

"Who was the last holder of your Ring?" Kuyi asked Maghrurio.

Buhlo sputtered and raised her hand in interruption. "Sorry, that's a breach of Mystic etiquette. You can't ask about or communicate with a Mystic's predecessor. It's not polite." She chuckled, "I only know because I did it at my first meeting. Way to start on a positive note, right?"

They chuckled, and Kuyi apologized. "It was a dumb question, anyway. It's not like the answer would help anything," she conceded.

There was another flash of light, and Varka appeared nearby. Maghrurio excused himself and greeted the elder Mystic.

"No earth-shattering news for us this time, I trust?"

"No, Varka, nothing of that nature. Are you well?"

Varka gave him a curious look. "I must admit to feeling apprehensive of late. With Abner dead, it feels like I have a target painted on my back."

Maghrurio thought about his own problems with Duke Bileyo and Azak. "I can certainly empathize, having similar if less life-threatening issues facing me."

Varka seemed distracted. "Yes, the way of the Mystic, I'm afraid." He sighed. "It seems not so long ago that I was one of the juniors. Now, I'm the senior…" He seemed to catch himself and gestured toward the twins. "Obolan and Miya seem awfully chummy this morning."

"I tried socializing when they arrived, but they'd rather converse with each other."

"They both started before the deaths began, so they're probably experiencing the same uneasiness as I."

Maghrurio nodded absently, realizing that confirmed the two as potential Mystic assassins.

There was another flash, and Usnik appeared. As expected, he seated himself and didn't acknowledge anyone's presence.

"I see old grouchy has decided to join us."

"He actually spoke to me at the last Gathering."

"Really?" Varka hadn't noticed, apparently. "Consider yourself lucky, I suppose. He's never said a word to me."

Another flash signaled The Hidden One's arrival. Masked as before, he joined the twins in their whispered debate.

"I'll give it another few minutes before we begin in case we get any more new faces." Varka paused and added, "Or old ones."

The group chose seats while a few silent minutes passed, and finally, Varka stepped forward. "It appears we are all of the twelve that could make it tonight. As the longest-serving Mystic here, it falls to me to convene the Gathering." They went through the opening ceremony as before, each Mystic producing an elemental at the appropriate altar. Buhlo intercepted Kuyi, who looked lost and had no idea how to conjure anything. They walked the altars regardless and joined their fellows by the wind altar. Varka named each Mystic in turn and lastly turned to Kuyi, who repeated her earlier introduction.

Maghrurio raised his hand. "I have a question, if I may." At a nod from Varka, he continued. "I see eight of us here today, yet as I understand, in the beginning, there were twelve Mystics. What happened to the others?"

The Hidden One stepped forward, gesturing toward Kuyi. "Some apparently died before they could take apprentices." Glancing in Usnik's direction, he added, "Others may have decided to keep their own council and forgo the Gatherings. Who can say? But yes, I have also heard our number should be twelve."

Buhlo, ever the talkative one, stepped forward. "But that means we have three distinct groups of Mystics. The absent ones you just described, the newest ones like us," she included herself, Maghrurio, and Kuyi in her sweeping gesture, "and the rest of you older ones. You speak of the deaths of other Mystics. Are we being stalked?"

The Hidden One again spoke up. "It is true we have seen deaths. I have been attacked more than once, which is why I wear a mask to protect my identity. I have suspicions but nothing more solid than that."

Maghrurio caught Usnik's eye and stepped forward with an ever-so-slight nod. "I must confess I was not completely forthcoming at the last Gathering." He shared his suspicions about Abner's death and described the strange package with the Graavtish writing.

Concern evident on his face, Varka asked, "So you believe Abner was murdered?" At Maghrurio's answering nod, he continued. "The others who died were all senior Mystics, as is The Hidden One. It sounds like you're suggesting the seniors among us are in danger."

Maghrurio would have preferred to deny this but could not. "That would seem to be the case."

Several Mystics started speaking at once, and Maghrurio couldn't make out anything clearly in the tumult until Varka clapped his gesturing hands together with a boom like stones clashing.

"Friends! Order, please!" The cacophony died down, and he continued. "Obviously, we all need to be on our guard and watch for any mysterious boxes like the one Maghrurio described. Does anyone else have anything to add?" Silence. "Any other new business? No? Then I declare this Gathering closed. Go forth and serve." He paused and added, "Please be careful and keep your eyes open."

Maghrurio made his way over to Miya and Obolan, who both looked concerned and angry. "Have either of you encountered anything out of the ordinary?" he asked.

Obolan shook his head, but Miya snarled at him. "Go play detective with the other infants." She vanished in a burst of light, and Obolan followed soon after.

Maghrurio saw that Varka and The Hidden One were in a heated discussion, so he joined Buhlo and Kuyi.

"We don't actually accomplish much in these meetings," Buhlo was explaining to Kuyi. "Mostly, it's just a chance to highlight anything important we encounter and to make sure we're each still alive."

"Are we really in danger?" asked Kuyi, her attempted casual demeanor betrayed by the all-to-familiar anxiety in her voice.

"I don't think we are," soothed Maghrurio. "If senior Mystics are in danger, I suspect we're too poorly trained to be a threat to anyone. I wouldn't worry."

"It wouldn't hurt for us to work hard at getting better, though." Buhlo was uncharacteristically somber. "A threat to any Mystic is a threat to us all." Brightening, she turned to Kuyi. "Oh yeah, let me tell you how to get out of here…"

Maghrurio saw The Hidden One flash away, so he approached Varka, whose face was etched with lines of deep concern. "Can I do anything to help?"

Varka eyed him, his scowl firmly placed. "As I said before, we need to keep an eye out. For myself, I will likely curtail my activities until we can figure out this mess. Do you know how to contact another Mystic directly?"

Maghrurio thought of how Usnik had called him days ago. "I'm aware of the possibility but not of how it might be done."

"Just concentrate on the one you're trying to contact. Like most Mystic spells, the oftener you do it, the easier it becomes. Contact me if you learn anything important, and I will do likewise." Varka took his leave and vanished.

Maghrurio scanned the Circle. Only Buhlo and Kuyi remained; Usnik had apparently left unseen. With a farewell to his fellow 'infants,' he vanished as well.

EQUILIBRIUM

Upon waking the following morning, Maghrurio checked on Jaysel's sleeping form. The bandages were relatively clean, which was good news, so he dug out his slate to check on Bacarus.

NEED TO LOSE AZAK'S MEN HERE, WILL ADVISE

Maghrurio wondered what she meant. He assumed Azak had already reached Ober City by now. He must have left a small contingent behind to guard against him circling back, or else he saw through Bacarus and Sheru's disguises and wanted to keep them under surveillance. Either way, they might be in danger, so he chalked a concerned reply.

BE CAREFUL!

It wasn't terribly helpful, but at least they would know he cared and was thinking of them.

He packed up his bedroll and greeted a returning Usnik.

"I was just taking down my defenses," Graavt explained, stoking the fireplace embers to warm some breakfast porridge. Jaysel woke and, after a tentative trip to the outhouse, joined them at the table for a hot meal. He appeared sore and tired, and after they finished eating, Usnik gave him some valarkian root tea to aid in sleep and healing. Maghrurio helped him back to bed before joining Usnik on the front porch.

"About the Gathering, I'm afraid I didn't get much from Varka or the twins."

"I figured as much. Can't pump someone for information if they won't talk to you."

Maghrurio thought about mentioning Varka's request to keep in touch but decided against it for now. At least, until Varka actually followed up on it. So there wasn't anything left to discuss in regard to the Gathering, which left the issue of training.

They stood in silence for a few minutes, Maghrurio watching the soft rain in anxious anticipation. Usnik appeared uncomfortable, unsure of what to say. Finally, Usnik scuffed the floorboards and muttered, "You understand this goes against principles I've held to for decades…"

"I understand."

"Mystics never teach each other what they've discovered, not past the basics."

Maghrurio understood that this was so but didn't grasp the why. So, with a nod, he let the statement pass. "Would it help if I showed you something first?"

Usnik looked up with surprise and curiosity on his face. Maghrurio did his rain shield spell and stepped out into the morning rain. He walked around a bit, his arms and hands raised to ward off the falling drops. When he returned to the porch, he was completely dry apart from his shoes.

Usnik smiled. "That's a good one. Simple, but one I'd never thought to do."

Proudly, Maghrurio smiled. "I included a fire gesture to add some warmth to the interior."

Usnik nodded, thinking. "I've used something similar but in a different way. Let's see whether you can master it as well. Try it again using stone instead of fire, and hold it in front of you."

Maghrurio stepped back, giving them some distance, and conjured wind and stone directed forward. He'd tried this before with only wind and had conjured a breeze, but with the addition of stone Usnik's hair wasn't moving at all.

Usnik gestured, scooped, and pushed, causing a nearby pile of twigs and leaves to rise up and fly directly toward Maghrurio. All the leaves and many of the twigs rebounded inches from him and dropped to the ground. It was weak and would be next to useless in a physical confrontation. Still...

He had learned to conjure a shield!

"Not bad for a beginner. Let's see if you can do better." Usnik conjured a dozen small stones and tossed them, one by one, at the shield. Maghrurio tried concentrating harder but only managed to deflect a couple of stones. Usnik seemed able to hit his face and chest at will, injuring little but Maghrurio's pride. "You're shaping it as a flat surface in front of you. Try angling your hands and fingertips together, like you're diving into a lake."

Maghrurio fought his frustration and angled his hands. Again came leaves and twigs, only this time he could see his shield was shaped more like the prow of a ship, at a point in front and angling back to either side. This configuration deflected to either side all the leaves and twigs thrown at him. Usnik again conjured and tossed stones, and this time Maghrurio was encouraged to see fewer than half the stones strike his chest.

Maghrurio smiled broadly, and Usnik waved him over. "You saw how the shape of your shield improved its effectiveness?" At Maghrurio's nod, he continued.

"That's an example of how you need to view these spells. Sometimes you need the right combination of elemental gestures, other times, you need an extra hand or arm motion, or sometimes you just need to change how you approach the problem. Your most powerful weapon is creativity, which you appear to have. Use it wisely, and you should survive."

He gestured to one of the chairs arrayed on the porch, and they sat. "Probably your second most powerful weapon is confidence, which you sadly lack. Sit here and think about your successes and failures as a Mystic. Try to identify what you did well to achieve the successes and what you did wrong in your failures. Don't beat yourself up, though. The goal here is to appreciate your triumphs and improve on your missteps. I have a brief errand and will be back soon. We'll talk more then."

Usnik stepped into the house and returned with a sack. As an afterthought, he added, "If your friend gets restless, he's free to walk about this hill. It has… protections." He turned and strode from the house without a backward glance. Maghrurio closed his eyes, breathed deeply, and tried to achieve a calm state, but his mind raced wildly.

He made a shield!

But half the rocks penetrated it.

But half the rocks didn't!

He kept going back and forth, with every high slightly overbalanced by every low. Pretty soon, he was lamenting his poor performance and doing exactly what Usnik warned him to avoid--beating himself up.

He began again, taking deep breaths to find his calm space. He thought back to his first attempts at summoning magic. Had it only been three weeks ago? Abner had shown him the basics, the four elemental spells. The idea of casting spells had frightened him at first, but he found with a little practice, he actually could do it.

In the days that followed, he had practiced diligently, slowly gaining a measure of confidence in his ability to cast the spells successfully. Always, he realized, was the gnawing sense of doubt as to whether his minor magical abilities could amount to anything. Then there was that horrible moment on the road when, against his better judgment, he tried to use magic to defend himself and his friends, and his magic had let him down badly. He examined that moment with the dispassion of distance and saw the fear beneath it--fear that he couldn't measure up to the task. His fear had been justified, as it turned out.

Or had it? If he really thought about it, maybe the fear was getting in the way. He thought of the few times he'd done well. The "Follow the Knave" dealer? He was pretty angry then. Was that it? Was being angry the key to making this stuff work? Or was it that being angry overcame his fear, and fear was keeping this stuff from working? Then how to explain his success against the tentacled pi'pala? That was all fear, fear for his life and for his companions. And what about the rain shield? He wasn't afraid or angry then, he was tired of being cold and wet.

Maghrurio sighed. He had hoped for a simple answer. Be afraid or be angry--those he could believe. Hell, if anxiety was the answer, he'd be the best Mystic in the land. But it seemed this riddle was far more complex.

He stared at the falling drizzle and pondered the possibilities.

• • ● • •

When Jaysel eventually woke up, Maghrurio helped his friend get cleaned up and accompanied him to the porch, where they sat contemplating the dwindling rainfall and their next steps.

"I should be well enough to travel by tomorrow. What are your plans?"

Maghrurio shrugged his shoulders. "I'm not entirely certain. I guess that depends on Usnik."

"He's not very friendly, is he, even for a Graavt? Still, he was nice enough to help an injured stranger."

They sat silently for a while until Jaysel became too fidgety and could sit still no longer. Maghrurio passed along Usnik's recommendation about remaining on the hill, and Jaysel departed at a slow but determined walk through the chaotic gardens and into the thin tree line. Maghrurio breathed deeply and tried to resume his meditation.

His mind wandered back through the myriad of jobs he'd taken during his adult life. In just about every case, he began with some interest, but sooner or later, when things started to get difficult, he'd lose interest and move on. With a start, he realized he'd assumed the Mystic mantle three weeks ago with much the same attitude. He doubted his spellcasting ability, and his failures magnified that doubt. His doubt fed his fears, and his fears contributed to his failures, and so on.

So what was he to do now? Could he shake the fears that hobbled him? Was there some way to rally his confidence? He pondered the answers to those questions for a long while.

When Jaysel eventually returned, Maghrurio asked for his assistance. He conjured a pile of small stones, and Jaysel tossed them one by one at his shield. Maghrurio tried to focus his attention on his past successes, but his shield performed little better than it had previously. This made it harder to focus, which made the shield even less effective. Maghrurio's frustration grew until he swore in a fit of temper. A stone struck his shield at that moment, and rather than fall meekly to the ground, it rebounded over Jaysel's head and struck a tree in the distance. Both men halted, stunned by the sudden and profound boost in the shield's efficacy.

After a moment, Jaysel broke the silence. "I didn't realize 'shit' was such a magically powerful word." That broke the ice, and the two had a good laugh.

"I didn't realize you had a sense of humor, Jaysel."

"I am a Graavt of many surprises. Do you wish to continue?"

Maghrurio could see the fatigue on his friend's face. "Thank you, but I think I should meditate on what just happened. As for you, my friend, the day has been long, and you should rest." Jaysel returned to the house, and Maghrurio resumed his seat on the porch. He had one thought paramount in his mind.

What the hell just happened?

He'd been performing as usual, meaning not so well, and he'd become frustrated. Angry. And his anger manifested itself in a dramatic boost in power. Once again, he had to ask himself… was it the anger itself, or had the anger overpowered the fear? Maybe success meant keeping the fear and anger in balance?

While he contemplated the conundrum, another thought crept unbidden into his mind.

What if 'shit' really was a powerful magic word?

THE ADVERSARY

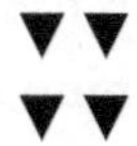

Eventually, Maghrurio grew tired of thinking and decided to explore Usnik's hill. The terrain was a rough mix of scrub and rocks, with occasional clusters of trees to break the monotony. He spied all manner of birds and small beasts going about their lives, as well as lesser predators--foxes and badgers and the like. Wild patches of sage, rosemary, and other aromatic herbs grew in abundance. It was a peaceful, idyllic environment, one he could grow accustomed to quite easily.

Scattered throughout the hill but more prevalent on the periphery was a strange stone statuary depicting mythical and actual predators. Snarling gûr-i, majestic dragons, grasping pi'pala, the statues were exquisite works. They seemed not so much sculpted as organically grown. They nonetheless evinced a watchfulness and warning.

Magical sentinels guarding Usnik's home, perhaps?

He wandered in no hurry and eventually returned to the house to find Jaysel relaxing on the porch. They chatted for a few minutes about things they'd seen on the hill.

"By the way, a courier dropped off a package while you were walking."

Maghrurio stiffened. "Where is it?"

"Inside, on the table."

Maghrurio looked in through the window and saw a box. It was wooden and unadorned and small enough that he could probably carry it if needed. Something about it, though, made him instantly suspicious.

"Have you gone near the box since he dropped it off?"

Jaysel looked at him oddly. "Yes, a couple of times. It's just a box, right?"

"I'm not entirely sure. An exploding box killed my former master…"

Maghrurio recalled the exact scenario. The box had been delivered to Sheru and had sat in her store for hours without incident. Then, when Abner showed up to examine it, the box exploded. Perhaps the box could somehow sense if a Mystic was nearby. Or perhaps whoever sent the box could tell? It was a working theory, and Jaysel's inconsequential approaches supported it. Of course, he could test the theory by approaching the box himself, but he wasn't quite so foolish.

He was still pondering what to do when Usnik returned. Maghrurio and Jaysel quickly filled him in on what happened and what they suspected.

"I expect you've divined the truth of it, Maghrurio. If either of us gets too close to the box, it will likely explode."

"We'll need to figure out how to remove it from your house without either of us getting near it."

Jaysel piped up. "I suppose I could just carry it out if it isn't a danger to me."

Usnik and Maghrurio stared at him and then glanced at each other. It was an appallingly simple solution if one didn't mind potentially putting Jaysel in harm's way, but Maghrurio would have none of it.

"Jaysel, you're brave to offer, but I couldn't in good conscience accept that. If we were wrong in our assessment, I'd never forgive myself for getting you injured or killed."

Usnik spoke hesitantly. "I may have an idea, but let's test it out here first." He moved a good distance from the porch, then beckoned Maghrurio to join him. "There's a spell I learned to lift things without touching them, but you have to be close. Watch what I do."

Usnik glanced at his feet to a rock the size of his head. He cast the wind spell with one hand and made a palm-up lifting motion with the other. The rock floated off the ground. He then turned his palm down, and it dropped again. "Give that a try."

Standing next to Usnik, Maghrurio copied the wind spell and palm-up motion and was able to duplicate his colleague's results. Usnik grabbed the rock and heaved it away from them.

"I know that weight is too far away for me to pick up. Why don't you try it?"

Maghrurio tried and was unsuccessful. He noted with grim amusement this was the first time it was acceptable that he had failed at a spell.

"Now, let's try to lift it together."

Usnik and Maghrurio executed their spells and gestures simultaneously. To their great relief, the rock rose and floated along.

Jaysel laughed aloud, "You've done it!"

"Good," said Usnik as they dropped the rock. "Now comes the hard part. Let's see if we can get the exploding box out of my house without killing ourselves."

The Mystics positioned themselves in sight of the open doorway, a dozen or so feet away from the box within. Once again, they cast their spells and made their gestures, and this time the mystery box floated above the table. At Jaysel's signal, they slowly backed away from the porch, guiding the floating box through the front door and easing it onto the open ground.

They maintained their distance as they discussed their next move.

"Obviously, it doesn't react to magic directly," opined Usnik.

Jaysel said, "So what do we do with it?"

"Usnik, what if we carried it to the Circle of Friends? You said no violence could happen there. Wouldn't it prevent the box from exploding? Or, at least, from killing us if it did explode?"

They agreed it was worth a try and so recast their spells and proceeded to carry the box ever-so-carefully to their destination. Jaysel led the procession, clearing the path of anything that might trip them up. The box floated along behind him, supported by the two Mystics a dozen feet behind it. What was normally a relatively short walk became a long and nerve-wracking trip. Each stubbed toe and slip threatened death for them all.

After what felt like forever, Maghrurio finally caught a glimpse of the Circle of Friends in the distance. His attention wavered for only a moment, and that was all it took. His shoe caught a half-buried rock, and he fell face-first onto the ground. Unable to support the box by himself, Usnik watched in horror as it slipped from his magical grasp and fell to the ground.

Everyone froze where they were, Maghrurio cursing his clumsiness. The box just sat there, intact and oblivious to the danger it represented.

"Um, sorry about that," an embarrassed Maghrurio muttered as he rose to his feet. He took a moment to compose himself, and at a nod from Usnik, they raised the box again and proceeded into the Circle.

Usnik spoke up first. "I believe we are safe here, but to be sure, let us both cast shields and approach the box. If we've been mistaken, hopefully, the shields will provide some protection."

Maghrurio thought about his own meager shield and doubted it would stop an explosion. Still, he was unwilling to embarrass himself in front of Usnik, so he nodded his agreement. The two cast their spells and slowly approached the box. One step, two steps, three… Pretty soon, they were standing right in front of it. Usnik caught Maghrurio's eye and winked.

"I think you were right about the Circle's protection. I'm going to drop my shield."

Maghrurio held his breath as Usnik's hands dropped to his sides and, with them, his shield. When nothing happened, Maghrurio dropped his shield as well.

They were safe for the present.

Carefully, they eased the lid from the box and examined its contents. To Maghrurio's untrained eye, it was filled with dirt and rocks. Usnik reached into the box, grabbed a fistful of the mixture, and rubbed it between his fingers.

"This is no ordinary pile of dirt. What it is exactly, I should be able to determine." He wiped his hands together and added, "As an adept of Elayrue, I can read the type and nature of a quantity of stone or minerals. You might have some similar ability with the wind." He placed his hand upon the soil in the box, closed his eyes, and concentrated.

"There is sulfur from the Blade Mountains… saltpeter from the Black Marshes… and charcoal from the Zod Hills. This mixture is highly combustible and lacks only fire to make it explode." His face grew grimmer and more focused as he concentrated harder on his magic. "I'm also sensing a magical flame. Come, Maghrurio, can you feel it too?"

Maghrurio extended his arm and grasped a handful of the mineral mixture. He closed his eyes and concentrated and felt a sensation similar to when he first located the slates at the library. He focused on that feeling. In his mind, he could see a flame, a flame struggling to feed and grow. "Yes, I can feel it!"

Usnik stood, his face more bleak than usual. "The flame knows a Mystic stands nearby and is trying to magically ignite the mixture. The magic inherent in the Circle is the only thing preventing it from doing so."

The trio stared at the box, wondering what to do next. Maghrurio spoke up first.

"Our mystery Assassin must not be able to see us; otherwise, he wouldn't try to ignite the box here. So how can he know we're close enough to the box?"

"It can't be just any person next to the box because nothing happened when I was near it."

"True enough," said Usnik. "It must react to something unique to Mystics." He glanced down at his Mystic Ring. "Perhaps our assassin enclosed a flame in some sort of magical shield and placed it in the box. When a Mystic Ring gets close enough, the shield is breached, and the flame ignites the contents."

Maghrurio couldn't think of a more plausible explanation. "The Circle prevents the box from exploding. So what happens if we float it just outside of the Circle?"

Usnik smiled. "I see your point. It should explode out there, while in here, we'll remain protected."

The pair repeated their earlier spells and floated the box ahead of them toward the Circle's boundary. As soon as it crossed into unenchanted space, the box exploded spectacularly, scattering debris everywhere except within the Circle itself.

Maghrurio cleared his throat. "Our Assassin must know the box exploded and must assume its target has been, uh, eliminated." He glanced at Usnik and continued. "That means you are free to act, so long as you don't reveal yourself. Perhaps you should forgo the next Gathering, and I'll see if anyone implicates themselves."

Usnik stood outside the Circle, staring at the debris. His face contorted in anger. "I always suspected it, but this is proof. A Mystic just tried to kill me. A Mystic! And that Mystic likely killed Abner and who knows how many others!" He stormed away from the others in his fury.

Maghrurio shared his sense of outrage. He'd not been a Mystic for long, but the idea that one of his brethren would assassinate another was shocking and outrageous. In fact, the Mystic must be someone in this area of Sonoduhl, given the source of the ingredients--Decra was in the foothills of the Blade Mountains, and he had passed through the Black Marsh on his journey here to the Zod Hills. Whoever the Mystic Assassin was, he or she may have been someone he had already met.

Which meant he might already know Abner's killer. The idea was almost too much to bear.

The disturbed trio left the Circle in silence. Their return trip passed far more quickly than the tense walk with the box, and soon they were back at Usnik's table eating dinner. The evening passed with little conversation as each was consumed by their own dark thoughts.

• • ● • •

It was quite late when Maghrurio woke to darkness. He'd drifted off to sleep while sitting on the porch, and the others had gone to bed without disturbing him. Still uneasy and suddenly wide awake, he dug out his slate to see what was happening with Bacarus and found a single word:

EMERGENCY!

A TIME TO STAND

Bacarus awoke at the usual hour, checking the slate before getting ready for her day. Sheru joined her for brunch, and they took their daily stroll around the area. It was all part of their regular routine, and she saw no point in tipping off the soldiers by deviating from it.

Afternoon stretched toward evening, and they had a quick supper at the inn. Nothing had happened during the day to change their plans. That evening, they agreed, would be their last under Dhalil's thumb.

Sheru departed first, her belongings concealed in the carryall she often bore. While committed to their plan, she was sad about leaving her job. She liked her work, genuinely enjoying the opportunity to help the sick and injured. She liked being free and uninjured even more, though, so she accepted the need for their swift departure.

Bacarus left shortly after, her meager possessions concealed in Sheru's carryall. She spied her escort easily and made her way to the tavern. Her shift passed without incident, as she had become quite adept at keeping things running smoothly.

I'm going to miss this.

Shortly before Sheru's typical arrival time, Bacarus beckoned the owner to his office to resign her position. He was quite sorry to see her go and tried unsuccessfully to entice her to stay. She collected her pay, extracted his promise to hold any announcement until the following day, and returned to her perch before Sheru's appearance shortly thereafter. Seated together, they awaited their plan's next step.

Dhalil arrived soon enough. Waving to Bacarus, he sat with his men at a table near the entrance. Bacarus left her perch and approached, and Dhalil was so focused on her that he didn't notice Sheru taking her carryall into the back room.

"Good evening, Lieutenant. Taking a break from babysitting us?"

Dhalil smiled broadly. "Bacarus, my dear, you exaggerate. Watching you is no chore for me--indeed, I would volunteer for it."

"Careful," she responded. "You'll teach your men bad manners." Smiling, she retraced her steps to her perch. Silently she counted to five hundred and then stood, calling out to the bartender that she'd be checking the storeroom.

Bacarus slipped out the back way, pleased that their ruse was working so far. She glanced around for Sheru, who should have been waiting right by the door. The streets, at this late hour, were empty.

"Sheru?"

Nearby she spotted a dark mass and rushed over. It was Sheru's carryall; she'd know it anywhere. Panic began to take hold, driving her to and fro in the streets and back alleys behind the tavern. No other trace or hint of Sheru's whereabouts turned up.

Frustrated and frightened for her friend, Bacarus rushed back into the tavern to find Dhalil hurrying toward her.

"Dhalil,' she shouted, "Sheru is gone!"

"My corporal just told me he saw Sergeant Vasagh carrying your friend in the direction of the docks."

Her eyes narrowed, and her fists bunched. "You!"

He threw up his hands in supplication. "No, you misunderstand. Vasagh is not following my orders. He's gone rogue, and I don't know why, but I will track him down and get her back."

"No, Dhalil. *We* will track him down and get her back."

Dhalil noted the determination in her voice and bearing and nodded. With a gesture to his men, the group left the tavern at a run.

The hunt was on.

They hurried to the eastern docks, intent on finding the sergeant before he could catch a boat out of town. By the time they arrived, though, there was no sign of him. While the soldiers searched the area, Bacarus approached a stout, grizzled older man who was tending his boat.

"Sir, we're looking for a soldier who kidnapped a woman. We believe he intended to catch a boat here. Have you seen them?"

The man stopped what he was doing and eyed her. "I did see a man show up a short while ago, dressed like them." He pointed toward Dhalil's men searching the docks. "He had a woman with him, trussed up like a sheep for the butcher. Loaded her into a small boat and took off downstream, not twenty minutes ago."

Bacarus called out to Dhalil, who rushed over. The pair quickly negotiated passage, and pausing only to load the soldiers, they departed the dock in pursuit of the fugitive Sergeant Vasagh.

"We're just floating with the current. If speed is what you want, grab a pole and start pushing," the old man called out. With a nod from Dhalil, the men jumped to the poles, and the boat picked up some speed. Still, it was going to be a long trek. Bacarus sat in a corner, tired, frustrated, and anxious, hoping Sheru was safe. She'd never really made friends easily, but with Maghrurio and Sheru gone, she never felt so alone.

Maghrurio! She fumbled through her carryall and produced the slate. Wiping it clean, she wrote one word:

EMERGENCY!

The sampler remained in Sheru's bag, so once she reached him, he should be able to magic himself to her. Clearly, she was more of an offensive threat than Maghrurio was, but somehow she'd feel more confident about getting Sheru back if he was around.

She passed agonizing minutes waiting for a response to her plea. Finally, her message vanished and was replaced with the following:

ARE YOU IN DANGER?

She quickly responded:

SHERU KIDNAPPED ON THE RIVER IN PURSUIT

There was no response, and Bacarus wondered why.

$$\bullet \ \bullet \ \bullet \ \bullet \ \bullet$$

Maghrurio was shocked. He always figured that, of the three of them, he was in the most danger. That friendly Sheru had been kidnapped angered him more than he thought possible. He rushed into the house and hastily collected his things. Jaysel awoke and immediately sensed something was wrong. Maghrurio gave him the abbreviated version of events.

"Jaysel, please accept my thanks for your assistance so far. But I am returning to my friends by magical means and cannot take you with me."

"I can find my own way back home. I'll let Usnik know what happened."

Maghrurio flashed his friend a sad smile and whispered to himself, "Dangers strike, troubles come; seek the solace of hearth and home."

• • ● • •

Bacarus let out an involuntary yelp as Maghrurio appeared beside her in a flash of light.

"Tell me what happened," he asked urgently.

She quickly related everything they'd seen and heard and speculated. Maghrurio closed his eyes for a moment and tried to find a calm center.

"It seems, for whatever reason, Vasagh decided to take Sheru. If he's gone this way, it's probable he's headed for Mosel. Where is your Lieutenant?"

Dhalil stood nearby, exhorting his men to push faster. She called him over.

"I assume we need no introduction," Maghrurio smirked at the lieutenant.

"Obviously, my orders are to place you under arrest, but circumstances have me questioning them. Let us call a truce for the time being. Please know that Vasagh has acted without orders. Indeed, his eastward heading is proof of his treachery. I'm treating this as a kidnapping by a rogue soldier, and when we catch him, I will see him punished severely."

"You'll excuse me if I don't give a cow's fart what happens to your soldier, Dhalil. I'm interested only in Sheru's return. If she is harmed in any way, your soldier will answer to me."

The two men stared at each other in a silent battle of authority, and Dhalil blinked first. "We will focus on retrieving your friend. What happens afterward will take care of itself."

Bacarus asked, "Why would Vasagh be heading east when the Duke is to the west?"

Dhalil frowned. "I suspect Vasagh may no longer be working for the Duke. Someone must have bought him along the way, but I will teach him the error of his ways."

Maghrurio turned away, really seeing his surroundings for the first time. He was, once more, aboard the *Saucy Susan* led by the enigmatic Captain Gav. Still wide awake from shock and fear, he offered to take the wheel for a while to let Gav catch a quick nap.

· · ● · ·

The night passed in a haze, a series of catnaps interspersed with intense inspection of the waterway ahead. Unfortunately, the boat they pursued stubbornly continued to stay well ahead of them and out of sight. As the light of a new day broke over them, the *Saucy Susan* slipped into the malodorous Black Marsh.

Gav was awake and at the wheel and ordered torches be set around the boat. Recalling the slithering horror that attacked them last time, Maghrurio hurried around instructing the soldiers where to place the torches, lighting them himself with a gesture. With their defenses in place, Maghrurio felt exhaustion fall upon him like a mountain. He found an uncluttered corner and fell into a dreamless sleep.

Time passed slowly, and still, they did not catch any sight or sound of their quarry. They had little food with them due to the hasty departure, but thankfully Gav's fishing lines provided ample sustenance to keep them going. Otherwise, the journey was as frustratingly unending as their first had been, with not even a sign of a pi'pala to break the tedium.

For Maghrurio and Bacarus, the waiting was cruel. They had no idea what had happened, or what was happening, to their friend. Every passing minute was torture, and the growing anxiety kept them from the comfort of sleep. Bacarus spent her time silently berating herself for allowing Sheru to be captured while Maghrurio tried reviewing his spell options in case things turned violent.

As the day passed into night again, Gav placed torches around the boat. They didn't want a visit from the pi'pala and had no time to waste on it anyway. Maghrurio tried catnapping when he was able, and

Bacarus spoke quietly with Dhalil when she gave up trying to rest. The night passed slowly but uneventfully, and by morning they'd left the confines of the marsh and entered Gladwater Lake.

A MAN ALONE

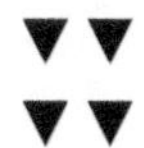

As before, Gav provided fish for breakfast which Maghrurio and Bacarus volunteered to prepare. The chase dragged on, but the morning fog over the lake obscured any sign of their quarry.

As the day progressed and visibility improved, they could see traffic on the lake but couldn't say for certain which boat held Sheru. Maghrurio guessed they were no more than an hour or two behind, but there was little they could do on the lake to close the gap. He thought of all Vasagh could do with his head start--head east to Ober City, strike out west into the forest, or go to ground in Mosel. It would be a challenge picking up the trail again.

With little to do but wait, Maghrurio decided the time was ripe for another visit with Abner. They'd not talked for over a week, and much had transpired in the interim. He returned to his corner, curled up, and sought his former master in his dreams.

• • ● • •

"Abner?"

Once more, the transition was abrupt, from dark nothingness to a lush forest. The air was resplendent with wholesome, woodsy scents, and Maghrurio felt like the weight of the world was lifted from his shoulders. He had no idea where he was, but the woods exuded a tranquility he'd never experienced before, and he longed to be transported here in the waking world.

"Good day, Maghrurio."

He smiled at the approaching Abner, who was robed in blue as usual. Looking around, he asked, "Where are we?"

"Ah, this is the Elf Wood to the north of Nahrein. It's quite a mysterious place, populated by mysterious people. No one I know has ever journeyed here and returned, and no one knows what manner of people live here. I'm fairly certain, though, that a Mystic does live within these woods. Long ago, I had a dream conversation with a Mystic named Chawi. Among other things, she warned me of trouble within the Mystic group. Our discussion turned contentious, though, and I'm afraid I didn't do much to follow up on her suspicions. Naturally, I wish I had."

This reminder brought Maghrurio back to himself, and he put aside his enchanting surroundings for the matter at hand. He glanced at Abner and prepared for serious discussion but was brought up short. Abner's appearance seemed off, with hints of the surrounding underbrush showing through his body.

"Is something wrong, Abner? I can almost see through you!"

"Yes, I'm afraid my time is running out. I expect this may be our last training opportunity."

"But… there is so much I don't know yet!"

"Maghrurio, you already know everything I can teach. What remains is for you to internalize that teaching and build upon it. It's going to mean some trial and error for you, I'm afraid. You'll just have to work it out on your own."

Maghrurio fought the impulse to complain. If his time with Abner was drawing to a close, he needed to make good use of every remaining minute. He related all the developments since their last meeting--his discoveries in the libraries, the artifacts, Usnik's revelations, his own spell discoveries, and Sheru's abduction. "Now we're pursuing the kidnapper, and I'm afraid it will come to some kind of armed conflict. I'm not prepared for that."

"As I've told you before, you already know the basics. You need to work on your confidence, and that means building on all the successes you've already achieved. It means letting go of the fear, of not letting it infect your thinking." He smiled at Maghrurio. "You can do this."

Maghrurio was tired, confused, and frightened for Sheru and just couldn't pull together his flagging spirits.

"Here is my last lesson for you. Even if something works, don't be afraid to fix it. Take the rain shield you thought up. It worked perfectly well, right? And when you moved it in front of you, it still functioned as a shield. But when you changed the position of your hands, it changed the shape of the magic, as well as changed how you thought of what you were doing, which made it more effective. That's what I'm talking about, Maghrurio. Don't be afraid to think differently."

Abner's image had definitely begun to waver, and Maghrurio feared their time was almost over. He thought of last-minute advice he could request or hints of next steps and realized it was too late for that. He'd been prepared as well as he had any right to expect. From here on out, things were entirely up to him. He straightened up and met Abner's transparent eyes. "Thank you, Abner, for your teaching and encouragement. I will do my best to justify the faith you have placed in me."

Abner began to dissipate like the morning fog, but his smile lingered long after his image faded. "You have always justified my faith in you. Justify your faith in yourself as well."

Maghrurio wept alone amidst the trees.

• • ● • •

He awoke, sad at the loss of his mentor but strangely refreshed. It was mid-afternoon on the lake, and there was much traffic coming and going around them. They still had no idea on which of the boats Sheru might be found, but at their present pace, they would reach Mosel well after Vasagh did. Maghrurio knew they needed to go faster. What was it Abner had said? "Even if something works, don't be afraid to fix it."

Bacarus was standing beside him. "What did you say?"

He glanced at her, lost in thought. "Something Abner told me. He was encouraging me to think differently." He looked around the boat, but nothing made itself obvious. It had a central mast but, at present, no sail. There was little following wind in any case. The wheelhouse was tiny, and the deck stretching from the wide stern to the tapering bow was strewn with an assortment of tools and ropes. What could he do?

He walked back to the stern. It was a good eight feet across and fairly high, presenting a large flat surface from the back. Could that be enough for a tailwind to push? Would he be able to produce one?

We need to catch up to Vasagh. Sheru needs us.

He raised his arms dramatically, made the wind gesture with one hand and the water gesture with the other, and pushed with both toward the front of the ship. Instantly a tailwind picked up along with a stronger current, and both propelled the *Saucy Susan* forward. Maghrurio nearly lost his balance but kept the spell working, and a cheer went up as the boat easily doubled its speed. If he could keep this up long enough, they just might have a chance at reaching Sheru before it was too late.

• • ● • •

Maghrurio dropped his arms in exhaustion. Apparently, prolonged use of the magic took a physical toll, but he had propelled them all the way to the docks of Mosel. It had been a long final leg, but they put into port far sooner than they might have otherwise. Dhalil rallied his men and sent them swarming across the town in search of the traitorous sergeant. Dhalil and Bacarus helped the recovering Maghrurio off the boat. They called farewell to Gav, who offered Maghrurio a job as his first mate if he ever became tired of 'fooling around with your Mystic stuff.'

Mosel was a fairly spread-out town, and it would take hours to scour it all. Maghrurio paused to consider while his companions kept their eyes peeled for suspicious signs. Vasagh came to Mosel for one of two reasons--to meet someone or to move on somewhere else. If he was meeting someone, then that could be anywhere, but if he was moving on, he'd need to be here at the docks.

"We need to cover the docks. He may be here to arrange passage."

The three split up and started asking the various boat owners about their availability, hoping to uncover a hint of Vasagh's plans. Time flew by without success, and Maghrurio's concern for Sheru's welfare grew.

Until his luck changed.

"Friend Maghrurio!"

Maghrurio turned in surprise to find his friend approaching him. "Vodi! I'm glad to see you. I'm looking for my friend Sheru, she's been kidnapped by a soldier, and we tracked him here."

"But my friend, I just saw soldiers carrying an unconscious woman not two minutes ago on the other side of the dock." Maghrurio described Sheru's appearance. "Yes, that sounds like the woman I saw. Come, I will show you!" He sped off, weaving through the sailors and merchants. Maghrurio followed, hot on his tail. Along the way, he spied Bacarus and called to her. "We think we've found her!" He raced along without waiting and soon caught up to Vodi.

"In there."

Vodi pointed at a dingy warehouse around the corner, one of the dozens arrayed between the docks and the town proper. While Maghrurio paused to consider his options, Bacarus and Dhalil caught up with them. He brought them up to speed, and Dhalil left to collect his men.

Maghrurio grunted impatiently, "We can't wait for Dhalil. We need to get in there now."

Bacarus shook her head. "We don't even know what we're up against."

"What do you think, Vodi?" Maghrurio turned to his friend, who was no longer standing with them. He looked around and saw Vodi walking boldly up to the warehouse entrance. Without stopping, he opened the door and entered.

Nothing happened for a minute, and then Vodi was unceremoniously shoved through the rapidly closing door. "I'm sorry to bother you," he shouted, "I'll keep looking." He wandered across the street, taking time to inspect each of the warehouses he passed until he turned the corner where they were hiding.

"I told them I was looking for my business partner down here. They threw me out pretty quickly, but not before I got a good look. Your friend is tied up in an office near the back, and a dozen or so men are in there with swords and crossbows. They appeared to be waiting for someone."

Now that it came down to it, Maghrurio was scared. His mastery of Mystic magic was by no means extensive. *What do I know that could take out a dozen men?* He looked helplessly at Bacarus and felt the fear inside him transform into something hard. Sheru needed him, and he'd just have to figure it out.

"Is there another way inside?"

Vodi thought for a moment and said, "I think I saw side entrances, and there are windows in the back."

They hastily assembled a plan, not knowing how much longer Sheru had.

"This had better work, or we're all dead," Maghrurio muttered.

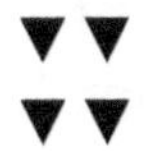

KNOCK KNOCK.

Vasagh and his mercenaries turned to the front door. "Is that idiot back again? Go see who it is," he shouted, pointing at one of his men.

The mercenary opened the front door and peered through. "Nobody here," he called out.

KNOCK KNOCK

Vasagh spun around. That came from one of the side doors. "You three, stay on the front door. You four check the side door. Everyone else, stay alert."

The four men checked the side door and reported it empty as well. Annoyed, Vasagh wondered what was happening.

Was it kids playing tricks or something more?

He was impatient waiting for his employer and just wanted to turn over the prisoner and get paid. He looked at the five men that stood around him and barked, "Go check the other entrances!"

Vasagh remained in the middle of the warehouse floor while his men fanned out to cover the entrances. Something was going on, and he again cursed his employer for making him wait. He was planning to use his payday to start a new life here in Mosel, and he wanted it to start right away. To hell with soldiering for the Duke.

A resounding crash yanked back his attention. A side door had just burst open.

What the hell was going on here?

• • ● • •

Maghrurio waited as long as he could and then made his move. With a stone gesture, he punched the door with a booming crash, sending it flying into the interior and knocking down two of the approaching soldiers. Two more quick stone punches, and his way was clear. As the remaining soldiers raised their crossbows, he conjured the angled shield Usnik had taught him and hoped it would be sufficient.

Eight bolts flew at him. A couple flew wide from poor aim. Several were deflected around him, but one breached the shield and pierced his right shoulder. He gritted his teeth and ignored the pain. He had seconds before they reloaded, and he made them count. He conjured wind and fire and sent forth a jet of flame. It wasn't much, but it was enough to give pause to his attackers and sufficient to set nearby timbers ablaze. He then recast his shield as the crossbows were brought to bear again.

• • ● • •

Bacarus made her way around the back of the warehouse, searching for a window midway along the wall that should open into the office where Sheru was being held. She found a likely candidate and pulled herself up to take a look. The room beyond the window was empty. Another window proved more productive, revealing her friend bound and gagged on a chair. She worked the window lock but was unable to get it open, so she waited for the noise signifying Maghrurio's attack.

The echoing boom of the side door imploding was her signal. She used a large rock she'd found to break the glass and released the lock to throw open the window. Pulling herself up, she tumbled into the room to Sheru's muted surprise. She yanked out Sheru's gag and drew her pocketknife.

"Thank the gods you found me, Bacarus! What's going on out there?"

Bacarus busied herself, cutting the bonds securing Sheru. "Maghrurio is buying us time to escape." There was definitely some kind of action happening in the warehouse, but she couldn't spare a moment. Finally, the last rope fell, and Sheru was free. "Let's get you out of here," she said as she hustled Sheru through the window to safety.

• • ● • •

The second crossbow volley was more accurate than the first and more painful. There were now two glancing thigh wounds to go with his shoulder wound. He had run low on options and had fallen back to swinging his flaming sword until Vasagh called for a halt to the fighting. A smiling Vasagh strode up from behind his men, dragging a reluctant Vodi and holding a dagger to his throat.

The damned fool wouldn't stay back after his diversion. He just had to try to help. Frustrated, Maghrurio dropped both magic and dagger. At Vasagh's command, he allowed himself to be taken.

Vasagh was inordinately pleased with himself. He expected to be paid for turning over the woman, but how much more would his employer pay for the Mystic? "You have caused me great inconvenience, Mystic." He waved his dagger in Maghrurio's face. "I will enjoy taking it out of your hide."

Maghrurio lacked the courage to present a brave face, but anger served well enough. He could only hope that Bacarus had freed Sheru.

There was a sudden crash, and the front and side doors burst open at the same time. Dhalil and his soldiers stormed into the warehouse and caught the mercenaries by surprise. Paid soldiers though they were, they proved no match for professionals with wrath on their side. Within minutes, Vasagh and his men were subdued and stripped of weapons.

Dhalil himself examined Maghrurio's wounds and treated him. Vodi smiled in relief, congratulating Dhalil on a well-timed rescue. Bacarus and Sheru joined them, Sheru expressing her gratitude as she examined all the wounded. Maghrurio just smiled. They had done it-- Sheru was safe!

Dhalil questioned the prisoners but grew increasingly frustrated with the results. The mercenaries were quite willing to talk but didn't seem to know anything. Vasagh, on the other hand, certainly knew something but wouldn't talk. He just sat there smiling at them, although Maghrurio couldn't comprehend why that was. He decided to question Sheru, who was remarkably whole and unharmed by her ordeal.

"I ducked out the back way from the tavern," she told Bacarus and Maghrurio. "I moved across the street and hid in an alley as we planned. Only instead of Bacarus, I met him." She gestured toward Vasagh, kneeling and smiling before an increasingly angry Dhalil. "He had a rag soaked in sovewort that he forced over my face, and I passed out. The next thing I knew, I was tied up in a boat with him and some goons. They were rowing like crazy, looking to put miles between them and their pursuers."

"That was us," Bacarus smiled.

"Yeah, well, you certainly got them nervous. They mostly ignored me and focused on getting downstream as fast as they could. Something attacked the boat in the marsh, and he lost one of his men, so Vasagh had to do some rowing himself. When they finally hit town, they tossed me in the back of a wagon and brought me here." She paused for a breath and continued. "I don't need to tell you how scared I was, but I knew you'd come for me." She smiled at her friends. "Both of you."

As Bacarus and Sheru shared their relief at being reunited, Maghrurio couldn't help but feel he was missing something. Turning to Sheru, he asked, "Did they mention anything about why they brought you to Mosel?"

"Sure," she replied. "They were supposed to turn me over to their employer." Her eyes widened in horror. "You don't think he's coming here, do you?"

"Dhalil," called out Maghrurio. "We're about to have company." He quickly explained what Sheru had told them, and instantly Dhalil had the captives locked in a side room, and his men deployed throughout the warehouse, covering the entrances. He sent Vodi and four of his men to accompany the women to the nearest inn for safety, but he insisted on remaining. He wanted to know who it was that had suborned his trusted sergeant.

Maghrurio also was interested to know who had ordered his friend kidnapped, but he was nervous about who it might be. Vasagh's dozen mercenaries suggested the newcomer would not be bringing his own muscle. That suggested he didn't feel he needed it, which in turn strongly suggested the newcomer was not Azak at all, but a Mystic.

Was this the Mystic Assassin we've been searching for?

Maghrurio reviewed his combat spell options, both offensive and defensive. If he survived this encounter, he promised himself he would think up some additions to his repertoire. His choices had hardly sufficed against Vasagh's crew and would certainly be insufficient in a fight with another Mystic. While he waited, he took out his slate and chalked a message to Bacarus.

NOTHING YET. ARE YOU SAFE?

They waited a while longer, with Maghrurio incessantly rechecking his slate. Finally, he saw his writing vanish to be replaced by a new message:

SAFE AT THE INN. BE CAREFUL!

He echoed her own response back to her:

ALWAYS

Satisfied, Maghrurio stowed the slate in a deep pocket.

Maghrurio had advised that their target was probably a Mystic, but Dhalil stuck with standard military practice. He arrayed his men strategically about the warehouse, covering all the entrances. His one concession to Maghrurio's urging was to keep his men farther back so the new Mystic couldn't use the doors against them as he had. At least, that was the hope.

As it turned out, they weren't far enough.

ONCE MORE INTO THE BREACH

When he came, he came with lightning and thunder. With a deafening crash, the Mystic Assassin punched down the side entrance. The door flew half the length of the warehouse, taking out several soldiers in its wake. Mahrurio, positioned near the front entrance, could see him across the room--a tall, menacing figure in a flowing black cloak with a hood obscuring his face. A volley of crossbow bolts flew in his direction, but with a gesture, he seemed to grab them mid-flight and, spinning about, sent them hurtling back from whence they'd come.

He'd arrived literally seconds before, and already half their number was down.

Maghrurio knew he was outclassed, but he had to at least try. He hurled a cold lantern at the intruder and, with his own gesture, fired the pool of oil it spilled. The resulting inferno momentarily engulfed the Assassin in flames, but an instant later, a flood of water snuffed them out. Turning, the Assassin impaled him with his gaze like a raptor on the hunt.

And he, Maghrurio, was the frightened rabbit.

Frightened, perhaps, but determined. He conjured wind and gestured at the bolts scattered about, seizing and hurling them at his enemy. The Assassin, in turn, cast a windstorm that blew the bolts back at Maghrurio. He hastily threw up his shield and barely missed being struck by several of them. The Assassin, meanwhile, turned his windstorm on the remaining soldiers, tossing them like leaves in a stiff wind and driving them headlong into sturdy walls.

With the soldiers dealt with, the Assassin proceeded across the warehouse to Maghrurio, who despaired of leaving this confrontation alive. "You've caused me some trouble, pretend Mystic," the Assassin snarled. Advancing, he conjured large stones and pushed them. Flying at high speed in a cluster, they overwhelmed Maghrurio's shield and knocked him to the ground.

Staggering to his feet, Maghrurio drew his dagger and conjured a flaming sword. "I plan on causing much more."

With a casual gesture, the approaching Mystic conjured a torrent of water that knocked Maghrurio off his feet again and doused his sword. "Pathetic. Didn't you get any training?" Not waiting for an answer, he hurled a fireball that barely missed a rolling Maghrurio but left him scorched and smoking. Casually, the Assassin conjured large stones he used to pin Maghrurio's arms to the ground. "Not much in combat, are you?"

Maghrurio could only lay there, bruised and defeated.

"Your investigation alerted the other Mystics to my plan. I don't imagine you've discovered anything of value, but I need to make sure." Another gesture and Maghrurio's leg was struck by molten rock. He screamed in pain until it was doused with water. "Just a taste... So, what shall we talk about?"

Maghrurio refused to answer, staring daggers at his enemy.

"Still need convincing?" He gestured, and Maghrurio was buried under a pile of stone. His head free but unable to move, he could only stare impotently as the Assassin crouched beside him.

"You and I will become great friends," he whispered.

"And I suppose you promise to release me when I've told you everything?" Maghrurio asked with all the sarcasm he had left.

"Oh no," he replied. "That's when I'll kill you."

The Assassin turned and loosed fireballs around him, setting the warehouse on fire. Maghrurio shouted, "Damn you, there are men in here. You'll kill them!"

"Yes, I expect I will," came the Assassin's casual reply.

As the inferno swiftly grew around them, the Assassin returned to Maghrurio's side. "Now tell me, what have you discovered?"

"I have nothing to say, you murdering bastard!"

"Tsk tsk, name calling is unworthy of a Mystic. Tell me, did Abner suffer? Please tell me the arrogant buffoon suffered?"

If looks could kill, Maghrurio would have been alone in his torment.

"No matter. I've taken care of him and Usnik, and Varka will be next. Oh, and I'll dispose of The Hidden One soon enough," he laughed. "The rest of the Mystics are too stupid to matter. They'll fall in line quickly enough."

The smoke and heat were becoming uncomfortable, so with a gesture, the Assassin threw a shield about them. "That should make things easier. I ask again, what have you discovered in your investigation?"

"I have nothing to tell you."

"That's unfortunate." Another stone gesture and the weight on Maghrurio's body increased. Breathing grew difficult, even with the smoke and heat shielded.

"Has your memory improved?"

Beneath Maghrurio's look of defiance was a genuine fear for his life. He wasn't sure how much longer he could survive before being crushed to death.

"Ah well," the Assassin muttered, rising. "I guess we'll be doing this the hard way."

Maghrurio didn't see the gestures, but a shower of stone encased his head, and, with a lurch, he realized he was being carried magically-- probably like he and Usnik had carried the booby-trapped box not long ago. Hoping against hope that the magic would still respond, he gasped the words he needed to free himself.

"Dangers strike, troubles come; seek the solace of hearth and home."

• • ● • •

Bacarus, Sheru, and Vodi were arguing with the soldiers and each other. Sheru wanted to return to the warehouse to help Maghrurio. Bacarus also wanted to return but insisted that Sheru stay behind. For his part, Vodi insisted that both women remain safely behind and that he should go in their place.

Following Dhalil's orders, the soldiers were trying to prevent any of them from leaving the safety of the inn.

The arguments grew louder and hotter until they were startled by a flash of light and the sudden appearance of a battered Maghrurio, who held out a hand briefly and then collapsed before them.

Sheru screamed, Bacarus gasped, and Vodi loudly thanked the gods. Recovering her wits, Sheru quickly took charge of her patient. She barked out orders, and the soldiers lifted the injured Mystic and carried him to bed.

Sheru stripped the burned, bloody clothing from his barely conscious form with care. "The leg is badly burned. There are four, no, five puncture wounds and severe bruising and contusions."

Maghrurio struggled to speak. "Warehouse... on fire. Dhalil and his men… still there."

The soldiers looked at each other and dashed from the room to rescue their comrades.

Sheru focused on the patient but addressed her friends. "I'm going to need supplies. Water, bandages, a basic healing kit, and something for burns." She described the specific items she required as she worked on Maghrurio's injuries.

Bacarus and Vodi ran from the room to find what was needed. In the meantime, she tore strips from her own shirt to staunch the bleeding as best as she could. Thankfully Maghrurio had already passed out because she knew her restorative actions would be painful.

Bacarus returned first with water and bandages, which Sheru put to immediate use. "These burns are severe," she said, the worry plain in her voice and on her face. "He's been through hell." She worked on cleaning and bandaging the worst of his wounds, and when Vodi returned with the healing supplies, she bent to work on the burns. "I don't know if I can heal these properly, not with this stuff. The best I can do is stabilize him and keep them clean."

Bacarus was angry. True, she had helped rescue Sheru and hurried her to safety, but she should have been there to help Maghrurio in his fight. Fighting was her thing; no matter that magic had been involved, she was convinced she could have helped.

Vodi felt ashamed. He had willingly accompanied the women to safety, knowing he was no match for a Mystic. Still, he had abandoned his friend in his hour of need. Somehow, he had to make it up to him.

Maghrurio cried out once and lapsed back into unconsciousness as Sheru completed her treatment. "I've done all I can," she sighed. "We can only wait to see what happens next."

Part 3

SHATTERED MIRROR

Pain… pain and confusion. Danger, worry, anxiety, a cacophony of sensations. But through the darkness, pain most of all.

After a long time (hours? days?), a sense of calmness appeared. Not all at once, just a kernel, a tiny speck. But it took hold and grew. Slowly. And it drove the pain before it until the pain was no longer the dominant sensation in his universe.

There was still pain, but it became increasingly manageable as his surroundings coalesced into familiar shapes. Tall, ancient trees. Low granite wall. Benches all about. He was back in the Circle of Friends.

Only this time, he was alone. No more would Abner appear to council and train, to succor and advise. He was completely on his own, and whatever advances he would make would be due to his own efforts and insight. He felt the loss like a missing tooth. Or, more accurately, like a missing limb.

But he was not here to reminisce. He had work to do.

Concentrating, he called for Usnik. He waited, quietly absorbing the calm this ancient site exuded. Eventually, Usnik appeared within the Circle, anxiety plain on his face.

"Maghrurio, are you well?"

"I'm alive, at least. And I am sorry for leaving in such a rush." He shared his tale of Sheru's rescue and his subsequent battle with the Assassin.

"So my suspicions about him being a Mystic were correct, it seems."

"Yes, and there is more. While he gloated over me, he let slip details of his plans. 'I've taken care of Usnik, and Varka will be next.

Oh, and I'll dispose of The Hidden One soon enough. The rest of the Mystics are too stupid to matter. They'll fall in line quickly enough.'"

Usnik ruminated on these words. "Well, that tells us some things. First, he thinks I'm dead. That means he knows the box he sent me exploded. Second, it confirms Varka is in danger."

"I'll need to warn him, as he asked me to do."

Usnik nodded. "It also confirms that The Hidden One is the next target. You'll need to warn him, too."

"Will do. On a separate note, what happened with Jaysel? I didn't have time to accompany him back through the hills."

"Jaysel is fine, I had some business in Ober City, so we traveled together. He's an interesting man. I'm glad to have met him."

"If you see him again, please extend my apologies."

"I'll tell him. Now go warn The Hidden One and Varka, and get well. Quickly!"

And just like that, Maghrurio was alone again.

He focused on the next Mystic. This time, Varka appeared in the Circle. Maghrurio described the Assassin and the means he used to kill. He mentioned he was with Usnik when the box arrived, but he left out the part where Usnik wasn't impacted by the explosion. He then told Varka about his battle with the Assassin and the clues he'd let slip.

"So you were right. You are being targeted."

Varka was disturbed but thankful. "Now that I have an idea of what to look for, I may yet survive this threat. Take care of yourself, Maghrurio, until the next Gathering."

Alone again.

His last attempted contact was unsuccessful. He repeatedly tried to summon The Hidden One but received no response. He even tried contacting Miya and Obolan, hoping they'd pass along the message, but neither bothered to respond either. He'd have to try again another time, assuming the Assassin hadn't reached him first.

He closed his eyes, drinking in the peace and tranquility around him. He had work to do, though, and friends to reconnect with. With a last wistful look, he released the Circle and returned to consciousness.

• • ● • •

On the morning of the third day since the battle, Maghrurio awoke, battered and sore but on the mend. His friends were relieved to see him return to the ranks of the living. They had mostly remained sequestered in their rooms and were short of news, but they filled in Maghrurio on what they had determined.

Dhalil and most of his men had been killed in the warehouse fire, and the room where they'd locked Vasagh and his mercenaries was filled with bodies burned beyond recognition. The remaining seven soldiers, led by a mere corporal, abandoned their mission and returned to Nahrein. Maghrurio felt bad for Dhalil and his men, but he wasn't sad to see their fellows leave. One less thing to worry about.

As for the Assassin, nobody had any idea of who or where he was.

Vodi was pleased with Maghrurio's recovery, and Sheru was relieved that her treatment had proven efficacious. Bacarus, on the other hand, was distracted and reticent. She was friendly with Dhalil and was shaken by his untimely end. Maghrurio tried to be supportive, but she likewise needed time to heal.

As for him, he had a few things to think about. He ticked them off mentally.

One, he needed to figure out the identity and location of the Assassin. Unless he was missing something obvious, the list of impending targets narrowed down the suspects substantially by eliminating all the senior Mystics. The Assassin was a tall man-- eliminating Obolan and Miya--which meant he must be an unknown Mystic who somehow knew the rest of the Mystics and how to find them. At least some of them that is. And he possessed recent knowledge; otherwise, Maghrurio wouldn't have been a target. Would his identity yield a clue to his whereabouts? Or would his location help identify who he was?

Two, he needed some better spells for the next time. He had no doubts he and the Assassin would meet again. He had to admit that, despite his preparations, he had been woefully outclassed at the warehouse. The only reason he wasn't dead was that the Assassin wanted to interrogate him first, and he had no intention of finding out what that might entail. He needed some better offensive and defensive spells to counter the Assassin's obvious superiority. Which led to…

Three, he needed to improve his execution of spells. Those spells he cast were easily swept away or overwhelmed because the Assassin's powers were so much stronger than his own. As Abner had told him, he needed to find some way of instilling confidence in himself--a challenge, considering he'd just had his ass kicked so profoundly.

Four, he needed to decide what their next step should be. While he was currently convalescing and could do little but think, action would be required before long.

There were supposed to be twelve Mystics total, which meant if the Assassin wasn't someone he knew, then he was one of the four anonymous Mystics. Actually, maybe three--Abner had mentioned a woman named Chawi, but who knew if she was still around. He sighed; with so many unknowns, there was just no way to think through this one.

New spells… how the hell am I supposed to come up with those? Confidence… yeah, I think I have some in my other pants. As for what to do next? Umm…

Maghrurio drifted off to sleep as his mind churned through problems without solutions.

• • ● • •

Dhalil was dead, Bacarus thought with a frown. Why did this affect her so? They weren't linked romantically, but he seemed to be an honorable man and true to his word, and she liked that in him. He was genuinely offended by Vasagh's betrayal and was beginning to question the Duke's orders. It seemed tragic and pointless for his life to have been snuffed so casually, so wastefully.

She caught herself, realizing she'd wallowed in melancholy for too long. She needed to do something, and she knew exactly what.

"Vodi, we can't stay cooped up in these rooms forever. We don't know where the Assassin is, and we need to find out. Are you game to try?"

His absence from the warehouse battle still smarting, Vodi found his courage and agreed to accompany her. They waited until after the dinner hour and slipped from the inn, making for one of the more popular taverns in town.

Some things remain constant, Vodi thought. Regardless of the culture or terrain, people everywhere tended to build taverns the same way. Large doors to let in the willing (and toss out the over-willing.) Small tables for more intimacy, a large bar for collective revelry. And noise, always too much noise, but that, too, was something to hide in. Yes, taverns were the same all over, and this one was no different.

They had decided on their line of attack on the way over and set to work immediately. They made for opposite ends of the bar, mixing with the patrons and buying a round or two to make friends. With some chit-chat and a few pointed questions, their goal was to identify the tavern ringleader. Every bar had one--one of the most connected people in town, one who could be counted on to "know a guy" who could provide whatever item or service one might need.

In Mosel, that person was Red.

He was bald with dark brown skin and wore mostly black and gray clothes. His eyes were always moving, and when they landed on you, it seemed he burrowed into your soul. Bacarus wasn't sure why he was called Red and didn't bother to ask. She and Vodi approached him, having been directed that way from their separate inquiries. Vodi took the lead, asking permission to sit. Red nodded, and they seated themselves.

"So, how can I help you?"

Vodi leaned forward. "There is a rumor of a Mystic in town, tall, cloaked, and hooded in black. We're wondering if you know where he might be found."

Red's face grew grim. "Mystics are bad news, bad for business. They follow their own rules and don't understand the concept of free enterprise. They're like Sonoduhl's conscience or something. Why would you want to get mixed up in that?"

Vodi kept his smile plastered to his face. He didn't want to give away anything for free. "We understand he's looking for someone. We might be able to help him."

Red stared at Vodi, trying to fathom his secrets. He sighed and waved a hand in dismissal. "I've already tried sending an intermediary and got nowhere. I doubt you'll fare any better."

Vodi and Bacarus rose and thanked the man. An associate walked them back to the bar to ensure their departure from Red's table.

"What a wasted effort," said Bacarus.

"Perhaps not," replied Vodi, nodding behind her. Bacarus turned to find Red's associate approach. Slipping a scrap of paper into Vodi's hand, he whispered, "The Mystic has left town, but if anything should come of this, Red would like you to remember his assistance." He nodded at Bacarus and returned to his table.

Vodi glanced down to see an address scrawled on the paper. "This is down near the docks, if I'm not mistaken."

Bacarus replied, "We should get back to the inn and tell the others."

With a quick glance around, the pair departed the tavern and returned to the inn.

CHRYSALIS

The following morning, Vodi discussed their discovery with Sheru and Maghrurio.

"The address is on the dockside of town. It's near the old library, I think."

Maghrurio's ears perked up. "Library?"

"Yes, it's a rather poor one, I'm afraid. They have many books and scrolls, but it's more of a storage house than a library. Very little organization and it is almost impossible to find anything. It's a real mess in there."

"I would like to have a look just the same. I might find something to aid in my research."

Sheru checked on his bandages. "Are you sure you're feeling up to walking around outside?"

Maghrurio smiled at Sheru. "Why don't we all go down there together? We can check the address to see what it is, then we can swing by the library on the way back. I won't stay long, and I may need some assistance moving boxes and books."

They quickly agreed to this plan, provided that Maghrurio disguised himself in a hooded robe, and settled down to breakfast.

Before long, they were out in the daylight and making their way through the town. Maghrurio felt warm and awkward in his robe but endured in silence, knowing the trouble they could get into otherwise. The town was spread out, so it took a while to reach the docks. Vodi asked passersby for directions, and they soon found the address belonged to a small inn.

"I've stayed here before," Vodi recalled. "It caters to merchants, so it's small but well-appointed. Let me see if my friend is on duty this morning."

Vodi left the group hiding in a curio shop across the street while he strode openly into the inn. They picked over the various oddities for sale while awaiting his return. After what seemed an eternity, Sheru spied Vodi hurrying across the street toward them.

"My friend was indeed on duty today. He said the robed stranger checked out yesterday morning and has not been seen in town since."

Maghrurio breathed a sigh of relief. "Does that mean I can lose this ridiculous costume?" To the chuckles of his friends, he removed the robe and hood and reveled in the warm spring air. "Great, now let's go check out the library!"

* * * * *

Vodi was right, Maghrurio thought. The building looked nothing like the splendid libraries he'd visited before. The exterior door opened into a single large room piled high with dusty books and boxes of scrolls. It was as if someone collected the works together and stored them here, then forgot to build the grand library they'd envisioned. It was rather disappointing.

With his friends remaining just inside the front entrance, Maghrurio closed his eyes and cast his senses throughout the room. There were no clear aisles, so searching would be a challenge, but he hoped that whatever secrets the room kept would yield themselves to him. There was something… He moved slowly, stepping gingerly over decrepit boxes as he tried to find his target.

There! He could sense something coming from the large pile on the left. He signaled to his friends and indicated the pile he wanted, and they helped him dig through it. The task took a while since the books were stacked in a rather haphazard fashion and tended to collapse readily, confusing his senses. Eventually, they cleared enough of the right books to uncover his prize.

It was a battered journal, much like the others he'd found. There was no furniture or anything else to sit upon, and he wasn't sure how much there was to read. Checking once more that there were no further signals in the room, he pocketed the journal and gestured for the others to depart.

• • ● • •

Now that they no longer needed to hide from the Assassin, the group decided on a late lunch at a small neighborhood eatery. It felt good to be out of their rooms, and the lovely spring weather was a balm on their battered nerves.

There was much talking and laughter over the meal, with each sharing a bit of their background. Bacarus told some amusing anecdotes about her early days with Abner, and Sheru told some stories about her days at university. Vodi regaled the group with a tale of yet another merchant mission in which each turn went terribly wrong until the end, when somehow everything turned out perfectly. Maghrurio obliged with stories of some of his earlier jobs and the horrible ways they went awry. It was a relaxing afternoon all around.

Vodi noted the change in the wind, heralding rain to come, and gathered his friends to return to their rooms. As they walked, an odd feeling overcame Maghrurio as if he was being watched. He glanced around and saw nobody familiar and no one looking at him, so he dismissed it as an overactive imagination. He was eager for their temporary home, as he had a book to examine.

Before long, they had reached the inn and bustled up to their rooms. Tired but curious, Maghrurio excused himself to his bed and dug out the journal. He flipped through the pages until he found what he was looking for.

"...Offensive and defensive spells are much more difficult to devise and more challenging to master. The trick, I am told, is to broaden your imagination to what is possible. I once witnessed a Mystic take on a killer dragon, a fire-breather with jaws of iron that had terrorized the city for some time. Now a swordsman would use his own strengths and seek to pierce the dragon's hide, but dragonskin is tough enough to endure all but magically sharpened blades. Such a swordsman might flail uselessly until the dragon, weary of the distraction, bit him in twain."

"The Mystic, however, was a master of intellect as well as magic. He knew to keep his distance from the jaws, but if he wished to prevail, he needed to negate the danger of the flaming breath. The Mystic first drew forth the fire from the dragon,

leaving him vulnerable. Then he summoned a blast of icy wind that froze the dragon's heart and killed him on the spot."

"Again, the trick is to broaden your imagination. Don't just think about doing things. Consider undoing them as well. Examine your foe's strengths and weaknesses, and devise offenses and defenses that take advantage of them."

"Drew forth the fire?" wondered Maghrurio aloud. "What does that mean?"

He considered the possibilities. You can make fire with the proper finger gesture. You can throw fire by conjuring it while using a throwing motion. Could drawing it out be as simple as using a pulling motion? He glanced over at the small fireplace in his room, then thought again and grabbed a candle instead.

Don't want to burn the place down if I mess up.

He placed the candle on his table and lit it. He looked around his room for the least flammable place and chose the bay window. He stood in front of the window and faced the candle, trepidation and excitement warring within him.

Will this work?

With a deep breath, he moved his fingers in the fire gesture while his other hand pulled. Instantly, the flame leaped from the candle and flew at him. With a strangled yell, he dodged the incoming flame, which bounced off the window and snuffed out before hitting the floor. He had done it!

He quickly grabbed the book and looked up the other tactic, eager to try that as well. It mentioned an icy wind… How might that work? He already knew how to create wind… Maybe he should try the same fire-pulling maneuver.

He crossed the room and turned, thinking ice on the window was probably safest. He conjured fire with one hand and wind with the other while pulling back his fire hand and pushing his wind hand. He could see a rime of frost form on the window, which was cold to the touch. Close, but not quite there. If he had to guess, he had just conjured a frigid wind.

What was colder than cold air? Ice.

Maghrurio tried again, only this time conjuring fire with one hand and water with the other while simultaneously pulling the fire and pushed the water. He was rewarded with a blast of ice that struck the window and loudly broke it asunder.

His friends burst into the room, thinking he was under attack and were surprised to find him laughing. He pushed them back into the sitting room and placed a glass of water on their dining table. Rolling up his sleeves, he repeated his cold wind spell. To their utter surprise, a blast of cold wind struck the glass and froze the water within.

His friends were suitably impressed, and he accepted their congratulations with pride. True, these spells were more complex and required his concentration to get the movements in the correct order. Still, their success meant his goal of devising better offensive and defensive spells was well underway.

TRIBUNAL

Maghrurio felt much stronger after breakfast and decided to return the book to the library. Sheru agreed that the walk would be beneficial but advised him not to overtax himself. He left the inn with promises of restraint on his part.

It certainly felt good to be out in the sun again. The late spring weather was a bit warm, hinting at the summer to come, and the cloudless sky suggested it would remain comfortable for the remainder of the day. He wandered somewhat aimlessly, taking in the sights, sounds, and smells of the town, and eventually found himself back at the library.

As yesterday, the building appeared abandoned. He slipped inside, relocated the box from whence the book had come, and left it behind for the next reader to find. For lack of anything better to do, he took another circuit of the interior but sensed no further sensations of Mystic lore. Mildly disappointed but unsurprised, he exited the library.

As he wandered in the general direction of home, he once again experienced the feeling of being watched. Like yesterday, he glanced around periodically but could see nothing to suggest a reason for the feeling. Regardless, he couldn't seem to shake it.

It had been several hours since his late breakfast, and he was feeling famished, so he stopped by a streetside cafe. He took a table in front of the establishment and ordered a fish dish and some tea. The streets were crowded, so he relaxed with his tea and observed the passing pedestrians.

There were a great many laborers and sailors this close to the docks, but that was hardly all. He spied merchants, farmers, children, travelers, even a Graavt or two, as well as a handful of people he couldn't quite categorize. He was pondering those when his lunch appeared, so he gave himself over to focus on his meal.

He had finished his lunch and was relaxing with his tea when a man approached. He was short and thin, with a beaten-down look to him as if life had been difficult. Maghrurio realized he'd seen this man several times on his walks.

"You've been following me the past couple of days, haven't you?"

The man was tentative as he nodded, "Please, sir, I apologize for disturbing your meal. Are you the new Mystic?" He seemed frightened of what he might hear in response.

"I am a Mystic, yes."

"Thank you, sir. My master has instructed me to request your assistance in resolving a dispute at the market, sir. Will you come?"

Abner had frequently been called upon to mediate disputes between merchants, townsfolk, farmers, and government officials. It was one of the primary duties of a Mystic to help maintain justice and order in the land without preference for class or country. He looked down at his mostly finished tea. *If I'm to be a Mystic, I may as well act like one.* He placed his napkin upon his dish and gestured for the man to lead the way.

• • ● • •

The man led him to a large building in the market area. They passed through the double entrance doors and entered a large interior meeting room filled with merchants and assorted others. At his entrance, his escort ran ahead to whisper words to a man at the front of the room who called the assembly to order.

"Assembled merchants, please pay heed! The Mystic has graced us with his presence. We will convene a judgment shortly."

He approached with an unctuous smile on his face.

"Greetings, Mystic. I am Hagah, the chairman of this merchant association."

"I am Maghrurio. How can I be of service?"

"We have two prominent and influential merchants in a dispute we are unable to resolve. We ask that you hear their arguments and pass judgment. Will you help us?"

Maghrurio kept his face calm, but his anxiety blossomed anew. He had no experience doing this sort of thing. Sure, he had watched Abner do it several times, but watching was not the same as doing. He longed to decline the request, but he knew he could not. This sort of thing came with being a Mystic, and a Mystic was what he was supposed to be. He nodded his assent.

Hagah beamed with pleasure and possibly relief. His nervous whisper belied the confident smile he wore, "I was just elected to lead this group and was afraid this conflict would splinter it apart."

Great, inexperience leading inexperience. His luck was appalling sometimes.

He stood at the forefront of the room and hoped for the best as Hagah assembled the merchants. Maghrurio was looking around for a chair when he heard a familiar voice boom.

"What's he doing here?"

Maghrurio's head whipped around. *Surely it wasn't…* But yes, it was. Burindar. He'd spent an few unhappy months working for the mediocre blacksmith many years ago. He was an obstinate, argumentative, unpleasant man who'd fired Maghrurio before he had a chance to quit. Apparently, he'd traded his anvil for a merchant's life, and he was not pleased to see Maghrurio now.

Nor was his apparent opponent, another employment fiasco that had ended badly. This one was a merchant at the time and blamed Maghrurio and his fellows for his own foolish choices.

Both men began yelling at Hagah, adding their objections to his choice of arbiter and continuing to denigrate each other. Others rejoined the arguments, and the scene devolved into an auditory riot of insults and threats. Maghrurio's initial fear quickly gave way to anger. Both men acted childishly and allowed their previously unfair treatment of him to color their present judgment.

What he needed was a dramatic gesture, one that would quiet the arguments and demonstrate his qualifications. He seized a plain wooden chair and slammed it dead center in the front of the room. Flipping his left hand in the stone gesture, he passed his right hand over the chair's contours, covering it in an even layer of stone. He worked slowly and carefully, applying a considerable thickness of stone until he'd transformed the simple wooden chair into a large stone throne. He even added some small embellishments so it wouldn't look too plain. Satisfied with his craftsmanship, he sat upon it and looked out over the room.

The silent and respectful room.

Looking out, he eyed a quietly smiling Vodi in the back. Maghrurio winked at him and spoke in a quiet voice. "Shall we begin?"

He listened to the arguments from both sides, and it quickly became apparent that both men had been caught trying to cheat each other. He asked them a few questions for clarification, and their responses were surprisingly deferential. He called for a short recess and beckoned to Hagah.

"Why did you need me for this?" he whispered. "These men obviously cheated each other. Anyone can see this."

"You don't understand. Both men have many friends in this association. My own position is tenuous, and any hint of favor to one side or the other would lead to chaos."

Maghrurio considered the pleading look on the man's face. Hagah was as uncomfortable and unprepared for his new position as Maghrurio. He felt a stab of pity and empathy. "Let me see what I can do."

Maghrurio loudly called the assembly back to order. "Hear now, my judgment," he began. "It is no crime to seek advantage in business dealings, but you both have done far worse. You shamed yourselves with your abysmal conduct, and you brought dishonor to your peers by dragging this dispute before the group. My judgment is this. Your original trade agreement is void, and you are free to dispose of your trade goods in whatever manner you are able. Further, you will publicly apologize to the group and each other for your conduct. Lastly, in recompense for the damage you've done to this association, you will each contribute half the value of the original deal to a local charity to be selected by your peers."

There was some grumbling, both from the pair and their friends. Maghrurio continued, "I will appoint a trustee to ensure your compliance with this judgment. Satisfy these conditions, and you may remain a member of this association. Refuse, and you will be cast out."

He briefly considered the idea of making an overt threat but decided not to push his luck. Standing, he declared, "So have I judged."

The grumbling continued as Maghrurio left his stone chair, but the worst was over. His initial anxiety had been misplaced, and he felt validated by the approaching Hagah's broad smile.

"Thank you so much, Maghrurio. Your judgment has saved this association."

Maghrurio accepted his thanks and excused himself to find Vodi. His friend was also smiling.

"You handled yourself well, friend Maghrurio."

"Thank you, my friend. Tell me, will the pair comply?"

"If they cannot bribe your trustee, then yes, they will comply."

"Then I'd better find an honorable trustee. Will you accept the charge?"

For a moment, Vodi was speechless. "What… I am but a minor merchant here, Maghrurio. This is an honor beyond my status!"

"Then it is time to raise your status. Will you accept?"

Vodi nodded, and they shared the news with Hagah.

HEART OF STONE

Over the next several days, Maghrurio returned to the meeting hall and judged disputes, moving beyond merchants to include the full range of Mosel's citizenry. Regardless of who was involved, he strove to be fair and impartial and, when necessary, to exact penalties appropriate to the offense.

Vodi reported that both merchants had repeatedly attempted to bribe their way out of their judgment but eventually made their contributions to a local orphanage and healing center--the very establishment, in fact, where Sheru and Bacarus had found employment. His time was otherwise spent at the merchant association, conducting his business as usual.

For Maghrurio, his days were increasingly split between judging disputes and enjoying his minor celebrity status. Vendors of all sorts were anxious to be seen with him, and he was never at a loss for offers of free goods and services. He tried not to take undue advantage and spread his patronage throughout the town's many establishments.

And any time he was too pleased with himself, Gazto's laughter echoed across his memory to cut him back down to size.

One afternoon, the day before the Vadha Gathering, he chose a restaurant for lunch that featured a trout dish he quite enjoyed. His morning judgments had included artisans, laborers, and a town official who might have been the most stubborn, hide-bound individual he had ever met. Maghrurio wasn't physically tired, but he felt mentally drained and in desperate need of respite. When the waiter appeared with his lunch, he cleared his mind and focused on his savory meal.

He didn't notice the approaching footsteps until a shadow fell across his plate. He looked up and saw a familiar face staring down at him.

"We meet again."

Azak pulled out a chair and seated himself opposite Maghrurio at the table, a smug expression plastered across his face. Maghrurio regarded the captain evenly, his own face betraying nothing of his inner turmoil.

Am I angry, worried, or afraid? Yes. I'd better play it cool.

"You've led me on quite a merry chase," Azak continued. "Cost me several of my men as well, in the swamps and at the warehouse."

"Tell me, was Vasagh following your orders, or had he gone rogue?"

Azak's face darkened. "I thought I knew the bastard. If he's not dead already, he'll wish he was."

Maghrurio picked up his fork and continued to eat his lunch. "Please excuse me; it's been a long and hungry morning. Feel free to order something for yourself."

Azak smiled again. "Thank you, but I've already eaten. Although," he paused, signaling for the waiter, "I could use something to drink."

Maghrurio couldn't figure out Azak's game. Was he stalling for some reason or just being discreet? He decided to continue his own approach of playing it cool. "Try the herbal tea. It's quite refreshing."

Azak followed his suggestion and sat silently watching Maghrurio eat until the waiter returned with his tea.

"That is good," he admitted. "So."

"So."

Azak drew a deep breath. "Let's not mince words, Maghrurio. You know why I'm here. Duke Bileyo doesn't appreciate your refusal of his hospitality and wants another chance to persuade you to his way of thinking."

Maghrurio put down his fork and wiped his mouth with a napkin. Inwardly he was outraged at the baldness of Azak's falsity, but he continued to exude calm. "Your Duke tried to rob me and threw me in a cell when that didn't work. I'd hardly call it hospitality."

"Nonetheless, the Duke asked me to accompany you back to his home to continue your conversation." He gestured vaguely at the town around them. "You may have bamboozled this lot with your tricks, but we both know where you'll end up."

Maghrurio paused and looked down at his half-finished lunch. His appetite was quite ruined, and the tea had gone lukewarm. Clearly, Azak had no respect for him, and he needed to change that. Inspiration struck, and he conjured fire while making a pulling gesture over his cup. The liquid within was instantly dotted with chunks of ice. He lifted the cup and took a sip. "This is quite good, cold. Would you like to try some?"

Azak's surprise was poorly hidden, but he tried to appear nonchalant. "It's fine as it is, thank you."

Maghrurio calmly put down his cup. "And I assume your soldiers surround us, waiting to take me with them?"

"When I rise from this table, I'm afraid."

"Ah... Well, I must admit you are entirely correct."

At Azak's raised eyebrow, he continued. "It *has* been a merry chase. You know, I was also attacked in the swamp. In fact, I've been attacked several times now by various people and things and have somehow managed to emerge in one piece."

"It isn't my fault if you've had a hard time, Maghrurio. You chose your path."

"You misunderstand, Azak. I'm not pleading my case with you. Rather, I'm pointing out that while the road has been a stern taskmaster, it has also been an effective teacher. I'm not the unskilled amateur who visited your Duke weeks ago." He leaned back in his chair and placed his hands on his lap, trying to act more confident than he felt. "You would be wise to note that."

Azak smiled. "Your words are bold, but they fit poorly in your mouth. Stop playing these games and accept your fate for what it is."

Maghrurio's hands moved discreetly under the table, and he pushed his plate forward. "Well, I'm afraid this fish won't fit in my mouth." He stood up. "I'm through running from you, Azak. The Duke will never get my Ring, and he won't get me either." He drew himself up to his full height. "I'm leaving now, but I'm afraid you won't be."

Azak grew angry and rose from his chair. Or, at least, he tried to. Unfortunately, his feet and lower legs were encased in stone and attached firmly to the ground, courtesy of Maghrurio's concealed spellwork. Speechless, he eyed the Mystic with wonderment on his face.

Maghrurio tossed a few coins on the table and left Azak behind. His heart pounded a staccato rhythm in his chest, outstripping his measured footsteps as he walked away. The stone trick he'd first used at the merchant association would keep Azak trapped for a while, but would the soldiers converge on him and try to take him down? He wasn't sure he could overcome them all, especially since he didn't want to kill them. They were only following Azak's orders, after all-- they didn't deserve to die just because of Azak's stubbornness.

Luckily, it seemed Azak spoke the truth. The soldiers wouldn't move until Azak walked away from the table.

Thanks to his Mystic magic Maghrurio could make his escape, knowing that Azak would remain at the table until his soldiers found a way to release him.

• • ● • •

Maghrurio was in good spirits when he reached home. He'd managed to settle the question of Azak pretty firmly without actually hurting anyone. He shared his encounter with his friends, and their reactions were predictable. Sheru and Vodi were pleased he had acquitted himself so well, while Bacarus was furious that Azak tried to take him again. They all agreed Azak had received what he deserved.

Yes, Maghrurio was quite pleased with himself. He'd performed actual magic and accomplished his intentions, and the best part was he'd managed to solve one of his problems.

Hadn't he?

VISIONARY

Maghrurio lay in bed that night, pleased with himself. Of course, he wasn't letting success go to his head, not when his bruises and burns reminded him painfully of his limitations, but he was learning to take what pleasure was earned. He reviewed once more his list of problems.

One was the identity of the Assassin. No help there, but they had at least determined he was no longer in Mosel.

Two, getting better spells. The cold blast and icy blast he'd learned were a good start. The stone covering might also be of use. He'd need to keep working on that one.

Three, improving his spellwork. He certainly felt more confident now, probably more than he had a right to be. So there was some improvement, but so much more was needed.

Four, what to do next. That was a hard one. He was mobile again, so they weren't necessarily stuck here. In fact, he wasn't sure where they should be, especially since he didn't know yet where the Assassin was. In the absence of a better alternative, Mosel was as good as anywhere else.

As for what to do that didn't involve one of these points, he tried to examine the big picture. This campaign of the assassination wasn't just an attack on certain Mystics but an attack on all Mystics. While he'd given a warning to the targeted ones, he hadn't yet warned the others. Maybe he should do something about that.

With the full Vadha rising outside, he focused his mind and brought himself back to the Circle of Friends. He found Varka already present and nodded to him in greeting. The balance of the Mystics turned up shortly thereafter--Buhlo, The Hidden One, Kuyi, Obolan, and Miya. Varka called the meeting to order and moved quickly through the opening ritual. At the request for new business, Maghrurio raised his hand, and at Varka's acknowledgment, he stood.

"Some may have noted Usnik's absence today. I must report an attempt was made on his life. I had visited him and was away from his home when a package was delivered. It exploded with killing force when he approached it."

Maghrurio wore a pained and saddened expression on his face. In his discussions with Usnik, they'd agreed it would be best to maintain the charade of his passing until they'd identified the Assassin. Still, he had no wish to lie to his fellow Mystics, so he made certain that his statement was entirely true.

As expected, his announcement brought an immediate reaction from the Gathering. Questions flew back and forth, and he held his hands up for silence. "There is more to the tale. I later encountered the Assassin myself and barely escaped with my life." *No exaggeration there, certainly, but it didn't hurt to keep the Assassin confident--whoever it might be.* "He did share something with me, though, something you all should hear." He related the Assassin's comments about his targets, looking suitably embarrassed at the slights against the lesser skilled among them. "Those who were named have already been warned, but I thought it only right for the rest to be aware as well."

He sat, leaving the other Mystics stunned yet silent. They were processing the news he'd shared, each working out their reaction. Except, of course, for whichever of them was the Assassin, who would be working out how to take down Varka and The Hidden One.

No, strike that. He had reconsidered the possibilities, and the Assassin had to be an as-yet-unknown Mystic.

He'd warned them all, so his duty was executed, but was there more he could do? He eyed The Hidden One, whose masked face was inscrutable but seemed to be returning Varka's worried stare. Their glance shared the unspoken acknowledgment that they were next. Varka had already said he was going to ground, and The Hidden One had dismissed Maghrurio's concerns. He could do nothing to help them, it seemed.

He stared at the other Mystics--skilled if distant colleagues like Miya and Obolan and friendlier semi-skilled peers like Buhlo and Kuyi. They continued to follow the age-old Mystic practice of training and learning in isolation from each other. They were, all of them, islands unto themselves.

Maybe it was time to change that.

He sidled over to Buhlo, seated near him, and whispered in her ear. "I think we junior members should talk a few things over after the Gathering breaks up. Pass the word along," She nodded and casually leaned over to Miya and Obolan on her other side. Maghrurio repeated his suggestion to Kuyi.

Varka stood and called out, "Let us all stand in silence to honor our colleague one last time." Maghrurio stood with the others, hands over hearts, as they all said goodbye. After a minute, they retook their seats.

Miya stood and addressed the Gathering. "We here and the unfortunate Usnik number eight. There should be twelve. Does anyone know anything about the missing four? One of them must be the Assassin."

Maghrurio raised his hand and shared what little he'd read of the mysterious Chawi.

Varka spoke up, "I recall Abner mentioning her once before, but we never discovered anything apart from her name." He sighed deeply. "It seems we continue to have cause for concern. Our Assassin must be some unknown Mystic bent on destroying our order. We must all keep our eyes open for him, thanks to Maghrurio's description."

Miya snorted. "A tall, hooded guy. That should narrow it down."

The Hidden One rose. "If we have no other business, Varka, we should adjourn this meeting. You and I must see to our defenses."

"Agreed. This Gathering is adjourned. Go forth and serve."

Varka and The Hidden One put their heads together for a hurried discussion as Maghrurio looked to gather the rest of the Mystics together. Kuyi and Buhlo seemed friendly and open, while Miya and Obolan were dubious at best.

"Friends, it appears while we are not in immediate danger, we are nonetheless affected by the Assassin's intentions." He tried to wear an encouraging face, but Miya's frown made it difficult. "I'm wondering whether we should pool our resources and help each other improve our skills."

Miya snorted in disgust. "You're still infants in the ways of Mystics. What could we possibly learn from any of you?"

Maghrurio responded. "True, we haven't spent as much time training as you two, but that's why it's important we help one another. Can't you see we're sitting ducks otherwise?"

"What I see is you want me to share everything I've learned. That's not going to happen." Miya threw up her hands. "This is insane. I'm leaving." She vanished, followed quickly by Obolan.

Maghrurio tried to rally himself. "Well, we three can still help each other. Are you willing?" He looked hopefully at his colleagues. Kuyi looked at Buhlo, who was examining her shoes with some discomfort.

She met his eyes reluctantly. "Look, Maghrurio, I know you're trying to do good here. I didn't spend that many days with my master, but working alone was something she drilled into me from Day One." She shook her head, "I'm going to have to think about this."

He smiled with some regret. "I understand, Buhlo. All I ask is that you do think about it. And, if you find you're ready, I'm willing to help."

Kuyi replied eagerly, "I'm ready; sign me up. I can barely get here and back. I'll take all the help I can get!"

Maghrurio smiled at her, pleased at her willingness to work together. He doubted he'd learn much from her, at first anyway, but he did recall from past jobs that training someone else was a great way to reinforce what you already knew. Plus, a fresh perspective often reveals new approaches and ideas. They bid Buhlo goodbye, and she vanished with a promise to consider his offer. Only Kuyi and Maghrurio remained in the Circle.

"So you have never met your predecessor?"

"No," Kuyi answered. "Like I said, I found this Ring in a cave and have no real idea what to do with it."

"I know how you must feel. I felt quite inadequate when I first began. Actually," he admitted, "I still feel that way from time to time." He smiled warmly at her and continued. "I won't overwhelm you with guidance this first time but let me suggest this. Compose your mind, as you do to come here, and call out for help from your Master. That may be enough to connect you with your predecessor."

"Thanks, Maghrurio. I'll let you know how it turns out."

• • ● • •

When Maghrurio finally awoke, the sun was climbing toward noon. His friends had left for their jobs, so he sat alone for a late breakfast in the dining hall. He had already advised Hagah he would not be holding court today, so his afternoon was free. As he finished his meal, he heard his friend Jaysel call out to him from the doorway.

"Well met, Maghrurio!"

"You're looking much better than when we last met, my friend. How are you keeping?"

"I'm working for our mutual friend now, in case he hadn't mentioned it. I'm just running errands for now, but he's considering taking me on as his apprentice!!"

"Nothing would please me more, Jaysel. I'll put in a good word if it will help."

Jaysel inclined his head in thanks. "In the meantime, I'm picking up supplies and other items for him. He's staying at home until he can decide a better course of action, so I'm his eyes and ears, and hands out in the world. Once I take care of his needs, I'll be relocating to a place in Ober City to be nearby. Although," he wondered aloud, "I'm not sure how he's supposed to let me know he needs me if he doesn't leave his home…"

Maghrurio considered for a moment and decided Usnik's need was greater than his. "Take these," he said, handing over the pair of slates he'd used with Bacarus. "They are magic. Anything written on one appears on the other. That way, you can still communicate."

Jaysel was speechless. "I cannot accept such a useful gift !"

Maghrurio shook his head. "I insist. These were of great help to me when Bacarus and I were separated, but we are together again. Your need is now greater than mine." He pushed the slates back into Jaysel's hands.

"I thank you for myself and for my master," he replied. "We are in your debt."

RIVALS

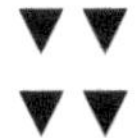

The afternoon was pleasantly warm, and Maghrurio enjoyed a purposeless stroll about town. He was greeted by many of the townsfolk, those he'd met in the course of his judgments and strangers who knew him by reputation only. It had clearly been a long time since a Mystic had last visited Mosel. He contemplated a future where his current difficulties were successfully resolved, and he could choose his own residence. There were worse places to live than Mosel, he imagined.

Despite the pleasant, carefree afternoon, the list of problems was ever on Maghrurio's mind. Find the Assassin, improve fighting, better spellwork, and what to do next. They were interrelated and, for the moment, intractable except, perhaps, for better spellwork. While he hadn't noticed any appreciable improvement lately, his first day of judgments and his handling of Azak certainly helped him feel better about his capabilities. In fact, now that he considered it, he hadn't seen Azak or his men since the encounter.

He stopped short. Since his successes with Azak and the merchant association, he realized that he'd been walking around town with little thought for his safety. At any point, the Assassin, or one of his hired goons, could have easily captured or killed him. Had he forgotten so soon how impotent and helpless he'd been at the Assassin's hand? Did the burns on his legs he still treated every morning count for nothing? Maghrurio resolved to pay closer attention to his surroundings as he reached the inn.

He found Vodi had returned in his absence. The two sat on the balcony fronting their sitting room, sheltered from prying eyes yet ideal for watching the neighborhood.

"How is business these days, Vodi?"

"My stock has risen since being appointed trustee for your judgment," replied a pleased Vodi. "People who wouldn't give me the time of day before are now clamoring to include me in their business deals. It has been oddly refreshing."

Maghrurio smiled. He was glad to help one of his friends.

They remained on the balcony for the balance of the afternoon, exchanging small talk and commenting on the weather. Maghrurio's mind gradually drifted from the conversation, and he found himself focused on the sights, sounds, and smells around him. His gut instincts had served him well recently, and today his gut was warning him to be careful.

He abruptly changed the topic. "Vodi, let's pretend you are the Assassin. You tried to interrogate me about my investigation, but I escaped you. Why would you then leave town rather than continue trying to find me?"

"Please take no offense, my friend, but not because I was frightened or intimidated. Perhaps I decided you had nothing of value to share? No, I hadn't heard anything yet, so how would I conclude that? Hmm… Perhaps because a more valuable target became available?"

"A more valuable target…" As far as the Assassin knew, Usnik was already dead, so the next most valuable target had to be Varka--the Senior Mystic. He came to a quick decision. "Vodi, I think you've nailed it. He must have finally figured out where Varka can be found." He stood up and stretched his stiff back and legs. "I should warn Varka." He left Vodi on the balcony, his face a mask of concern.

Maghrurio settled himself into his bed and relaxed his body. He could have done this on the balcony, but he was unwilling to risk letting down his guard in public, however physically sheltered the balcony might be. Clearing his mind, he called out to Varka and waited. His mind calmed, his body relaxed, and he nearly drifted off to sleep. When Varka's response came, however, he was instantly alert.

"What do you want?"

They were alone, once more within the Circle of Friends. Maghrurio explained his reasoning and his conclusion. "This time, I think he's coming for you, and it won't be remotely like it was with Abner. He's figured out where you are and wants to make sure to finish the job."

"I've certainly not publicized my location, but neither have I been a hermit like Usnik. People talk, and word gets around." He sighed, "I suppose this was bound to happen sooner or later." His face grew grim. "But he won't catch me unawares, that's for sure. I made arrangements with The Hidden One, and he's joining me here for mutual defense. The Assassin may be prepared for a fight, but he won't be expecting two of us."

"I hope The Hidden One will be a great help to you. He's survived an attack before, and he didn't seem overly concerned with my warnings."

They talked a while longer, Maghrurio relating the blow-by-blow of his own battle with the Assassin in the hope that Varka might glean some nugget of technique or strategy that could be of help. Maghrurio tried engaging Varka in a discussion of offensive and defensive tactics, but Varka wasn't in a sharing mood. Maghrurio wished him luck as he departed.

Maghrurio remained in the Circle of Friends for a while longer, instinct warning him his world was about to change. He drank in the tranquility he could only experience there, knowing he would be yearning for it before long. A flash from behind jolted him out of his dormancy, and he spun around to see Kuyi standing before him with an eager look on her face.

"Maghrurio, I'm so glad I found you here. You'll need to show me how to call other Mystics. I couldn't figure it out, so I just showed up. Sorry, I'm babbling." She stopped for a breath. "I did what you suggested and found my Master, and she showed me some stuff. I'll continue to learn from her, but if you're serious about training together, I could use all the help I can get."

Maghrurio found her garrulous nature somewhat draining, even more so than Sheru. But he could understand her excitement, especially given that she knew nothing at all before. The fountain in the middle of the Circle caught his eye, and he wondered whether it worked here as it did in the real Circle.

"Let's try something." He led her to the fountain and explained. "The Circle of Friends is a real place you can visit in the Zod Hills. When I was there last, I placed my Ring hand on the fountain and discovered which of the gods was my patron. I don't know whether it will work here as well, so why don't you give it a try?"

He turned his back as she approached the fountain and, after a few moments, heard her gasp and step back.

"It is Mystic etiquette that I do not ask what you discovered unless we both agree to tell each other. I would tell you of my patron. Would you honor me by sharing yours?"

"This is sort of weird, but yeah, sure," she replied.

"I thank you. My own patron is Wehni, god of the winds."

"My patron is Ufnal, the goddess of birth."

"Ufnal is of the water triad. I take it your Master showed you how to create water?"

Kuyi looked surprised. "Yes, that's all she showed me so far. It wasn't hard to learn, but it surprised the hell out of me the first time I did it."

Maghrurio worked with her for a while, going through the other three elemental spells. She had some trouble at first, but no more than he'd experienced. He tried to be as encouraging as Abner had been, and she seemed to appreciate it. For good measure, he also told her how to call other Mystics to meet at the Circle of Friends.

"You should continue to work with your Master and learn what she will teach. We can continue these sessions as well, so long as you are willing. Most importantly, practice what you've learned so you can master the skills."

"This is all so overwhelming. Can I ask one question?" At his encouraging nod, she continued. "How can I get my spells to be as powerful as yours?"

Maghrurio was taken aback by the idea that his spellwork could be considered powerful by anyone. She was a novice, of course, and had much work ahead of her. He recalled a similar conversation at his first Gathering, "Practice builds confidence, and confidence builds capability. Work hard, and you will exceed your wildest expectations."

Kuyi beamed at him. "Thank you, Maghrurio. You've been incredibly helpful. I can only hope to pick this up as well as you have."

Maghrurio smiled at her. "We are all learning here. Steady work will yield steady improvement." He paused and added, "For both of us."

THE COLLABORATOR

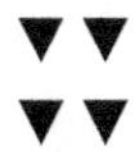

The following day was dark and stormy, consistent with late spring in this part of the world. Sheru and Bacarus bustled themselves off to work after breakfast, and Vodi and Maghrurio left for the merchant association headquarters. After a busy week, the demand for Maghrurio's judgments had dropped dramatically. He instead spent the morning chatting with local merchants and other citizens, most of whom just wanted to be seen in his company.

He realized he was starting to get comfortable, so perhaps it was time to consider moving on. But to where?

He and Vodi discussed this over lunch but had no sudden inspiration to guide them. They had chosen an indoor restaurant today, partly to placate Maghrurio's gut instinct about approaching danger and, practically, to stay out of the rain. Mid-conversation, he felt a familiar sensation indicating another Mystic was trying to contact him.

"Vodi," he interrupted his friend. "Please accept my apologies, but it seems I have another Mystic trying to contact me." He smiled sheepishly, "I usually contact them within my room, so I'm not sure what I'll look like while I speak with them. But can I ask you to keep watch and give me a shake if anything important arises?" Vodi nodded his assent, and Maghrurio closed his eyes and descended into the mental state his communion required.

● ● ● ● ●

He opened his eyes to the Circle of Friends under a clear afternoon sky and was surprised to see several familiar faces--Kuyi, Buhlo, and even Obolan and Miya. Kuyi began talking almost immediately.

"Hi Maghrurio, I hope you don't mind, but I contacted everybody. You talked about collaborating on training, so I thought…"

"Thank you, Kuyi. I wasn't sure anyone wanted to share. But all are welcome," he smiled at his peers. "Can I ask what changed your minds?"

Buhlo spoke frankly, "My master talked about tradition but, in the end, left it to me. It can't hurt, I guess."

He turned to Obolan and Miya, who looked uncomfortable and traded glances as if each expected the other to speak. Finally, Miya answered. "We haven't heard from The Hidden One in a while now. He usually contacts one of us every few days, but it's been weeks." She seemed to dig deep to find the courage to continue. "I'm not the kind that accepts help easily, but," she glanced at Obolan, "we're starting to think maybe we're not as safe as we thought."

Maghrurio tried not to smile too much. "Whatever your reasons, I think our joining together is a good thing. If I may ask, has everyone identified their patron god?" Kuyi was quick to nod, but the others shook their heads. He explained the real Circle of Friends and how to use the fountain to find their patron god. "It is customary among Mystics to conceal the identity of one's patron god. I don't know why this is, apart from perhaps more Mystic secrecy. So, for propriety's sake, I ask that everyone turn their backs so one by one, we can consult the fountain. If anyone cares to share their results, I would be honored to share mine as well."

Buhlo and Kuyi nodded their agreement. Obolan and Miya glanced at each other and, with a shrug, agreed to disclose theirs as well.

"If all have agreed to share their results, I'll go first. I am of Wehni, the wind god."

Kuyi followed, "Ufnal, the goddess of birth."

The others glanced at each other, and Miya strode up to the fountain. She scanned around the rim until she reached the fire sector. "Thebar, goddess of plants." Obolan took his turn and found a match almost immediately. "Sarnas, god of animals."

Kuyi asked, "Why would plants and animals be in the fire triad?"

Miya's answer was clipped with impatience. "Plants and animals both possess the flame of life within them."

Maghrurio jumped in. "Thank you for your answer, Miya. I wasn't aware of that," he fibbed, hoping to take the sting out of her response. "I hope everyone continues to feel free to ask questions. Learning is why we're here."

He gestured to Buhlo, who took her turn at the fountain. She passed each sector until she stopped in the Wind sector. "Ellast, god of wisdom. Wow, definitely not intimidating…"

"So now we know our patrons. It appears Obolan and Miya are natural allies, as are Buhlo and I." He smiled at Kuyi, "But we can also ally across triads, so you're not alone." He turned back to the others. "Can I ask you to gather some pinecones? We'll need them for the first thing I'd like to demonstrate."

The others, with varying degrees of enthusiasm, collected pinecones from within the Circle. When they each had a small supply, he continued. "We all started with the basic elemental spells--water, fire, stone, and wind. Incidentally," he said as an aside, "it seems the sector you belong to dictates the first elemental spell you get taught." He received a couple of nods. "Of course, things get far more interesting when you combine the elemental spells--with each other, with non-spell gestures, or both. We'll try one of those today."

He stepped back a few paces, then called up his angled shield. All they saw was him standing there with his arms outstretched, hands angled and touching at the fingertips. "Please throw your pinecones at me and watch what happens."

They were only pinecones, and besides, the Circle of Friends would prevent any serious harm from befalling him. Still, he felt a twinge of anxiety as the other reared back and began to throw. One by one, the pinecones flew, and one by one, they were deflected by his shield.

The Circle erupted into a cacophony of commentary. Miya muttered, "I've been using a flat shield."

Maghrurio nodded, "I also started with a flat shield, but the angled surfaces deflect objects better than a flat surface can." He explained the mechanics of his shield spell, casting as he talked. "Now, why don't you pair up and try this yourself?" The group spread out and collected more pinecones while he approached Kuyi.

"Have you mastered all the elemental spells yet?"

"I worked with my master, and I've been practicing, so I think I can do it."

"Keep in mind that this is a bit more advanced than anything you've tried so far. It was a while before I was able to do this, so don't get too concerned if it doesn't work as well as you'd like. With practice, you'll get it."

Kuyi nodded and turned toward Buhlo and her armful of pinecones. Kuyi took a breath and summoned her shield. The first throw struck her chest, the second bounced off her head, but the third struck the shield and glanced away. Kuyi's exuberant outburst was infectious, and Maghrurio felt truly happy for her. Buhlo's grin was ear to ear, and even Miya and Obolan spared her a smile.

Maghrurio let them continue to practice, watching their progress from his vantage point near the fountain. Granted, pinecones weren't exactly lethal, but he could see they were all improving steadily. After a while, he called the group back to order.

"I'm going to pick on Buhlo for a moment to demonstrate a point. Buhlo, can you please shield against Miya?"

Buhlo turned around to face Miya and cast her shield. Instead of asking Miya to throw a pinecone, however, Maghrurio picked one up and tossed it at her back. It struck her easily, bouncing off her head.

"My apologies, Buhlo, but I wanted to demonstrate an important point. The shield faces forward. It does not protect your back. Take care of how and when you use it." The group nodded their understanding.

"But no matter. Remember, as with everything, practice makes perfect. If you don't have anyone to help you, try casting your shield upwards in the rain." He heard a few chuckles.

"I have one last bit of advice to share today. If the town where you live contains a library, go visit it. I have found that some libraries contain snatches of Mystic lore that can help give you a better understanding of spellcasting and other aspects of Mystic life. Next time I will share what I've learned, but until then, please go to your own libraries and see what you can find. If there is something there, you'll feel a weird pulling sensation in your chest. Just follow it, and you'll be able to tell which book or scroll has what you seek."

He looked around at the nodding faces. "Thanks again for coming, and let's shoot for tomorrow around lunchtime."

He motioned to Miya and Obolan as the others talked about the meeting. "I spoke with Varka yesterday. He said The Hidden One was traveling to join him against the Assassin, so that's probably why you haven't heard from him."

Miya looked stiff as she acknowledged his news, while Obolan looked frightened. "Thank you," she conceded.

One by one, the Mystics extended their thanks to him and each other and vanished. Maghrurio, with a large smile on his face, was the last to go.

• • ● • •

Maghrurio found himself back at the restaurant facing Vodi.

"Welcome back," Vodi said with a smile.

"That seemed to go quite well. How long was I gone?"

"You sat unmoving for perhaps ten minutes? I just had time to finish my tea. Did you learn anything useful?"

"No, but they did." He related the particulars of the training session and couldn't help breaking into a broad grin.

"Ah, my friend, that is what fellowship can do. That is why I frequent the merchant association, despite the occasional unpleasant interaction or social hiccup. It just feels better knowing you are a productive member of your fellows."

Maghrurio found he couldn't argue with Vodi's observation.

TO THE DEATH

Their shifts completed, Bacarus and Sheru walked slowly through the streets on their way back to the inn. Sheru chatted away happily, with an occasional response from Bacarus, until she stopped short at an intersection.

"Bacarus, what are we doing?"

Nonplussed, Bacarus replied, "We're going home?"

Sheru shook her head. "No, I mean, what are we doing in the broad sense? Are we staying here in Mosel? Are we heading somewhere else? I feel adrift again like I've lost my purpose. Maghrurio has his investigation, but it feels like we're no longer part of it. I feel like I'm not part of anything."

Bacarus sighed. "I know what you mean. I don't feel connected, either." She drew herself up. "But that's going to change tonight. It's been a while since we've discussed this case, and it's time we do it again."

When they returned to their suite, they found Vodi and Maghrurio in a quiet discussion over tea in the sitting room. Bacarus wasted no time.

"Maghrurio, we aren't happy."

Concern erupted on his face, and he noted the crossed arms and stiff postures. "What's wrong?"

"What are we even doing anymore? You've been doing your Gatherings and talking with important people, and we've been shunted aside. It's like you don't even need us any longer."

He sighed. *Here was Problem #4 coming to a head.* "Please believe I'm not shunting aside either of you. Vodi and I were just discussing what our next steps should be. Please, join us."

He talked for half an hour, laying out everything he'd learned so far. Then, he covered his Four Problems and the progress, or lack thereof, that he'd made on each. When he was finished, he suggested they break for the evening meal so each of them could give thought to his report.

Dinner passed with a minimum of discourse, each lost in his or her own thoughts. Afterward, they returned to their sitting room with a bottle of wine and resumed their discussion.

"Let's go through them one by one," began Bacarus. "First, who is the Assassin, and where is he? You say he's a Mystic, but not one of those you know?"

"That's correct. He's a tall man, which eliminates most of the lot. Both Varka and The Hidden One have been threatened and are joining together for defense. In fact, The Hidden One had been attacked before and survived."

"How did he survive?" asked Sheru.

"He won't say, but he wears a mask during our Gatherings because of it."

Vodi jumped in, "And you say there are three unknown Mystics?"

"Well, the original number was twelve, so there should be three more. There was once a Mystic named Chawi, away to the west, but she hasn't attended any Gatherings in Abner's memory. So one of the three must be our Assassin."

"As for where he is, nobody knows. I don't think he's in the vicinity of the Gladwater; otherwise, we, or Usnik, would have heard of another Mystic. I don't think he's back in Nahrein either since Abner didn't know about him."

"Great," muttered Bacarus. "That only leaves all the rest of Sonoduhl to search."

Maghrurio shook his head in helpless agreement.

"OK," said Sheru, "let's move on. I know we can't help you with spellcasting, but might it be helpful to talk through some spell ideas?" At the bemused stare from Maghrurio, she conceded, "Fine, we can come back to that. Your last question is related to our first question… what do we do next, and how can we help?"

"We've been talking about that," said Maghrurio. "We think the Assassin left Mosel for a more tempting target--Varka." He related the news he had shared with Vodi about Varka and The Hidden One. "So, unless they can somehow kill him, I have to assume he returns here to pick up our trail." His face grew somber, and he corrected himself. "Or, should I say, my trail?"

None of them spoke. Through the window drifted the sounds of children playing, parents yelling, and drunks calling to each other. Typical sounds one might hear in any town at night, Maghrurio thought. They could easily mask the approach of a spy or worse.

Bacarus broke the silence. "It seems like we should prepare to leave town, but where do we go?"

They spent the next hour throwing ideas around, but no suggestion was compelling enough to act upon. Their voices eventually trailed off. The silence was interrupted by the sound of heavy footsteps climbing the stairs. Bacarus and Vodi flanked the doorway as the steps approached. Maghrurio and Sheru stood their ground and awaited the inevitable.

There was a knock at the door, and Maghrurio moved to answer it. Everyone tensed as he opened the door, only to find a short heavy woman--the inn's night maid--bearing a letter.

"Begging your pardon, sir, but this arrived for you just now. The courier said to tell you, and I quote, 'There were two bodies,' whatever that means."

Maghrurio accepted the letter, muttered his thanks, and closed the door. Everyone breathed a sigh of relief as they returned to their seats.

The plain brown envelope was devoid of any markings, but nonetheless, the letter evoked a feeling of dread. He tore it open and removed the letter within. Neat, precise handwriting filled the pages, which he read aloud in the darkening room.

"Greetings to you, Maghrurio. I am leaving this letter with my apprentice as insurance. If you are reading this, then it means I was unsuccessful, and the Assassin has killed me."

"As I write this letter, our colleague The Hidden One is traveling to my location in Arnhem at the foot of the Long Falls. We fully expect the Assassin to come for me, but we hope The Hidden One's arrival turns the tide in our favor."

"Since I am, as I said, already dead, I must confess a certain apprehension about needing to rely on The Hidden One. I can't decide whether it's the idea of relying on someone else or that the someone is him, but it keeps me up at night nonetheless. The Assassin has managed to kill some powerful Mystics, and while I have some talent, I was never in the same league as Mystics like Abner. Whatever may transpire, know that The Hidden One's assistance was not enough, at least not for me. I cannot speak for his fate."

"My advice to you, at this point, is to trust no one stronger than you. Look out for yourself and those around you. I do not trust this Assassin for many reasons (not least of which is because he has killed me.) If it comes down to a fight, try to arrange for it to be on terms and grounds favorable to you."

"Make friends and take time to enjoy life. I wish I had done more of both."

"Your fellow Mystic, Varka"

Maghrurio clutched the letter, his thoughts dark and worrying. He excused himself and retreated to his room. *Varka was dead.* What of The Hidden One? He had to know, so he closed his eyes and tried to calm himself. He called out to The Hidden One, hoping for an answer but somehow knowing he wouldn't receive one. He waited for a long while, repeating the call several times, but his instincts were true. There were two fewer Mystics in Sonoduhl tonight.

With a heavy heart, he rejoined his friends in the sitting room. What little conversation they had halted immediately at his approach. "I am unable to contact The Hidden One. The messenger said there were two bodies, so we must assume both have been lost."

Sheru's hand covered her mouth in dismay, and both Bacarus and Vodi bowed their heads in respect. They shared a moment of silence for his fallen comrades.

Vodi spoke first. "My friend, I am powerless against a spellcaster, but I'm ready to do what I can to assist you."

Maghrurio watched his friends all nod in agreement, to his great sorrow. He couldn't ask them to risk themselves. It was bad enough that he'd likely have to risk himself. Still, he knew he had to wear a brave face.

"The Assassin said after Varka and The Hidden One, everyone else was 'too stupid to matter.' I suppose that means I should be safe from imminent attack. But he must have plans beyond killing Mystics, and with all the top ones gone, he has a clear field to execute them. I need to find out what those plans are."

"You mean *we* need to find out, don't you?" asked Bacarus, her eyes and tone daring him to disagree with her.

"Bacarus, please. The Assassin nearly killed me, and I have some degree of magical defense. I shudder to think what he could do to any of you."

The response was swift and voluminous, each of his friends clearly and loudly attempting to convince him their participation was not optional. He could not interject with the shouting until he brought two stone hands together with a resounding clap.

Before he could speak further, he was interrupted by a familiar sensation in his head. One of the Mystics was trying to contact him. "One moment, please… a Mystic," he explained, pointing at his head. He closed his eyes and concentrated on making contact.

"Hello again, Maghrurio," said a frightening yet familiar voice.

DISTANT VOICES

There was no visual, only a voice drifting out of the darkness. But there was no question in his mind that, once again, he was speaking with the Assassin.

"What do you want?" asked Maghrurio as a chill crawled up his spine.

The Assassin chuckled. "You know, for a know nothing charlatan, you can be quite the troublemaker--first your so-called investigation and now Varka's letter. What did he tell you?"

Maghrurio's heart seemed to rise to his throat. *How did he know about the letter?* "I don't know what you're talking about."

"Don't play games with me, simpleton. I'm not in the mood. What was in the letter?"

Maghrurio thought for a moment. There seemed little point in denying it further, so he changed tactics. "We correspond regularly; it is no different from any others we have exchanged."

The Assassin grew angry. "Do you take me for a fool? He admitted sending you the letter before I killed him. I have big plans, and I need to know what he told you!"

"Sorry, I'm afraid that was between Varka and myself." He was playing with fire, and he knew it.

"Listen, you insignificant worm. You will tell me what I want to know NOW!"

"I won't be intimidated or bullied!" The words were defiant, but Maghrurio's gut churned with fear.

There was a long pause before the Assassin replied in a cold and barely audible whisper. "As you wish. Know this, then. In three days, I will come for you. We will have much to discuss."

The conversation ended abruptly, leaving Maghrurio shaken and fearful.

• • ● • •

The others waited while Maghrurio sat in a trance, communing with whichever Mystic had contacted him. They glanced at each other nervously, but no one broke the silence until Maghrurio awoke.

"He is coming!"

His words had a strangely calming effect on them all. While before they wrestled with unknown possibilities, the certainty of the Assassin's arrival sharpened their focus because now they had to decide.

"What about that Circle of Friends you mentioned? He couldn't hurt you there," Sheru asked.

"We couldn't stay there permanently. He would need only to starve us out," observed Bacarus.

Vodi suggested Ober City as a possibility. "Lots of people live there; it would be harder to find anyone."

Maghrurio thought it over. "Perhaps, but if he did find us, then more people might get hurt."

Bacarus asked, "What about Varka's letter? He said to find favorable terms and grounds. Any idea what that might be for you?"

Maghrurio frowned. "I'm afraid I'm not much of a military man. But you've had combat training, even if it's only personal combat. What would you suggest as favorable?"

"If it was me, I'd pick solid ground with sure footing and little cover for concealing long-range attacks. Our combat styles are not exactly similar, but for you, I might suggest familiar ground at the very least. It would be even better if it was familiar to you and not to the Assassin, but we have no idea where he's been."

Maghrurio poured himself a glass of wine and downed it. First, he needed to fortify his courage and settle the fearful rumbling in his stomach. "Familiar ground would suggest heading back the way we came."

"Should we consider returning to Decra? It seems like you've settled the score with Azak, so maybe the Duke is no longer an issue.

Of course, given the choice, I'd much rather deal with him than the Assassin."

"That is another possibility, Bacarus."

They settled into an uneasy silence, each lost in his or her own thoughts. The hour grew late, and the wine bottle yielded its last before Maghrurio rose.

"I think perhaps we should go to bed. He won't be here for three days. There is still time to decide what to do."

The friends said their goodnights and drifted off, each to their rooms. Maghrurio lay awake in bed for what seemed like forever, rehashing his choices and failing to come to any new conclusions. One thing he did decide was to apprise his Mystic colleagues of the latest developments.

He quickly found himself in the Circle of Friends and called out to Buhlo. She responded instantly as if she was standing by awaiting his summons.

"Hey there, Maghrurio. What's happening?"

He filled her in on the latest news.

"You don't mess around. Where will you go?"

"We haven't decided yet. Listen," he started. He had promised to keep Usnik's secret, but somebody else should know in case… well, in case. Hell, he'd trusted Buhlo since he first met her. He told her the real story about the attempt on Usnik's life.

"I just wanted you to know in case the Assassin gets me."

"What if Usnik staged the whole thing? What if he's really the Assassin?"

Maghrurio stopped short. He hadn't considered that. He'd been pondering the idea of running east to seek Usnik's assistance but realized that might put his friend in danger. If Usnik was, in fact, the Assassin, he'd only be helping to hasten his own demise.

"But no, you said the Assassin was tall," she said. "Usnik isn't tall, even by Graavt standards."

Maghrurio chastised himself. She was correct, of course. The Assassin was quite a bit taller than the diminutive Mystic.

"You're right, of course. Usnik is far too short and quite old for a Graavt besides."

"So what can I do? If it helps, I live in a small town in the Western Wall."

Maghrurio shook his head. "I'm traveling in Mosel, down near the Gladwater Lake. It would take you weeks to get here. What would be most helpful, though, is to pass the word along to our group." He gazed into her dark, concerned eyes. "And promise me you'll try to continue what we started? Share our learning with each other so you don't end up like me?"

Buhlo nodded her assent, then gave him a quick hug. "Be careful and may the Twelve watch over you." She flashed a worried smile and vanished.

Composing himself, Maghrurio next called out to Usnik. His response took longer, but soon enough, they were staring at each other within the Circle.

"Well met, Maghrurio. What news have you?" After hearing the tidings, he frowned. "What would you have me do?"

Maghrurio hesitated. What he most wanted to ask was for protection, but he knew he must not do so. "I cannot ask you to risk your life for me, but I would request a favor. The shield you taught me was helpful when last I faced him, but my own spells fared poorly against his defenses. Is there anything you could suggest for when I confront him again?"

Usnik stood motionless for a long time, his face a study of uncertainty and indecision. He was clearly torn between their budding friendship and centuries of Mystic tradition, but he had to choose. And choose he did.

• • ● • •

A torrential thunderstorm woke the group early the next morning, and they made their way to the dining hall in bleary-eyed fashion. Tea and a hot breakfast helped to revive them, and they returned their attention to the question of their next steps.

"So last night, we discussed Ober City and Decra as possible destinations. Has the night brought new ideas, or are these still our choices?" Maghrurio waited for dissenting voices but heard none, so he continued. "Then we must choose between those two. Should we hope to get lost in Ober City or return to Decra?

Sheru toyed with her tea. "I, for one, wouldn't mind seeing home again. This journeying has had its fun moments, but mostly it's been a pain. But I know that wasn't what you were asking."

Bacarus frowned. "The Ober City choice sounds a lot like hiding to me. I prefer to meet the enemy squarely."

Maghrurio had to smile. She could be so predictable at times.

"I have contacts throughout these parts, so one place is as good as another to me," replied Vodi. "The real question is, which option works best for you?"

"I've given serious thought to that and consulted with some of my fellows. I think our best bet is a return to Decra. I'll have to deal with any fallout from the Duke straight away and then prepare to face the Assassin after."

Sheru brightened. "Great, we're going home! So how do we get there?"

Vodi broke out his professional smile. "Leave that to me."

MOVE ALONG HOME

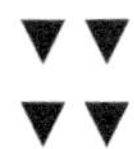

They spent the balance of the morning gathering supplies, and by early afternoon Vodi had them boarding a sailing vessel under clearing skies heading north for the Black Marsh. "The plan," he shared with the others, "is to sail north and ride the Marane River all the way to Decra. I know it took you over a week to come out this way, but that was on foot or with the current. We'll have the wind at our backs, so we should reach Decra in just a few days."

Maghrurio was pleased with the arrangements. The speed of travel was helpful, and unlike his last boat trip, he wouldn't have to work as a deckhand. This left him free to contemplate tactics and strategies for facing the Assassin when the time came. And he knew with certainty that the time would come, far sooner than he would like.

He gazed out at the afternoon sun on the rolling waves and tried unsuccessfully to calm himself. The setting was quite tranquil--firm breeze, pleasant weather, lightly rolling deck, and good-natured shouts between the working sailors. His eyes recognized the tranquility and tried desperately to convince the rest of his body to unwind, but his gut knew the truth and remained clenched in anxiety.

No, let's not mince words. Fear is what I have, not anxiety. Fear. Fear of what the Assassin could do to me. Fear of being unable to stand up to him. Fear of not being good enough to master the magic that could save me. Fear of letting my friends down.

I really need to relax. Instinctively, he abandoned his attempt at solitude for the comforts of friendship.

His companions had given him space, but at his approach, they welcomed him into their conversation. They mostly talked about the weather and the strange birds that followed, hovering nearby and waiting for scraps of food the passengers threw to them. The words themselves didn't really matter. It was the spirit of camaraderie that helped to diminish the fiery knot in his belly. He found himself breathing more easily, and his taut muscles slowly loosened.

They approached the Black Marsh as the sun dipped below the western horizon, and the captain ordered the anchors to be dropped. This made sense, as the sailboat was making good time, and the marsh was no place to be speeding in the dark. A simple dinner of stew and bread was served to all, and blankets were distributed so passengers could bed down on the deck.

Maghrurio lay quietly, staring at the stars and contemplating his future. He was headed toward a confrontation he was ill-prepared for, and nothing he could do would change the fact. He thought back to all the jobs he'd held before and realized he'd quit most of them when things had become too difficult or too challenging. Sure, he'd talked about wanting to find his true passion, but the reality was he'd never been willing to commit to anything in his life.

He was committed now, though, and he had too many people counting on him to back out. Abner, his friends, and the remaining Mystics. Well, except for the one Mystic that was trying to kill him. Who knew what the Assassin planned for the long term? All Maghrurio knew was he seemed to be the only person left in a position to hinder that plan.

If he could only gather enough courage to make a stand, that is.

If he could only hope to survive his stand.

At first light, the crew began preparations to resume their journey while the passengers were served a thin gruel for breakfast. Once the last dirty dish was collected, the crew hoisted the anchors and set forth into the Black Marsh. The following wind was as strong as yesterday, and the boat sliced through the vegetation-laden waterway. Maghrurio noticed the lookouts stationed at the crow's nest above, positioned to view their surroundings for a long way on every side. He imagined they were watching for all sorts of hazards, pi'pala not the least of them.

The day passed without incident but always with the unspoken threat that marked any passage through the Black Marsh. Several times the lookouts spied movement in the waters but, apart from surface ripples, no threat revealed itself. Lunchtime came and went, and the steady wind continued to drive them westward. When they finally left the Marsh behind, there was still an hour of daylight that remained. There would be no offshore anchoring that night, though, and after a few more hours, they docked in Acyfala.

Glad for an opportunity to sleep on anything but a cold hard deck, Maghrurio and his companions took rooms for the night at a nearby inn. The boat would be leaving the following morning at noon, so they planned on a late sleep before heading back. They bade each other goodnight and turned in.

As tired as he was, Maghrurio lay awake in the darkness. He had so many worries his mind refused to consider sleep. He went over the problems again and again with no new insights. Finally, bowing to the inevitable, he calmed his mind and revisited the Circle of Friends.

He was curious about how the group learning project was going, so he first contacted Buhlo. Her smiling face greeted him fairly quickly as if she had also decided sleep wouldn't come.

"So far, we've tried every day, and most of us have continued to attend. We've been taking turns teaching with a different person every session. Much of what we cover is familiar to at least some of us, but it never hurts to practice. Besides, sometimes someone points out a variation or different approach that turns out to be useful. How are you doing?"

Maghrurio's face lost some of its sparkle. "We decided to head back home, where we lived with Abner. I'm hoping familiar territory gives me some sort of advantage, although I don't have a clue what it might be. We have an overnight layover, so I thought I'd check in to see how you were."

Buhlo smiled warmly. "We're missing you and sending you all the warm thoughts we can." Concern etched around her eyes. "Do be careful. I'd rather not lose your friendship."

He held her hand, and smiling once more, she vanished.

The next half hour was probably a wasted effort, but he wanted to be sure about The Hidden One. The letter hadn't said anything about him, but the deliverer had mentioned two bodies. Unfortunately, his attempts to contact The Hidden One amounted to naught.

His next attempt was Usnik, who, as usual, took a while to answer. They exchanged greetings, and Maghrurio caught him up on his progress. With nothing new to discuss, Usnik gave his customary parting nod and vanished.

Maghrurio remained for a while, taking in the peace and tranquility while he still could.

• • ● • •

Maghrurio awoke from a troubled sleep, the memory of Gazto's taunting laughter ringing in his ears. The morning dawned cloudless and warm, but he couldn't quite shake the sense of impending danger. Not wanting to cause undue worry, he composed himself before rejoining his companions.

The quartet chatted over breakfast and afterward strolled around Acyfala, enjoying the unmoving land before catching a quick lunch and reboarding the boat. A few short hours later, they were back in Cyrchan. The arrangements were similar--lodging at a nearby inn and departure at noon the next day.

They enjoyed a quiet dinner in the inn's dining area. With the end of their journey drawing ever closer, the conversation grew sparse. What discussion there was centered mostly on the same theme--what to do to survive the coming confrontation. Maghrurio had no doubt the Assassin would soon figure out where he'd gone and come for him, if he wasn't already on his way.

The exchange accomplished little, being mostly a rehashing of suggestions they'd made multiple times since departing Mosel. Frustrated and tired, Maghrurio retired to his room for the night. He was preparing for bed when he felt the familiar sensation of being summoned by another Mystic. He composed himself and shortly was joined in the Circle of Friends by his friend Buhlo.

"I hate to bother you, but this might be helpful. We were discussing our library trips today, and Kuyi shared something interesting. She'd already visited her local library and found some lore--stuff already found and shared by you and others in our group. It turns out she'd dropped an earring there, and when she returned this morning to retrieve it, she picked up an entirely new signal that hadn't been there last time. When she hunted it down, it was a new piece of lore none of us had heard yet."

"The Twelve Ules honoring the gods were sundered from each other and scattered throughout the land. What their capabilities might be, none know for certain, but it is conjectured that reassembling them into their triads could yield immense power."

Buhlo could hardly control her excitement. "I don't quite understand what that means. If the Ules are scattered, how likely will it be to find more than one? Never mind managing to bring them together… But that's not important. The really interesting thing is the library had new lore after she'd already been through it. Maybe other libraries can produce new lore as well. We think each of us should revisit our libraries to see if anything new turns up."

Maghrurio listened with keen interest. This was indeed an important development. Could it be that the answers he needed were, in fact, already waiting for him? The Cyrchan Library was impressive, and there would be time to search tomorrow morning.

"That is a brilliant bit of deduction. I'll test it out tomorrow morning. Thank you, Buhlo. You may have just saved my life."

THE CHANGING FACE OF EVIL

Maghrurio rose early and skipped breakfast. He left a note for Bacarus that he had an errand in town and would return before the boat departed. He departed the inn, made his way through the morning commuters, and found the library he had visited weeks before. He passed within and marveled yet again at the artistic stylings in the structure and furnishings.

Within the library proper, he relaxed his mind and felt a familiar sensation calling to him. Excitement built as he found the source, a bookshelf tucked away in a corner. A moment of further concentration identified the shelf and specific book, which he retrieved and carried to a tattered wingback chair that had seen better days.

The book was written in a language unfamiliar to him, but he paged through it, confident that the lore he needed would be accessible. Sure enough, he found a legible section at the end of a chapter that appeared as if someone had scrawled it after the book was bound.

"The key to a Mystic's power is their force of will, which channels magic from the gods. Think of it like a river, in that a wide river can carry so much more water than a narrow one. For an experienced Mystic, force of will is primarily manifested as self-confidence. This includes a belief in one's own abilities and in the righteousness of one's cause."

"Force of will can take other forms, but these should not be relied upon. Fear or desperation can sometimes lead a neophyte to bursts of power, but such bursts are short-lived and unreliable. A Mystic's best hope is to cultivate a superior self-confidence in their abilities through practice and accomplishment and to invest in a superior cause such as justice and the protection of life."

He sat and contemplated the passage. He had several accomplishments to his credit but still lacked sufficient self-confidence to defeat the Assassin. As for having a righteous cause, he was pretty sure 'staying alive' wasn't terribly righteous.

He rose, replaced the book on the shelf, and continued wandering the aisles, casting about for another hour. Unfortunately, he failed to detect anything further. A quick glance out a window showed a sun that hadn't climbed very high, so he still had plenty of time before he had to return to his friends. He meandered among the shelves and thought further about what he'd read.

The sensation of Mystic contact intruded on his meditation, so he found a chair and dropped into his calm state. A cold, familiar voice greeted him.

"Good morning, Maghrurio."

Anger burned bright as he responded, "What do you want, murderer?"

The Assassin assumed a mock injured tone. "Now, now. Name calling doesn't become you. I would like to confess if you wish to hear."

If he talks long enough, he might accidentally tell me something useful. "Whatever, I'm not busy."

"Splendid! First, I would verify some facts you have no doubt pieced together. Yes, I am a Mystic, but my fearsome visage has not graced the Gathering in the living memory of anyone there now. Which, sad to say, isn't saying much."

Maghrurio bit his tongue. *Keep talking, you bastard.*

"I put up with the blowhards and the do-gooders for long enough and finally decided to seize my own destiny. You understand how that can be an attractive option, can't you?"

Maghrurio made a noncommittal noise.

"Oh, it took some clever work to be sure. I had to sow the seeds of discontent quite carefully; otherwise, the seniors like Abner would catch onto me. And then one day, nestled in a book I found in a library, was the hint I needed to perfect my weapon." He chuckled without humor. "I had already developed a formula of minerals that exploded when exposed to flame. Sulfur, saltpeter, and charcoal all packed tightly into a container. All it needed was a flame to make the weapon complete, and the book showed me how to place a shielded flame within the container indefinitely. All it took was the magical emanations from a Mystic Ring to disrupt the shield, and BOOM!"

So that's how he did it.

"My victims had no chance at all. I only had to figure out where each one lived and ship a surprise package. Once they got close enough, I had one less senior to worry about." His voice took on a sharper edge. "That is until you blabbed about what you knew, and I had to find a new method. Still, I'd gotten rid of everyone but Varka, so he required a different approach."

What about The Hidden One, or did I miss something?

"He was on his guard, so the exploding package wouldn't work. I had no choice but to physically attack him." He chuckled. "He'd been around a while and had grown skilled, so a frontal assault might have been problematic. I had to use cunning to trick him into letting me get the jump on him."

Maghrurio gasped in horror as he finally realized the only answer that made sense. "You're The Hidden One!"

The Hidden One laughed. "So you finally caught on, have you? Riddles within riddles! Your surprise is nothing next to Varka's, I can guarantee. I distracted him with a noise at the door, and when he turned his back on me, I blasted him. Oh, I so enjoyed killing that pompous fraud!"

"You are a monster, Hidden One. One day soon, you will atone for your crimes."

"Please, spare me the histrionics. The eternal brotherhood of Mystics is a stale organization and needs to be remade."

"And I suppose you think you're the one to do it?"

"Oh, yes," replied The Hidden One, his voice confident and self-assured. "I've set myself a lofty goal and have made it my life's work to achieve it for the good of all Sonoduhl. You would do well not to hinder me."

Maghrurio tried to hide the tremor of doubt in his voice. "I'd hate to break it to you, but I've made it my mission to hinder you."

"I assumed as much, you neophyte. Oh, I'm sure you're quite capable of parlor tricks that fool the rubes." His voice dropped into a lower, more menacing tone. "You stand no chance against me." Resuming his normal voice, The Hidden One continued. "I must confess, though, you've led me on quite the merry chase."

"I'm happy to have caused you trouble," Maghrurio retorted, his voice dripping with sarcasm.

"You've been a distraction, it's true. But no longer. I've decided to offer you a choice. Walk away and forget about me and my work, and I promise to leave you alone."

"How magnanimous of you. Hard pass."

"Ah well, I thought you'd feel that way, but I had to make the effort. You won't like the alternative."

"Why does that not surprise me?"

"You've caused me a certain amount of pain, Maghrurio. I'm happy to say I can now return the favor." He chuckled again. "I'd run home if I were you. Say hello to Duke Bileyo for me."

A cold feeling of dread crept up Maghrurio's spine, and he snapped out of his trance with the threat ringing in his ears.

He leaped from the chair and ran from the library. It was still early for the boat, but he had a premonition for disaster that fueled his pumping legs. He ran all the way back to the inn and bounded the stairs two at a time. Breathless, he burst through the door of their suite.

It looked like a tornado had blasted it. Furniture was strewn about, and there was some blood as well. He saw no sign of Bacarus or Sheru, but he found a badly beaten Vodi sprawled on his bed. He rushed to his friend's side, who opened his eyes and rasped, "Vasagh's men took the women."

Maghrurio's mind raced as he applied first aid to Vodi's wounds and listened to his accounting.

"We had planned to walk down to the market, but when Sheru opened the door, they were waiting for us. Bacarus put up a hell of a fight, but they overwhelmed us. I recognized Vasagh from the warehouse, and he must have recognized me, too, because he had his men beat me. They tied up the women, and he made sure to tell me his master sent his regards and that you'd chosen poorly." He looked distraught. "There were too many of them, Maghrurio. I'm sorry I couldn't do more."

Maghrurio placed a comforting hand on his friend's shoulder. "You did all you could, and now I must do all I can." He turned away, his mind racing.

Where would Vasagh have taken them?

His mind latched onto the magic sampler. He blurted out, "Dangers strike, troubles come; seek the solace of hearth and home," before he'd given any thought to what he might do. In a flash, he reappeared in an unfamiliar room and realized it was Bacarus' bedroom. The sampler was still in her pack, lying on the floor. He dug through the pack and removed it from his pocket against future need. *Wait, it doesn't make any sense for me to hold it.* He placed it on the bed instead.

He returned to Vodi's room. "I'm going to assume I can bring along anyone I touch, so when we find them, we can use the sampler to escape." He stared into his friend's eyes and added, "And we will find them, Vodi. We will find them."

APOCALYPSE RISING

Maghrurio recalled The Hidden One's parting words and realized what they meant.

"Vodi, Vasagh has taken them back to Decra. I must follow, even though that almost certainly means a confrontation with Azak and the Duke. I have no choice but to follow, but you…"

Vodi's damaged, bloody face turned adamant. "I must also follow. I owe it to our friends, and I will gladly face whatever is to come."

Maghrurio looked into his friend's eyes and recognized his resolve. "Then we will discuss it no more. Come, let's get you into traveling condition." He helped Vodi into fresh unblooded clothes and retrieved the sampler and the balance of their luggage. Realizing the time was running short, they hurried down to the boat and barely reached it before it departed upstream toward Hasa.

His mind was awash with thoughts of combat and defense. He'd been puzzling over strategies these past days in preparation for The Hidden One, but now his next confrontation would be with Vasagh and his men instead. He talked through possibilities with Vodi, keeping in mind that his friend, who was not a wielder of magic himself, could still play a part in their rescue operation.

In a few short hours, they arrived in Hasa. As per their prior agreement, Maghrurio secured lodging while Vodi scoured his local contacts for news of Vasagh's men or the captured women. They met outside the inn and exchanged news.

"Vasagh and less than a dozen men have been through, but my contacts tell me they were passing eastward, and no women were in their company, nothing of the captives."

"That must have been before they arrived in Cyrchan," answered Maghrurio. He gazed into the evening sky, trying to decide what to do next. "Does that mean they weren't noticed coming back, or does it mean they went on foot, and we've beaten them here?"

"In other words, do we go on, or do we wait? That is what you ask," Vodi reflected. "I don't think they are ahead of us because my contacts say ours was the first boat of any size to arrive today."

"Which means they are behind us, either on foot or in a later boat. We should head down to the docks to see."

They remained at the docks well into the night, but nothing further came upstream. Vodi slipped a few coins to the night watchman. "He will inform us if anything comes along," Vodi assured Maghrurio, and they returned to the inn.

The following morning was blustery, with wind-whipped rain splattering the town. After an early rise and a rushed breakfast, they returned to the docks, where Vodi consulted his contact.

"No new arrivals since our boat yesterday," he announced after more coins had changed hands. "It would be best to take shelter here and await their arrival, although if they left Acyfala at dawn, they wouldn't arrive until lunchtime."

The two hunkered under a warehouse overhang, sitting on their luggage and keeping mostly out of the rain. Maghrurio could easily have shielded them from the precipitation, but he wanted to keep himself free to think and act. Mostly, though, he just worried. At some point, Vasagh and his men would appear with his friends in tow, and he'd have to take action to free them. As angry as he was with Vasagh, he had no real desire to kill him--much less his men, who were likely mercenaries and only in it for the money. He had the morning to decide how to approach this latest problem.

Until he didn't.

One of Vodi's contacts approached, and Vodi excused himself to go talk with him. Maghrurio watched them exchange tense whispers, and Vodi returned with a grim look on his face.

"We have a problem. My contact tells me Azak's men are in town and looking for us. They've already found our trail at the inn, so it was fortunate we checked out already."

Maghrurio was exasperated. He had neither the time nor the patience to deal with this, and now he had another group of soldiers he didn't want to kill. "Maybe we should move undercover?"

Vodi scanned the area and approached an old man seated in front of a nearby fishing shack. They spoke quietly, and after coins changed hands, he motioned for Maghrurio to join him inside the ramshackle structure. It was small, a working fishing shack filled with equipment and the detritus of a lifetime of river fishing. It was a mess, and it stank badly of fish and dust, but it had a dirty window that looked out at the dock.

"Our host will keep an eye out for anyone approaching," Vodi whispered. "We should be safe enough here." He remained by the window while Maghrurio sat on a battered tackle box.

Maghrurio's thoughts returned to his latest dilemma. How was he to overcome a dozen armed soldiers without killing any of them? His musing was interrupted by the sensation of another Mystic trying to contact him. Relaxing his mind, he responded with his willingness to communicate.

"Good morning, ignoramus," said The Hidden One in his taunting manner.

Maghrurio replied angrily, "What do you want, Hidden One?"

"I just wanted to let you know I haven't forgotten about you. I have your friends here, nice and safe, while I decide what to do with them. And what to do with you."

He has them? Assuming it wasn't a lie, it suggested either he was traveling with Vasagh or that Vasagh himself was a ruse. *Which was it?* "How do I know you really have them?"

The Hidden One sighed. "You want proof? Fine… Speak to Maghrurio, woman!"

"Bacarus and I are safe for now, but I don't know--"

The Hidden One interrupted, "That's enough for now. Satisfied?"

Maghrurio's mind spun. Sheru was safe, and Bacarus too. But where? And how could he hear her voice? "For the present. Are you enjoying boating in the rain?"

"Still trying to weasel information from me," his adversary chuckled sadly. "I am inevitable, and you still think you can do anything to stop me? Even with all the clues at your disposal, you continue to flail about for answers." His voice took on a harsher tone, "Look, I told you already. I have great plans for Sonoduhl. It is my life's work, and all of your pathetic investigations are just water to a pi'pala."

The connection ended abruptly, leaving Maghrurio confused and afraid.

Maghrurio related the conversation to Vodi, and the pair remained watching through the morning until the noon arrival of the boat from Acyfala. They scanned the debarking passengers closely but saw no hint of Vasagh or the prisoners. The doubt and fear nestled in his gut threatened to consume him, but he fought back against the rising panic. The answers were right in front of him. They had to be!

Vodi could see the turmoil on his face. "This Hidden One says you have all the clues to solve this. Why don't we go over them again?"

Maghrurio sighed. *It couldn't hurt, could it? Besides, it's not like we have anything better to do.* "Very well. He has them prisoner with him. So if we can figure out where he is, we'll know where they are."

"And he says he has plans for Sonoduhl? That doesn't sound good."

"He probably has delusions of godhood or wants to make himself emperor. It's his life's work, apparently…" His mind thought back.

What was it he had said about water to a pi'pala? The phrase seems oddly familiar…

"You know, we came down the Marane River, but the Black River crosses it between Acyfala and here. Vasagh could have switched back and disembarked on the other side instead."

Maghrurio barely heard Vodi's words. His mind was searching back through his memory, trying to place those words. With a start, he recalled just where it was--back at Acyfala when he had first approached the metalsmith from his vision. The crotchety neighbor Gazto had uttered them.

Realization hit him like a thunderclap. *The blacksmith is the key to the beginning and end of your search*, the vision had said. The blacksmith himself wasn't the end of his search; the neighbor was. Gazto!

He stood up, the shock evident on his face.

"What is it, Maghrurio?"

"Half a moment, Vodi," he whispered, then dropped into the communication trance. He had always wondered why he could never contact The Hidden One, but now he understood why. The Hidden One was merely an alias for...

"Gazto!"

An answer came almost immediately. "Ah, perhaps we aren't so stupid after all."

Maghrurio poured out all of his anger and outrage. "Hear me, Gazto. I'm coming for you."

"Bring it."

BLOOD OATH

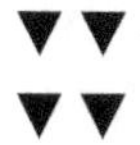

Darkness and pain encompassed her whole world. Eventually, a sliver of light and thought intruded. The sliver grew broader as the light grew in definition, and finally, Bacarus regained consciousness. *Where am I?* A lone candle on a small table lit the cage. She was in a cell that took up half of a large stone-walled room without windows and opposite the single wooden door. On the dirt floor beside her lay Sheru, unconscious and facing the other direction. No sound permeated their environment, and the room reeked of dust and disuse.

She was tired and sore and quite confused. She tried to stretch her cramped muscles and found she'd been bound tightly, hands and feet in front of her. She struggled against the bonds without luck; not even her teeth could budge the knots. Her head was clearing, though, and she recalled the sequence of events leading to their captivity.

Maghrurio had bolted from their rooms at the inn, intent on some quest or other at the library. With nothing else to do, they packed their bags in preparation for the boat's noontime departure. There came a knock on the door, and Sheru opened it before anyone thought twice. Soldiers burst into the room, and she fought without thinking, fierce and desperate and, ultimately, unsuccessful.

She remembered Vasagh's ugly face gloating and Sheru knocking out one soldier's teeth with a well-swung elbow. They beat Vodi savagely, and she could do nothing. Then Vasagh placed a rag over her face, wet and sour-smelling, and her brain swirled until she passed out.

She looked around the room again, seeing everything more clearly, but nothing new presented itself. They were captives and almost certainly of Vasagh's master. Vodi was not here, and she hoped, wherever he was, that he was still alive. She squirmed over to Sheru and saw that while unconscious, her companion had no apparent injuries. That was a small relief. She shook her friend to wake her.

"Ugh, my head. Where are we, Bacarus?"

"It looks like somebody's cellar. Probably the Assassin. Are you injured?"

"I don't think so, but my elbow is sore."

"I don't doubt it, but I bet it's not nearly as sore as the soldier you brained. I saw his teeth rattling across the floor."

Sheru cast a tight smile as her eyes swept the room.

"There's nothing to see. Looks like we're stuck here for the time being."

The floor was uncomfortable, so they wriggled over to one of the walls and propped themselves against it. They remained there in silence, working futilely on their bonds and waiting for who knew what.

Their wait wasn't long. The muted but clear sounds of approaching footsteps froze their escape attempts. A lock snicked, and the door opened to reveal Vasagh and two of his cronies. Behind them strode a face from their past.

"Gazto," Bacarus snarled.

Vasagh unlocked the cage and made a menacing move toward her, but she regarded him with indifference. Her eyes were all for Gazto. He was clothed in pants, a tunic, and a cloak of high quality and wore a bulky cloth glove on his right hand. On his left lay a Mystic Ring. His eyes were half-open, and his face bore an odd combination of concentration and confusion. He just stood there like that for a while. Then smiling, he strode forward, reached out with his ringed hand, and grabbed Sheru's bound ones.

"Speak to Maghrurio, woman," he growled.

Sheru hesitated for only a moment and said, "Bacarus and I are safe for now, but I don't know--"

Gazto pushed her back down. He stood a few moments more, with his men keeping a watchful eye on them until his eyes refocused and his expression transformed to one of grim satisfaction.

"Your choice of friends is unfortunate. He is as stupid as he is unskilled."

Bacarus eyed Vasagh and replied, "I was about to say the same to you."

Vasagh's response was swift, and Bacarus slowly sat up with a newly bloodied lip. "Case in point," she responded.

Vasagh raised his hand again, but Gazto froze him with a gesture. "Leave us and get some rest. The fool will come, but not before tomorrow afternoon at the earliest." Gazto thought for a moment and added, "Set a watch for the local troops. I don't want anyone sneaking up on us. Have them stay sharp and inform me of anything unusual."

Vasagh saluted, casting Bacarus an evil eye. He then turned and departed the room, his men in tow. Gazto glanced about and, seeing there was nowhere for him to sit, conjured a stone stool which served adequately.

"Your friend has continued to Hasa and will take some time to return. Assuming he doesn't just keep on running."

Bacarus ached to mouth off, to insult him and respond in a belligerent manner. But she knew that wouldn't help anything, and the most helpful thing she could do for Maghrurio would be to get some answers. "What do you want with us?"

Gazto smiled. "You, my dears, are bait for my trap. One I will use to catch your friend."

Confused, Sheru asked, "But why? He hasn't been a Mystic for more than a couple of months. He's no threat to you."

Gazto sighed, "I have a vision for the future. For too long, we Mystics have denied our true power and capabilities and resigned ourselves to remain arbiters and policemen. Our gods-given abilities raise our heads and shoulders and elevate us above mere men. They should look up to us, and we should rule them for the good of Sonoduhl!"

Bacarus sneered. "And I suppose you should rule over the Mystics?"

He smiled at her. "Naturally, the most powerful among us would be the obvious choice."

"You've abandoned your calling and sacrificed your humanity for a shameless power grab. You aren't superior. You're just a regular asshole like so many out there."

His temper flared. "I would choose my words carefully if I were you."

Bacarus glared daggers, and Gazto seemed poised to strike her when Sheru interjected, "I don't understand; why would anyone want to be ruled by Mystics?"

Sheru's question succeeded in distracting Gazto from Bacarus' insolence. Bacarus gave Sheru silent thanks--her last comment had pushed him a little too far.

"What people want most is stability. Safety. Prosperity. They'll follow whoever is best able to provide those things. And that would be the Mystics."

"Led by you," Bacarus muttered, her voice thick with sarcasm.

"Yes, led by me," he responded seriously. "Sonoduhl's current leaders will recognize that we can do a far better job than they can, and we can keep the peace. They will undoubtedly step aside in favor of our rule."

"If not, I'm sure you can easily persuade them. All it would take is a few choice executions."

Gazto rose in a fury. "You try my patience, woman! Our world will be transformed into a utopia. Why can't you see it?"

Bacarus' anger also rose. "Because tyrants like you always start with good intentions, and next thing you know, the people are oppressed, and corruption runs rampant. You've betrayed your fellow Mystics!"

Gazto's rage boiled over. He raised his hand and gestured, conjuring a stone collar that began to squeeze the life out of Bacarus. She tried pulling on the collar to no effect and started turning blue as her airway was constricted. Sheru screamed, and Gazto's madness dissipated. He waved his hand indifferently, and the collar vanished, leaving Bacarus sputtering and gasping on the floor.

Crouching to her level, he grabbed her chin and forced her gaze to meet his own. "You will bow to me, woman. After you lure your friend to his demise."

Her throat was raw and graveled, but she stared defiantly while she deliberately bit her own lip. The blood flowed down her chin as she growled, "By my own blood willingly shed, I swear I will see you dead before you ascend to rule."

Gazto snickered. "Your blood oath means nothing to me, nor do the ridiculous superstitions of your order. I will rule." He turned to leave, then stopped and glanced over his shoulder. "And since you seem so fond of predicting executions, perhaps my first act will be yours." He smiled and continued out of the room, closing the door behind him.

"That could have gone better," said Sheru.

CROSSOVER

Maghrurio severed the Mystic connection. He shared the exchange with Vodi but couldn't keep the anger from his voice.

"But my friend, I know of this man. Gazto of Cyrchan is a merchant who travels far and wide over Sonoduhl. I have not dealt with him myself, but I know others who have."

Maghrurio considered this as his temper simmered. Mystics, as a rule, don't advertise their location to each other. Still, everyone in Decra knew Abner lived there, and most could have escorted you to his home. It would make sense that, in traveling about Sonoduhl, Gazto would have run across most of the Mystics. But how was it that he was not known as a Mystic?

He thought back to his brief physical encounter with the man and realized the answer. Gazto had worn gloves, which could easily hide the telltale Mystic Ring. Without a visible Ring, no one would realize he was a Mystic if he chose not to announce his profession.

So that settled the identity of the Assassin and also where he probably was now.

"Damn! He's still back in Cyrchan. Sheru and Bacarus must be there too!"

"So we must return. But remember, Vasagh will be in Cyrchan as well, and Azak is right here in Hasa searching for us. You remain here; let me see what can be found." Vodi had words with the old man and then left the shack with a determined stride. While he was gone, Maghrurio followed up with Buhlo and Usnik, sharing his discoveries and intentions. He then reclined against his pack and tried to sleep. His problems, and lack of adequate solutions, made sleeping difficult but, thankfully, not impossible.

Vodi returned eventually, bringing with him some baked fish balls for lunch. "The return trip to Cyrchan is about two days on foot or eight hours by boat. Normally there are no boats leaving this late in the day, but I found one who could be convinced to take us. Do you want to leave now or tomorrow morning?"

Maghrurio chewed thoughtfully. Leaving tomorrow morning would give them a chance to plan out a strategy, but he'd been wrestling with strategies for so long that a few more hours were unlikely to be of much help. Besides, there was no guarantee this shack would be available for that long, and they didn't need a run-in with Azak to delay them from rescuing their friends. He shared his thoughts with Vodi, who agreed on all counts.

"It will be a bit more expensive to convince the captain to leave now, but Gazto will not expect us to arrive until tomorrow. Getting there late tonight could provide us some advantage."

Maghrurio gave a thin smile and nodded, but in his heart, he had little faith that advantage would matter much. He collected his belongings and motioned for Vodi, who led the way along the docks to the captain in question. Once more, Vodi did his thing, and thanks to an excess of coins, the pair boarded the boat as the crew prepared to cast off.

Vodi scanned the dock area, seemingly searching for something. His eyes fixed on something. "Maghrurio," he asked, pointing, "would you be so kind as to wave to the man near those scales?"

Maghrurio looked across the docks and saw Azak shouting furiously at one of his nearby soldiers. A fey mood struck, and Maghrurio smiled and waved to Azak. The boat eased from its mooring and began drifting downstream in the direction of Cyrchan.

"Vodi, why did you want me to piss off Azak?"

Vodi told him.

$$\bullet \; \bullet \; \bullet \; \bullet \; \bullet$$

The trip to Cyrchan was both ponderous and swift. Their progress seemed to be nonexistent unless Maghrurio gave thought to the upcoming conflict with Gazto, in which case the miles seemed to fly by. But thinking about strategies didn't yield any new insight, which gave him such a panic attack that he had to force himself to think about something else. And once more, time would slow to a crawl.

Eventually, day passed into night and they finally arrived in Cyrchan. They disembarked and found an inn close by the docks.

"This is convenient," said Maghrurio.

Vodi shook his head. "Too convenient. We don't need to make Azak's job quite so easy. Let's find something a bit farther from the docks."

The pair found another inn more to their liking and secured a room. They laid low for an hour or so, resting while they could, and returned to the streets under cover of darkness. They headed in no particular direction but simply walked back and forth, midway between the center of town and the docks. They were looking for someone and expected to find him in this area. They just hoped they found the right person because there were far too many wrong people in the darkness.

The night wore on, and they grew fatigued, but fate would not be denied. They turned a corner and ran headlong into Vasagh, leading a group of soldiers spread out across the road. A second passed while each party eyed the other, and another as recognition dawned.

"It's the Mystic!" yelled Vasagh to his men.

"Run for it, Vodi!" cried Maghrurio. The pair turned and bolted back the way they had come. Vasagh's men shook off their surprise and bounded after them.

"Now we're in for it," Maghrurio shouted at Vodi as they ran in the general direction of the docks. They were gambling here, and he hoped things worked out. He didn't want to have to kill anyone, though he doubted that Vasagh shared his attitude.

At first, they distanced themselves from their pursuers, but all too quickly, Vasagh's men closed the gap. Maghrurio and Vodi were no athletes, and both knew that soon they would be caught.

Unless they were lucky, that is.

Luck, it seemed, was a funny thing.

As they rounded a corner, they found themselves face-to-face with Azak and his men, who froze in surprise. Not stopping, the pair continued running directly for Azak. "We found him," Maghrurio shouted, "he's right behind us."

Azak hesitated for just a moment, and that was enough. Vasagh rounded the corner; his eyes locked onto his former commanding officer. Azak roared in fury and charged, and his men followed his lead. Vasagh's men, following close behind him, found a horde of charging soldiers and attacked without thinking.

Maghrurio and Vodi staggered off to one side, clutching their sides as they fought to catch their breath. Vodi's plan had worked perfectly. Azak was angry with Maghrurio, but that was nothing compared to his rage at Vasagh's desertion and betrayal. Vasagh, on the other hand, knew capture by Azak would mean pain and confinement in the Duke's dungeons. The rest of the men were soldiers or hired thugs and needed little reason to fight.

"Come, Vodi, we must help the good Captain. We can't afford to let even one of Vasagh's men bring news back to Gazto."

Maghrurio brought his magic to bear selectively against Vasagh's men--a burst of wind to topple, a random stone to trip, or a burst of fire or water to divert. Vodi likewise added a few strategic blows to the cause. Before long, Vasagh had been captured, and each of his men had surrendered either their freedom or their consciousness.

Azak barked an order to bind the prisoners and then stood before Vasagh, fury twisting his countenance. "You are charged with desertion, disobeying the orders of a superior officer, abandoning your post, and striking a superior officer. There may be more charges, but those should be enough to see you hang."

Vasagh said nothing in his defense but regarded Azak with deadly intent as he addressed Maghrurio instead. "You think you are oh, so clever, but he will have you before long."

Maghrurio drew himself up. "You have poor taste in masters, Vasagh. I suggest that you spend your prison time reconsidering your life choices."

Soldiers bound the prisoners and led them away to the local jail. This left only Azak and a corporal to face Maghrurio.

"Maghrurio," he greeted cautiously.

"Captain Azak."

"You understand I'm still under orders to escort you back to the Duke?"

"Captain, you and I both know why the Duke issued those orders. His assessment in this matter is no longer valid, as I demonstrated at our last encounter and again tonight."

Azak regarded Maghrurio coolly but said nothing in response.

"Also, we delivered a deserter into your hands, one guilty of actual crimes. You won't go home empty-handed."

"I suppose I should grant you that point."

"Captain, there is a merchant here in town named Gazto. He murdered Abner and other Mystics. He has taken captive two of my friends--fellow citizens of Nahrein--and has threatened to kill them. You know these women; you've met them before."

Azak's face reflected the memory of the first time he'd met Maghrurio and of the women accompanying him. "I see. He's in town, then? Here?"

Maghrurio nodded. "He's holed up in the market square next to a burned-down smithy."

"I know the place. What do you propose we do?"

Maghrurio looked at Vodi, at a loss as to what to suggest. Vodi jumped in. "Captain, I assume you have lodged with the town's garrison?" When Azak nodded, Vodi continued. "Good, we have a room ourselves at an inn nearby. Gazto won't be expecting us to have found passage downriver until tomorrow morning and won't expect our arrival in town until tomorrow evening. He won't be expecting your presence at all. May I suggest we retire for the evening and reconvene for breakfast tomorrow? We can decide then how to approach him."

Azak considered the suggestion. "Meet us at the inn's dining hall an hour after sunrise." He fired a cold glare at Maghrurio and growled, "Do not disappoint me."

With both sides in agreement, the pair slipped away and returned to their room at the inn. They had accomplished enough for one night. What the morning might bring would be a completely different story.

FIELD OF FIRE

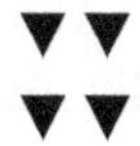

Sunrise came far too soon for Maghrurio after a night of little sleep. He dragged himself out of bed and, accompanied by a similarly lethargic Vodi, went down to meet Azak in the dining hall. All bore grim faces, fully aware of the gravity of what they would be attempting that day. Rescuing Sheru and Bacarus from a skilled Mystic would be a grave challenge, and none of them had any illusions of accomplishing the task completely unscathed.

"The first thing we should do is to reconnoiter the target," Azak began. "We have to be sure they're in there and see what to expect when we go in there after them. I have men monitoring who goes in or out of his shop. Gazto also has men watching the approaches, but they aren't terribly skilled."

"That's a good idea, but they should be careful," Maghrurio answered. "Gazto is a powerful Mystic, and he has killed before. Several times."

"My men know how to handle themselves."

"The question remains, then. What are we to do?"

"My men can take out his without leaving him the wiser. But afterward…" Azak trailed off, unsure how to complete the sentence. "Look, I am a military man with military training. Give me an enemy fortress, and I can rattle off numerous strategies for victory. But a Mystic?" He shook his head. "I've had enough trouble with you, and you've only been one for weeks. You tell me this Mystic killed Abner. I'm not sure how we can tackle him."

The three sat in silence, pondering which strategy might accomplish their goal of freeing the women. Maghrurio spoke first.

"I can provide a diversion at noon that should draw him out of the house." He described his plan to them.

Azak grunted, "If it doesn't kill everyone, that might work. While he's diverted, we'll use an alternate entrance and extract the prisoners."

"I volunteer to do that," said Vodi.

Azak looked askance at Vodi and replied, "My men and I will take the lead, but you can come as well. Just keep quiet and be careful. You," turning his attention back to Maghrurio, "should remain outside, ready to confront Gazto in case your diversion doesn't work."

Maghrurio and Vodi nodded, accepting their assignments--not with enthusiasm, certainly, but with a resigned acknowledgment of necessity. They glanced at each other, wondering which, if any of them, would survive to day's end.

· · ● · ·

The morning passed swiftly as they waited in the deserted dining hall, and Maghrurio worried the whole time. Were his friends still hale and whole? Would his arrangements pan out? Would the diversion work? There was no way to know; they could only execute the plan and hope for the best.

Noon approached, and with it came guests looking for lunch. To Maghrurio's relief, it also brought an expected messenger. Obscured by hood and cloak, he found them at their corner table in the dining hall. He drew up a chair, placed his small package on the table, and removed his hood. It was Jaysel.

"Well met, Maghrurio."

"And you, Jaysel." He gestured toward the package. "Is this what I hope it is?"

Jaysel nodded. "My master sends his regards and hopes his gift will prove satisfactory."

"That is my hope, as well."

They were joined by one of the soldiers, who whispered into his captain's ear. Azak nodded and dismissed the man.

"It appears our target has his men arranged about the house, but we can't confirm whether anyone else is in there with him," said Azak.

Maghrurio set down his tea and pushed it away. "I suppose it's time to set our plan in motion, then?"

A nod was all they received from Azak, and they rose from the table as one and headed for the door. In a short time, the uncertainty would resolve itself. They would rescue the women, or they would be dead. There seemed little likelihood of any other outcome.

They proceeded toward their target without words. Azak led them to a rendezvous with one of his scouts, and with a gesture, the scout disappeared to pass along word to his fellows. Shortly after that, Maghrurio knew, those of Gazto's men that remained on guard outside would also disappear.

Maghrurio whispered to Jaysel, "You've had some hard traveling to get here in time. Are you sure you are willing to do this?"

Jaysel replied with a sour look, and Maghrurio held up his hands in resignation.

They remained within their place of concealment for several more minutes until the scout returned and flashed them a thumbs-up signal. Gazto's men were no longer a threat, so the next phase of their plan could proceed.

With a glance at Maghrurio, Azak and Vodi headed for the rear of the house for their phase of the operation. Meanwhile, removing his cloak, Jaysel left their hiding place and meandered down the street. His gait suggested a weary, footsore messenger who would like nothing better than to complete his delivery and perhaps visit a tavern. He made his way to Gazto's home and walked up to the front door. He knocked twice and waited for a response.

After a short time, the door opened a crack. Maghrurio couldn't see who was inside, but whoever it was exchanged words with Jaysel. He removed his pack and fished out a wrapped package about the size of a smallish loaf of bread. More words were exchanged before the door was closed again. Jaysel shrugged and bent down to place the package on the doormat. He gave a half-hearted salute and walked away from the house.

$$\bullet \; \bullet \; \bullet \; \bullet \; \bullet$$

Usnik waited in an alley across from Gazto's house, watching his apprentice play his part in their plan. It had taken much arguing to convince Maghrurio to accept his help. Taking a cue from Varka's original plan, Gazto expected Maghrurio but not Usnik as well.

I'm not a violent person. It's been a long time since I fought anything other than predators in the hills. Even then, I fought to drive away, not to kill. Still, a threat to one Mystic is a threat to all.

He was determined but realistic about their chances. He wasn't sure he was Gazto's equal, but he couldn't leave Maghrurio to face him alone. He'd just have to do his best.

If it must be to the death, then to the death it will be.

• • ● • •

Once Jaysel had disappeared around a corner, the door opened wide to reveal Gazto. He was dressed more finely than the last time Maghrurio had been in Cyrchan, but this time he had only a single glove covering his right hand. On his left, Maghrurio could clearly see a Mystic Ring. Gazto checked up and down the street but saw nothing to rouse his suspicion.

Maghrurio waited, tense and expectant. The street was silent and quite empty. Gazto looked around once again and bent down to examine the package. Then the trap was sprung.

Usnik called out a challenge to Gazto and launched a fireball at the rogue Mystic. Gazto raised a hasty shield to block it. Forgotten, the package lay at his feet. Prepared by Usnik, it contained the same explosive mineral formula Gazto had used against other Mystics. While the shield blocked the fireball from touching Gazto, it didn't protect the package from the flames. The explosion rocked Gazto's front porch and sent him flying back into the house.

As Maghrurio expected, Gazto stormed back out again, casting his own spells at where Usnik had been. Usnik, meanwhile, renewed his attack from a different position in an attempt to draw his foe away from the house.

Maghrurio waited anxiously while the Mystics traded spells. Usnik had warned him to wait until Gazto had committed himself away from his house before attacking from a different side. From where he stood, though, it seemed the Graavt was no match for Gazto, and Maghrurio wondered why. Was Usnik less powerful than a Mystic? Did his permanent detachment from his fellow Mystics work against him? Or was he playing a dangerous game, deliberately underperforming to trick Gazto into overconfidence?

Whatever it was, Usnik was getting manhandled. He continued to fall back as his attacks were rebuffed, and his defenses took a beating. The pair didn't waste time on advanced magic, as they mostly alternated throwing fireballs and stones. Gazto had progressed to the middle of the street, moving forward as Usnik fell back, and Maghrurio prepared to enter the fray.

When Gazto crossed the street, Maghrurio knew his time had come at last. Fighting his fear, he gestured with both hands and conjured molten rock, spreading it widely in front of Gazto's house and blocking access to his door. Gazto, for his part, was focused on Usnik's retreating form.

Until he wasn't.

Maghrurio glanced toward his enemy and saw him looking back. They locked eyes for a moment, and the moment was enough for Usnik to go back on the offensive. He redoubled his attacks, hurling fireballs and stones at his enemy. Gazto blocked the spells easily, deflecting them in Maghrurio's direction. Maghrurio ducked and cast a blast of icy wind, intending to freeze Gazto or knock him off his feet. Gazto countered with a wall of fire, which sublimated the ice directly to steam. Back and forth, the spells flew, each attack seeking out a gap in the defense, some vulnerability to exploit.

Dodging a hail of fist-sized stones, Gazto conjured a massive fireball that missed badly and passed harmlessly over Usnik's head. Harmless, that was, until it struck the brick warehouse behind Usnik, and the building collapsed onto the surprised Mystic. In an instant, their two-against-one advantage had become a repeat of Maghrurio's prior showdown with Gazto. Outclassed, he knew what he had to do, which was what Usnik had warned him to do earlier when they made their plans. He must abandon the field, or else Gazto will catch and kill him.

Maghrurio turned and ran, hoping against hope that Gazto would give chase. He desperately wanted to escape but needed to draw his opponent far enough away from his house so the prisoners could be rescued. He dodged in and out of shops and cut down side streets to confuse his pursuer.

After several minutes of frantic running, he slowed to a walk. He had heard pursuing footsteps at first but nothing for the past minute. Where had Gazto gone? Was he still being chased, or had he remembered his prisoners and circled back? Maghrurio couldn't tell, so by prior arrangement, he returned to the inn to await his accomplices.

The wait was intolerable. Maghrurio had reluctantly agreed to Usnik's plan, and now he feared the Graavt may have been injured or even killed. He was hot and tired and anxious, afraid for his friends' lives and, truth be told, afraid for his own. He never should have allowed them to risk themselves. If any of them had been harmed, he'd never be able to forgive himself. Worse was the realization that, regardless of the outcome of their attempt, he still needed to confront Gazto for justice and for the honor of the Mystic order. He paced the room incessantly, his mind awash with worry, his footsteps ticking out the inexorable passage of time.

There was a sound beyond his door, and he stopped short. He could hear multiple footsteps climbing the stairs. Were his friends returning? Were Bacarus and Sheru with them? Or was he hearing the approach of Gazto and his men? He stared anxiously at the door, listening to the approaching footsteps, which came to a halt just outside. The knob turned, and he readied his spells.

Friend or foe? He'd know in a moment.

IN PURGATORY'S SHADOW

As Jaysel wandered down the street toward Gazto's house, Azak signaled his men to move out. He nodded once to Maghrurio and left. Vodi, looking nervous but anxious to do a good job, smiled briefly at Maghrurio and followed.

The group made its way down the street, keeping under cover where possible until they came to the rear of Gazto's house. There they paused in the shadows and awaited the signal. To Vodi's eyes, Azak and his four men were experienced professionals who could do stuff like this in their sleep. He, on the other hand, was so anxious he could hear his own heart beating. He hoped he'd calm down once things started.

Vodi considered what had brought him to this point in his life. He had been given a second chance by a Mystic and had taken full advantage of it. When the opportunity came to help another Mystic, he grabbed at that too. But this went beyond commitments to Mystics. He had befriended Maghrurio and, in turn, Bacarus and Sheru and considered them good people. He tried to maintain a positive attitude in life. He cared deeply for his friends and hated when people bullied or intimidated others. Those were his core values; they motivated his thoughts and his deeds. Rescuing his friends from Gazto, he realized, hit all three.

The silence was shattered by the woosh of a fireball and the ensuing explosion. Azak grunted, "Let's go." The team broke cover and proceeded to a window at the back of the house. After a quick glance inside, one of the soldiers broke the glass with his dagger and dug out the larger shards. He then lay a thick cloak over the windowsill for protection and, one by one, they climbed in. Vodi came last and most awkwardly, not being accustomed to climbing through windows or, for that matter, most kinds of strenuous physical activity. He wondered again what had possessed him to volunteer for this, but not for the last time.

The sounds of battle filtered in from outside, and Vodi wondered how Maghrurio was faring. He kept close behind Azak as the soldiers spread out from the window and searched for the prisoners. The house was fairly large, and there were many rooms on the ground floor. A kitchen, food storage, sitting rooms, and office space were what you might expect in any merchant's home. They eventually encountered a staircase, and at a gesture from Azak, two men took their position at its foot while the rest of the group ascended.

Upstairs likewise boasted many rooms, but they were mostly living quarters and closets and such. At every door, Vodi felt like they'd finally located his friends, but each time he was disappointed. When they had searched the last of the upstairs rooms without finding any sign of the prisoners, they were forced to admit they must have missed something.

They descended the stairs and found the soldiers at its foot with their fingers to their lips, signaling for quiet. Vodi could hear someone moving slowly through one of the sitting rooms at the front of the house. Azak's men moved silently in that direction and surprised one of Gazto's guards as he walked into a hallway.

Quick as a flash, Azak had his hand over the guard's mouth and pinned his arms against the wall. The guard had no idea who they were and was clearly frightened, a condition which only grew worse when Azak drew his dagger and pressed it against the man's cheek. He leaned in close and whispered in a clear yet threatening voice.

"If you want to live, tell me where the prisoners are."

The guard's eyes threatened to burst from his face as he looked from one soldier to another. He clearly felt Azak to be the icy hand of death, and his reply came out in a strangled gasp. Azak tried again.

"Take a breath. Tell me the truth, and you shall live. Lie, and you die."

The guard inhaled and whispered, "Downstairs."

The guard directed them to a hidden door leading to the cellar.
Two of Azak's men bound and gagged the guard and stuffed him in a
closet, but not without a last word from Azak.

"If you lied to us, if you make a sound, we'll be back."

He locked the guard in the closet, and the group opened the hidden
door and descended the stairs.

The cellar was dark, with only the occasional guttering candle to
provide any light. A smallish room lay at the foot of the stairs, with a
hallway extending ahead and behind them. Azak signaled two of his
men to wait there, and the rest followed him forward down the hall.
Here the darkness was thick, and they had only a discarded lantern to
light their way. The floor and walls were of dirt, rough-hewn, with an
occasional door on either side. The soldiers investigated each door
they encountered but found only disused storage, dirt, and more dirt.
Eventually, they found a door at the end of the hallway, which led
outside.

"An escape route," Vodi whispered to himself.

They returned the way they had come and passed the soldiers at the
stairs. Continuing down the hallway, they found much the same as
before--dirt floors and occasional doors leading to boxes or furniture.
Vodi's nerves were on edge. They had chewed up a good deal of time
in their search so far, and there was no telling how much remained to
them.

At the end of the hallway stood another door. When they opened
it, they found a small room with a couple of Gazto's guards
languishing over a card game. Everyone froze for a moment, too
surprised to act. Azak's soldiers recovered more quickly, though, and
by the time the guards realized what was happening, they were face
down in the dirt, bound and gagged.

The room contained a small table with cards scattered upon it,
three chairs currently upended, and a single door in the far wall. With
a glance at Vodi, Azak moved to the door and tried to open it.
Locked, as they all expected. He rummaged through the guards'
pockets and found a key ring, and fitting one to the lock, was able to
open the door. The inner room was dimly lit by a candle, but clearly
visible was a cage at the far end of the room containing two people.

Bacarus and Sheru stared back at them.

Vodi rushed in and exclaimed, "I'm so pleased to find you alive!"

Sheru was likewise overjoyed. "By the Twelve, am I glad you found us. Where is Maghrurio? Is he alright?"

"Slow down," answered Vodi. "Maghrurio is fine, or he was when we last saw him." He found a keyring lying on a small table next to the candle and unlocked the cage door. "We need to get out of here before we're spotted, so let's go."

Azak followed him into the room, produced a knife, and cut their bonds. With a gesture for quiet, the group followed him back through the outer room into the hallway. They'd taken two steps down the hall when they heard a sound they'd been dreading... the boom of a door upstairs being slammed shut. They froze where they were, holding their collective breath and straining to hear what happened next on the floor above.

Footsteps were loud and unmistakable; whoever it was made no attempt at stealth. Vodi grew afraid and thought for sure that Gazto had returned to the house and was searching for them. Azak must have had similar thoughts because he signaled to the others they should break for the exit door at the other end of the cellar hallway.

They'd taken a single step when the door at the top of the stairs burst open.

$$\cdot \ \cdot \ \bullet \ \cdot \ \cdot$$

Spells poised, Maghrurio had a split second to decide whether to attack as the door opened. He needn't have. The figures in his doorway resolved themselves into Jaysel carrying a badly wounded Usnik. He rushed to help, and they lay Usnik's unconscious form on a bed. He was covered in blood and bruises where the building had fallen on him. One arm was broken and had been set in a rough manner. His breathing was labored, and Maghrurio suspected some internal damage.

No one else accompanied them.

Maghrurio fetched water and some linens, and the pair tried to provide what first aid they could, but the more they cleaned him up, the worse his condition appeared. Usnik's eyes flew open, and he gazed wildly about, eventually settling on Maghrurio's.

"He is… powerful," Usnik gasped between spasms of pain.

Maghrurio could only nod, not trusting that his voice wouldn't break.

"You will have to face him, you know."

Maghrurio nodded, "I knew I would have to, eventually."

Usnik broke into a series of wracking coughs, each sounding worse and more painful than the last, and several accompanied by splatters of blood from his mouth. He grasped with his good arm and found Jaysel's hand.

"My friends, we have known each other far too briefly, and I have lived far too long. I can only fix one of those. Jaysel," he turned to him, "you have been a good apprentice in our short time together. I bequeath to you your heritage and your right." Somehow, he managed to remove the Mystic Ring from his finger and placed it in Jaysel's disbelieving hand. "Don't repeat my mistakes. Embrace your brethren. Achieve greatness for our people." He grasped Maghrurio's arm with a weakened grip and whispered, "Help him."

For the second time within two months, a Mystic died in Maghrurio's arms.

THE RECKONING

Jaysel sat at Usnik's bedside, too numb with grief to say or do anything. Maghrurio covered the body with a sheet and said a quick prayer to the gods. The pair sat in silence for several minutes, paralyzed by grief. The reality of the situation filtered through the sadness, though, as Maghrurio recalled that his friends had not yet returned to the inn. He rose to check at the window. The usual foot traffic paraded past the inn, but he saw no sign of them.

Jaysel arose in silence; his head hung low. Maghrurio could see him staring at the Ring in his hand.

"My friend, if it helps any, I know exactly how you feel. Your master has been killed, and an unbearable burden has been placed in your hands." He put a comforting hand on Jaysel's shoulder. "Know that I will help you if I can. You are not alone."

Jaysel looked up at him, tears threatening but his face hard. "I will make him proud," he declared, and he placed the Ring on his finger.

"We cannot wait any longer. It seems this rescue has met with disaster, and all of our friends are captive. It will be up to us to make another attempt, and we must not fail."

The pair descended the stairs and exited the inn. They had no real illusions that this would succeed, but they owed it to their friends to try.

Before they left, Maghrurio contacted Buhlo and gave her the bad news about Usnik and how Jaysel had replaced him. She was sympathetic and concerned for his safety but could do nothing to help him now. He hoped if things didn't work out well for him, she'd be able to rally the other Mystics to resist Gazto.

When they were still several streets away from Gazto's house, Jaysel took a different path. Gazto would probably recognize him from earlier, but he wouldn't know Jaysel was now a Mystic and pledged to oppose him. The plan was for the Graavt to find a rear entrance to the house and try to free their friends while Maghrurio engaged Gazto. While this had been Azak's unsuccessful plan, they understood they had no other options.

Maghrurio paused to gather his courage. Somehow he'd always known it would come down to this, a direct confrontation between him and the Assassin, Gazto. The man had murdered multiple Mystics by stealth and subterfuge, then killed Usnik in a straight-up fight. He had been a Mystic for less than two months, and yet here he was, preparing for a death match.

There was fear in his heart, but anger also. The thought of Gazto holding his friends captive and of corrupting the Mystic order filled him with outrage beyond belief. But deep down, he knew his abilities as a Mystic were insufficient to do much about it. He dearly wanted to hold Gazto accountable but recognized the harsh truth that he could not possibly force that particular outcome through magic alone. He looked ahead to the most hopeless task of his life.

It was almost funny. Thinking back, he had to admit he'd quit or sabotaged almost every job he'd ever had when things started to get tough. How ironic that this job was far and away the toughest he'd ever faced, and yet he could not bring himself to quit. Somehow, the thought of walking away and letting Gazto have free rein was an affront to his sensibilities. Whatever transpired, he would not run from this confrontation while his enemy remained alive.

The distance to Gazto's house seemed like a million miles, but it felt as though he'd crossed it in seconds. He ducked into the back of Munpi's ruined smithy next door, recalling the prophecy that had started his journey. *"The blacksmith is the key to the beginning and end of your search."* Little had he realized that the prophecy had been correct after all. He began his journey at this smithy, and he would end it from here with the coming confrontation.

From his vantage point, he regarded his adversary with renewed fury. Gazto was sitting on his front porch, exactly as he had been the first time Maghrurio met him weeks ago. He seemed relaxed and extremely sure of himself.

He has every right to feel that way.

As much as his anger allowed, he closed his eyes and contacted Gazto.

"I was wondering when I'd hear from you, fool."

"You tease me as you did the blacksmith the first time I met you."

"I teased him because he was an idiot. Just like you."

"Did you kill him for that reason as well? Or just because you could?"

"He annoyed me for too long, and I grew tired of his backtalk."

"So you don't like dissenting opinions. Is that why we have so few Mystics today?"

"All the Mystics I killed were antiques, unwilling to consider new ways. We're better off without them."

"You know, for someone advocating change, you seem quite intolerant of it. In fact, little of what you do seems to change."

Gazto's voice grew harsh. "You want change? How about changing the enslavement of our order? I'm tired of serving Sonoduhl's people like second-class citizens when we Mystics are head and shoulders above them. Our brothers didn't agree with my ideas, but they are no longer in a position to object."

"You have done murder, Gazto, and have worked to bring down our order. Were I to judge you, I would find you guilty of that."

"Well, how fortunate for me I don't recognize your authority to judge me."

"I am a Mystic, as you are. I have the authority to judge everyone, from kings to commoners."

"Instead of judging actions, wouldn't Sonoduhl be better off if we directed those actions beforehand? To rule is a natural extension of judgment, Maghrurio."

"It is not the servant's place to rule, Gazto."

"Some Mystics can't help but remain servants, especially the stupid ones."

"Crude insults do not become a ruler."

Gazto chuckled, "This chat has been amusing, of course, but the afternoon progresses. I imagine you are curious about your friends' health. Or would you prefer to play more word games?"

Maghrurio's anger bled into his voice. "You have no right to hold them!"

"I have every right, as any ruler would. But see here," he added, "I am magnanimous in my kingdom. I will let you see for yourself they are unharmed."

"I have no need for your assurances. Release them!"

"Ah, that poses a small problem. You see, I don't really need them for anything, but I do need you. Surrender yourself to me, and I promise to release them."

Maghrurio breathed deeply and firmed his resolve. "Release them first, and then I will surrender myself."

Gazto laughed, "You seem to be laboring under the illusion that this is a negotiation. Let me clarify. You will surrender yourself, and then I will release them. Or, if you'd rather, I will kill them all, and then I will kill you. I've grown weary of this conversation, fool. Choose quickly."

Maghrurio felt a familiar mental tickle. "Give me a moment to consider," he asked before dropping out of the conversation and connecting with Jaysel.

"I found them, Maghrurio. They are alive and locked in a cage in the cellar. I'm sorry, but I cannot open it."

"Thank you, my friend; then we move to the final stage. Remember what I told you. Farewell."

He signed off with Jaysel, thinking of how mismatched a direct conflict with Gazto would be. He sighed in resignation and reconnected with Gazto.

"I grow impatient. What is your answer?"

"Do you swear my friends will be released if I give myself up?"

"Would you believe me if I did?"

Maghrurio had no response.

"Here's what you will do, fool. Remove your Mystic Ring and place it in your pocket. Approach my front door with your hands in sight. I will accompany you to your friends, and you can watch them depart. Then... we can continue our chat."

• • ● • •

His adversary stood on the porch, eyes fixed on Maghrurio's approach. His naked hands were held up for Gazto to see. His heart pounded in his chest, his stomach roiled, and his nerves screamed at him to run far and fast. But Maghrurio knew that his friends depended on him for their lives, and he would do nothing to further endanger them. Gazto seemed to know this as well, as evidenced by the broad grin creasing his unpleasant face.

"Welcome to my humble abode!" Gazto pointed at a porch chair. "Please, have a seat while I check your bag."

Maghrurio handed over his knapsack, and Gazto rummaged through it quickly. "Traveling light, I see. Nothing but a single change of clothes and personal effects." He kept hold of the pack with one hand and gestured with the other toward the door. "Shall we greet your fellow guests?"

Maghrurio preceded him into the home, his hands still raised, and followed Gazto's directions until they came to the hidden cellar door. Gazto tripped the latch to open the door and extended his arm in mock courtesy. Maghrurio descended the stairs with Gazto close behind. The stairs ended in a long hallway, and they turned right and continued to the end. Gazto opened the door, and they entered the guardroom, crossing through a second doorway into a smaller room.

With a gesture, Gazto lit torches arranged along the walls. Maghrurio saw the cage on the far end of the room, filled with his anxious but still living friends. He rushed over to Sheru and Bacarus, drawing strength from the mere touch of their hands through the bars.

Maghrurio turned and called out to Gazto. "I've come. Now do as you promised and release them all."

Gazto stood at the opposite wall, with the cage to his left and Maghrurio facing him. An unpleasant smile gave his face an evil cast. "You've interfered with my mission from your first day as a Mystic, and I can't have that. So if you want your friends released, you'll need to hand over your Mystic Ring."

Maghrurio stood in shock. He'd agreed to remove his Ring from his pocket as a sign of faith but turning it over was something else entirely. It would leave him utterly defenseless against Gazto's already proven murderous tendencies.

Gazto correctly interpreted Maghrurio's hesitation. "Come now, Maghrurio," he shouted, freeing his hands by tossing Maghrurio's pack against the wall behind him. "Hand over your Ring, or the prisoners will die as slowly and painfully as I can contrive."

Maghrurio saw the hunger in Gazto's face and knew he wasn't bluffing. With no other choice open to him, he reached into his pocket and pulled forth the Ring. He made a silent apology to Abner before tossing it to Gazto, who caught it cleanly.

"There, that wasn't so difficult, was it?"

"Release them, Gazto!"

Gazto's smile grew even wider.

THE WAY OF THE WARRIOR

Gazto stared hungrily at the new Ring in his ungloved hand, ignoring Maghrurio's demand. "Is this from the Fire triad?"

Nonplussed, Maghrurio replied, "No, it's Wind."

"Pity, I was hoping to complete a set." He pulled off his glove with his teeth, revealing three more Mystic Rings adorning his left hand. "Multiple Rings will increase the power of your spells, you see. They're harder to control, but I've learned to live with that. My original Ring didn't like sharing a hand with the others, though. Gave me a nasty burn when I tried it. Still, I'll find a Fire Ring someday, and then we'll see if it increases power even more."

Maghrurio grew impatient, "Gazto, the prisoners. You promised."

"Ah yes, I did promise to release them, didn't I? Hmm… no, I don't think I will after all."

"Gazto!"

"Put yourself in my shoes, Maghrurio. If I release them, they'll try to rescue you, and I'll just have to kill them anyway. It's better this way. No, it's better if they remain locked up. In fact, I should probably just kill the lot of you."

Maghrurio was numb with shock. He'd come to accept the possibility--no, the likelihood--that he would die, but the idea that his friends would also be killed was just too much. And the cavalier way in which Gazto announced his decision was like oil on the flame of his outrage. This was too much to bear, especially after surrendering his Ring and his powers.

Somehow, he had to stop Gazto.

Time slowed to a crawl. He saw Gazto turn toward the prisoners--his friends--and raise his hands. The killing spell would no doubt be cast in a heartbeat. What could Maghrurio do?

Gazto's hand raised a fraction of an inch, and Maghrurio recalled Abner's comment from his first training session.

"The Mystic Ring helps to focus your power and makes the magic easier to learn, but anyone sufficiently skilled and practiced can do it."

Abner had insisted anyone could do magic. Could it be so? Could he actually cast spells without his Ring? His spells were underpowered with the Ring. Would they even work without it?

Gazto's hands started forming the gestures that would end his friends' lives. Maghrurio had no choice but to try.

His thoughts and deliberations took a fraction of a second, but now was the time for action. Maghrurio took a deep breath and summoned a burst of wind aimed at Gazto. The gust was raw and powerful, fueled by his righteousness, and it knocked Gazto off his feet into the wall.

Gazto's expression of surprise was nothing compared to Maghrurio's. He had cast a spell without his Ring, which had been stronger than anything he'd ever cast. In an instant, he realized the reason why.

His past attempts at magic were diffused and diminished by conflicting emotions and motivations. This time, however, his emotions and motivation were pure. All his outrage, sense of justice, and certainty of right and wrong had galvanized into a powerful, overriding directive. Gone was the fear, the indecisiveness, the hesitance. He was perfectly aligned and perfectly focused.

Focused enough to perform like a real Mystic.

No. He was focused enough to BE a real Mystic.

Gazto recovered himself and went on the offensive. He summoned stone and encased Maghrurio's hand, but in a burst of inspiration, Maghrurio formed the stone gesture and drew it back with his other hand, dissolving the stone in an instant. Gazto cast stone projectiles at Magrurio, who ducked, rolled, and came up, casting his own sheet of flame. Gazto conjured a shield to dissipate it, then returned a blast of water that knocked Maghrurio down.

As he struggled back to his feet, Gazto attacked again. He cast a freezing wind that transformed the water instantly to ice. Maghrurio slipped on the puddle beneath him and went down again, but that fortunate accident meant most of the icy effect missed him. From his position on the ground, he countered with a shower of stones that Gazto ducked. Once again, luck saved him as the stones rebounded off the wall and struck his target from behind.

Both men struggled to their feet and faced each other. Maghrurio had pretty much used his entire arsenal of offensive spells yet hadn't made a dent in Gazto's defenses. Still, he remained relatively undamaged, and that was encouraging.

"It seems you've done some studying," panted Gazto.

"You have no idea," replied an equally exhausted Maghrurio. He had survived so far trading spells, but he knew it couldn't last. It was time to try something different. He recalled the dagger tucked into his cloak, which Gazto had missed earlier. He drew it out and cast the flame spell, transforming it into a flaming sword. Gazto's eyes went wide, and he cast a stone shield in time to meet Maghrurio's attack.

They thrust, parried, pushed, and blocked each other's attempts, with minimal physical damage but increasing fatigue. Finally, Gazto paused long enough to cast his own wind spell to push Maghrurio back across the room.

"You cannot win, Maghrurio," Gazto snapped. He was stalling for time to catch his breath, but Maghrurio couldn't take advantage until he caught his own breath.

"I've learned a thing or two since our last encounter. You see, I'm no longer the pushover you expected." Maghrurio was pleased to see a glimmer in his opponent's eyes, a recognition of the truth of his statement. "There is still a way out for you. Free the prisoners. Return the Rings you stole. Forswear your traitorous plans and help me rebuild the order."

Maghrurio desperately wished Gazto would accept his offer. The pure confidence that had driven him was draining away, and he feared the power of his spells would suffer. It would be better for Gazto to continue considering him a worthy opponent and yield before his substandard skills betrayed him.

Maghrurio could see the hesitation in his opponent's eyes, overrun by anger. He realized he was wasting his time--Gazto would never agree to yield. He would fight to the death, convinced of his destiny and unwilling to accept any other outcome. Maghrurio could almost hear the response before Gazto spoke the words.

"Mercy? Is that what you offer? Crumbs!" Gazto scowled. "I am your better, you fool. I wasn't expecting much from you before, but I will end this now. Prepare to join Abner, Maghrurio!"

Maghrurio wasn't sure what kind of attack to expect, so he cast a shield for protection. It was a good thing because Gazto conjured a devastating wall of flames. His shield blocked most of it, but he could feel the heat passing by, and the wall behind him was scorched badly.

He scooped up the scattered rocks in the room and hurled them at Gazto, who was already casting a shield. He followed up the rocks with another wall of flame, forcing Gazto to continue his shield a little longer. He followed that with a stone punch, gambling that Gazto would be quick to drop his shield and go on offense. He was partially correct, landing his punch a fraction of a second too soon, so it did little damage except to knock Gazto off-balance.

Enraged, Gazto arose fighting. He cast wind to unbalance Maghrurio and followed it with his own stone punch, which was far more effective. Maghrurio's shield was a fraction slow, and he took a heavy blow, throwing him into the wall. Gazto cast another stone spell and once again encased Maghrurio's hand in stone.

With only one hand free, Maghrurio gathered the loose stones and bombarded Gazto again to give him time to free his hand. In this, he failed because Gazto dodged the attack and cast another stone spell, missing Maghrurio's other hand but encasing his foot.

Bound hand and foot to the floor did more than limit Maghrurio's maneuverability. It rendered him unable to cast a shield, effectively leaving him vulnerable to a killing strike. Yet Gazto withheld that blow, satisfied to re-encase a hand whenever Maghrurio managed to free one. Eventually, Maghrurio succumbed to the futility of the situation and sat back as best he could, with two of his limbs immobilized.

"You see, Maghrurio, how useless it is to resist me," Gazto gloated.

"It is never useless to resist evil," declared a beaten but defiant Maghrurio.

Gazto laughed. "You took your shot and gave me a good run, I'll grant you, but you lost. I suggest you make peace with the gods because you're about to meet them. Do you have any last words?" He raised his hands to cast the final, fatal spell.

Maghrurio shouted at Gazto, "Dangers strike, troubles come..."

Several things happened in quick succession.

Flying stones struck Gazto, hurled from within the cage by Bacarus and Sheru. With a snarl, Gazto turned his attention to the prisoners with the intent to kill.

Across the room, the door was thrown wide, and Jaysel burst in shouting, "This is for my master," as he cast his own hail of stones at Gazto.

Gazto reacted instinctively to Jaysel's spell by conjuring a shield, which easily protected against the elementary spell.

Maghrurio, having waited for Jaysel's appearance, finished the phrase "...seek the solace of hearth and home." Instantly he found himself free of his stone fetters, sitting next to his knapsack lying behind the distracted Gazto.

All of Maghrurio's emotions--outrage, desperation, sense of justice--poured through his flame spell, and Gazto was struck from behind. Caught between the hammer of the flames and the anvil of his own shield, there was no escape. A single cry escaped Gazto's lips as the fire consumed him. His dry husk dropped to the floor, lifeless.

Maghrurio's exhausted form collapsed, grimly satisfied.

The dead were avenged.

TACKING INTO THE WIND

Maghrurio could hardly believe it.

Abner's murderer had been brought to justice. The Mystic order was free from Gazto's poison. He had actually performed exemplary spellwork.

He wasn't a failure after all.

The stresses of the recent past, both physical and mental, conspired to overwhelm him at last, and he lost consciousness to the cheers of his friends.

• • ● • •

His faint was brief, and when he awoke, he found himself surrounded by familiar faces. Sheru was examining him for injury and pronounced him fit enough, whatever that meant. Vodi and Bacarus helped him to his feet.

I did it! I really did it!

Bacarus placed a concerned hand on his arm. "Jaysel found the key and released us."

"I'm so pleased you are all alive."

"Not quite all," Sheru replied. "Azak and his men fought before Gazto overpowered them, but all were injured, and a few died. Azak has a concussion and a broken arm."

The remaining ranking soldier, a sergeant, explained that his men preferred to convalesce with the Cyrchan garrison, but as Azak insisted on returning to Decra, they didn't want him taking his road alone.

"We will take him," Maghrurio decided, "because we must return to Decra ourselves." Bacarus and Sheru nodded their agreement, but Vodi hesitated. "Vodi, I realize Decra is a bit out of the way for a man of your ambitions. But I do have a task for you elsewhere if you are willing."

"I would be pleased to do whatever you require, my friend."

The Mystic rose and crossed to what was left of Gazto's body. It was a distasteful task, but he poked through the charred remains until he recovered the four Mystic Rings. Despite the condition of their former master, the stolen Rings were surprisingly whole and unharmed. The single one on Gazto's left hand was his original Ring; Maghrurio stored it in an inner pocket.

"I'll need to consult with my peers to decide what to do with his old Ring."

He examined the remaining three. He had yet to learn where two of them had come from, but one had been stolen from Varka. He held and concentrated on each Ring in turn and was able to sense which was Varka's. He offered it to Vodi. "Varka lived in Arnhem, at the base of the Long Falls, according to his letter. He had an apprentice who deserved to have this Ring back. Would you be willing to deliver it?"

Vodi accepted his charge with a flush of pride. "You may consider it done."

"Excellent. Please extend my condolences and ask the apprentice to contact me when he or she is ready."

Vodi embraced his friends, said his goodbyes and left to complete his mission.

Maghrurio turned to Jaysel next. "My friend, I thank you for your assistance. If you ever need my help, you just have to ask."

Jaysel bowed deeply. "I will take my leave and return Usnik to his home. He will need funeral rites, which I am sorry to say are closed to all but fellow Graavt." He saluted, hand over heart, and added, "I will keep in touch."

Maghrurio watched Jaysel depart and then turned around to his closest friends. "Are you ready to go home?"

Bacarus and Sheru burst into grins.

• • ● • •

In bed that night, Maghrurio contacted Buhlo and shared the developments of the day. She was, of course, pleased to hear from him and especially relieved to learn of Gazto's demise. They briefly discussed possibilities about the future of their order and made plans for further discussion with the group at the upcoming Gathering a few days hence.

The following day, Bacarus purchased a used wagon from a local merchant. They were surprised to learn it was, in fact, the same wagon they had sold weeks before. The merchant admitted she'd been unable to sell it, as it seemed to generate uncomfortable feelings in any potential customers. Reunited with Snowfall, who was glad to see them again, it was more than sufficient to bear the three friends and the injured Azak to their destination.

Azak bid farewell to his men, and the party departed for home the following morning.

They took things easy on the road, content to allow the horse to set its own pace as they discussed the events of the previous day.

"Usnik recreated Gazto's formula for the explosive minerals, and he thought it would be sufficient to overmatch Gazto. Their battle turned out to be more than he'd anticipated, unfortunately, and he died of his wounds."

"Before we mounted our rescue, though, he reminded me the shield only faces one way, and that might be a vulnerability I could use against Gazto. It was ironic, of course, that the very same vulnerability ended up being Usnik's own downfall." He was silent for a moment, a wistful expression marking his face. His friends withheld their questions in respect for his loss.

"After he died, Jaysel and I had to decide how to attempt your rescue. We knew if Usnik and I couldn't overcome Gazto directly, then surely Jaysel and I could not either. That meant we needed an angle to give us a chance."

"The sampler," answered Sheru.

"Exactly. I realized it could place me behind his shield in position to deliver the killing blow. Jaysel volunteered to cast a distracting spell to give me an few extra seconds. It was risky, but we decided we had no other option. He waited outside the room, the first part of the sampler spell his signal to launch his attack. Your stone throwing added to the confusion, giving us the additional seconds we needed to put the plan into motion."

"An excellent tactic," opined Azak from the rear of the wagon. "Are you sure you never served in the military?"

Maghrurio chuckled.

"One thing I can't figure out," puzzled Sheru. "Where did your spellcasting power come from?"

"Ah," mused Maghrurio. "I've been thinking about that. I believe the power came from the purity of thought and purpose, undiluted by conflicting feelings like fear or doubt. My motivation was justice. Gazto's actions up until that point, his plans, were an affront to everything fair in the world. I couldn't allow such injustice to continue."

• • ● • •

They passed the remainder of the day without incident and camped under a copse of trees in the pleasant evening. Dinner was prepared, watches were set, and the night passed in peace.

Clouds threatened the following morning, and they hurried to get back on the road before the rains began. It never became torrential and often tapered to a light drizzle, but it stubbornly continued to rain to some degree for the balance of the day. Sodden and weary, they finally reached Hasa just as twilight set in. They stabled the horse and wagon and spent the night in a warm, dry inn.

Early the next morning, Azak suffered a relapse, so Sheru delayed their departure for one more day in order to procure additional supplies to stabilize his condition. After a quiet dinner in their rooms, Maghrurio decided to visit the common room for a glass of wine. Halfway through his glass, he heard a familiar feminine voice gushing to a friend--Nepri, the woman he had encountered during his last visit to Hasa.

"That man is so enamored of me; he'd do anything I ask. Give me the moons and stars, he promised."

Nepri's friend joined her laughter. "You should hold out for the biggest rock he can manage."

Maghrurio smiled. He was no longer as mortally embarrassed about their incident, but he couldn't resist a tiny bit of payback. He approached their table, and before either woman could speak, he conjured a large rough stone in the middle of their table.

"Would this rock be big enough for you?"

Smiling, he left the stunned women behind and went off to bed.

• • ● • •

The following morning, Sheru pronounced Azak fit for travel, so they loaded the wagon and set out once more. The weather was beastly hot and humid, and while rain threatened throughout the day, the clouds never delivered. They made good time and halted for the night in a clearing by the road.

Dawn broke over the last leg of their journey to Decra, and they were anxious to be on their way.

"If I never have to sleep on the ground again, it will be too soon," grumbled Sheru. Bacarus, who was hardier about such things, nonetheless didn't disagree.

They loaded the wagon, made sure Azak was comfortable in the rear, and set out. The weather had cleared as the clouds and heatwave had both dissipated. The landscape was unimaginative one day out of Decra--tree, rock, bush, tree, bush, rock--and the hours and miles passed in a repetitive numbing haze.

Until they crested a shallow hill and encountered a band of horsemen.

Maghrurio looked around from his position in the rear of the wagon, seated next to a drowsing Azak. The men looked familiar, and he realized this was the same band that had challenged them weeks ago when they had first fled Decra. The ruffians didn't seem to recognize them, and he was content for now to watch what played out.

The leader addressed Sheru, who was driving the wagon, "Good day, miss. We're collecting taxes for the good Duke and would ask that you cough up your fair share." A few of his mates laughed at his cheek.

Sheru secured Snowfall's reins and sat back, cool and unafraid. "We're transporting one of the Duke's officers back home, so you can see we're not interested in your lies."

Maghrurio imagined what the leader was thinking. A wagon with two women, an injured man, and his healer… clearly no threat to them.

"No, I think we'll be taking those taxes anyway." He spurred his horse toward Sheru and added, with a leer, "Perhaps we'll take a little something besides."

Sheru stiffened, but this time with anger and not fear. The leader reached for her, and she swept her right hand in a circular pattern that deflected his arm. Her movements definitely lacked Bacarus' grace and fluidity. Nonetheless, she thrust forward her left hand with all her anger and fear and was rewarded with a satisfying *crack* as she connected with his elbow. The leader fell howling from his saddle, holding his broken arm close to his chest.

Maghrurio stood and addressed the ruffians. "You have been judged and found guilty of attempted highway robbery." He made the wind gesture and moved his arms in broad, circular waves, and the group found themselves in the midst of a whirlwind. One of the horses panicked and bolted into the wind, and both horse and rider were thrust back into the interior of the swirling tumult. "Dismount and lay down your arms," he commanded.

One by one, the ruffians obeyed his order. Using rope from one of their horses, Bacarus and Sheru tied each of their hands in a long line from the rear of the wagon. When the prisoners were secured, Maghrurio negated his spell and tied their mounts in a second line.

Azak had roused during the brief fight and was understandably angered by the ruffians' behavior. "We have been trying to catch this group for a while," he grumbled.

Sheru returned to his side to check on his wounds. "The prisoners are secured and remanded to your custody, Captain," she answered, winking at him. "You're welcome."

On the road once more for Decra, Bacarus leaned over to congratulate Sheru's performance.

"I just did what you taught me," insisted Sheru, blushing just a bit.

"You did well," answered Bacarus. "You'll never have to be frightened again."

THE HOMECOMING

The sun set before them as they approached the gates to Decra. The guards on duty were pleased to find Azak in their company and quickly took charge of the ruffians and their horses. "No doubt at least one will talk, and we'll find their hideout soon enough." He turned to Maghrurio and continued. "I thank you for getting me home, but I fear that will not change the Duke's intentions."

Maghrurio was touched by his concern. "I've done my duty to you, Captain, and forgive your slavish adherence to the orders of a tyrant. I will go to the Duke myself and educate him on current events." He saluted the captain, "Good health to you, sir, until we meet again."

Azak returned the salute, and his soldiers took him away. Sheru guided the wagon through the streets and back once more to Abner's home.

No, strike that. His home. The home of Decra's Mystic.

They re-entered the house with a sense of disjointed reality. Two months ago, Abner was alive and walking these halls, but now Maghrurio was the master here. Bacarus grumbled about the cleaning she'd need to do as they unloaded the cart. Maghrurio rubbed down and stabled Snowfall after parking the wagon and entered the kitchen to find his friends seated at the table. He joined them quietly.

"You know the Duke will send for you," Bacarus warned.

"I know," he nodded. "I don't intend to give him the satisfaction, though. I am going to see him right now and put an end to this foolishness." He rose, confident at last. "Decra once again has a Mystic, and it isn't him."

He made his way through dark but familiar streets. He passed through the marketplace, noting that Sheru's old store still hadn't been rebuilt. Eventually, he spied the Duke's castle ahead and could see its guards had likewise spotted him.

He stopped and addressed the approaching guards. "I am the Mystic Maghrurio, newly returned from Albiona and lands to the east. The Duke has requested my presence. Please take me to him." The guards, confused but pleased with his compliance, escorted him into the castle. They passed through hallways and rooms until he found himself in the same audience chamber in which he had met the Duke the first time.

"Please wait here," a guard requested, and he was left alone.

He looked around the room, taking in once again the large bookshelves on opposite walls. One of the books called to him in that special Mystic way, and he retrieved it. He sat in an easy chair and began to read.

"Mystics should always be on the lookout for their replacement. Sometimes a candidate is marked by positive qualities--hard-working, disciplined, and compassionate. Other times a worthy candidate may be helpful yet fearful but, over the course of time, demonstrates the strength of character to face that fear and triumph over it. Still, others might be undisciplined and unserious about anything in their life but somehow harbor a spark of goodness within them. These are the hardest to find but often make the best Mystics."

"But take care with these and train them carefully. They are prone to anxiety and doubt and can be slow to accept their abilities. Pretend to have a limited time to share with them and force them to stand on their own. This will seem harsh, but in the long run, will almost always produce strong Mystics who are masters of their own destiny."

Maghrurio replaced the book and considered what he'd read. Clearly, he was the third candidate type. *So, Abner deliberately deceived and abandoned me for my own good, eh?* Still, seeing the wisdom in Abner's approach, he didn't feel terribly disturbed by the revelation.

We will have some words later tonight, he and I.

He pondered the rest of the text and the idea of replacements in general until the door burst open. The Duke blustered into the room as usual and approached Maghrurio eagerly.

"Well, Maghrurio, I see my captain has not been totally inept in fulfilling my orders."

"Captain Azak was industrious in his attention to duty and kept at it even in the face of pain and death. He should be commended."

"Yes, of course. I trust you have had the chance to review our conversation and reconsider your position?"

"I have given long consideration to our conversation, your Grace."

"Excellent. Now that you are here, I will ask you again." His face glowed greedily. "Give me what I want."

Maghrurio reached into his pocket and revealed the three rescued Rings. "In my absence, I fought and killed a rogue Mystic responsible for many deaths, including Abner's. I retrieved these Rings from him and intend to bestow them upon worthy candidates." Duke Bileyo's eyes grew wide as saucers, and the greedy look intensified.

"You, however, will not be one of them." He thrust the Rings back into his pocket and stared at the Duke, awaiting his outburst.

He was not disappointed. The Duke flew into a rage, cursing Maghrurio and calling him all manner of vile names. He summoned his guards, and six rushed into the room with swords drawn. Maghrurio gestured, and each sword was encased in stone, rendering them too heavy to wield. Another gesture and the Duke was enfolded by a small whirlwind. His face was lined with terror as he was immobilized and lifted slightly off the ground.

"Hear me, Bileyo. Your behavior has been reprehensible and insulting to me and the entire order of Mystics. You are quick to demand respect for your office, but you failed to show respect to mine. Therefore, I will recommend to the Nahrein Confederacy Council that you be stripped of your lands and title and removed as Decra's leader. So have I judged."

With a wave of his hand, he dissolved the whirlwind and released the Duke. He stared at the soldiers until they gave way before him, and he walked from the room with his head held high.

He departed the castle without incident, certain that he did not need to worry further about the Duke. The Council would hear his recommendation and would likely act upon it, and Decra would be spared the rule of an idiot. As he made his way back home, he fingered the Rings in his pocket, contemplating the words he had read.

Maghrurio returned to find Sheru and Bacarus enjoying a late tea in the kitchen. They were his dearest friends in all of Sonoduhl and had repeatedly proven their worth.

Bacarus put down her teacup and asked, "I take it things went well with the Duke?"

"Well for me; not so well for him."

Sheru laughed. "So what happens now?"

Maghrurio grinned and pulled out the Rings from his pocket. "Who wants to be a Mystic?" he asked.

COMING SOON…

LEGACY OF SONODUHL

Mystic apprentice Dina knows that someday she will become the new Mystic to a people who generally avoid her. Frustrated and lonely, she tells herself she'd trade her destiny for one true friend.

Haman-ji is a displaced aristocrat with a dark secret. Descended from deposed royalty, he inherited his family vow to reclaim what was once theirs. He also inherited a family talent for a magic unlike anything Mystics had ever seen.

When Dina's routine mission ends in a deadly attack by mutant creatures, Haman-ji rescues and befriends her. They bond over their shared magic as Haman-ji works to convince Dina to help him restore his stolen heritage. If she agrees, Dina will be forced to choose between friendship and destiny, with the fate of two nations hanging in the balance.

Legacy of Sonoduhl will be published early 2025.

ABOUT THE AUTHOR

Rudy Lopes was born in New York City of immigrant parents. Growing up a Bronx kid, he developed a love for playing guitar, watching baseball, and reading thousands of fantasy and sci-fi novels.

With a strong librarian mother, three sisters, a wife, and two daughters, his writing naturally includes women striving to find their own place in the world.

As a technologist and erstwhile entrepreneur, Rudy's mind is always attuned to what might be. He remains on the lookout for the bright blue police box, the unexpected party, or the shimmer of a transporter to signal the start of an adventure.

MYSTICS OF SONODUHL is his debut epic fantasy novel.

Say hello to Rudy:
Threads – rudylopesauthor
Facebook – RudyLopesAuthor
Instagram – RudyLopesAuthor
Website – www.rudylopes.com